C000146970

A MODERN FAIRY TALE

PUSHING COTTON

DARRAN NASH

The Book Guild Ltd

First published in Great Britain in 2021 by
The Book Guild Ltd
9 Priory Business Park
Wistow Road, Kibworth
Leicestershire, LE8 0RX
Freephone: 0800 999 2982
www.bookguild.co.uk
Email: info@bookguild.co.uk
Twitter: @bookguild

Typeset in 11pt Adobe Garamond Pro

Printed and bound in the UK by TJ Books LTD, Padstow, Cornwall

ISBN 978 1913913 755

British Library Cataloguing in Publication Data.
A catalogue record for this book is available from the British Library.

For Clare, my beautiful wife.

Best wishes,

Damian Nash

Chapter One

The creak on the stairs, the click of the latch,
He sits on your chair, he's ready to snatch.
Cares not how you do, for you'll make him rich.
He's coming for you…
Behold, Mr Critch.
– traditional Edwardian rhyme, 1903

2003

"…cock! Itchy cock!"

The boy remained impassive. It was a technique that served him well with Jasper, the mad mongrel that hung around his street. He would catch you by surprise, bound black out of the bushes and nuzzle a snotty, sniffy nose into your terrified crotch. Mum said he was after Jaffa Cakes. It was the only time in his life the boy felt relieved to be poor.

Jasper was notorious on the estate. Everyone recognised him and nobody knew him. Why was he convinced that Jaffa Cakes came in underwear, rather than boxed and cellophane-

1

sealed-for-freshness? It would not have been so bad if he stopped at your pockets, but to rummage… there. What if he had nipped, for God's sake?

Those in no particular hurry – schoolchildren and pensioners, mostly – would stand motionless and let him get on, secure in the knowledge they had no tangy orangey bits secreted about their Scooby Doos. Then morning rush hour spawned a rival 'executive semaphore': a risky flipping of palms accompanied by the rumble of a double decker and a soothing, 'All gone, Jasper'. That Number 26 was full of just-made-it commuters with nibbled knuckles and slibbery slobbery flies.

Jasper's dad, Dwyn Collins, was dead. That was when the trouble started. He had succumbed to an age-old complaint; he was ninety-four. There was no family and less insurance, so a patch of undergrowth was cleared for him at the back of the town cemetery. While they were there, grounds maintenance gated off the neglected chapel next door and now no one visited, not even last-orders lovebirds on a bone hunt.

Lemon-lipped Glendalers pinned the ensuing mayhem squarely on the old man, though he could hardly help dying. Some claimed he had weaned Jasper on orange juice. Others, only too aware the departed are seldom litigious, tapped noses and remarked in all innocence that, 'Mr Collins never possessed (nod and a wink) a *proper* biscuit barrel'.

It was not long before local youngsters, egged on by the red tops, had christened Jasper 'The Devil Dog'. Suspicions of Satanic incitement were bolstered one wet Wednesday when he knocked a Jehovah through a rhododendron in a dispute over a can of Tango. The police had been summoned, of course, but the Witnesses had seen nothing and, besides, Jasper was away like a shadow in a storm.

So, the carnage continued and sales of Jaffa Cakes plummeted: it was simply not worth the risk. Only commuters condemned to public transport continued to purchase from Noah, and those were not for human consumption. Those were to crumble up and scatter about like an aircraft dropping chaff. He was a bad cat, that dog.

Jasper was stood in front of him now, snuffling and truffling, nudging and budging, head glinting like an eight ball. *All that Vitamin C.* Presently, he raised two drawn eyebrows and peered up. The boy smiled down. Jasper did not frighten him; he saw the best in everyone.

"No Jaffas today, Jasp. No Jaffas any day, come to think of it. Sorry, old fella."

Both heads dropped.

He knows I'm useless, thought the boy. *Even the mad mongrel has sussed me out. No friends, no money. Never any Jaffa Cakes. If only you could talk, eh? We could be mates, you and me. You'd have someone and so would I. Man's best friend. Boy's only friend.*

The dog was evidently sticking around and so, abstractedly emboldened, the boy began to caress its head. It was the first time since Mr Collins that Jasper had let anyone stroke him. He was usually far too streetwise for that. It is a common knowledge the first thing you are taught at mad mongrel school is that any human who actually wants to touch you most likely works for the dogs' home. And Jasper was careful all right. Not a living soul knew where he lived. Some said the Meddy among the wild rhubarb, or even the cemetery; others an abandoned orchard, but a search there by an impromptu lynch mob proved fruitless (on both counts).

The texture of Jasper's crown was not at all what the boy had imagined. Instead, it was clumpy, nylon almost, and the skull supple. Nevertheless, the young man felt elated, enjoined. He had become a pair.

"I wonder what you would say, Jasp, if you could talk?"

Without warning the animal gulped and blurted out, "Itchy cock!"

The dog was talking to him.

"I'm talking to you!"

The dog was talking to him! He *could* talk. Brilliant! They could joke and laugh, go to the park, fly a kite, carry out missions, run after things and bring them back. Wait a minute… a talking dog? They could make a fortune together: *This Morning with Fern and Phil, Des and Mel, Terry and Gabby, Paul and Barry Chuckle, Pets Say the Funniest Things.* Even Kilroy! (How would *that* make you feel?) In fact, any one of the shows he loved watching at his aunty's during the holidays. He could buy something nice for his mum, too. For as long as they lived they would dine on ruddy Jaffa Cakes for breakfast, dinner and tea.

"Oi! Itchy cock!" He said it again.

Yet this time the voice was more insistent. A sort of '*I know you can hear me so don't pretend otherwise*' tone.

"I do hope you're not going to be rude…"

Wait a minute… that was not Jasper's voice at all. Jasper's voice was a little *rough*. Come to think of it, Jasper never had a voice. *That* was Norton.

"Daydreaming again, Itchy?"

Norton's voice.

A shudder.

"…Love your new friend!"

Back now among the sentient, the boy gazed down. His hand was resting on the head of a plastic doll cradled roughly around the neck by a young girl, maybe two years old. She had been happy enough to share her baby with the big boy in the misshapen jumper, yet Father, alerted by the raised voices, was less impressed and flashed one of those menacing 'get your own dolly' stares before dragging the child away arm upstretched, small palm wrapped within big.

By the time the boy had snatched back his own limb it was too late. Everyone – his classmates, the Ray Gun, anonymous faces looking elsewhere, even the statues and portraits – had seen it all. And each stared and shook and smirked while he longed for instant oblivion.

The most feeble museum in the world had just taken a turn for the worse.

Make yourself small! Instinctively, he hunched – grinding his knee – and kept his breath. Eyes darted the room for refuge. With the gents back at the entrance and Norton policing the exit, there was little option but to brazen it out. How he wished he could melt into this maddening crowd. It should have been easy in a room teemed with fellow Year Nines and rampant regulation: identikit hair, all substance and precious little style; grime-ringed shirts; ties as wide as a pterodactyl; pine pullovers plucked senseless while A Knight Won His Spurs; and the entire ensemble topped off with a blazer. *The blazer.* Bought to last, yet always threadbare before the occupant grew to fill it. Coach-driver green; double vent, or fart flap, depending on familial aspiration; faux-silver cuff buttons (a phrase the cause for much befuddlement as there were never more than two); and a breast pocket majestically adorned with the unicorn and mermaid of St John's. How the boy envied those oversized jackets and the sense of belonging they afforded. How he ached for the *uniformity* of it all.

Instead, here he stood like a clown at a funeral. He knew they had to manage on slender means, but even so… was it entirely necessary for his mum to take up knitting to save money? And could it really be pure fluke she was so prodigiously awful at it? When expert tuition was gently suggested she said if she could afford knitting classes she would not be knitting in the first place. His latest mutterings, over breakfast that morning, had prompted a lengthy discourse about the *homogeneity* of sheep. Mum was always using big words; he would not have been surprised if she made half of them up. He listened politely and was even secretly impressed with the wool association she had dexterously conjured, but he was not won over. It was all right for her. She was at least thirty-six and what is the point when you are that age?

"The wally and his dolly!" A last hurrah from Norton's crowd. Mum had always told him to turn a blind eye to name-calling. They had been doing mixed metaphors in literacy. The problem was the boy was asking for trouble. Or, more precisely, Mum was asking for it on his behalf. She may as well have knitted a target on his back, though it went without saying the finished attempt would have resembled nothing of the sort.

It was then it happened.

He heard it.

It was as faint as the breeze and there was a second or two while his brain percolated it from the bubbling hubbub. He glanced about to pinpoint the origin. A window left ajar? An echo of a conversation on the other side of The Gallery?

It came again and this time he was ready for it. It sounded desperate, urgent. Grave.

"Help me…"

A scream swathed in a sigh.

Who was it? Where…? Bobbing on the balls of his feet he looked for clues to the adults in the room. Scanning eyes, reading lips. Finding nothing.

"Please! Help me…"

Intuitively, the boy began to roam, sound crowding his head. He found the courage to tap a passing shoulder. "Did you hear something just then?" It shrugged and turned away.

Again, the voice: "*Help* me!"

What was the matter with everyone?

He searched for a reaction in the faces around him. Grunting boys were barging each other towards the ladies, each secretly hoping they might tumble in. A clowder of girls honed dirty looks, while others spiralled spearmint and poked sticky strings into motor mouths. There was the hiss of barely stifled sniggers as young hands fondled cold, bare buttocks and, beyond the statues, best friends linked arms and swayed like a tipsy three-legged race. And at the edge of the room, among the philistines, Sir, anxiously eyeing his watch for the welcome signal to leave.

Mr Reagan was wearing his usual face: one that looked every minute of every day, and never more so than just before bed, like he had recently risen. He had long since dispensed with any pretence of enjoying the profession. Days marking time instead of books. Whispers in the staffroom had Old Bridgey fingering him for capabilities. *Good. Put them both out of their misery.* Leaning into a pillar, arms wrapped above the hemisphere of his stomach, a tic in his wrist monitoring the clinging seconds, he had the air of a man awaiting a detonation.

The boy moved gingerly on, wandering and wondering, now beyond the crush of the Greeks and towards Flat Cap Corridor. As the moments ebbed, his private whisper seemed to have passed: a development – employing powers of deduction freshly gleaned from a dog-eared *The Sign of Four* one wet playtime – he narrowed to two possibilities.

One: he had strayed to the wrong side of The Gallery.

Two: he had imagined the entire episode and was, in fact, a real-life mad person.

He paused to consider the facts.

In support of Possibility One: he had been hearing voices over *there*, but not over *here*.

In support of Possibility Two: he had been hearing voices as a result of being a real-life mad person. As addenda to '*Two*' he felt it only proper to present the following, since he had not thus far enjoyed the sanest of days: alighting the coach at the museum he had slipped in front of the entire class, landing in a heap at the kerb; he had made friends with a doll; and, perhaps worse, during a designated 'comfort break' had discovered an interloper from Mum's laundry basket in the back of his Scoobys (for one horrific moment he imagined he had actually passed a peg). Still, he felt... *normal*. And, on reflection, each of the above just about made for par.

Starting back across The Gallery, he rounded a sweetie-popping boy nested with blond curls, discombobulated a trio of head-counting teaching assistants and eased beyond the solitary pupil – a freckled, buck-toothed swot poring over an official visitors' book – actually paying attention to the exhibits. She did not seem the shoplifting sort (and anyone stealing from souvenirs would surely go for the pencil with Tutankhamun rubber on the end) so most likely secured that guide with her own spending ration. *This Sherlock stuff was infectious.*

"Help me, please…"

It was back.

By now the boy's senses were midnight-sharp. All distraction screened. Only the plea.

"Where are you?" his own voice said. "You can't be far…"

He weaved around clots of contemporaries; between affairing lovers, eyes only for each other (and friends and neighbours at the doorway); and through this Friday lunchtime's teetotallers and tightfists. On he went. Past the Greek warrior who had seen better days, past the low-slung rope guaranteed to keep him confined should he ever rise, Talos-like, from his plinth and beyond the glass cabinet that housed a motley collection of gravel pit duckers labelled 'Stone Age Arrow Heads – Do Not Touch'. *Do Not Bother* was more like it.

Then he stopped.

Dead.

It came from beside him and seemed so close it nuzzled his ear like a warm lick.

"Here," it breathed, "I knew you'd come."

Adrenaline tore through him causing every fibre – even those in his pullover, the boy imagined – to stand on stiffened end. Where before he had reeled about, now he was rooted to the spot. All he could muster was the squeeze of his eyes into the outer orbit of their sockets.

"Who's there? Does somebody want me?" he whispered.

"Here," came the reply, "I am here."

When he considered it later there was little of the next few seconds he could recollect with any coherence: one of those familiar journeys of departure and arrival and nothing in-between. And when realisation finally struck, he gaped like a ghost train. *This had to be a joke.* They would not get him a second time. No way. Not again.

Too late.

The laughter reeled in on a roar. Norton and his gang, high on teen testosterone, bellowing simian. The boy braced.

They were prodding and pesting as before. But this time no one bothered meeting his gaze. This time, the room's attention was on the warrior. Amid the rising heads, Norton, all gurns and grins, was clambering back across the safety rope, falling into the arms of conspirators. And the Ray Gun, tone set to stun, was moving in to redden ears. ("*I slipped tying my laces, Sir!*" Norton was a compendium of excuses.)

In the shade of the diversion the boy, head flitting, stepped forward. A rushed, "Ehlow?"

"What?" *A reply!*

"Ehlow. Ish it yew? Torking tummee?"

"Is it what?" There was a ready impatience. "Are you afflicted?"

Forget it, thought the boy. He was never any good at ventriloquism, anyway. Not that he hadn't tried. He'd had his own dummy once and took it everywhere until watching a film where one of them inveigled its owner into murdering all and sundry. Nowadays, Malcolm only saw the light of day on Penny for the Guy nights.

"Is it you, talking to me?" the boy enunciated softly. "Is it a joke?"

"A whimsy!" snapped the voice. "Do I look a picture of delight?"

The boy shifted side to side. Everyone doing the everyday. Everyone except him. He wanted to reach out, to touch, to take a just moment to reason, but instead his head was a castanet of clatter. Was he even awake? Forefinger and thumb nipped wincing into the flesh of his own hand.

"I understand, my friend." The voice had calmed. "I, too, find all this monstrous to comprehend."

The boy pirouetted to scan for hidden cameras. No obvious indications. *Obviously.* Instinctively, he stepped forward to press a cheek against the chill of the wall.

When you have eliminated the impossible, whatever remains, however improbable, must be the truth.

"Who are you? What do you want? How do you do that—"

"Year Nine, can I have your attention please?" That *would* be a first. "It's time to leave." Mr Reagan's round-up raised a weary cheer from the chronically underwhelmed. "Can we make our way *sensibly* to the exit, please?" They had been doing rhetorical devices, too. The stampede for the back seats almost lamped a papier mâché Florence Nightingale clean off her plinth.

"Stay close, my friend," urged the voice.

"Listening for woodworm!" joked Mr Reagan, a man transformed now the ordeal was nearing its end.

The boy bolted upright. "You made me jump then, Sir."

"Come on, lad, we're back to school."

"I'm not going to school, Mr Reagan," he said jauntily. "I've got to go to the dentists, Sir. It was on my slip."

"I must say, you seem very pleased to be going to the dentist. Let me check. Name?"

This was a good sign. He knew his name, all right. He just said things like that when he was in a good mood. Hometime, mostly.

"Come on, Mr Reagan. It's me, Nelson."

A bouquet of permission slips was extracted from a carrier bag and a wetted finger flicked at them, first-day teller dexterous. Within seconds the gulling pile had cascaded to the floor to be recovered in a feathery bunch. As the 'Dear Parent/Carer' say-sos were realigned ("Nelson... Nelson... Nel-serrn..." the mumbled refrain) the dregs of the school party shuffled by. Yet Nelson sensed a hovering presence, eyes watching, waiting. He looked up and caught Norton across The Gallery, staring into him. *And just beyond.* Gazes were momentarily matched and the boy turned swiftly to his feet. When next he dared, eyes were seized and Norton grinned heavy.

"Aah yes, Nelson... Hitchcock. Says here you're getting the bus straight to the dentist."

"Pard...? Oh yes, Sir. I'm meeting my mum there, Sir."

Another glance and Norton had vanished.

Mr Reagan posted the slips back into his bag and took a sunny stride. "Can't say I'm all that familiar with the timetables, Hitchcock."

Nelson stood his ground.

"Well, what are you waiting for, lad?"

"Can't I stay here, Sir, just a bit longer? My bus isn't due yet."

"Sorry, lad. Counted them out and I'll count them back in again."

"Sir?"

"Your slip says 'catching the bus to the dentist', not 'has permission to stay unattended in the museum until further notice'. I can see the bus stop from the pick-up and that's where I'll be leaving you."

Nelson's shoulders fell.

"By the way, Hitchcock."

"Sir?"

"I just wanted to say, you've been one of our better behaved today. Not like that Edward pillock. Pity that bloody statue didn't topple on him." Professional etiquette usually dictated that this opinion was not one Mr Reagan should necessarily be sharing with a pupil, but what did he care?

"Saw you walking around," he went on. "Appeared very interested, looking at all the exhibits, staying out of bother. Good for you."

Nelson smiled.

"Did you manage to buy the pencil with the King Tut death mask? Noticed you admiring it earlier."

"No, Sir."

"Here, take mine. Only had it in the old earhole once." Mr Reagan returned the grin. "Call it the prize for Pupil of the Trip."

"Really?" said Nelson, holding out a hand. "Thanks, Sir!"

"You're welcome. But don't let it go to your head, lad, there's one for Hill, too." And the gift was presented. "Watch out there, Hitchcock, losing a thread on your jumper."

Nelson pulled at the straggly string of his cuff, hoping the entire creation might unravel. As he fussed, the pair of crescent indentations, one of which had begun to weep watery-red, caught the teacher's eye.

"Something nipped you, lad? Some sort of miniature hound?"

Nelson scissored the nails of forefinger and thumb. "Did it myself, Sir. Got carried away playing initiation scars, after the Zulu display."

"Deary me," exhaled Mr Reagan. "Hey, don't be nipping that dentist this afternoon, lad. One slip of his drill and your soup days could be over." And they both grinned more. "Come on, I've got a head count to do. Let's hope we've lost a few, eh?"

The pair began the slide towards the exit, Mr Reagan pausing here and there so Nelson could catch up.

"What *have* you done, lad?"

"Banged my knee, Sir. Getting off the coach."

"Deary, deary me…"

The museum felt more serene now that four dozen of St John's finest had been extruded, yet in negotiating each dwindled gallery the lull silence had grown unnerving. Should Nelson tell the Ray Gun about what had just happened? About what he had heard and seen? About the voice? A glance across. Sir looked the type who could be trusted. He looked teachery. *Respectable* – that was the word. And it was probably best to say something, anything.

14

Nelson rehearsed what he intended to report. There were a lot of 'what if's, one 'just supposing' and several references to 'a boy who he knew, but who Mr Reagan did not know at all because he didn't go to our school'. So, that was it. Tell teacher. Like a good boy. Not just yet: as soon as they reached that crack in the floor, over there.

Arrival was sooner than anticipated so Nelson opted to count from three instead.

Three... two... no, make it five. Five... four... ten. Ten. Let's go for ten. Like a rocket. Ten... nine... eight... sev—

"When I was a lad..."

Ruddy hell!

The moment was gone. It was just as well: he barely believed it himself.

"When I was about your age..." Mr Reagan continued, "to get in the Meddy Gang you had to eat a frog's leg. Tough lot, that lot. Anyway, Boxing Day this lad turns up with what was clearly a turkey drumstick."

What is he on about? thought Nelson.

"Coloured green it was! We never found out how he'd done it. Got a paint set for Christmas, or rubbed it on the grass, or something, I don't know. Anyway, didn't fool the gang for a minute and, of course, his mum went mad when she found out. Full turkey drumstick! Daft, really. Frog would've been the size of a sandpit."

Mr Reagan spied Nelson's politely puzzled expression. "Initiation rites, lad! Zulus! What we were just talking about."

Just talking about! That was ages ago. Still, Nelson smiled and nodded. "I had a frog-shaped sandpit once, Sir," he explained, helpfully.

15

And that was it. They landed in silence at the main entrance, right by the security guard's office.

"Have to go and get my bus, Sir."

"All right, Hitchcock. Have a good weekend."

"Bye, Sir."

"And Nelson?"

"Sir?"

"Don't worry about the doll thing. All be forgotten by Monday."

They stepped outdoors to find the empty autumn sky had filled. Mr Reagan squinted up through the first of the rain and, raising his carrier bag high, mourned a different life when those drops would not have caught so mockingly against his scalp.

"Come on, lad…"

Having made a mental note of tomorrow's opening Nelson followed, easing his way down the stone steps. Moving warily – they sagged in the middle and the shower already had them shiny as shells – he reached ground level without further mishap. The pair paused at the kerb where the school coach waited like a bronchial bonnacon, black smoke spewing from its backside.

"Off you go, Hitchcock. Make sure you get that bus. Museum'll be here in the morning."

"Yes, Sir."

Nelson did not possess a school coat – it was only half-knitted yet from a pattern that looked terrifyingly, he thought, like a poncho – so buried his neck into his shoulders and shuffled away, resolutely ignoring the flattened palms slapping the dry side of the coach windows. 'Undercrackers

16

weather', his dad called this: wet and windy. Said it made him feel primeval, like a caveman. Then he would fire up the central heating.

Adopting a peculiar gait designed to keep the ball of his left foot off the ground, he loped towards his destination, though all hopes of a dry sock were scuppered when he was momentarily pursued by a discarded tissue. Finding the bus stop deserted, he assumed an insouciant lean – wet rested upon right – against its mottled post and waited for his ride to trundle into view.

*

Doors hissed and he made his way down the aisle, screening passing seats for chewing gum. Selection made, he edged over to the glass and flipped the flap of his rucksack to admire his new pencil. Within the canvas gloom he caught glimpse of his lunchbox and it occurred to him there was a biscuit waiting. The lid of the container – an old ice-cream tub that had multi-skilled – was eased and he fumbled among scrunched-up papers and crushed cartons of own-brand concentrate. Out came the rectangle. Nelson ran a finger, Braille-like, across its surface. A steaming teapot. He would take his time with it: bereft of a moistening drink, there was little option. A bone-dry taster was snapped off and he grimaced anew.

Morning coffee, he thought. *Not daft, that ruddy Jasper.*

Finally downing the first bite Nelson craned towards the rear bench. *Empty.* The entire bus, notwithstanding a shuffle of shoppers clinging grim to tartan trolleys and the front-seat handrails, was deserted. Why had he not sat there?

Before taking so vehemently against local transport, Mum had once theorised that sitting on a bus was a metaphor for the circle of life. During a particularly long (or so it seemed) journey she insisted that the very young always wanted to be at the front, inquisitive, set up high, anticipating the road ahead. By teens the rear rows offered excitement and a distance from authority. Middle age brought the inevitable drift to the sensible seats and then, in our dotage, she concluded, it was back to the front – not now for the view, rather to offer driving advice and afford the best chance of escape should the vehicle spontaneously combust.

So, there he was: two stops from the dentist watching raindrops tadpole down a bus window. What did settling in the middle say about him and his thirteen years? Late developer? Or old before his days? Next time, he determined, next time, the back seats would be his.

A thunderclap drew gasps from the front-end travellers and roused Nelson from his reverie. Outside, a conga of umbrellas danced the pavement, hunched figures splittered and splashed, and pinked streetlamps noseyed into puddles. He raised his eyes. The sky was muddy-brown and the streets blue-grey. A world turned upside down.

"*Only you…*"

He recalled the words that chilled him as he turned to leave with the Ray Gun.

"*Only you can save me.*"

Perhaps it was not real. Perhaps everyone was laughing yet behind his back. Perhaps tomorrow everything would return to normality, or at least the skewed simulacrum he inhabited.

He would sleep on it. That's what grown-ups did. Perhaps he was in the appropriate spot after all.

"*Museum'll be here in the morning.*" Nelson knew he was coming back. First thing. He had to. He had been chosen. He had no idea why and what it meant, but that did not matter. Something – *someone* – in there needed his help.

Maybe Mum had been right after all. Nelson Hitchcock was not one of the flock.

And now, for the first time, he was glad of it.

Chapter Two

Nelson squinted at the clock. He had not looked at it for twenty-one minutes. And nineteen before that. 07.10, red digits read. Take off the fifteen minutes fast it was always set and the real time was 6.55am. *A-ruddy-M.* Thirty-five minutes earlier than a school day and yet, today, he did not feel tired. If he'd had to get up in the middle of the night during the week he would have pretended to be dead. Sleep – good, old-fashioned restful sleep – did not easily find Nelson. The only time he ever got his head down properly was just after the alarm went off and several times during double geography. Scree and alluvial deposits; they could hardly complain. The rest of the time there was too much to think about. Too much to worry about.

They had tried all sorts: smearing onto his chest leafy unguents that left him ponging like a dunghill; or damping Mavis-from-the-market's exotically monikered concoctions onto his pillow, triggering hives and sneezing fits. He even had a clock that promised to soothe him to sleep with the roar of a distant ocean. That did not last; he was up and down to the bathroom all night.

Nelson decided to get up. It was probably earlier than necessary, but apparently you could never tell with buses. 'Untrustworthy from top to big fat bottom', Mum reckoned. He heaved back his quilt and the cold rushed in. Resisting the chill, he lay frozen, wide eyes slaloming floaters down the cracks in the ceiling. The coving finishing gate negotiated, extremities were clenched and crunched, and he yawned white.

Speed was the key when it came to getting dressed at this time of year. Nelson was always the last person in the entire school to feel the benefit of central heating, or so he imagined. He would arrive early to class – first in bags the radiator! – and watch his classmates steam behind, each with that happy Pop Tart glow only he could divine. The clocks were a day from falling back and the first of the frosts already stiffening the ground and yet, despite Nelson's pleas, Mum refused to countenance throwing the switch. "Not until October's out," was her default response. "It's like living in ruddy Narnia," was his.

"Remember, remember, the first of November." He shivered to himself as pyjamas fell to the floor. A stippled arm reached into his underwear drawer and grabbed an optimistic handful. He loosened his grip in retreat and spare pairs tumbled back into the pit until a single prize remained tightly clutched. A squint through the energy-saving gloom. Scoobys. Good pick.

Nelson had a treasured collection of briefs featuring Scooby Doo. They were his undergarment of choice. Dad had bought them; Mum thought them crude. The elastic that sealed waist and legs was embossed 'Scooby, Scooby

Doo!!!' – the triple exclamation only adding to the sense of wonderment. They were almost as old as him and yet Nelson refused to throw them out. These were once his purples. Originally, they sported a mucky cartoon ('Shaggy' featured prominently Mum occasionally recalled, mortified), but that had long since washed clean away.

In one movement he poked through feet and snapped the waistband into his stomach. '!!!ooD yboocS ,yboocS'. *Inside out.* Off and back on. Then jeans, then casual jumper. Casual! This had a neck tighter than a wetsuit and off-beam horizontal hoops that created the illusion the wearer had one leg shorter than the other. The alternative was a tank top patently cobbled together from dozens of colour-clashing ball ends. That was stuffed back into the cupboard for tomorrow's party.

A rattle-tat-tat on the door.

"Can I come in?"

Mum. Already up, even at this smudgey hour. "Come in." His voice muffled.

She entered to find Nelson wriggling to free his head from the pullover.

"Come over here, Nelse."

Easily locating Mum's outstretched arms – the holes in the remainder of the garment were wide enough to warrant a police escort – he found himself jolted, jerked, puffed and pulled. She was just about to insist his head was in the sleeve when Nelson emerged purl-cheeked. Breathless, she ruffled her son's head and he watched in horror as a helter skelter of fair hair spiralled to the floor.

"Bigger collar next time." She smiled.

*

Twenty minutes later Nelson was sitting at the kitchen table tenderly mouthing volcanic oats. Too late, each steaming spoonful was being methodically blown. The anticipation of the morning ahead must have caused him to rush because breakfast at 53 Glendale Terrace was never the tastiest way to start the day. Porridge, porridge, porridge. What was he, one of the three bears? Why couldn't he have Honey Nut Loops, or chocolate toast, or crisps, like normal hyperactive, attention-deficient kids? Of course, all the fibre was good for him (he was reminded at regular intervals) and Mum *had* endeavoured to add a little la-de-dah by chopping prunes into the mix. But, still, it looked – and tasted, for all he knew – like the underside of a rabbit's foot.

"Waiter, waiter, there are droppings in my breakfast."

"Very funny, Nelson."

He was always having to eat things that were good for him – one of the perils of living in a vegetarian household. Cabbage, carrots, every type of bean (bar baked), stalks of sprouts that appeared overnight like triffids and, worst of all, the dreaded tofu. Nelson equated that experience to chewing a PE mat. Mum had once told him that tofu was curdled soya milk. He wished she had not.

The eight o'clock chatter from the listing radio with its coat-hanger antenna was damped. "What's the plan for today then, Mr Early Bird?" asked Mum, scraping a snaggle-toothed afro comb about her frizz.

"I'm going to the museum."

"Don't tell me you've left your jumper again."

"No."

"Well, I am impressed. You must have enjoyed it yesterday. Not got a date, have we?"

"Mum!" Nelson hated questions like that. He had never been on a date and, even if he had, that's the sort of thing he would tell Dad.

"Talk to anyone while you were there?" she continued, hoping he had.

"No," he lied, hoping she could not tell.

"Well, I'm delighted that you're taking such an interest". *How had Thom described him? 'A planet in want of an orbit'.* "What time's your bus?"

"Twenty to. Should get me there for about half nine, just in time for opening."

Nelson's spoon plopped wearily into the mortar lining the bottom of the bowl. The nuggets of prune had gone, and with them all remaining enthusiasm. Mum eyed the crockery until he took the hint.

"So what are you doing today?" he called back from the sink.

"I thought I might do a bit of knitting."

"Good God!"

"I think I heard that, young man!"

"I said 'good, good'." Nelson squirmed. "Like… couscous." And he rattled his bowl heartily in the hot water.

"I'll let you off." She winked.

For a moment Mum almost smiled, and Nelson fleetingly considered taking her into his confidence. He returned to the table wringing his hands around a thinning tea towel. *Let's see what today brings first.*

"I might set off for the bus a bit early. Make sure I don't miss it."

"Good idea. You know what they're like."

Nelson sidestepped up the stairs for his birthday bubble jacket. It was one of the few items of clothing he enjoyed wearing and had been earmarked exclusively for weekends to make it last. Mum had spotted it at the market and had secured it as a surprise with weekly payments. Bright yellow, it even boasted the Helly Hansen logo as a sort of tribute.

"I'm off!" he called from the hallway, wrestling a jammed zipper.

Setting down clumsy needles Mum came to kiss him. She always insisted on a proper goodbye, just in case he was killed during the day, or for some reason never came back. She never actually articulated it, but Nelson knew.

"Here's a pound for your lunch."

She wished it were more. *He* wished it were more.

"Thanks, Mum."

Nelson wiped the peck from his forehead, plucked his fob from the Burglar's Delight key tidy on the wall and was away.

Marching down the pavement, knee easing as he went, he was a man on a mission. He did not know what to expect, and did not expect what he would know, but in this moment he felt alive. The ice air burned his chest and fogged out in front; it nipped his lips as it passed and hung dew from his nose. He loved these mornings. He generally liked any morning on a Saturday, but today was different. Today he was special. He cleared the length of his street without troubling a crack, even the sections of crazy paving where the rapacious – *PersonalMishaps4U* on speed dial – routinely flung themselves down; a perfectly dribbled stone tipped down a grid momentarily big as a crater; and he even outpaced an old lady sharing his flight path, zipping out of her slipperstream and diving back in front as a lamppost scraped by. The pensioner was wheezing a happy tune all the way to the stop but need not have felt afraid: as a rule, Jasper did not work the bus route at weekends. Not enough passing trade, the populace reasoned. A nodded acknowledgement to the singlet-dressed man blowing smoke rings beyond his doorstep (with more of a care for his ceiling than his lungs) and Nelson was there.

The empty single decker slinked up a mere ten minutes late. Ordinarily, Nelson would have tackled the two miles ahead on foot, but he'd had stay-at-home stomach-ache on Monday so there were a couple of journeys spare in this week's fund. He climbed aboard, negotiated Mr Grumpy and made his way to his usual spot. The old lady was next up (Nelson's wafted invitation to the front of the queue graciously declined), but even her porcelain beam failed to sparkle the sourpuss at the wheel. It was only when the third and final passenger – possibly mid-twenties and certainly oblivious to October's capricious nature – bounced up, that the charm alarm activated. D1063 evidently could not do enough for the blonde, or her halter neck. He even cupped her manicured hand while handing over the change instead of swooshing it down the plastic flume like everyone else coppered for.

For a ridiculous moment, the new Nelson hoped Number Three might share his seat then panicked as she sashayed straight towards him. Fortunately, she drifted on, leaving a trail of scent and his cool hand against a glowing cheek. She made herself comfortable and the bus finally pulled away with at least two of its passengers crossing fingers the driver would at some point consider the road ahead as well as the rear-view mirror.

Half a mile – and several near misses – later she was gone. "It's your stop, sweetheart!" misery guts called out in his jauntiest tone. She wiggled to the front, ponytail swaying like a hypnotist's watch, breathed, "Thank you" (though it could well have been 'Do-do-be-doo') and was down the steps under the driver's concentrated gaze. It seemed all he could do to stop himself carrying her off and setting her gently down.

All eyes front at last, Nelson took the plunge and sprung up.

Yet the remainder of his journey passed with him dabbing a porridge-seared tongue against the roof of his drying mouth.

*

Though this moment had been anticipated all night, the museum grew into view too soon. Slowly – any sense of triumph strangely absent – he negotiated the *entire* length of the bus to begin the minute-long stroll to his destination.

Quarter of an hour later he arrived, feeling as though someone had stolen the bones from his legs. He looked up at the steps descended so warily yesterday. *Count them.* That did not help. The clock above clicked to nine thirty and a huge timber door began to groan like a casket lid. Inside. Waiting.

Breathe. For the first time, his eyes observed the thorns spiking the high window ledges. He assumed their objective was Keep *Out* – rather than *Off* – until a careless pigeon almost weathervaned itself. He deliberated on the portico and its columns: giant fluorescent tubes exhausted by traffic fumes. *Breathe.* And he attempted several times to decipher the banner strung crooked and twisted beneath, enticing passers-by to visit the Egyptian exhibition. 'K ds – Br n yo dad i s to ee our mum es!'

Breathe. As he lingered, a bush-bearded drifter, a matryoshka doll of overcoats, hacked alarmingly by for the warmth within. Nelson had promised *he* would be first. Dismissing the returned gripes from his patella he bounded the thirteen steps and paused at the top, shrouded within his own personal cloud.

Breathe. Deeply.

His rival barely halfway, there was a moment to look around from this gasping elevation. He shuttered his eyes, hoping to fix a picture of the world as it was this very second. He was sure it would be changed forever next time he saw it.

Then, inhaling fierce, he was in.

Chapter Three

The room was exactly as Nelson remembered. Statues, paintings, profusions: the art deco ballerina forever bronzed; the faded watercolours in their mish-mash of chrome, carve and dust; those unsettling masks of weather-beaten exotics; and the accumulation of Lilliputian cottages, holiday thimbles and clay pot Westies that suggested the consolation shelf at the amusement arcade.

"Thought I'd find you here, Nellie-bobs."

Nelson turned to find Aunty Thomasina in the doorway. She stood motionless for a moment, the biggest portrait in the room. He was becoming obsessed.

Stepping from her frame, she reached out a ruffling hand. What was it about Mum's family? Still, better than a kiss. "Heard you'd clunked your knee."

Nellie-bobs? He wasn't a child. *Not now, he wasn't.* "It's all right, thanks," and he lamented another few strands tumbling from his scalp.

He liked Aunty Thomasina, and her front room, in particular. It was a lost world, a Brigadoon existing only at Christmas, Easter and occasional red-letter days. From where he was standing net curtains repelled prying eyes and sieved the sunlight that dared glance the mahogany dining table. A glassy sideboard heaved with treasures from the four corners of the world – Murano (they had been to Venice for her fortieth), Taiwan, Woolworths and Carbootia. Near the window, the brawn of a writing bureau was summitted by a photo of Gran. And then, in pride of place, atop the sliver-streaked tiles of the mantelpiece, was the old lady herself.

Aunty Thomasina had bought Gilda Close from her and maintained this room, her mum's favourite, in case she visited from the sheltered accommodation. Gran died before she had chance to return, and Aunty had not the heart for a revamp.

"Too soon," she would say, "too many memories." Nelson understood.

Nelson guessed Aunty Thomasina was forty-something, and knew for certain she was the eldest of three sisters. The middle of the trio was Aunty Dick, though Diane was her real name. She was not coming today. There had been some garbled message about a blocked soil pipe and waiting in for a man to look at it: a tale that, for reasons utterly beyond Nelson, tickled every grown-up within earshot. His own mum had been the baby of the household and so, at the sisters' insistence, he would always be the baby's baby.

"Have you seen it, then?"

"Is it that furry thing?"

"Where?"

Nelson pointed it out.

"No, that's a bit of Clemmie fluff. Your Uncle Henry's dusting is beyond useless!"

For as long as Nelson cared to remember, his aunty had played a game where she added a new ornament to the sideboard collection especially for his visits and challenged him to unmask the interloper. It bore a passing resemblance to *Where's Wally*, except Nelson had already spotted him – garishly tank-topped and staring back from the mirror above the lacquered walnut.

A second examination revealed the mouse. One of those fiddly Swarovski numbers with whimsical dickie bow. Nelson was about to claim the point when a hand snaked out to fang his cheek.

"It's the mouse! I thought you'd have spotted that!"

"Oh yeah."

A notepad was retrieved from a drawer that opened in rattles. "Seventeen-sixteen to me. How about we play for double Christmas Eve?"

"Has Nelson told you about yesterday?" Mum, paper-plated, at the threshold. "Went to the museum. On his day off."

"Really?"

"And it wasn't any ordinary visit was it, Nelson?" she said between mouthfuls.

"I can't wait to hear," Aunty replied, a disconcerting keenness in her voice.

"Did something a bit special, didn't you?"

"Special?" he replied, finally.

"Don't be shy. Tell your aunty who you met."

"Met? Nobody…"

"Mumbling in your sleep?" *A hint.* "A name?"

"Ooh, now I'm very interested." Aunty Thomasina was always a sucker for a snippet. "Was it a boy or a girl?"

"A girl," replied Mum.

"Oooh, a *girl!* I thought he seemed a little distracted."

"He fell asleep on the couch yesterday afternoon; the early start must've caught up with him. Anyway, that's how I heard about…" Mum stared Nelson in the eye, gleefully letting the tension tickle before announcing, "…Pippa!"

"Ooh! Did he go into detail?" His head re-ruffled. *Stop that!*

"That was all I could make out. *Pipp-pah.*"

"Well, I think that's wonderful news. You used to have so many friends. Coming out of your shell at last, Nellie-bobs?"

Nelson was about to protest when it struck him that neither inquisitor had the faintest idea why he had returned to the museum. Yesterday's secret – the biggest, most amazing secret in the whole world – remained his alone. And a bout of teasing was a small price to pay for that.

"Pippa, eh?" continued Aunty. "She sounds a doll." And, delighted at her own joke, she nudged the nearest elbow at her sister's midriff.

*

"Clemmie's got the chicken!" A yell from the party's far border abruptly halted the ribbing. "Grab that mutt!"

By the time Nelson and the sisters reached the scene the West Highland White was haring around the back garden with Uncle Henry in stocking-soled pursuit, both combatants sporting a chicken leg clamped to their mouths. Nelson had just secured a spot on a concrete toadstool when Clementine – barely beyond a second circuit of the rockery, and to a chorus of disappointed groans – ran out of juice. Relinquishing her plunder at the doorstep, she bounded panting through the house for the sanctuary of the staircase.

Two drumsticks firmly seized, Uncle Henry called off the caper and was gleefully engulfed in backslaps as spectators dispersed for drinks. Then he propped up the wall with a dozen knuckles, waiting for his breath to catch up.

*

As it was a pleasantly mild October Sunday, the forty-fifth birthday celebration had spilled onto the patio. It was not that there was a large number of guests in attendance – mainly immediate family, neighbours and a trio of hangers-on from Uncle Henry's work who were keeping themselves to themselves – it was just that there was nowhere else to go. The kitchen-cum-buffet area was short and narrow, the front room cordoned off like a crime scene, and the rear lounge contained a three-piece suite, all tapestry and timber, so uncomfortable that no one could perch for more than five minutes before cramp set in. Yet this was the room that was Nelson's all-time favourite because it was dominated by the largest television set he had ever seen. Silver and sleek, like an intergalactic lander, it was guarded by a bank of surround-sound speakers that boomed disapproval at anyone who dared make contact. Underneath nestled the trimmest video recorder and a VD player (as Aunty called it), gleaming like a pool of mercury. He was allowed to watch sometimes. Today was not one of those times. "Too rude," ruled Mum, "not at someone else's party."

The thrill of the chicken chase at an end, Nelson resolved to stay occupied; keep his mind from the relentless rewind to Saturday's museum. A quick reconnoitre revealed, as feared, that he was the only guest with parent in attendance, notwithstanding Gran's ashes on the front mantelpiece, and with his two cousins beholden to the terrors of a stuffed soil pipe there wasn't anyone remotely his own age to seek out. Aunty Thomasina had no children: a situation, both her sisters had separately concluded, probably not unrelated to Uncle Henry's lack of stamina. A penguin had been adopted, though they had to leave it at the zoo, much to her nephew's disappointment. They did visit once, but it just ignored them then waddled off when the man with the fish arrived. *Gratitude for you.* Uncle Henry bought Clemmie after that. Two legs bad, four legs good. Apart from the chewing, and the scratching. And now the chicken drumstick.

After stopping off to pluck at the buffet's vegetarian selection – cheese and onion pie, cheese and tomato quiche, and cheese surprise sandwich, which was actually egg mayonnaise (Aunty's little joke) – Nelson meandered back through the patio doors and into a conversation he deduced, rather smartly, he thought, about continental pen-pals. He arrived to snorting laughter that died away into synchronised throat-clearing.

One of the trio of work mates pretended to spot the newcomer.

"Oh hello! Who's this little soldier?"

"Nelson."

"Little sailor, then!"

"Actually, I was named after Nelson Mandela, the South African president."

"That's the chap. He likes bright clothes, too, doesn't he?"

And this from someone with the effrontery to parade a Disney waistcoat in public. *Ruddy cheek!*

"I think you'll find, young Nelson," the man continued, "that President Mandela was, in fact, named for Lord Horatio. Thus my 'little sailor' statement indeed holds water, so to speak."

The threesome guffawed between gulps from old-fashioned half-pint mugs that resembled amber hand grenades. Nelson smiled politely, secretly hoping at least one might explode. It gradually became obvious no one had anything else to say as the chortling ran on to a ridiculous degree. Then, just when Nelson thought it was all over, one of the others piped up, "Anchors aweigh!" and it began anew.

"Going so soon?" Aunty had appeared.

"Not yet, Tomaszewski. Having far too much fun. Cheers!"

Movement at her rear.

"Henners, old son!"

The host, patting the nape of his neck with a handkerchief, was beckoned over. Aunty Thomasina pounced.

"Ah, there you are. Don't get settled, birthday boy. Just nip upstairs and fetch the cardboard box from the wardrobe, will you?"

Nelson knew exactly what was coming next and slid back inside to claim the armchair nearest the television. ("Where was I?" asked The Waistcoat as soon as the coast was clear. "Oh yes, the French letters story...") He had just about plumped the cushions and settled down, legs dangling and an arm flat against the chill timber, when Uncle Henry returned, laden.

"Do we have to do this now, Thomasina?"

"Of course not," she replied, "but we're going to."

"Well, I'm off to find the chaps, then."

Looking through old photographs was a sort of tradition whenever Aunty was entertaining. Not a tradition like weekly pocket money; more like foxhunting. Everyone had seen them dozens of times, of course, but Thomasina had a system where she replaced recently viewed packets to the bottom of the pile. That way, long-forgotten snaps came to the surface to be discovered afresh like ammonites.

She took the box from Uncle Henry and placed it reverentially on the floor. Battered, bruised and held together by masking tape bandages, it slumped as the daylight slashed at it through the plumb blinds. Nelson could just about make out the ancient '*Stardrops*' image on its side. A mummified bottle of disinfectant grinned from behind the yellowing stripes that hid the '*St rd op* ' of the logo. In his mind, Nelson always added an 'e' onto the letters that remained. And smiled.

The women at the party began to swirl into the room like water at a plughole. Nelson's scheme to claim his seat early was paying dividends until Mum wandered in last, steadying a glass of wine. Still, he could tolerate being squashed: the important thing was that he could hear. He thrilled at all the tittles and tattles and confidences. And, more than that, he delighted in their acceptance of his presence. Nelson, the honorary adult.

"Are you comfortable there?" asked Thomasina. A handful of heads nodded. "Don't worry about resting glasses on the arms. Full of scratches anyway. Scrooge says I can't have a new one till the dog dies."

She dipped into the box and pulled out a plum-coloured envelope, '*SunnySnaps*' emblazoned across its flap. As the pouch was unfolded a scatter of negatives emptied onto the carpet, from where they were pawed into a pile with scant regard to touch-on-the-edge-only protocols.

"And who have we here?" she invited at last, holding aloft the first photograph. The five women crammed onto the three-seater, only lower arms free, began to flip it down the line, lap to lap.

"Is it your Dick?" suggested Three, squinting.

"Same ears," confirmed Five, spinning it over to the armchair.

Mum made a red-lipped grin as the photo arrived. Her son shrunk for the shadows. "It's not Dick. It's Nelson!"

"No!" the crowd cooed.

"Why's he wearing a dress?" enquired Four.

"We were here," she explained, "when Mum was alive, and Nelson had an *accident* and," she turned to Nelson, "all Nan had was one of my old dresses, didn't she, Nelse?"

Barely into his teens, Nelson's life in clothes had so far been one great tragedy. He was too young to remember wearing the dress, which is probably just as well because Dad was working that day and they'd had to get the bus home. But he had seen the picture before. In fact, he had seen it only the last time they had played 'Family Photos', during the summer holidays. And the time before that, come to think of it. Either Aunty's filing system had gone awry, or she was dealing from the bottom. Reddened, Nelson leaned out as far as he dared without jeopardising his position and jettisoned the oblong backstabber.

Next out of the box was a selection of less familiar memories. There was one of Mum, aged perhaps ten, standing at the top of the driveway of Gilda Close holding aloft a goldfish in a bowl. *Must have been taking it for some fresh air.* There was a photo of Nan and Grandad defying a moonscape beach. Then there was a shot of Nan looking bereft on an empty couch. Aunty Thomasina reported that Grandad had run away with Mrs Trott who lived next door. Everybody gasped and a hush descended.

Eventually, Mum inhaled a deep slurp. "We've never had much luck with men in this family."

"Oh, I don't know," said Aunty defensively as Uncle Henry appeared, tilting a beer and carrying Clemmie, tufty as a popped swan, under one arm.

"Brought this naughty girl to see you," he said. And as he placed the dog down it dived headlong into the photos and snatched a mouthful.

"Sit!" boomed Henry.

The instruction went unheeded and the second chase of the day was underway.

"Hmm…" said Aunty as the pair disappeared.

The quiet returned, and a sense of unease about the next few minutes began to bubble in Nelson. As a rule, Mum usually refused to engage with the 'men' topic, but exceptions had been noted when wine was at large. Happily, though, further conversation was curtailed by a racket from the hallway that signalled Henry's return. Creaking berry-faced through the door he halted gauchely perpendicular to the room. Nelson could see that his uncle was attempting to conceal a spectacular grass stain down the beige of his chinos.

"I've got your photos back," he panted. A handful of prints were held out, and he retreated backwards through the door.

"Clemmie's had a right go at these," Aunty moaned, flicking through scraps. "Oh, hang on. Not a scratch on this one. Nelson in the dress!" Almost everyone in the room cheered.

The hostess was soon back rummaging at the box. She put the incriminating evidence back in its envelope and made to feed it to the bottom of the pile, or at least pretended to. Yet as the stack was lifted, Nelson caught sight of something that did not quite belong. Among the gaudy envelopes with their desert-island shores, hot-air balloon rides and windswept donkey derbies, was a glimpse of crimson that embered with the faintest lustre.

"What's that, Aunty Thomasina?"

"What's what, love?"

"At the bottom there, the red thing."

"Oh, this," she announced, outstretched arms counterbalancing a Bacardi Breezer and a leather-bound journal, "belongs to the one man this family can really be proud of."

But she did not know what Nelson knew.

*

Nelson moved to cross-legged on the rug and sat the book delicately on his lap. He smoothed his hand across the rivulets of its surface then traced its foolscap perimeter with a tender finger. Gently, he tipped it over and around. A silk thread burrowed inside, and gilt-edged pages dazzled his curiosity. He rested it down again and the sun sparkled a puff of dust that rose to his musty nose.

"It was among your gran's belongings when we moved in. We had no idea she had it. I'm not sure *she* knew she had it. Look inside, Nelson."

Curator-careful, he gingerly eased it apart so the spine settled between his knees. Attached within was a portrait – not black and white exactly, more caramel-brown – of a man in a uniform. Almost hidden behind a moustachioed lip was a stiff-backed presence, chest in profile, head turned towards the camera. On his near breast a medal gleamed; to the front, he awkwardly cradled a picture frame. But the observer was drawn elsewhere, to the eyes: dark, doleful.

"Now, there is a handsome lad," said Four, swan-necking.

"Is he a fireman?" asked Two.

"A policeman," Aunty replied.

"I wouldn't mind him taking down my tippiculars…" And the sardine settee shook.

Encouraged that the volume had not crumbled in his grasp, Nelson was now skimming the pages within. It was a diary begun, according to the initial entry imploring God to save the King, January 1st 1903 Anno Domini ("*That's 'In the Year of Our Lord', Nelson. We did a bit of Latin at Corpus*"). The handwriting was the most beautiful he had ever seen: great sweeping loops of ornate italics, flourishes of deep blue curlicue. Nelson drew his thumb across a blur of pages, days breezing by. And then, finding the final entry, he gasped. This last of the leaves was catastrophically altered. What had once been calligraphy – Mum had been through a phase with a special pen – was now disjointed and spattered, the dimpled surface stabbed and scarred. Amid the foul, shuddering scrawl letters could barely be deciphered, let alone words, phrases, paragraphs. Nelson pitched pages back and forth, searching for an explanation, but there was none to be found. And beyond there, time and reason ended: thoughts, feelings – secrets – lost to the emptiness that remained.

He returned to the photograph at the front and looked again into those eyes. *What had they seen?* It occurred to him that some of Aunty's photos had commentary on the back, reminders of the scenes they captured: '*Harry's Bar, Venice 2000 – SIPPING! a 20 Euro Bellini!!!*'

"Can I take the photo out, please?"

A nod of assent. Nelson pinched the edge and lifted it from its binding. As it came away, a vellum rectangle, tucked behind, loosened into his lap.

It was a commendation, embossed lettering reading: 'Presented for Long and Meritorious Service to Caleb Fitzgerald, Sergeant in His Majesty's Police Force, Upon His Retirement This Day November 11th 1903'. The certificate from the frame in the portrait.

"Who is he?"

"That, Nelson, is your great-great-great-grandfather, Sergeant Caleb Fitzgerald. One of the finest policemen to walk God's earth."

"Did he solve any murders?"

"He'd have caught Jack the Ripper given half a chance."

"Did you ever meet him?"

Everybody laughed.

"Cheeky monkey! How old do you think I am?"

"I'm really not sure," he replied, truthfully, "but you look very young."

Off the hook.

"Little charmer, you. I know where you get that from." Thomasina instinctively glanced up at her sister and pulled a 'sorry' expression. "No," she went on quickly, "your great-great-great-grandad was long before our time. We do know something about him, though: Uncle Henry began reading the journal when we first discovered it, but he ran out of steam, as usual. It seems our ancestor had a hard life, though."

"How do you mean?"

"From what we can gather Caleb and his wife, Ella, your great-great-great-grandma, already had a daughter when, quite late in life, they discovered she was expecting again. Now, medicine wasn't as advanced as it is now and shortly after the birth Ella died."

"No!" The afternoon's second collective gasp.

"Well, you can imagine. The only thing that kept Caleb functioning was the baby. Doted on the boy. Brought him up alone, which was unusual for a man in those days. Then one morning, Caleb awoke to find his son, seven years old by now, missing. Not a trace. Disappeared into thin air. He searched night and day. Became an obsession."

"But he found him, though?"

"No, he didn't. And it seems others had disappeared, too. Taken from their rooms at the dead of night. They became known as The Vanishings."

"I've never heard of them. What was it?"

"No one knows who, or what, it was. It is a mystery without resolution."

42

A cram of questions began to coalesce; there were facts to be established before St John's' greatest-ever Show and Tell the following morning. But reciting 'great-great-great-grandad' was clearly too cumbersome. A shorthand was required. Nelson pondered options: 'Grandad Fitz' – not strictly factual, and verging on *diagnostic*; 'The Sergeant – too impersonal; 'Caleb' – too impertinent.

"So," said Nelson, clearing his throat, "what happened to him, *4G*?"

"Who?"

"4G."

"Who's 4G?" asked Mum.

By the time he had explained it all, Nelson began to think it would have been quicker persevering with all those 'greats'.

"Well," said Aunty Thomasina, "*4G…*"

Nelson grinned.

"…4G disappears from the pages of history, literally. You've seen for yourself the final entry, and the photograph, and after that no one knows. We asked your gran, of course, but lucidity had long left her by then. There was just one occasion when something seemed to spark in her: she rambled away about him '*setting a house afire*' then spent the rest of the visit insisting he was harmless. What *is* perfectly clear from the journal is his desperation to get his boy back. He went so far as employing mysticism, apparently."

"What's 'mysticism'?"

"Mumbo jumbo," said Mum, draining her glass. "It's séances and incantations, ghosts, the occult and… and mumbo-jumbo—"

"It is," Aunty interjected, "a belief in an existence beyond our own reality. A bridge between the living and the dead, where supernatural forces can be harnessed to effect things beyond our comprehension."

"Mummbo. Jummmmbo."

"We're very arrogant, you know," Thomasina replied as Uncle Henry materialised. "We can't see everything. Have you just changed your trousers?"

"Hoo-ray Henry! Be my spirit guide and point me in the direction of the vodka." And Uncle was back out again as Mum swam away to the kitchen. Amid the embarrassed silence, Nelson looked again at his forebear. He was not the same as before. Now there was a shock of hair, streaked-grey, lines ravine-deep gouged into flesh, downturned mouth undeniable. And those desperate, desolate eyes. It was the face of a haunting.

"Would it be all right if I borrowed this book please, Aunty Thomasina?"

"Course it would, Nelson. See if you can solve the case, eh?"

There was a sudden crash and a splintering of glass. Aunty patted Nelson's forearm and, heading for the door, quietly suggested it was time to tidy away. "Everything all right, Henry?" she called.

The room swiftly emptied, leaving Nelson to replace the photos into the arse box. A little rifling later he had located his target. He held it to his face and grimaced. A furtive glance to check no one was peering through the vertical blinds and it slid perfectly between the outer cardboard and the hideous paisley wallpaper that someone, enjoying a criminal amount of spare time, had used to line the box's interior. He was still congratulating himself on the success of 'No More Nelson in the Dress' when something new seized his attention.

Nestling loose between 'Henry asleep in a chair 1992' and 'Puppy Clemmie wearing a kilt 1999' was a snap of a young boy, aged about seven. Nelson scanned its fringes, searching, then turned his attention to the image's foreground. It was a blustery, colourless, winter's day, yet the boy glowed against the gloom. He had just reeled in a kite flapping and squirming. He was trying to hold it steady as it fought to be free and his aunty was shouting, "Cheese!" But the boy in the picture was not interested in his kite, nor the lens. His gaze was elsewhere. He was looking up to his right at the man crouched alongside; the man cradling his shoulder with a tender, tethering arm. And the boy was smiling sharps and flats. And the man was laughing, too. And the smell was warm and safe. And the wind was making his eyes water. And he wanted to stay there forever. And his eyes were watering now.

"Dad…"

"Nelson…" Uncle Henry had reappeared.

His back to the door, Nelson sawed at his eyes with index fingers and turned around. There was now a burgundy stain down his uncle's grey trouser leg.

"Red wine," he said, looking down, "slight accident. Are you all right, Nelson?"

Nelson nodded.

"We've ordered a taxi. Your mum won't be able to walk home."

"But we can't affor—"

"It's all taken care of."

Aunty Thomasina joined her husband and a quick turn of charades established that Mum was sitting on the stairs hugging a coffee.

"Aunty Thomasina?"

"Yes, Nelson?"

"You don't have his medal, do you?" And he pointed out 4G's chest.

"I think it's in the bureau. I'll get the key."

She returned within the minute and presented Nelson with a fistful of scarlet box. He held it in clammy hands, then prised it apart. The medal was smaller, though heavier, than he imagined and attached to a rainbow of resolute ribbon, with a pin for a proud chest. The king's head was in relief on the obverse and haloed by Roman numerals. Nelson read, "Em, cee, em eye-eye-eye. Is that 1903?"

"It is."

The medal was pressed against its portrait. The disc's sheen had long since faded, yet Nelson was dazzled to the marrow.

"Is it valuable?"

"I doubt it. It's certainly not gold and probably not even silver, although there might be a little of that mixed in with pewter or tin and a few other things," Henry guessed.

"Can I borrow this too, please?"

"Well…"

"Oh, don't be so silly, Henry! It's only stuck in a cupboard and you just said yourself it wasn't valuable."

"Thanks!"

"You will look after it, though? It might not be worth a great deal, but it's a part of us, and that counts more than any money. Check with your mum, too, when she's feeling better;

there was a box of keepsakes she took at the time and I'm not too sure she's felt up to sorting through them yet."

Nelson nodded and trailed a cheered droplet up his forearm. As he pocketed his bounty the taxi honked its arrival.

At the bottom of the driveway Uncle Henry passed the address to the driver and attempted to pay with a book token. He returned to the house for cash then tottered back with Aunty Thomasina – and Mum draped between.

"Oh nooo, I've made my baby cry," she was whimpering above the chug of diesel. Nelson, abashed, scampered for the farthest seat. Mum was poured into the kerbside belt and Uncle Henry pushed his head within to retrieve the coffee cup. *Whittard.* One of a set of six. Not even in the sale.

"Thanks for coming," he said jauntily. Nelson suspected he was just being nice.

"Shpleashure."

"And thanks for the lovely cardigan."

Now he knew he was.

"Everything's sorted, Nelson. The driver'll help you get your mum in if… erm… if needs be. I'd have taken you, but I've had a drink." And with that the door was shut, the roof double-slapped and they were away in a choke of fumes.

Mum was snoring before third gear so Nelson spread the day's assortment in the space separating them. He weighed the medal in his palm then returned to consider 4G. So much in common, a century apart.

Love. Loss. Quest.

There was something else. Checking first to his left, he rummaged under his tank top and T-shirt and pulled out the kite photo. The driver had his window down, air rattling at his shirt sleeve, and Nelson's hair was blowing and his mum had started to mutter in her sleep. *That* ran in the family. The boy was holding on and his fingers were pale and aching, but he did not want to let go.

"Hello? Erm, Nelson, is it?"

Nelson lifted his lids and they sluiced salty once more.

"We're here." The driver craned into the mirror. "You all right? Wind in your eyes, was it? You should've said, *son*."

Nelson glared.

At the rake of the handbrake he stared down at the photo of his dad and scrutinised once more, as schooled, the distance beyond their figures. A marquee, mini-fairground, rows and rows of cars to be trailed around for hours. Wait. Was that someone? *There*. Staring in their direction. Watching.

A photograph. So they had not got every one after all.

Something, somehow, had begun.

Just as he had been promised.

Chapter Four

"What's this shite?"

"Muesli, Heath. It's good for you."

"Good for me if my name was Mr Ed. You'll have me running at bastard Newmarket next. Where's my Coco Pops?"

"You had the last on Friday."

"I know I *finished* a box on Friday, so where's the new one?"

"At the shop. I forgot to get one."

"I forgot to get one?" This was the 'tell' that Heath was about to be displeased: the return of your previous statement as a question. "Jesus Christ!" The *Mirror* cracked down on the table. "I take it you also *forgot* to get that new frock you've been on about?"

Heather pretended she had not heard, but her quiet merely cranked up the volume.

"No, I didn't think so! Cocos. All I want is a bowl of bastard Cocos! Is that too much to ask when I'm out working all week?"

"Look, why don't you just try some muesli? It's all natural. Better than all those 'e' numbers."

"Well, yes, I can see it's doing you a power of good. What have we plummeted to now? Twenty stone? You'll soon be down to just having tits on the front at this rate."

Heather didn't rise to the bait. *It'll be his trouble*, she thought. *Must be playing up this morning.* She had long since – after several painful rounds, it had to be admitted – reached the conclusion that there was no sparring with her husband when he was in one of his moods. Anyway, she was nowhere near twenty stone. More like twelve.

"No, what I meant was it'll help, you know, your…" The missing word was '*bottom*' – they all knew – but it was silently mouthed on account of her proximity to the breakfast table.

By the time Heather's slice of wholemeal jack-in-the-boxed from the Dualit, Heath had reverted to hunter-gatherer mode ducking, sniffing and scratching into cupboards. As he stooped, the crack of his backside grinned out hairily between T-shirt and towelling shorts. *Oh, to rake this toast ferociously, like sandpaper, down that furrow. That would make the miserable sod jump.*

"You buy some shite," he eventually mumbled.

No reply.

"I say!" The secret sneer slipped back into its sanctum as he rose to his full 5'4", shine-faced, and now light-headed, clutching a bottle. "I say! You buy some sh…"

"I heard you," Heather dripped with despair.

"Olive oil? Olive oil! In my day that was for washing your tortoise."

"Look, why don't you sit down and let me get you…" and she reeled off a menu fit for a tyrant.

"No, I'm having nothing now. On principle. And if I get in a bad mood just remember whose fault it is. I could faint at my desk. Who's going to sub the paper then, eh?"

"Dad?"

"What?"

"If you think about it, your name actually is Mr Ed. Do you get it?"

"Pipe down, Norton. Little tit."

Norton, too, was well versed in defusal tactics and he returned to gently scraping preserve – what else? – across his cream cracker.

The kettle toiled and bubbled, and three mugs of decaf decamped at last to the table. The momentary lull suited everyone.

Working from home today on account of the builders, Heath was now rifling his way through the *Daily Mail*, pausing occasionally to scribble notes on a shorthand pad. As editor of *The Respecter*, a weekly freesheet, his morning ritual included skimming the nationals for stories that could be lifted and re-written with a local angle. Cheap news for a cheap operation. House prices soaring – ring Mike at the Royal Bank; firefighters grumbling – call Derek at the station; bubonic plague making a comeback – any cases at the walk-in centre? And so it went.

Heather watched the great man as she exhaled across cupped hands. Twenty years, this year. For bitter or worse, she had vowed. Half her forty summers. It had not always been like this: he had mellowed. Still, the money came in handy. There had never been a mortgage. Their home, The Cottage, had passed down through generations to the first-born male (a regular boast for his local history vanity column). Heath was an only child. So was Ming the Merciless. He had also been left a moderate inheritance and so Heather, taking full advantage of the indulgences bestowed upon a second wife, had tended to view his wages as 'spends'. There was the MGF roadster, the annual cruise, the beauty regime. And at the end of the month, she could play the cards like a steamboat sharp. Heath's credit was good with everyone – especially her.

Nevertheless, the role of Edward homemaker, as all the best quiz shows now referred to her calling, did bring its worries. Numbed by the constant round of cheapskate cheque presentations, chip pan fires, bonny babies and clever pets – *not to mention treachery!* – Heath was lumbering towards retirement. It was the only thing that got him to work in the morning. But it was not merely the thought of spending unnecessary hours with her husband that was troubling Heather: it was his new-found interest in the family finances. He had actually started scrutinising the household bills. Units consumed, off-peak, on peak, don't peek. She had even caught him reading through their joint bank statement. And not just a cursory glance at the bottom line in case they had been cleaned out by a sticky-fingered clerk funding a secret life as a high roller. On many an occasion he had indeed thought this to be the case until assuaged by his wife: golf club membership, must-have Manolo's, six-week month, etc. If this assiduity continued, she would be saying goodbye to living like *Hello*.

He knew about the credit cards, of course. Most of them. And he had tried to rein her in. "Leave that thing in the house," he would growl. "If you take it out you know you'll have to use it. It's like a bloody Gurkha's knife."

Still, she knew roughly the days her statements were due and worked hard at intercepting them, though the early mornings were playing havoc with the bags around her eyes. Nothing a little prick could not sort out.

Yet in recent weeks her husband had seemed a little more perky on the finance front. Builders were due for a loft conversion and Heath had squirrelled himself away up there for a general tidy and prep work. Heather would arrive home late on (aren't the hours kept by tanning parlours far more agreeable these days?) to find him in his lofted lair, head down in a book and wittering excitedly to himself. The conversion was to become Heath's home office, overlooking the graveyard. The last of the attic junk – one hundred years of knick-knacks, doodahs and, for the most part, plain old doo – had been cleared out and the completion date was now set for three weeks hence, give or take a builder's month. Or two.

What was tickling Heath's fancy, as far as Heather could see, was the deal he had contrived on the funding. The work was costing £10,000 in total, and Heath had persuaded *The Respecter* to stump up half the final tab. He had convinced the Regional Director that the company could hive off its town-centre premises and ask/force* (*delete as appropriate) the staff – two reporters, one photographer, four advertising sales 'executives' – to work from home using the miracle of broadband and ISDN. Organise a PO Box for any correspondence and the money saved by this restructuring would more than compensate for the outlay on his new office.

Heath estimated the conversion would put £50,000 onto the value of The Cottage. Add to that the masterstroke, amid all this jiggery-pokery, of a phoney £30,000 invoice from the builder – a mate from the history buffs – and *The Respecter* was not the only one getting a good deal for its *fifteen* grand contribution. All that remained then, with the money banked and the snagging signed off, was for Heath to announce the surprise swansong of his illustrious career.

No wonder he looked pleased with himself whenever he climbed the steps and sidled off into his crow's nest. The family would tease him, disposition dependent, that he had uncovered a gold mine up there.

*

"We've had an e-mail from Heath." Heather was now bored with the quiet and one of her dietary tactics was to keep her jaw otherwise engaged.

"What did he say?" asked Heath.

"You know Heath, Heath. Moaning about his loan, as usual. Blah, blah, blah."

"Did he say when he's back next?" chipped in Norton.

"He's not sure. Doesn't think he'll be able to make this weekend, after all."

The Edwards' nineteen-year-old eldest was in his second year studying media at the University of Northumbria. In a giant leap of imagination they had christened him Heath: Heath Snr had claimed it as a family custom and no one was going to argue. The presence of more than one Heath was a ready recipe for confusion in the Edward household; even more so when *Little* Heath reached puberty and, in one of those strange quirks of genetics, sprouted to 6'2".

It often bothered Norton that his parents had not tried harder to maintain the letter string. Don't think it had not crossed his mind. *Why Norton?* What was wrong with Heathen? And any third sibling, he reckoned, could be Heathland, or Heathrow. Boy or girl.

This news of Little Heath's temporary indisposition put a spring in Norton's seat.

"It's Norton I feel sorry for," Heather fumbled blindly on. "I know how much he looks forward to big brother's visits."

Yeah, right.

*

On Little Heath's last appearance at The Cottage – which, as usual, coincided with him running out of ready clothes and clean cash – he had shredded with bare hands, just for the fun of it, five pairs of his younger brother's boxer shorts. Three were being worn at the time. The waistband on one pair had courageously refused to submit so Little heaved littler around the house like a human holdall until Norton snapped chin-first into the parquet. The chafing around his groin had him mincing orangutan-style for a week.

"Have they told you yet?"

"Told me what?"

"Oh, why can't people just be honest? Are they just going to let you find out in a few years?"

"What are you on about, Heath?"

"I'm on, Nort-on, about you being adopted."

"Am I balls!"

"Course you are. Just look at you. Does anyone else in this family have black hair?"

"Mum might."

"And how come you're so bloody thick?"

"Fuck off!"

"You must be the only Year Nine still writing in crayon. Bastard rescue dog, you are."

"Don't talk shite! And anyway, you're the one different to all of us."

Big brother let go a jab. "And don't you forget it. That's what's known as evolution, Mr Mencap. Mr *Nort-on*."

A throbbing deltoid was massaged, wincing.

"Oh, come on then. Shake paw."

The hand extended was cold-shouldered and a second punch hit home.

"Fucking stop it!"

Little Heath would often dispense 'digs' during these fraternal reunions. Just above sleeve level. His latest wheeze was to pummel the top of Norton's arm until he had been furnished with ten jokes.

"Funny ones!"

"Oww!"

"Funny ones or!"

"Owww!"

"Else!"

"Owwww!"

Enjoyed a laugh, Little Heath.

*

Heath Snr was now studying *The Sun*. He had picked it up and held it in front of his face like a spy. That way he could ogle Page Three without getting caught. Norton had finished his cracker and was warmly hugging his own shoulders. He watched wisps of his father's grey arc out from behind the paper like solar flares. *Bet Dad had black hair when he was little.*

"What's the plan for school today, Norton?"

Heather was *very* impressed. Heath had never before taken an interest in Norton's schooling. Perhaps this loft conversion had loosened him a little, given him new purpose.

"Oh, you know, Dad."

Norton caught his breath for the dreaded, "Who are you calling 'Dad'?", but it never came.

"He's doing well at this new place, aren't you, Norton?" Heather offered. "You could end up at uni, just like Heath, if the teachers give you a chance this time."

"And what are *you* up to today?" Heath asked nicely enough, but in hindsight Heather would have been better advised suggesting she was off to the shop in search of chocolate-flavoured breakfast cereals.

"I'm meeting June. We're having our nails done."

Heather was particularly particular about her grooming. She liked to make the most of her natural beauty. A perma-tan accentuated ice-blue contact lenses and glacier crowns; an immaculate (and outrageously expensive) coiffure, ribboned with all the reds of autumn, poured over her shoulders; lips were plumped like a paddling pool and eyebrows were colour-coded and plucked pin-sharp.

She had been a blonde once, and before that no one could remember. Over the years she had ranged from platinum to yolk but had given it up for fear of appearing brassy like the buggy brigade from the estate: all chain smokes, tatts and greasy brown partings.

Her inspirations were the doyennes of the lifestyle magazines, delivered in heaps to her door. Although currently de rigueur, Heather was not too fussed about this working-mum trend but was very interested in the glamour, the clothes, the wealth and the hunky husband. Unfortunately, Heather's aspiration to the stick-thin glitterati was circumscribed by a couple of significant flaws. The first, the hunky husband. *Look at the state of him.* Puggy, puffy, gasping, grasping. Mind you, his face looked younger than his years. This she put down to the complete absence of laughter lines. He had been in mourning the morning they met. Their paths crossed again weeks later – she wearing a wimple, he packed into Werhmacht grey (what *was* it with her and uniforms?) – and their courtship began. She was the svelte, glamorous girl about town, he the classically educated widower widely regarded to be going places. He never arrived. From pretty boy to petty man. He had the world at his feet, and now time had tripped him.

And the second flaw? Well…

"Having your nails done? What for?" Heath thought it too cheap to enquire just yet about the price, though this was a concern.

"So I'll look nice," she called back from the dishwasher.

"So I'll look nice? You want to get your priorities right: 'My arse might be a yard across, but look at my lovely nails!' I doubt the first thing people in the street will notice about you is your bastard nails! You want to get to the gym. Thighs like a bloody brontosaurus. We could soap the Third World if we melted those down…"

Of course, Heather had tried to get trim, but it was just not that easy with her metabolism. She had dieted for years. Who hadn't? And there had been successes. Her record loss was five pounds in a single day, yet even that failed to impress. And, to be frank, she could have done without the gastroenteritis. At least her husband felt able to offer the occasional word of encouragement. "Just read a piece in one of these," he went on, rummaging through his mound of dailies, "about how housework's supposed to be an effective way of exercising. Just a thought, Idleweiss." *Loved* The Sound of Music, *did Heath.*

Heather's back remained turned while she stabbed – several times – a utility knife into the cutlery basket.

"And who's paying for this nail jamboree?" Heath had been known to exhibit 'letting go' issues.

"I am."

"You mean *I* am. I'm trying to retire here. Is that too much to ask? A bit of enjoyment in my later years? I've done my bloody whack and all you're doing is holding me back. How old am I now?"

"Fifty-four."

"Am I?" He sounded surprised. If he had been any good at maths he would have counted back to check. "Well, it's a good job I've got a pension plan lined up, see out my days in a modicum of comfort. It's a good job *I've* not been sitting around on a big fat wobbly arse."

Heather rolled her eyes to the cobwebbed ceiling and wished the old miser would shut up about that bloody loft.

"Just remember, son," Heath jabbed across the table,

"there's nothing – *nothing* – more important than funds."

Norton nodded as he slipped into shiny Rockports, zig-zagged his temporary tie to Adam's apple, popped a 'what's-the-worst-you-can-do?' baseball cap into his rucksack and lifted the blazer from the back of his chair. He had learned to remember everything his dad told him. The belt of leather on leg was something not readily forgotten.

"Right," announced Heath. "I'm off upstairs."

"Anything for the splash?" Heather's opportunity to extend some peace-offering curiosity.

"Sod all. Might get something from the police calls. If not, we'll have to go with the hamster that recognises all the Mister Men. We could do with a murder, or a nice kidnapping. Something to get our teeth into."

Heather watched on as her husband stretched for the banister, the dirty divot emerging for a final squint.

"That's awful," she grimaced.

"That's newspapers," he called back, oblivious.

*

Alone in the kitchen Heather located a blue feather duster, freed it from its crusty sleeve and wafted it about like a conjurer's bouquet. A plume of spores trailed behind as it collected a spider nest from among the plasterwork. *Ten calories.* She spied her toast, untouched and cold, and posted it in the pedal bin. *Two points.* If only she had buttered it; that would have been four. Then, contemplating the Danish with June that had just been earned, the tickling stick was downed and she headed for the shopping channels.

Norton, meanwhile, had swung his rucksack like a swag bag and yanked the front door behind him. As he marched the garden path a grin played his face. A grin that did not really belong on a Monday morning.

"*What's the plan for school today?*" Norton knew what it meant. They both knew. He'd had his instructions.

And he was going to enjoy this.

Chapter Five

Roland Grange emerged blinking from Noah's General Stores weighed down like Double or Drop. Pausing on the red-tiled step, he eased his burden by feeding the PS2 magazine into the gaping mouth of his satchel, which he had carefully floored between splats of spittle. That was for RE. The remainder of his purchases *would* be required en route. A Kit Kat Chunky nestled into his left-hand blazer pocket, company for the jelly beans. Cheese and Onion Walkers crinkled into the right, the savoury side, with the Chipsticks, and he would have his Strawberry NutriGrain now: get the healthy stuff out of the way.

At the start of the term Mr Noah, driven to the brink of bankruptcy by wanton pilfering – even the dog biscuits went walkies – had imposed a blanket ban on St John's pupils. Only Roland had been exempt, but even his stupendous outlay was never going to be enough to keep Noah afloat, so the owner rescinded and allowed the animals to return two by two: all the better to keep an eye on the cunning swines. Unfortunately, only permitting pupils through in pairs created a bottleneck at the entrance and there was nothing for those treading water in the doorway but gabbing and gobbing.

Roland was running late this morning on account of having a larger than usual breakfast. There was the regular basin of Golden Nuggets and the swim-float toast, all rinsed down by a mug of sugar with two spoons of tea. *And* a dotty banana (pockmarked, over-ripe was all he could stomach). Usually, he would skip the banana, but Nan was on the premises and she liked to see him eating healthily.

By ten past nine Mr Noah had been fighting a rising panic. Leaning into his counter, he alternated watching his watch and zooming in on the convex spy-mirror covering the door. He moved in to wipe its glass, as if Roland might materialise from behind the grime. Circling its newly polished curve, he rounded on his own reflection: its pudding-bowl haircut, the thick-rimmed glasses, bulbous nose and diabolical goatee. He resembled a disguise. Pearls of sweat formed strings in the deepening depths of his brow. *Don't tell me he's ill. Please don't let it be serious.* Then the doorbell clattered and in rushed Roland's swollen purse. A guaranteed score, more with the scratchcards and his mum's cigs. Of course, the snoopers from Trading Standards had crossed Mr Noah's mind, but the boy *looked* sixteen and, more to the point, Mrs Grange was on forty Chimleys a day.

Grabbing the opportunity for a final rehearsal before curtain up at school, Roland informed Mr Noah that he was behind time due to his sister hogging the bathroom in preparation for a work experience interview. Mr Noah, dusting the reduced to clear Jaffa Cake display, nodded sympathetically then suggested that Roland might exchange the narrative's premise for a hospital appointment.

Ready cash and farewells were exchanged, and back outside it was 9.20am. With St John's still ten minutes away and first register long gone, there was little point rushing. In any case, it was the kind of mild autumnal morn that had polar bears all of a lather.

Roland lingered to savour these extended minutes to his liberty. Peeling nimbly at foil he craned to the find-the-missing-angle contrails slowly dissipating against the sky; a backcloth of ever-deepening blue towering out of sight, a real spacescraper. He scrunched a fistful of wrappers into a trouser pocket and meandering off, Noah watching wistfully on, tackled the last of his five packs of football cards, quickly sorting new additions from doublers to be exchanged later in the playground. With a Twix already down the hatch, an approximation of cheese and onion now perfumed the air.

"Roland!"

"*Shit!*" Roland strode on.

"Ro-land!"

He was rattling his index finger around his ear when the blow struck. A heaving collision against the scapula, the shockwaves from which almost flipped the satchel off his opposite shoulder. The follow-up was a Spock-like death clinch on the soft rounds at the base of the neck.

"It's me, Rolls. Did you not hear me shouting?"

"I thought I heard *something*, but I've had a bit of glue ear lately, me." And he held up a discoloured digit as proof.

"Tell you what, your ears might be full, but there's fuck all between 'em."

"Good one!"

"Closer inspection, your neck's all red. Did I catch your skin?"

"Nah, it's fine thanks, Norton."

"So how come you're late?"

Roland went through his updated excuse. He would have it off pat by the time he reached the school office. They ambled a minute in arm's-length contemplation before superhuman resistance finally crumbled. Roland reached into his blazer and retrieved his half-eaten packet of crisps.

"I thought I could smell cheese, but I wasn't sure if it was your nob," said Norton. "Tax the sprinkles!"

"Course…"

Eyes burning into him, Roland took a last pinch, crushed what remained then presented the bag to Norton.

"Cheers. Very kind." Norton pulled the packet taut, raised it to his mouth and tipped the shards down his gullet. Seconds later Roland was flying backwards.

"You can't do that!"

"Why not?" asked Norton, askance.

"Save the whales! Weren't you listening in the Eco Warriors Assembly?" It was not until Roland heard the question himself that he realised how ridiculous it sounded. He climbed panting from the gutter and squeezed the freshly retrieved crisp bag into his savoury pocket.

"Actually, I'm glad I've caught you, Roland." Norton was now pulling on a newly lit cigarette.

"Really?" said Roland, sucking smartly on his inhaler.

"Yeah. I've got some good news for you."

"Wonderbra!"

"…And bad."

"Oh."

Roland and Norton were occasional classmates ('occasional' because Norton's attendance, even at this early stage in the school year, was worse than minor league relegation fodder). They were in the same set for maths and science, and possibly history and German. Set Three. There was no Set Four. Roland was trying his best to get out; getting in was where Norton's predicament lay. Roland sat at the front. Norton preferred the back, gazing through glazing.

"Which do you want first then? Good or bad?"

"Erm, good please."

"There's no rush for them jokes. He's not home this weekend, but I might need them the weekend after, if it's not too much trouble."

"Not at all. In fact, I've got a new joke book on order so it'll give me more time to choose some *extra* funny ones."

Norton winced. "Sounds like a good job Little Heath's not coming back. Sounds like you could have left me in the lurch with sub-standard material."

"I wouldn't do that, Norton," and Roland borrowed the wince.

"I know, Roly. That would never happen."

Roland racked his brains for something to lighten Norton's mood. "You said there was some bad news?"

"Well, it is quite bad, I'm afraid."

"Is it about that cough your guinea pig had?"

"Don't be soft. It's your game, Vice City. I've lost it."

"Lost it? Where?"

Norton adopted the air of a simpleton. "Derr! If I knew that it wouldn't be lost, would it?"

"Oh yeah, course. Still, can't be helped, Norton," and Roland smiled. Not his most enthusiastic beamer, but he hoped it would suffice.

"I've been dreading telling you," Norton continued, "but I feel a little better knowing that you've taken it so well. Tell you what, though, I might be able to secure a second-hand replacement for you to buy. Shall we call it twenty quid?" He grinned back. And as he did the sickle-shaped scar that scythed around his right eye pinched and whitened like the wink of an angler fish.

*

Norton Edward was a Jack Russell of a boy: a wiry bundle of muscle with a physical maturity that was still sweet anticipation for his contemporaries. When he joined St John's – was it only seven weeks ago? – rumour had it he was in fact an eighteen-year-old midget who would be claimed back by the circus before long. His voice growled with puberty, or tar, and on days when he neglected to shave his stubble was the envy of every boy racer's duckling down. That was not all. He had already lost his virginity (though only to a milk bottle) and he could do roll-ups with one hand, a party piece that delighted everyone bar the school cook, whose skins he regularly pocketed if she was careless enough to leave her tabard within reach. He also knew how to make money. Selling stolen PlayStation games for one. And his library of dirty magazines, loaned from Heath's not-as-secret-as-he'd-like-to-think stash, was much in demand, tidy fee notwithstanding.

There's nothing more important than funds.

*

"I'm a little embarrassed to ask this, Roly," Norton continued.

"Yes?"

"But," his stride was briefly interrupted to stamp out a beetle, "you haven't got that money you owe me, have you?"

"Erm…" Roland was momentarily thrown. "I th-ink so. How much was it again?"

"How much have you got?"

"About two quid, me. I think."

"Why don't you think again?"

Roland cupped his hand to the bottom of his pocket and scooped out a five-pound note, a two-pound doubloon and assorted shrapnel.

"On second thoughts, £8.63."

"Well, there's a coincidence if ever I heard one! The exact amount."

The booty tinkled, with the exception of the two-pound piece, into Norton's greedy money bag. Quick-sharp, Roland retrieved the fumbled coin and re-acquainted it with its new owner.

"Roly, my boy, you're shaking. You can't possibly be cold," said Norton, "not on a glorious day like today."

The pair continued continuing with Roland imperceptibly (he hoped) picking up the pace. At last, an infantry of railings arrived to escort them past the playing fields towards the main entrance. A games lesson was already underway on the dew-doused grass. Seven-a-side. Almost. Both goalkeepers – identical twins – were flat out soaking up the dregs of the summer; the centre-forward was giving his marker a piggyback; and the pupil-referee awaiting treatment to a broken whistle. Only the red bibs' bespectacled winger, a fast, smallish lad ('nippy', *The Respecter* would have pronounced) wanted to play. They watched on as he retrieved the football from the depths of the Nature Area ('tenacious'), passed to himself ('educated left peg'), pushed a teammate out of the way ('wayward genius') then skipped the length of the field to score ('one for the future'). All the while providing his own commentary ('fruitcake').

Norton had narrowed his eyes and was staring hard at the game, chinking out a slow beat on Roland's change.

"See those goalies?" Roland said cheerfully. "Their mum's got a doubler."

And the beat went on.

"I heard Wales played the other night," he continued. "It said on the radio, 'Wales 2, Serbia and Montenegro 3', and I thought to myself, *Fancy that! Wales had to play two teams!*"

"Shouldn't be playing footy—"

"The Welsh?"

"Shouldn't be playing footy with glasses on. Little speccy prick."

This revelation came as a surprise to Roland, as spectacle wearers were among the few generally exempt from Norton's 'charms'. In fact, a thriving black market had sprung up at St John's with Grandad's old models swapping hands for up to a week's worth of dinner money. *Remove the lenses, sit back and breathe.* The staff all wondered what was going on, of course, but hands were tied until governors could adopt the emergency uniform policy.

"People can't help it if they have to wear glasses," offered Roland.

"Most can't, granted. But what about those who've been fiddling with themselves?"

"You mean?"

"I do." And the change in Norton's pocket rattled hard.

"But isn't that just a—"

"A Readers' Wives tale?"

"…n old wives' tale?"

"Old wives? Never seen that one."

Never seen that one? What is he on about? thought Roland.

"Tell you what though, Roly poly."

"What?"

"People *can* help being fat."

Roland glanced ahead. How far to the gates? Norton was getting restless and the sanctuary of the main entrance was only loafing up. Into their margins crept, too slowly, the school sign: a large emerald board bearing the coat of arms that adorned a thousand blazer pockets, gold paint below announcing, 'Headteacher – Charles Bridge BA*D* (Hons) MA*D*'. Another tiresome mission for the caretaker and his green paint. Little did they know it was him appending the suffixes at the dead of night.

"You're a big lad, aren't you, Ro-land? A person of size."

Now, Roland was not exactly huge, not like some of the Humptys nowadays. And when he stood up straight, he was slimmer still, all his family agreed. (Mum's side was constantly trying to correct his posture. "*A matter of proportion,*" they would maintain.) But he *was* carrying a bit, and there had been that profitable time last year when he charged thrill-seekers twenty pence a time to plunge their little fingers deep into his belly button. Or to listen to the sea. His much-

70

departed Nan – she had passed on three times already this year – often described him as 'cuddly'. They had been doing euphemisms in Set Three. She also said that, in her day, men with Roland's physique were sought after. She didn't say what for.

"Some people have medical things," Roland replied. "Conditions." And anyway, he huffed (privately), Norton was quite short. *Vertically challenged.* Then he judiciously recalled that tit-for-tat name-calling never solved anything.

"Conditions? I'd say it was *lack* of condition that was your problem. Your arse must be a yard across. You could shit in the Olympics. My dad says your sort are a drain on the NHS. I'm just glad we go private. I wouldn't like to be behind you in the queue when the biscuit trolley comes around. The doctor would come back after a few days and all the other beds would be full of skelingtons. And now your sister's at it."

"What?"

"This appointment you mentioned before. At the hospi*tul*—"

"Oh, actually—"

"I hope she'll be all right. Your Lauren's my latest favourite in the sixth form."

Norton's gaze shifted towards the distance and for a moment Roland perceived a smile riding those stubborn, stubbled lips. Only a moment.

"Have you seen her tits?"

"No!"

"You must have. You can't fool me, Roly, my boy. I've seen you. I can tell. You're a watcher. A *voyeur*. I know."

"I am not."

"You've had a peek, all right. Bath-night, or on holiday…
no wait, they don't go topless in fucking Shivering-on-Sea."

How much further?

"Listen, I'll make you an offer: a game for one of her bras."

No response.

"Tell you what Roly, if her knockers are *half* as big as
yours…" Norton took a last drag on his second roll up and
exhaled creamily, eyes closed, mouth pursed like a suckling
runt.

A scuffle of footsteps from the rear caused Roland to start.
He was already wound tourniquet-tight and the last thing
he needed was a flight or fight episode. A Year Seven, keen
on, strapped to a rucksack and Quasimodo bent, arrived
alongside and slowed.

"Come on you two," he panted in step, "we're late!"

Without warning, Norton leaned in and dug the red
ember of his smoke about the youngster's ear. The boy yelped
but was unable flee because his rucksack tabs had been seized
like reins. Rummaging within, a calculator was pulled out.

"There it is!" Norton announced. "I lost that yesterday.
Thanks for finding it for me."

The harness was released and the victim shot forward
a dozen strides before outdoing his luggage's impetus. His
countenance on looking back, tearfully stroking scorched
flesh, realisation manifest, sent shudders through Roland.
Bad news travelled fast at St John's. Unless it was on its way to
school accompanying a travelling tuck shop.

"Stroke of good fortune, that turning up," Roland offered.

Norton pocketed the calculator, already passed clean for
Tippexed initials and distinguishing features. "Wasn't it just?"

"Bet it hurt, though. Could be scarred for life, his ear."

"He'll be all right. He could always grow his hair. Or put a plastic one over the top like Mr Potato Head."

"What if he has to go to hospital?"

"I just hope he's not on the same ward as you. He's only a skinny lad."

"What if he tells Mr Bridge?"

"I'll tell him it was you."

"Oh."

"And *you'd* say?"

Roland gulped. "I'd say it was me, too."

"That's right. You know, Roly, my boy, I'm beginning to believe you're a bit too smart for Set Three."

Roland followed intently the lumbering progress of the Year Seven up ahead, wishing he could clamber deep into that rucksack. Now roughly a minute into the distance, burned-ear boy had reached the school gate only to find his path blocked by a figure emerging from behind a redbrick post.

"Holy shiteus!"

"What is it?" asked Norton, trying to focus.

"I don't believe it!" Roland's chin was a ferment of dimples. "It's Mr Bridge. It's only Mr bloody Bridge." And he steadied himself at a spike.

"Are you sure, Roly?"

"It was me, it was me... I didn't mean it... It was me!" he began to mumble.

"Well, if he's snitched he's done it quickly 'cos he's just walked straight past old Mad Dog and gone in."

Roland opened his eyes to monitor the Year Seven, legs tripping away down the slope to the office.

"Oh, thank God for that." *Shake shake.* "You might not believe this." *Shake shake.* "But I've never been so nervous about something I didn't do." *Suck and hold.*

Roland emptied his lungs and returned his inhaler to his pocket. "Hey, Bridgey's not even following him so he probably hasn't asked for a private chat inside, either."

Panic subsiding, Roland began to ponder aloud exactly what the headteacher was up to, hanging around the front gate.

"Beats me," was Norton's response. "But," he added, "I'll tell you this for nothing."

"What?"

"I've been thinking. I've behaved rather badly this morning, been a bit of a bastard."

"Oh, I wouldn't say that…"

Norton curled a breath-freshening gum into his mouth, flicked the foil into the undergrowth and snapped a glance at Roland. "I know you wouldn't," he said, "but in my *own* opinion I've not been the best of friends today. The thing is, Mum and Dad have been arguing at home – in front of me, even – and the builders have been in measuring up and I keep thinking they might go in my room and nick my stuff, you know what these workmen-types are like, so I'm not sleeping very well, and now there's all this worry about your sister at the hospital—"

"Look, I need to tell you something about that—"

"So, if I could finish, to make it up to you, for the game and everything, I want you to take this."

"It's not the calculator, is it? I mean, I've already got one of those."

"Certainly not, I've only just got that back, remember?"

Norton delved into his trouser pocket. Roland failed to contain a gasp. Something was not adding up.

"Thanks, but I couldn't, really."

"Go on."

"But it's yours, Norton. You keep it."

"Look, I've no idea why, but I like you. So don't offend me. Take it. I *insist*."

Roland did as instructed. "Righto… th-thanks."

The boys were mere metres from the front gate when their attention was wrung by the bell announcing the end of Period One. Below their pavement pupils spewed out onto pathways connecting upper and lower school. Those trying to reach the lower – primarily Years Seven to Nine – swirled from all directions, forming a whirlpool of grease and hormones around the main entrance.

"Do you know that one down there?"

Roland tried to follow Norton's outstretched digit. "There's hundreds, Norton. Which one do you mean?"

"There. Charlie bastard Bucket. The pillock with the jumper, and the haircut that time forgot."

"Just getting to the door now?"

"That's the one. I was hoping I'd see him. I think it's about time me and him got to know each other."

Now, Roland was not at all adept at predicting the future; he was no pier-end soothsayer. But he required neither crystal ball, nor tassel-draped kiosk bedecked with grainy snaps of Frankie Vaughan to know what lay ahead for the poor unfortunate Norton had just fingered.

"I've seen him around," answered Roland truthfully, "but I don't know him."

Norton uncocked his arm as the gate – Sing Hosannas! – came upon them. It was at this point that Roland habitually turned right and Norton, with delectable irony, stayed on the straight, narrow path to Waggers' Wood. But this time the company had not parted. In the void between wheezes there was definitely a second fall of footsteps turning towards school. A downward glance confirmed a flash of Rockport.

"You… coming to school?" For the first time that morning Roland looked Norton in the eye.

"Yeah, why not?"

"N-no reason." And he looked away.

No reason? Norton did nothing without good reason. He would not have taken breath without first making sure there was something in it for him. It had to be Charlie. It was the only conceivable explanation. And it had to be something special to end a perfect run of Monday-morning absences.

"*And now a sad story. Charlie kicks the Bucket.*" Roland was just imagining *Newsround*'s solemn announcement of the boy's demise when he became aware of a third party pressing his personal space.

"Good morning, Mr Bridge!" he blurted optimistically, though his hand was already back at the inhaler in his pocket.

Chapter Six

"Ow, that hurts! You're twisting my arm!"

Nelson bounced through the entrance to the lower school and into the breathing space of the office foyer. Shaking the limb to confirm he had not accidentally taken someone else's, he turned back to the mêlée from which he'd just emerged: cheeks checked against the wired glass, faces red and misread, fingers starfishing towards the single open door. It was like a scene from *Day of the Dead*. Someone was going to get harmed. Hang on a minute, someone had been harmed; his elbow throbbed like radar.

Next at the birthing pool was a dark-haired girl he recognised. She was jammed shoulder to hip with Duane Pipe, school's tallest pupil. A Year Eleven (Nelson had spotted the concessionary blue tie in place of the regulation green and black button-hider), Pipe was his real name, but Duane was not. He seemed to contain the same ingredients as everybody else except God had rolled him out like a Plasticine sausage. His tubular head was high and narrow and often snow-capped, and his legs stuck like stilts from three-quarter trousers.

"Stop pushing!" she yelled up at him. "And we'll all get in."

"Piss off!"

Upping her head into his ribs – and availing herself of multiple tonnes per square inch at her back – she burst through ahead. Nelson had almost finished counting off his extremities when she fizzed into him, bounding him backwards as she stopped dead. They had been doing Newton's Cradle in science. She was bubbling still as Pipe lolloped in behind.

"Where's your manners?" she demanded indignantly.

"Fuck right off, posh cow," he replied, and gangled past for his citizenship lesson.

Her riposte was lost as the red metal Frisbee above the doorway blurred into deafening life. The ting of this bell, last call for the start of Period Two, quickened a panic outside and the race to avoid a late brewed stampede among the eager-to-please Year Sevens. Fortunately, Mr White the geography teacher was on hand, thirty centimetres of plastic rule brandished like a swagger stick, to unbolt the partnering doorway. 'Doc' – to those who'd already had the lessons in the history of feminine hygiene – had returned just this morning after fending off a virus that had been doing the rounds and was already back in the thick of it. If he carried on like this, he assured himself, the role of Risk Assessment Co-ordinator, and the management point remuneration that came with it, was in the bag.

Nelson had just about recovered his footing when the horde stormed the Doc's newly doubled doors, flinging the girl forwards once more. A battering of shoulders, elbows and knees at her back, she glanced up furious to see who was hindering her escape. "Oh, hello."

They briefly matched eyes before Nelson, embered, was absorbed by anywhere else. In his periphery he could make out her head bouncing against the surge, could taste his own panic at their rhythmic connection. With every push her breasts flattened against his withering chest; perilous lips neared his. And she was warm (*he* was warm) of airing cupboards and cake mix. And this close up, she – girls – thrillingly terrified him.

What he really wanted to do was throw a barrier around her. Instead, he froze scarecrowed until the crush subsided then scratched hopeless at his nose. Crazy-paving freckles on the girl's forehead huddled quizzically, producing an instant glow; green eyes studied him. For a moment she looked as if she was going to say something but, to Nelson's relief – and disappointment – opted instead to head for class. She had not gone a stride when he dragged her back. Or rather, his home knit did. Her badge, feline, enamel, had snagged in his pullover. *Cats like playing with wool.* Both reached for the tangle; fingertips touched then recoiled. She spotted a previous loose thread.

"Your arm."

Nelson rubbed his elbow bravely. "It's not that bad."

"No, the arm of your jumper. It's unravelling."

"Oh that! Oh, don't worry, I'll wear it as a tank top. It's summer in seven months."

"A tank top," and she giggled dimples.

Nelson laughed too, though he had no idea why.

"This is Bastet," she said, pulling forward her cardigan. "She's the Egyptian goddess of the home. She's supposed to be protective. I got her on the trip the other day."

"It's a nice badge."

"Thanks. I've got a real one, too."

"Sorry?"

"A real cat. Named Bastet."

"Oh?"

"You didn't stop long. On Saturday."

"*That's* where I've seen you," he bluffed. "It was your brother's birthday, wasn't it? Did you have a good walk in the woods?"

"The woods? What gave you that idea? We were off to the rugby for my *dad's* birthday. Got to get wrapped up."

"But the balloons—"

"That's a family jest, Mum's always calling Dad a Looney Tune."

"Oh."

Nelson eyed ears. *Still missing.*

"No luck with the search, then?" he enquired, tugging at his own lobes.

"No. Mum's hoping for a call today, but she's not holding her breath."

Nelson offered a smile, pleased to get something right.

"That reminds me," she went on, "I'm sorry about the accident – and all that blood! I hope it didn't put you off."

"I wanted to come and help, but—"

"Don't worry about it. You seemed engrossed anyway."

They were untangled now and she free to move off. And yet she had not.

"Do you go often? Twice in two days isn't bad."

"Mum and Dad took me once when I was little, but that was… a long time ago. I'll definitely be going again," he replied.

"I adore museums. I intend to be a historian when I've got my degree," and she lit as giraffe markings diffused.

The foyer had emptied now and Miss Lyttle, the school secretary – or Office Manager, as the prospectus had it – emerged from the sanctuary of her den wafting obligatory sheet of paper and asking after Mr Bridge. Twirling a spare finger about the butterfly necklace that never flitted her neck, she called out to a passing teacher for 'Charles's' whereabouts, prompting giggles from a gaggle admiring a Hitler moustache freshly appended to the Head's likeness at the staff photo board.

"There goes Smelly Tits."

Nelson's eyes widened.

"No, I wasn't being rude. It's an anagram," she went on. "I'll work one out for you, if you like. I love doing puzzles."

"Yes, I'd like that."

"Have you lot no lessons to get to?" The secretary, frustrated at failing to cross Mr Bridge, was lingering.

Nelson raised his wrist. "I've got to go."

"What time is it?"

"I don't know, haven't got a watch."

"What have you got?"

"I have a radio alarm at home, but it's not working properly."

"I didn't mean timepieces. I meant, what lesson?"

"Oh, numeracy."

"I've got double science."

"Experiments. Good."

"Yes... well," she laughed, "I'll be on my way. Probably got a late already. See you again."

"Hope so," Nelson mumbled as he turned away. Now it was too late, he wished he had said more. Then again, he had probably said too much. 'Experiments. Good'. *Idiot.*

The last of the loiterers were making their way through the front entrance as Nelson set off for 9RR. He was just about to initiate self-flagellation with the dangling wool when he felt a tiptap on his shoulder.

"You must think me terribly rude. I neglected to introduce myself. I'm Phillipa." She held out a hand, just like a grown-up. "My friends call me Pippa."

He knew that. He had heard her mum say the name in the museum. And he had blurted it out in his sleep.

Nelson took her hand, firm and strong. His slightly damp. For a marvellous, mad moment he imagined he was going to raise it to his lips and drop a hummingbird kiss onto it. In reality, he waved it up and down stiffly.

"Pleased to meet you, Phillipa," he said.

"Pippa." And she gave him a look of approval.

"Pippa," he echoed. "I'm—"

"Nelson Hitchcock," she said triumphantly. "I've done my research."

As her fingers slid from his, Nelson tried to work out what *his* friends knew him as, then recalled that he had none. Instead, he took a pace, or several, backwards (he had forgotten how to count) and floated away down his own corridor. Reaching the fire doors, he spun around and teetered on tiptoe to watch Pippa bobbing out of sight, hair high and dark, like the changing of the guard. *A girl knew his name!*

He had not gone much further when he sensed renewed presence to his rear. What had she forgotten now? But this time there was no tap on the shoulder, just a crunch at the kidneys as a diminutive figure barged unapologetically by. Nelson leaned into the sudden hurt and massaged the pain with his sore arm. That boy, disappearing into the distance, would have a better chance of seeing where he was headed if he pulled up his cap.

"Are you all right?"

Nelson turned, and his screwed gaze rested on a second familiar face.

Yet this time there was bad news.

Very. Bad. News.

Chapter Seven

"Okey cokey, we've just got time for some Show and Tell before we begin. The first thing I've been given is this."

A white plastic cylinder, roughly the form and gravity of a golf tee, was held aloft. "Any ideas?"

He didn't have a clue himself, but the class did not need to know that.

"It's hollow," he went on, and he raised it to a squinted eye to prove his point. After picking out several of the back row in imaginary crosshairs, he lowered the artefact to his lips and blew. "Extremely smooth. Could be some sort of whistle?"

Still no response. It was going to be one of those days.

"The boy who brought it in… the new boy… sorry, I've forgotten your name?"

"Norton, Doc. And I'm not new."

Not new? It *was* true he had been a little concerned about his memory of late. But the class did not need to know that.

"Doc?" said Mr White. "Doc? I fear you're crediting me with qualifications I don't possess, young man. No PhD here."

Unless? No… he would remember one of those. They are quite a big thing, aren't they? Nevertheless, better check the old CV at home – just to be on the safe side. Might be worth a management point.

"And please, for the *third* time, remove that ridiculous American whatsit. I think we're all aware they are not allowed."

Norton lifted the peak from his forehead and punched the headwear into his blazer pocket. A hand was raised at the front.

"Yes, Roland!"

"Is it for playing blow football, Sir?"

"Could be!" And Mr White sucked and blew a last-minute winner. "Or it might be one of those cigarette replacement thingies, for people trying to, you know, give up." Warming to his role play, he exhaled a Hollywood plume.

"Any other offers? Nope? Well, in that case I think it only fair that we let young Norman tell us what it is."

Nobody dared laugh. They merely turned as Norton leaned forward, shifting weight from two legs to six.

"It's my dad's internal nozzle for his Anusol," he said, matter of fact.

Mr White cupped a palm to his ear and simultaneously ruched his forehead. "Your father's what?"

"The tube he sticks up his arse for his pile cream."

It was an age before the howls began to die away and all the while Mr White remained stone-still, the nozzle pincered top and bottom.

"My dad blames his grumpiness on his pile." Norton, anticipating a chilly half hour in the shade of the wood, was already returning the baseball cap to his head. "Says it isn't any fun waking up every morning with an aching arse, Sir. Says it proves what a misnomer the term 'gay' is."

While the rest of the class was still wrestling with 'misnomer', Mr White suddenly sparked into life like a cartoon electrocution and launched the nozzle in the general direction of the wastepaper basket. He was already scouring his lips with his handkerchief when Norton, deliciously affronted, piped up: "Hey, don't bin it! My dad'll go mad. He's only got the one and he doesn't want germs on it!"

The rattling of the bell was barely audible above the splitting of sides and the slapping of high fives; it was only with the scuffling of the cloakroom outside that it permeated the consciousness.

This was not the usual call to assembly.

*

"Pot Noodles!"

Leant across the empty table adjoining his own, temple rested on the heel of his hand, Nelson had been reflecting on his day so far...

On the downside, the word on the corridor was that Norton had taken a shine to him. Ordinarily, this would be the trigger for the rapid onset of a mystery ailment requiring immediate withdrawal to the sanctuary of home, followed by several days' isolation then emigration to more conducive climes. Nelson, however, was less concerned. Rorke's Drift heroics this was not, merely that he had persuaded himself it must be a case of mistaken identity. He did not even know Norton. He knew *of* him, of course – who did not, except, perhaps, most of his teachers? And what reason would he have? Nelson had no money, that much must have been obvious. The only possible explanation was that he may have unwittingly ignored him in the museum, but no one in their right mind would take umbrage at that, surely? No, he was not too fearful just yet.

Anything else of note? Oh yes, on arrival to class he had found his desk piled high with dolls.

Yet on the upside Nelson had brought in 4G's medal for Show and Tell, earning five house merits; he had spoken to two people his own age, one of them – Pippa! – a girl; and his knee was cured. And he had just spent twenty minutes on the playground while the fire brigade dealt with a freak cloakroom blaze (Blue Watch arriving so efficiently that some members of staff barely had time to apply fresh lipstick). Smoke signals reported a Year Seven's rucksack had spontaneously combusted, almost taking a Halloween wall display with it. Fortunately, the coven of witches lashed to stakes proved remarkably flame retardant. Initial enquiries pinned probable cause on a smouldering cigarette. The boy in question denied smoking – they always do – but parents had already been summoned to an audience with Mr Bridge. Their twisted firestarter was to join them as soon as he had been discharged from First Aid, where treatment on a nasty-looking burn to the ear was ongoing.

Then, to top off a morning to remember, numeracy had been cancelled: minus one sickly teacher. There had been no time to organise supply so a science department minion with a free period had been drafted in. *Pippa would be doing science now.* In quid pro quo of the last-minute favour, quadratic equations were out of the window to be replaced by a general chitchat, no recording and, subsequently, the happy by-product of no marking.

*

Ffion Ffortune, spinster, was on her knees at the front of class. She had a reputation for clumsiness. Already she had stumbled over the threshold and taken the head off Paula's lucky gonk.

"Now, 9RR, what do we know about space?" the teacher enquired as she at last stood upright to push the lens back into her spectacles, tearing a nail in the process. "Did you know, for instance, that the first astronauts had to wear nappies?"

Smirks all round.

"Or that to protect the men from radiation, their capsule was lined with a precious metal? Any ideas which?"

Silence.

"Four letters?"

Silence.

"Starts with a G."

Silence.

"G-o. Precious metal?"

Nope.

"G-o-l? Four letters."

A final, desperate scan of the room.

"G-o-l-d… Yes, Rocky!"

"Aluminium, Miss?"

"Nearly," and she turned to write 'Gold' on the board ('morons' was infinitely more tempting), but the chalk snapped.

The last thing Nelson remembered was some guff about the commercial spin-offs of dehydrated astronaut food. Leant across the empty table adjoining his own, temple rested on the heel of his hand, he began to reflect on his week so far…

Was it really only two days ago?

*

The first thing that struck him was the hush: the swish of an occasional car outside and, up ahead, the apologetic jangle of blind keys and the squeal of a distant door. It was only as the day's second visitor hacked indoors that he realised he had been walking on tiptoe. Moments earlier, though that time now belonged to an earlier epoch, Nelson had been steeling himself outside. He had stepped briskly through the entrance, partly because he feared his courage would leach, and partly because he was being harried by the down-and-out's reeking force field. Much to the relief of seared nostrils, the punch-drunk plodder had sunk uninterested into a quiet pew set before a sprawling canvas, growly snores already beginning to rise as Nelson moved out of range. If it was art that had drawn that man to the museum this raw Saturday, it could only have been the art of survival.

At the end of the foyer – flanked by flaky noticeboards straight-facedly extolling the virtues of Alcoholics Anonymous, Women Against Domestic Violence and happy hour at The Flying Tooth – Nelson funnelled through the walkway that led on to the displays. To the left, the first sign of life as the souvenir shop attendant, thread thin, shuffled a rack of postcards. To the right, Security. This office window was wafered by lazy vertical blinds that exposed, zoetrope-like, the scene inside. A desk fan irritated bakery bags and

Nelson could just make out horses on a portable so snowy that racing should have long since been abandoned. The guard reclined about his chair. Almost horizontal, he was a human waterbed. With fingers interlocked behind an unfeasibly large head, his face overflowed onto his chest and two jellyfish had settled into the mineral pools of his armpits. Shoeless feet lay crossed next to the television set and bursting like a Death Cap through one sock was a big toe for changing channels.

Alerted by the sound of impending approach – his elderly, hip-swapped boss? – Security suddenly sloshed upright, inadvertently pancaking the bacon barm that anchored his tabloid. By the time Nelson snatched a passing glance through the open door the man was a shine of sweat, fumbling furiously at the chaos of his desk. Eyes met. *Panic over.* A withering look was shot at the lame imposter and the guard tossed his pen back to the almost-ready report kept to hand for such emergencies.

Nelson made for the entry turnstile to be corralled into the café beyond. From here his objective was the building's far end. The Gallery. The dead end, where new additions rubbed shoulders with the second-rate overspill from earlier zones. And though the stiffness in his knee was easing (the charge to the top of the steps had been a little regrettable), this journey was completed no quicker than the previous day's retreat with the Ray Gun.

Arrived at last in the doorless gape of his destination, he stilled: the faint buzz of a demented bluebottle and the flick of a cold fluorescent tube; rising in him that exquisitely uncomfortable tingle-in-your-trousers sensation of being alone in a public building.

The spot was spied. It was there. *He* was there.

When Nelson envisaged this moment in his head for the thousandth time, he had pictured himself charging to the rescue, a vision of strength and verve. But now he was here, now it was real, a certain uncertainty was all he could muster.

He approached in a generous, collie-dog sweep. Drawing level with Talos, where such a commotion had ensued yesterday, there was the welcome distraction of a lost coin on the floor. Nelson genuflected to collect it and, for a moment, statue and boy were synchronised. *Heracles and Iphicles.* Father and son, he imagined.

In his cowed state he was unable to resist an inquisitive glance skirtwards. His eye was drawn to a white rectangle creased against the warrior's buttock. He rose closer. Handwritten with overlarge capitals, the sticker read,

Norton Edward Territory

'Tying my laces, Sir!' A likely tale, he wore slip-ons. Nelson had witnessed those silver buckles swing into unexpected flesh enough times: Norton had been tagging the statue.

All diversions now spent, the curve of the room was abandoned and Nelson stepped tremulously out.

"I'm back," an escaped whisper. "It's me, from yesterday. You… you spoke to me. Remember?"

The overhead hum was suddenly deafening. No wonder he could not hear. *Half a step closer.*

"I said I'd come back. Remember? I keep my promises, don't I?"

By now the tingling had mutated into an unremembered

urge to urinate, and a bobbing leg was enlisted to soothe his bladder.

"It was me. You chose me! Out of everyone – all of us – only I could hear."

Trembling took him closer still, searching. "I can't hear you. Please… don't abandon me."

Nelson wanted to shake him loose, to slap him to his senses, to rail at another loss, but… but what was the point? He was Nelson Hitchcock. Nelson Nobodyandalwaysruddywillbe Hitchcock.

"*You returned to save me.*"

Nelson stiffened. "Yes! Yes. I promised I would."

"I am glad of it. I'm afraid I took a great risk yesterday. I could have exposed us both, and I should not give you away for the world."

"Give me away?"

"Your gift. Does this not seem extraordinary to you? I can teach you to harness this wonder you possess. I can fulfil your very heart's desire, and yet—"

"Yet?"

"*Nunc non est tempus.*"

"What? What does that mean? I don't understand." The words tumbled out. "My heart's desire? Tell me again. Slowly, please… please!"

A toddler's cry gurgled fleetingly from cold walls to frozen marble. *No!* The last thing Nelson needed was company. He swivelled to watch the rising shadow of a six-legged monster: its flank a trio of jouncing humps, two great wandering eyes on stalks, a squirming child carried in its mouth.

Within seconds the family was sharing his end of The

92

Gallery. Mum, dad (or partner – *you never knew nowadays*), a girl he had seen before, and wailing younger brother in the pushchair. Above the chair danced duplicate helium balloons: Bugs Bunny, Daffy Duck and Porky Pig, all goofy grins hogging one side, and 'Happy Birthday!' the reverse. The strollers each sported matching wax jackets, dark blue jeans with phosphorescent stitching and hideous roll-sole walking shoes; the sort of garb that even the Sunday supplements – well-versed in the horrors of orthopaedic lingerie and absorbent underwear – would baulk at promoting. Nelson promptly fathomed it was the little one's birthday. *Watch and learn, Watson.* They were heading off to the woods for a family ramble-cum-picnic – those Waitrose carrier bags swinging from the back of the pushchair were a dead giveaway – before returning home for a children's party. Brilliant!

"So, you spent most of the afternoon in this room?" Nelson heard the woman ask.

"I told you!" the girl replied.

"There's no need for that attitude," interrupted Dad / partner. "We're all as upset as you, you know."

"Sorry, Dad."

"At least the security man told us the room hadn't been swept overnight so it might still be here. He was very helpful, Solsbury," the woman explained. "Even said he would have helped us search if it wasn't for that paperwork he had almost completed."

Nelson was willing the intruders – each now intently scanning the floor – to move along. As he held his ground those strange words replayed under his breath: "*Nunc non est…*" And more than anything in the world he knew his heart's desire. What would he not give for that?

Disregarding the impromptu search party sweeping his way, he stepped forward again.

"What must I do?" He may as well have addressed the wall. **"What must I do?"** he hissed.

As each of the family raised heads (and eyebrows) Nelson caught their collective glance, and smiled. There was even a follow-up nod of half-recognition in the direction of the girl: the swot scrutinising the guidebook on the school trip yesterday.

"Your gran will spin in her grave if we don't find that earring," moaned Mum.

"That's right, Primrose, make her feel better."

"Good Lord, Solsbury, she shouldn't have been wearing them for school in the first place. She knew they had sentimental value."

The bottle narrowly missed Solsbury's foot, but the startle of the shatter caused him to jolt backwards as if it had powdered his toes. Green shards arrowed in all directions, tinkling trills to mark each resting place; and at the rear of the pushchair, sailing torn upon an expanding pool of red wine, the bad ship carrier bag.

"Oh no," sighed Dad with admirable restraint.

A miniature finger helpfully pointed out the puddle. "Yuks yike byud!"

"That's right, George. Looks like blood," echoed Mum.

"Is your leg cut, Dad?"

"Your father's fine, Pippa. If you look in the other bag there's some tissues. Get them for me, please."

Pippa found the box and began, magician's assistant-style, to eject a cloud of wipes.

"Don't just stand there, Solsbury! Go find a cleaner."

Dad did as instructed and waddled down the corridor while Pippa drifted tissues to a gory end and Mum began recovering the larger of the bottle's remains. Nelson wanted to help, too, but when it was all over he feared conversation may have been expected.

Solsbury soon returned, both legs of his jeans rolled to the knee following a quick examination for lacerations to a major artery, and in his wake a brown-coated flunky carted an industrial mop and bucket.

"Not to worry," the cleaner reassured. "This room was on my list."

The family stood back as the mop's thinning dreadlocks scratched a figure of eight through the spill. Several crushing wringings later – the squeegee letterbox of the bucket clamped vacuum-tight by wrestler's forearms – the liquid had gone.

"I'll just get a pan and brush for the glass," she said.

"If you are going to be sweeping, *Dusty*," Mum interjected, having cast a peek at the name tag, "would you keep an eye out for a gold drop earring? It was lost yesterday and it's of great sentimental value."

"Of course, I will."

"We'd be very grateful," Mum confided, her hand cupping the dome of the cleaner's bicep. "There'll be a reward, of course."

Pippa. So that was her name.

An elderly couple made the scene, and the galleries began to murmur and move.

"Hello? Hello…"

No answer.

"Please, speak to me…"

No answer.

"You need me to save you…"

No answer.

No answer.

*

With the museum closed for the next two days it promised to be a long, lost weekend and more. At least tomorrow was the day of Uncle Henry's birthday party. That would help pass the time. And there would be the television to watch.

A final look, a dampened valediction and Nelson headed disconsolately for the long corridor to the exit. Pausing en route at a door ajar, he peered inside to find the cleaning lady in her cave emptying the mop bucket into a sink, the hand brush she had promised clenched across her teeth.

The jiggle in his leg had returned, and now there was a sense of other footsteps. A rising clip. Closer. Closer still.

"Nelson? Nelson?"

An icy touch on his hand.

*

"Welcome back, Mr Daydream. Don't suppose you've heard a word of what we've been saying."

Nelson peered up from his desk. "Pardon, Miss Ffortune."

Her hand, attention secured, left his. "Are you all right? You look like you've seen a ghost."

"Can I go to the toilet please? I'm desperate."

Nelson left the room to stifled laughter as Miss Ffortune capsized a pile of papers off her desk.

Outside, he quickened to corridor overdrive. He was in luck. The walkways were deserted apart from the occasional ejectee standing sentinel.

A ghost? No, it was a man, all right. His new friend was definitely a man.

Except, this was a man trapped in a painting.

Chapter Eight

The knife chopped through the air like a loosed propeller and clattered into the grey wall, releasing a puff of breeze block. Nelson was screaming at the top of his voice. A grey chip settled next to the French fry that Mr Jones flattened as he slid through the crowd to collar the culprit. The wood-stained deputy head was in no mood for messing and the miscreant, swirling up a cyclone, was hauled unceremoniously into the corridor.

"You'll have to be calmer, Sutra!" he bellowed. He had been *dying* to say that.

Nelson was yelling still – it was the only way to be heard in the dining hall.

"Pardon?!"

"Is anyone sitting there?"

Nelson surveyed the empty seats doughnutting him then glanced up to find his inquisitor already on the chair opposite.

"Did you see that? Could've had someone's eye out!"

A nod of assent.

"I mean," continued the boy, "we all lose our temper, but you can't go around throwing cutlery like that. Not when you're a dinner lady."

Nelson began to peel the lid from his former ice-cream tub.

"Tell you what though, it would've been mad funny if Jonesy had gone arse over tit when he skidded just then. Needs a good sweep, this floor."

There was a pause in the unpacking while Nelson scanned the flotsam at his feet: maudlin Smilies; 'Italiano' pizza, crust so charred it owed more to Pompeii than Napoli; and the grease-seeping remnants of pig's dicks, or Turkey Twizzlers, as the box contended. The only thing missing was the vegetables; they were safe in the tin coffins at the serving hatch.

His gaze returned to the features before him. It was the boy from this morning. The boy with the bad news.

"I'm Roland by the way."

Nelson suppressed a smile but recovered manners to offer his own name in reply. He resisted extending his hand, not before he had eaten his sandwiches.

"*There's a snake in my boots!*"

"Yeah, yeah… very funny," Roland shouted without the bother of turning around. Instead, he appropriated a look of grave concern. "Have you got a minute?"

Nelson laid his prophylactic bundle onto his upturned lid and nodded.

"I didn't get chance to speak to you properly this morning. Bridgey wanted a word."

"Thought you seemed in a bit of a rush," Nelson replied, fumbling blind for the clinging ends of the plastic.

"*Reach for the sky!*"

"I'll be back in one minute."

"Okay."

Usually, lunch was presented in brown paper, for its reusable properties, but the last remaining piece had crumbled like a scorched love letter. Nelson's groping patience now finally spent, any lingering prospect of recycling was off today's menu as its replacement wrap was hungrily yanked asunder.

The sandwiches were scrutinised: four rounds of thinly sliced wholemeal cut cheerfully on the diagonal. Party-style. Nelson lifted the uppermost to survey the seam and it frowned – heat exhaustion from the cling film. Looked like hummus. Again. His nose confirmed the diagnosis. Guaranteed death breath.

Ironically, this daily disappointment was readily avoided as Master Hitchcock was eligible for free school meals. Yet mother's pride insisted on packed lunches; she did not want anyone to think they were poor. Not that the home knits could keep a secret.

He took a weary bite and peered about the zoo of the lunch hall. In all directions, imprints of stray footballs dotted the room like a disorderly dado. At the far end was the climbing wall, used regularly the week the inspectors visited (and for the rest of the year its lower hand-holds made excellent ashtrays for staff and pupils alike). To his left, a whaling net for zoning off the badminton courts, drawn limp against the brickwork and currently snaring a flapping Year Seven. And still dangling from that lofty light fitting, the Dunlop Green Flash plimsolls strung together, tongues out like a taunting bolas.

Glancing around the islands of octagonal tables set out – appropriately enough, Nelson considered – like a test, he eyed the other packed lunch kids. One per table. *The sore thumbs*. Hunched, sensible, solitary figures. People like him. And crashing against them a maelstrom of open-mouthed school dinner mates sharing chips, springing beans from tined trebuchets, flicking garden pea footballs. Bawling. Bonding.

He found again the nest of curls in front of him and remembered Roland. The rounded face betrayed a zealot's devotion to the progress of Nelson's lunch, every mouthful eaten by proxy. Mutual mastication. The boy had a strange virtual chewing technique where his teeth chattered together in a vertical plane and his lips gathered and fell like a wine taster. Nelson recalled the first time he had seen it: demolishing secret sweets in the museum.

"*There's a snake in my boots!*" It came again, a different source.

Roland swallowed his imaginary mouthful, but this time remained seated. "Have you seen him?" he asked, dabbing non-crumbs from the corners of his mouth.

"Seen who?"

"Seen who? The invisible man. Who do you bloody well think? Norton!" The name was mangled through clenched teeth.

"Oh, Norton."

"What do you mean, 'Oh, Norton'? What's the matter with you? He's after your babycakes on a platter!"

"I'm not so sure."

"Well, I was there and I *am* sure. He pointed right at you. And he gave a description."

"Description?"

"Well…" Roland was not about to add to Nelson's woes. "I'd just watch my back if I was you. He's a nutjob. And a black belt."

"At what?"

"Like it matters."

"But what does he want with me?" protested Nelson. "I haven't done anything."

"That makes no odds with him. He's a bully. Comes from a long line of bullies. You know his dad's been married twice?"

"So?"

"They reckon his first wife drowned in a wishing well. And what about that time in the first week when his dad had the Ray Gun pinned to the wall…?"

"Whose balls are you going to chop off now?"
"Look, Mr Edward, the boy's got it all wrong. I merely stated that if he didn't do his homework I'd castigate him."

Preferring not to dwell on episodes of wanton Edward violence, Nelson abandoned the meditation to find Roland gazing longingly at the serving hatch. There, two PE teachers had pulled rank to jump the queue. Shellsuit tops were unzipped to reveal pale-green polo shirts and, lurking within, all manner of wheeze and woe (it is a truth universally acknowledged that PE teachers are the unhealthiest examples of humanity in school). All was tucked into high-hitched shorts selected by width rather than length and below these, football socks, shinpad-stuffed. Completing the athletic aesthetic were pristine white, and ostentatiously expensive, training shoes.

The pair were pointing in all directions, bar the salad bar, while loudly complimenting the servers on their generosity. Sated at last, Mr Sigsworth and Mr Finch shuffled off together nursing heart-stopping plates. Roland almost dislocated a vertebra in his admiration of the passing burgers, beans and pick-up-sticks chips.

"Are you not going for some?"

"No cash. Norton took it this morning. I wouldn't mind, me, I've not eaten a thing all day." His grumbling stomach triggering False Memory Syndrome.

Nelson swallowed hard. All this promise of torture and ritual death had diminished his appetite. *Mistaken identity.* What was he thinking? Who was he likely to be confused with?

He surveyed his leftovers. Two sandwiches, give or take the odd nibble, and a plum that looked like it had been in a set-to (and lost).

"You want these? I'm not really hungry."

"Wonderbra!"

A crafty check for cold sores and Roland introduced himself to the remains of Nelson's lunch. "They're all right, these," he said, twirling the sandwich and displaying his molars. "What is it?"

"Hummus. Homemade."

"Bummers? Get stuffed!"

Nelson used his best dining-hall voice. "Huh-Hummus!"

"I was joking." Roland paused to digest. "What's in it?"

Before there was chance to offer the recipe, the chair neighbouring Nelson's scraped across the floor. He looked straight ahead for a clue. Roland had stopped chewing.

"If it isn't the Loch Snot Chicken."

"I'm afraid you've got the wrong table," said Roland bravely.

"Don't think so. Mind if I join you, Nelse?"

He smiled red and hitched his chair sideways. *Nelse...*

"So, what do you think? Of your anagram?"

"Smashing."

"It could have been ruder. Got a head start with your name, after all."

"No, it's smashing."

Pippa chuckled. "My grandad says 'smashing'. Aren't you going to introduce us?"

"Yes, of course... this is Roland. Roland Bytheway."

"What?" Roland spluttered. "Where do you get that from? It's Grange. Roland Grrr-aange. Guh. Ruh. Ainge."

"I'm Phillipa. Howdy."

"Don't you start, please."

"So, what do you know?"

"We've just been talking about Norton," said Roland.

"Oh, him. I've just seen him on the car park, smoking for Arbroath."

"He was fagging it all the way to school this morning. I'm not surprised he's such a titch. Hey, he asked me for a match and I was that far," Roland closed index and thumb, "*that far* from saying 'my face, your arse'."

"Shouldn't that be the other way round?"

There was a second pause in jaw action while Roland re-ran the phrase. "Oh yeah!" He grinned.

"Anyway, what's so interesting about that idiot?"

"Well, for some reason he's taken a shine—"

"It's nothing," interrupted Nelson, "nothing—"

"In that case, let's talk about something else," said Pippa, "such as... do I smell?"

"Pardon?"

"I was merely trying to ascertain why," she added, eyeing Nelson up (and down), "you are sitting way over there?"

Nelson leaned upright. "Of course, you don't smell. Not at all. But I think *I* might."

"It's these," said Roland, thrusting a lank wedge at Pippa. "They're homemade bummers."

"Well, *you* certainly look like you're enjoying them."

"They're not bad," and a soggy morsel shot her way. "I'll eat anything really, me. Except red apples. Not after Snow White."

"Mmmm..." Pippa dismissed the crumb from her sleeve. "If you mind my stuff, Nelson, I'll get some lunch. Want anything bringing back?"

"No thanks," both replied.

Roland watched her go then tilted conspiratorially. "Your best option," he suggested, "is make sure you're always with your mates. Strength in numbers."

Nelson looked doubtful.

"So, who's in your crew?"

"Erm... you're it. If you want to be."

Roland rewound and ruminated on elastic crust. "Well..." He paused. "I have got one or two offers on the table at the moment. No offence."

"That's all right."

"*You're my favourite deputy!*"

Roland periscoped about, seeking the culprit. "I'm going to get really mad in a minute!" he boomed at the hall.

By now Pippa had reappeared with a mound of salad. "What are you up to after school, Nelse?" she asked.

"Detention for me." Roland was fast forward in his seat. "Listen to this for bad luck. Norton handed me a mobile phone on the way into school. Said I could keep it. I tried saying no, but he was having none of it. So, we get to the gates and Bridgey pounces, says he's 'received some information' and makes Norton empty his pockets. Then, yours truly. Turns out the phone's been stolen from Miss Ffortune. I knew it wasn't Norton's as soon as I saw the Groovy Chick cover—"

"Have they called the police?"

"I'll find out shortly. I've got to go and see Mr Bridge" – the headteacher afforded his proper title while Jones the deputy was patrolling within earshot – "before afternoon reggie."

"So, what about *you*?" asked Pippa.

"There's something my mum said she would help me with," replied Nelson.

"Well, that sounds rather mysterious."

"You can come to my house for tea if you're at a loose end, Phillipa."

"Thank you, Roland, but it's piano lessons on Mondays."

"Another time, perhaps?"

"Roland?"

"Yes?"

"Look, I know we've only just met and that," Pippa said, "and if I'm being personal, just say."

"Go on."

"But what's with the get-up?"

"Oh, this!" he said, tugging at the mustard shirt. "Norton."

"Norton?"

"Caught up with me in the lavs. Shoved my head right down the bowl and flushed. Then an arm, and then a leg. Said he was just checking I'd remembered to forget where I'd got the phone."

Arm? Nelson's decision to withhold the handshake exonerated.

"Wearing wet clothes," he continued, "is a dead cert for rheumatism – Nan told me that – so I went straight to Miss Lyttle. Told her the top had come off one of the taps. She suggested my PE kit, but I didn't have it in school. The best she could offer was the drama box."

"Right…" breathed Pippa.

"It's a bit snug, but… look at the time!" Roland straightened from his chair. "I'll be late for Bridgey. Good luck with Nort… y'know… see you around."

The pair watched in silence while Roland line-danced between tables towards the exit. At last, he shouldered the door and the bedlam of the hall found the corridor in a dam burst. Through the dwindling slot Nelson and Pippa spied the profile of Mrs Sutra Singh, slumped forlornly outside the headteacher's office. She turned as company approached and her shoulders blurred.

Their final glimpse was a bite on his Salbutamol comforter as he awaited his fate, clutching forlornly at the crown of his Stetson and dressed top to toe as *Toy Story*'s Woody.

Chapter Nine

"Can you hear me? Can. You. Hear. Me? *Please*. Why won't you talk to me?"

Nelson felt like he had been begging all night.

Four forty (*04:40* reported the scarlet digits reflected in the plastic of his bedside cabinet, then *04:41* sixty seconds later).

"Say something. Anything. 'I'm missing you. I love you.' *Say that*. Say anything."

Nothing.

He pressed the photograph to his smooth pillow and slumped beside. For a moment he supposed the blue – *Mum said Dad had Balearic eyes* – had followed him across the darkness.

"Please, Dad…"

A wait in the stillness.

Nelson turned his back onto the mattress. Through the curtain's gape the constellations had begun their retreat from the rising sky. Perhaps he was up there, watching. Like God. Waiting for his son to find him.

He would believe anything possible these days.

*

It would soon be time to get up and, all too late, tiredness began its cosy embrace. Nelson had not slept much. He had not slept at all. Another of those nights. He knew before lights out he would be wandering through the dark, and had dressed for the cold hours. Now, for the first time, he wormed beneath the weight of his quilt. The paperball lightshade, another Glendale Terrace original biding its time for a return to the fashion spreads, hovered nebulous between slow swipes of his eyelids. Welcome to Planet Nelson. A minor world of bedtime stories, warm chats, soothing milk and goodnight kisses. A world succumbing to the creep of an ice age in its teenage years.

Through the frustrated gloom night-eyes picked out books shelved for their narrator's return. Mum had continued to read to him afterwards. She really loved him, he knew that, yet it was not the same. There were no true-life adventures in unknown lands, no secret codes, no heroic missions to be accomplished. He was too old now for bedtime stories. *He wasn't a baby*. But what would he not give for such splendid embarrassment?

Up above, through his breath, he could spy James Bond. Sean Connery, back in action, with Honor Blackman as Pussy Galore (*Pussy!*) and Gert Frobe as you-know-who. Dad used to make him laugh by telling him he had an *Aunty* Gert when he was Nelson's age. Certificate A. They don't do those anymore. "Connery. Goldfinger. Best Bond. Best Bond," Dad would say. They must have sat through it oh, oh seven times. He still looked good, James, one arm clutching Pussy and the other poking his PPK at the whole world. Pulling the quilt snug to his chin, Nelson recalled again the choice in the poster shop. One version had James and Pussy stood before a huge golden hand; in the alternative the background was a gilt-skimpied Amazon. No guessing Dad's preferred option and Nelson went along. Mum was less than impressed when they arrived home, of course, but Dad just grinned and said she should be delighted: at least he had got their son eating broccoli. It was Nelson's favourite-ever poster and his dad had bought it. To cover a damp patch.

And there was little else. Slabs of woodchip monotony punctuated by an exclamation of Sunflowers – Mum's idea, it went with the yellowing background – and a yet-to-be-discovered art installation entitled Bedside Cabinet, Beaker of Bubbly Water on Coaster, and Radio Alarm Jammed for Eternity on Background Radiation.

The first of the day had still to infiltrate, but even the pre-dawn murk could not disguise the enforced shabbiness of the surroundings. Patches of threadbare carpet, mostly at the window, gave the game away like the roots of a cheap wig. Those curtains had not achieved a total eclipse in many a moon and where Nelson had been through a phase of gouging the chips from the wallpaper, surfaces were as scabbed as a lunar landscape. Mum accepted it all as a coping mechanism and said nothing. She had a friend down the road whose son was slicing chunks from his arms.

There had been attempts to decorate in the last three years, *cheer the place up*, but each had been repelled. Not that the room was anything less than clean. Mum demanded the right to vacuum on agreement that everything be left exactly how it was. Nelson understood instinctively how Aunty Thomasina felt. A time capsule of his own.

Six fifteen am.

*

Seven forty am.

"Nelson! Time to get up!"

Seven fifty.

"Are you up, Nelson?"

Nelson dragged himself dazed from his pillow. He must have rolled over during his all-too-brief drift and the photograph had attached to his cheek. He peeled it carefully away and stared again into the scene. Reaching up to his mouth, he ran a thumb along the ridge of adult teeth that had replaced those absent in the image. Once, he had thought nothing of showing all the world his broken grin. Now it had grown whole, he kept it hidden.

He tracked the kite's string into his tiny white fist, then gently traced the bare arm set bulwark at his narrow shoulders. (His father's preference was shirt sleeves whatever the weather). "Good morning, Dad," he whispered.

Footsteps on the stairs.

Nelson pushed the picture out of sight and crackled from his bed. Whipping off Gran's old housecoat – a bundle of her nursing home possessions was stored in his wardrobe and he was pretty sure Mum would not approve of him wearing it – he threw his grip into his Scoobys drawer. The swilling hiss of the bathroom flush was ebbing by the time Nelson pulled their waistband over and high, leaving a bend like Punch's hump.

A knuckle at the door. "Are you up, Nelson? Your breakfast's going cold."

*

Lumping down his porridge had pulled Nelson ahead of the clock and, back in his room, there was less urgency for filling his Tuesday bag. He would be travelling light today. French first thing (nothing required for that), followed by maths (in went Uncle Henry's old geometry set) and, a decision that could only have contributed to the sleepless night, he reaffirmed the PE kit would *not* be required for the afternoon. That done, he reached into his installation and retrieved a sketch pad, a leaf of notes in Mum's handwriting and, underneath, 4G's belongings. The last thing collected was his own diary. Pocket version, half price last March from Stationery Box. He found the previous day – Monday, October 27th 2003 – and scribbled, "Museum closed. Pippa! Mentioned 4G." There were too few lines for much else – an edition for the chronically uninvited – but Nelson's secrets were best unwritten anyway.

One last look at the kite picture. "If I can speak to a stranger in a painting, why can't I talk to you?"

But Dad was not listening.

The photo was entrusted to 4G, a police escort until it could be scanned and printed at Computer Club, and with everything bagged Nelson was down the stairs (the scent of disinfectant lingering) for his solitary kiss. He could barely recall the time when there had been two. *Why?* Why couldn't he have been like all the other dads at school. Builder, salesman, on the dole?

He should have put himself first.
He should have put Nelson first.
Why?
Why did he let them talk him into that last assignment?

Chapter Ten

"A plague on both your mouses!"

Another scuffle in the ICT suite.

"That's Francis Kitt," whispered Pippa as the boy harrumphed by, hitching his blazer back over his shoulders. "In my form," she went on, "adores his Shakespeare."

The flash of disbelief, that shockwave of silence that accompanies outbursts of random violence, passed and the corridor regained its voice. The long planes, home to images of outward bounds, last year's Godspell and unloved number crunching, bustled and muscled anew.

The odd teacher (were there any that were not?), stiffened by the head's first-light pep talk, trooped purposefully by, armed with a day's ring-bound illumination. Sydney, the caretaker, made his way to the front entrance gleefully swinging his patella-high tin of green paint, and knots of mustard-fingered youths conspired around doorways, ready for take-off as soon as they had checked in. Ninety-four per cent turned up last week, boasted the wall, 'up two per cent from the same time last year!' Another weary dose of creative accounting – Operation Smokescreen – as the whole of St

John's knew attendance plummeted once the nicotine pangs kicked in.

"I've got that stuff I promised…"

The pair departed the runway and banked into the classroom. A glance through the barren harvest of upturned stools confirmed they were alone.

"So, this is your form room, eh? Where the *top set* hang out."

"Everyone has different qualities. For all I know you may be a great artist, or something. I'm absolutely hopeless at stuff like that."

Nelson's gaze arced the room. "Which one is yours?"

"This one." Pippa pulled down a seat from the table closest the exit and levered herself into its hollows; wool-warmed legs filled its mould then poured over the edge like melted chocolate.

Nelson shadowed, sitting opposite. He heaved his dad's Army and Navy rucksack to the grey tabletop and unthreaded frayed straps.

He had often imagined what a top-set classroom must be like: full of little boffins with oversized heads – though Pippa's was in perfect proportion – and incomprehensible whiteboards crammed with equations for afternoon tea on far-off asteroids. Apart from its aura of tidiness, this one was disappointingly normal. Stacks of exercise books settled into an overwhelmed shelf, wide-eyed calculators peered from a plastic tub on teacher's desk, and vanilla walls were windowed by arty-farty posters. There was the *Mona Lisa* (he knew that one), one of a big brown pipe with foreign writing underneath, and one of a nude man in a square circle, sprouting four arms and legs. On second thoughts, this could only be a top-set room: that man's privates were full out and no one had gratuitously graffitied them.

"…Thought they might come in useful if you're doing Victorians."

Pippa reached over and wisped the treasures towards her.

"Well, this is definitely une peep!"

"Pardon?"

"A pipe. It's definitely a pipe."

"I know."

"What's the significance?" Pippa asked, rotating it end to end.

"The inscription. It's his."

The artefact was blackened and slyly deposited a charcoal patina around her curious grasp. She found a dulled glint ringing the splice of mouthpiece and stem, and rubbed. "*Always, I. 1896.*"

"A gift from his wife."

Next, the red case that shelled the medal (this inspection transferred a squabble of guilty fingerprints), then her palm and its piano fingers – hurriedly wiped clean across her skirt – flattened against the crimson hardback as if she could play out the journal's secrets. A curled thumb had barely lifted the front cover before she stooped impatiently to peer within. "My goodness! What's happened to the last page?"

As she spoke, the portrait fell into view.

"So, this is your great-great-*great*-grandad?"

"That's him," replied Nelson. "Sergeant Caleb Fitzgerald. 4G, I call him: everything else seems a mouthful."

"He looks a bit glum. Mind you, I'm not surprised after what you were saying."

"So won't Young Jonesy mind, then?"

"About what?"

"About you writing an essay on 4G, instead of Charles Darwin or Samuel Pepys."

"Pepys was 1666 and all that," she said without derision, "and, anyway, famous Victorians have been done to death. I mean, how many books must you have read about Brunel?"

Nelson pouted and shook his head as if he was unable to comprehend of a number sufficiently large.

"Modern historians," Pippa recalled from some previous discourse, "recognise the lives of ordinary people are just as valid as those of the *extra*ordinary. In fact, 4G can probably tell us more about the turn of the last century than any princess in an ivory tower."

Her spectacles took on a semblance of absolute transparency as she pushed them into the coal of her curls. "I don't think I've ever seen such melancholy," Pippa said. "It's the eyes. If they really are the windows to the soul, this is a man drowning from within. And yet…"

"What?"

"I detect something more, too. A defiance."

"There have been developments since I told you about 4G yesterday," said Nelson eagerly. "I found this."

He handed over an envelope franked 'British Gas'.

"Well, this is hardly Edwardian."

"It was all I could find."

"It's empty, Nelson."

"No…" He reached in and withdrew a hair. Black. Stiletto-straight. Held up to the light. "I found it tucked in the page 12th October 1903. I've written it on the back of the envelope. Looking at the photo it's not one of 4G's. I think it might be a clue."

"How so?"

"I was hoping you might work that out. There's something else, too."

"Go on."

"When Gran died there was a box of her papers along with some clothes and things. Mum had tucked it away, but we went through it after tea yesterday and found some information about 4G. That's where the pipe was. Mum jotted down a few notes."

"That was good of her."

"She owed me after getting drunk at Uncle Henry's party at the weekend. She was sick in the hall when we got home and I was left to clean up."

Nelson retrieved folds of paper from his back pocket. Reading past a fledgling shopping list – bean curd, beansprouts, Rich Tea – scribbled (thankfully) through, he began relaying the tasty parts.

"Notes from newspaper cuttings," Mum's staccato handwriting announced. "*The Harbinger*, Friday 13th November 1903, 'Retired officer found dead in bed'. Police alerted by former colleague unable to contact for two days. Recently retired. Missing son. Town in mourning. *The Harbinger*, Friday 20th November 1903, 'Unusual ruling on police death'. Coroner, Mr Thos. Williams esq. decided on Wed. against formal inquest into sudden death of Sgt.

Caleb Fitzgerald. Initial investigation, personally overseen by police commander Sir Wm. Josephs, no evidence of foul play, or self-intent. Protect Sgt. Fitzgerald's surviving family from further distress. Mayor, Mr Jos. Thomas esq., hoped 'natural causes' would draw veil over sad affair. Permit Sgt. Fitzgerald, malfortune well-recorded, dignity of resting in peace."

"I thought there always had to be an inquest when someone died suddenly," said Pippa. "Have you any more?"

"I've been saving the best till last." Nelson unhooked a newspaper clipping from the back of the notes.

"*Harbinger*, Friday 27th November 1903, Town's farewell to police hero," he read.

> Scores braved biting winds on Monday afternoon to attend the funeral of Sgt. Caleb Fitzgerald. Chief among the mourners at All Saints' Parish Church was Sgt Fitzgerald's 32-year-old daughter, Mrs Clara Turnbull.

"That's Great-great-grandma."

"*3G*," offered Pippa as Nelson returned to the report.

> The priest, Fr. Mr. P. Brody, gave a moving valediction that brought forth tears from many in the congregation. Much of

the aforementioned is kindly reprinted below:

"I have had the honour of knowing Sgt. Fitzgerald, as parishioner and officer of the law, for nigh on 30 years.

"He was the most honest of souls, at whose very core was a belief in the beauty and sanctity of human life. He was filled with the unshakeable conviction that everyone deserved justice: the weak, the old… the young. That was what made him such a dedicated servant of our community.

"But I also had the privilege of knowing him on a familiar level, just an ordinary man who loved his family more than life itself. And so today, on this most sombre of days, I should like to speak of Caleb Fitzgerald as a friend.

"I vividly recall Caleb's delight, some 8 years ago, when his beloved wife Isabella – 'Ella', to many of us here today – was with child again after so many prayers. 'A gift from God!' he told me. They had, of course, already been blessed with Clara, whom we welcome back from London and in whose sorrow we share today, and they had set their hearts on a son to complete their family. How overjoyed they were! Ella knew his name long before 'Christian' entered the world.

"Yet in a terrible twist of fate, the kind that hurtles faith towards a precipice, their bliss lasted but a few short hours. Poor Ella, Caleb's bright star, was called to God's side that very evening.

"'A life for a life'. That was how Caleb came to terms with his grief.

"With great rectitude, he set about raising his son in his wife's image. What pride both his children bestowed upon him. What joy! But tragedy was to strike anew and the mysterious disappearance of his precious boy, the first of four such vanishings to plague us this year, proved a heavy cross to bear. The search for Christian, and the others, consumed every moment. It is without reproach that I say his seat here in the congregation began to gather dust. The last time I spoke to him – though how could I know it then? – was at the well-reported meeting in the town hall to discuss the advancement of the investigation. During a brief interlude we took a welcome cup of tea. He confided he was sleeping little but said that was for the best. It was his way of keeping the demons at bay. I told him I wished he felt able to draw comfort from the church during his hour of need; he inhaled deeply and we instinctively understood each other.

"Yet after all had been said, and despite his evident exhaustion, his sense of propriety blazed like a beacon. I clearly recall he was adamant that no one but him should tidy the china. How typical that was!

"We parted, as ever, in friendship and shook hands. Lamentably, as if Caleb had not known suffering enough, that same hand would soon be lost to him following a terrific accident at home."

"What!" Pippa, incredulous, snatched up the portrait again. "Of course! That's why he's sitting sideways on. He's concealing his missing arm. There's no right arm!"

She pulled her stool perpendicularly towards Nelson so the pair could share the journal at the table's corner. The final entry: Saturday 31st October 1903. "It all falls into place! Look how childlike it is. He's writing with his wrong hand, just like your namesake after Tenerife." She stared with new eyes at the spidery scrawl. "I wonder how he lost it?"

"I thought that might interest you. The funny thing is, Gran had tried to tell Aunty Thom he was armless."

"'Terrific accident'? What kind of accident could cost you your arm?"

"Run over?"

"At *home*?"

"A knife!" and Nelson sawed at his forearm with the edge of his palm. By the second slice he sensed Pippa, rhythmically chewing her bottom lip, was not biting.

"A fall?"

"…Possible."

"A burn?" he continued.

"The rumours of him setting fire to a house—"

"Aunty Thomasina believes that was why they pensioned him off," said Nelson.

"But what if it was his own house?"

"Why would he do that?"

"Well, we seem to be assuming this fire was deliberate."

Pippa drew eyes tight and began to massage her temples. While she worked, Nelson marvelled unseen at the jet of her eyebrows, those soft fly-trap lashes and the mosaic of freckles bridging her nose. Her breath washed out and in, as he held his. Then she began.

"He was sitting in his armchair," she narrated, blind. "Almost November, but the hearth was warming. He'd had no rest, hadn't eaten. Perhaps he had taken a drink – who could blame him? Numbed by exhaustion, he slipped into sleep where the demons lurked. He was still holding his pipe – *this* pipe – when his hand slipped over the arm of the chair (and hers, too, fell from the table and swung). Embers escaped to the rug. The heat began to singe, to scorch, to catch. Too late, he woke screaming at the bitterness of smoke and burning flesh. In his stupefied daze he overcame the flames, but it was only as the fire died did he see…"

When, at last, Pippa opened her eyes Nelson was agog. How could he possibly belong on the same planet as this creature? "See? See what?"

"…see the charred, weeping stump that had once been his arm," and she bounced her own like a retriever's grouse.

Pippa returned to the journal. "It all makes sense. The difference in form…" She opened a random page and read aloud: "'Sunday, January 18th 1903. Church this morning with Christian. An uplifting sermon! Walking home I recited by heart a favourite by maestro Keats'." Ordinarily, she would have stopped there, but she could never resist poetry.

"He knew whose gentle hand was at the latch,
Before the door had given her to his eyes;
And from her chamber window he would catch
Her beauty farther than the falcon spies;
And constant as her vespers he would watch,
Because her face was turn'd to the same skies;
And with sick longing all the night outwear,
To hear her morning step upon the stair."

When, eventually, Pippa came to ("*So* beautiful!"), it was to slowly, desolately, find again Caleb's end notes.

"It's barely readable, isn't it?" she conceded. "Just look at the final line. 'Is… caned… wands…', is it?"

Nelson peered across and followed Pippa's fingertip beneath the double-height scribble. "It's all squashed together and pulled apart. 'If… eaned… wands'?" he read slowly. "…'talkf the mail', it looks like."

"That's an 'ell', 'Talkf the mall.' Talks the mall?" replied Pippa.

"Why don't you work at it for a few days? You're good with words and puzzles. Take the journal. You'll look after it."

"I'd love to. Thank you," she said. "Is there anything else?" and she eyed his newspaper cutting, balancing on its crease.

Of course, there was something else! The biggest puzzle *ever,* but only he could solve that.

"There is something mysterious the vicar said," Nelson offered as an alternative.

"Go on."

He lay out the clipping again, swiped the folds with the flat of a hand then recited…

> "There have been whispers within our community that Caleb would have no longer desired a Christian burial. It is true that during that fateful public meeting he proposed a course of action to shake every right-thinking man to the foundations. It is a matter of public record that I was one of many who could not, on strong principle, support his unholy petition to the assembled. But of that I shall speak no more, nor hear more, save to say that most of us, God willing, will never have to know what would become of us in those very circumstances. My message to the talebearers is simple: today we are here, and so is our dear friend, Caleb."

"What was all that was about?" said Pippa.

"He went off religion, Aunty Thomasina said. Believed God had let him down. Can't say I blame him."

"Well, he seems to have got a few backs up with something he suggested at that meeting. I wonder what he was up to. Any more?"

"That's everything."

"And you're sure I can take this?"

"Sure," Nelson confirmed.

Pippa gathered the notes and portrait, and opened the journal's back cover to deposit them for safe keeping. There, a second image was waiting.

"I need that," interrupted Nelson, sharply. He hastily claimed the photograph and cuffed closed the flap of his rucksack. An awkward silence fell between the pair.

"Look…" he fumbled. "I didn't… I didn't mean… look… I'm…"

Pippa held the journal close. "You know," she chirruped, "this is really invigorating. I want to be doing stuff like this for a living when I'm older."

"In that case, I hope the future's kind to you."

"Don't tell me you're a fatalist, Nelson Hitchcock. That wouldn't do. Your future is yours to determine."

Nelson contemplated the stains and scratches of their shared table.

"We all have choices," she persisted.

"But what if someone else's choice takes away all of yours by mistake? What happens then?"

"Then there's simply a new choice: do nothing or do something. And my advice, always, is do something."

Nelson did not need the clatter of the bell signalling the

start of morning registration to tell him it was time to leave. He pushed himself upright and slid the rucksack onto his shoulder.

"So, when would you like these back?"

"Take as long as you need with the journal," he said. "Aunty Thomasina would like the medal back pretty soon, though."

"How about we meet up later? Lunch?"

That would be exactly what he needed: the chance to make amends for that unseemly grab, the chance to stop her abandoning him.

"Sorry, I can't."

"Can't?"

"Computer Club, there's something I need to do. And after that…" but Pippa did not need to know the reason for the hollow in his rucksack.

The corridors had begun to rumble and the first of Pippa's classmates were bouncing in. "I'd better… y'know," said Nelson, almost relieved, "I don't want to be late." And he turned to dart downstream.

"Catch you soon?" called Pippa.

She watched for a reply, but his head never found the surface and he was gone. Perhaps he had not heard.

The form room was beginning to thrum with the beat of arrival: the click and clack of buckles and bubblegum. Pippa delved into the holdall at her feet and pulled out a PE blouse to wrap Nelson's mementoes. Bending to return the cushioned bundle, her head collided with a leg, sending spectacles winging to the floor.

"You ought to be careful, Bugsy. Could've sliced my trousers with those chompers."

Jade Greene, as in 'Deadly Night', stood at the head of a clutch of girls, hands on brawler's hips.

"Is this what passes as entertainment for you?" asked Pippa.

"It'll do," came the reply. And with that Deadly and her acolytes, only too pleased it was not them, swaggered snorting to their seats.

Pippa recovered her glasses and was tucking herself tight to the table when she caught a *Psst!* She looked to find Nelson back at the doorway. She forced a smile. He smiled back.

"Hope so," he mouthed.

Pippa nodded and he retreated.

'Hope so'. 'Hope'. 'So'. 'Ho! Peso', 'Soho PE', 'Hose op', 'Oo, Shep!', 'Soop, eh?', 'Oh, pose!', 'She poo!'. Pippa rolled the barrel of her pen fast and loose as she played with combinations and listed them on the back of her hand. A world of riddles, where words are for pleasure.

It was only when Nelson rejoined the swarming corridor that it struck him Pippa was sitting entirely on her own.

And it was only when Pippa glanced back from her anagrams, beyond the newly arrived and breathless Mr Jones and out through the open door, she realised – to her dread – that Nelson now had company.

Chapter Eleven

Sunday 9th August 1903

Ode on a Broken Urn

Thou still unmend'd fiend of dry-ness,
Thou foster child of parch and sapp'd bliss,
Silver Myrmidon, who can't thus express
A gilded sip yet sweeter than a kiss

Chapter Twelve

The scissors flashed cold against Nelson's bobbing throat. These were not the usual dreary school blades. These were pickpocket sharp: built to butcher. A no-contest. *A walkover.* Down at the event horizon of his vision, light danced towards him in a victory jig. Already a thorny foray had found a warm welcome at the clavicle. Now he was desperately fending off nervy hiccoughs with crazy thoughts of balmy beaches.

The steel again edged closer.

"Look, you don't have to do this," Nelson suggested.

"But I'll feel so much better if I do."

As the needle-tip began its work Nelson instinctively lifted his gaze like a supplicant. Short, stabbing breaths refused to leave, filling his chest chainmail-tight, and the weight and the wait began to crush his lungs. If this did not end soon, he would suffocate in fresh air.

"Nelson Pie all round for tea!" *He* was enjoying this.

"Look, just leave it, will you?" Nelson gasped at last. "I'm sure we can sort this out another way."

The scissors finally relented, to be replaced by Roland's pointed squint. "I doubt it. I don't think we're going to get that peanut out," he concluded. "It's one of the best I've ever seen, me. We'll just have to snip it, I'm afraid."

This was bad news. Nelson was not entirely sure what elicited most concern: the scissors back at his throat or facing Mum with a lopped tie. Particularly galling was the fact that this was the first time he could recall the knot being in the same county as his top button; it usually began its relentless slide south the moment the front door shut. Better let him get on.

The cutters engaged again and the tie was lost in a whisper.

"All done!" said Roland, proud as a midwife as he yanked it away. "Quality scissors these!"

"My mother's got a pair exactly the same. She uses them to spatchcock chickens," offered Pippa from the breakfast bar. (She had been closer to the action until Nelson complained he was overheating.)

"Well, these are for getting into packets of bacon. And pizzas," replied Roland, and he slid them back into their plastic tray. A splash of cutlery followed as the drawer, propelled by a casual stomach thrust, hit home.

Despite the oven, the hob, the wedding-day spice rack and the glockenspiel saucepans hoisted at the ceiling, this was an anti-kitchen, specifically designed for the avoidance of cooking. It was instead a homage to reheating, repackaging, repeeling and regurgitating. Fresh food: the great inconvenience.

Haste, or indolence, was everywhere. Alongside the microwave – piled high with ragged post – toasted crumbs cascaded from chopping board to non-working tops, crusted plates dotted like stepping stones to the dishwasher, and on the windowsill a frozen meat and potato sweated for the key in the door.

Nelson helped himself to a reviving swill of water. In the absence of coasters, he placed the glass within a handy tea stain at the timber-topped bar.

"These are a good idea." He winked conspiratorially, though that was so awkward it could have been confused with a minor spasm, or the onset of a palsy.

"What are?" asked Pippa, looking over Milk Wood.

"These circles that tell you where to put your cup."

Roland, out of earshot across the linoleum expanse, had succeeded in resisting the tissue about his chin long enough to reach into the deserted fruit bowl. He recovered a scrap of paper nuzzling a crisp £10 note. "Back about nine," he read aloud, "plenty of food in. Here's cash for a film and nibbles – nothing violent!! Have a good time, love Mum. PS: did you get my Chimleys? PPS: hands off the pie, I'm defrosting it for supper. PPPS: Stop slouching!!!"

He marched, grinning, to his comrades, wafting the booty like peace-for-our-time. "Bombay mix and Haagen Dazs all round!" he said, slapping the contents of his hand so giddily onto the table a dust plume spewed from a pumice-coned ashtray.

The 'hurrah!' he anticipated failed to materialise. Pippa was drowning in dreams of Captain Cat, and Nelson – face slumped about his bottom lip – was still mourning the passing of his neckwear.

"Don't worry," said Roland, "I'll give you one of mine. Or, better still, you can have one of Lauren's."

"Won't she mind?" asked Nelson, a quaver of optimism rising in his voice.

"She won't know," replied Roland. "She can't keep track of all the stuff she's got."

"Thanks."

"It's poor form rifling through your sister's private things, if you ask me."

"Don't get me wrong, Pips. It's not the sort of thing I make a habit of. It's just a one-off to help a friend indeed."

Pippa's expression on receiving her new nickname cautioned Roland that there, too, was a further example of a one-off. "Seems like theft to me," she added.

"Well, as a member of the school Eco Committee, I prefer to think of it as *recycling* and anyway," mine host continued in his most mellifluous tone, "let's not spoil our lovely, grown-up evening. Our little *dinner party*." He wagged his finger at Nelson opposite. "We wouldn't even be having this conversation if you could stay away from our little friend."

"I'm trying!" he protested. "It's not that easy."

"I must admit, I've never known him in school so much, me," said Roland. "Two days running now."

"You've seen him today, too?"

"Briefly," Roland replied and, had he been blessed with the wherewithal, he may have permitted himself a wry smile at the choice of adverb. "Hey, do you know that scar on his face?" he went on, curving a fingernail around his eye. "He got that from a knife fight – him versus some dad whose son he'd beaten up. They met in a park and had their wrists strapped together with zip ties. A *dad*! And everything!"

"How do you know that?" asked Pippa.

"I overheard him telling someone in the lavs."

"You spend some time in those toilets," said Nelson.

134

"I can't help it! I'm desperate when I get there, then Norton walks in and I can't go. I end up hiding in a cubicle for ages until he's gone. I'll burst one day."

There was a moment's meditation while the party queasily played out the vignette.

"Anyway, I'm starving, me. Who's ready for some grub?" Roland reeled across the kitchen and flung back the freezer door. Lost in a cloud of cold, he pulled and pushed, lifted, turned, and read and replaced, pausing only occasionally to rub his hands.

"I was going to do sausage salad, but we're out of salad," he announced, staring hard into the mist. "So I'm going for bacon and cheese doorstops instead. What do you fancy, Pippa?"

Pippa had bobbed Dylan to her bag and was engrossed in the note accompanying the ten pounds. Only good manners prevented her from making a quip about violent nibbles. She cautiously made her way to the rubble of the working top to inspect the dry-ice goodies on display, eventually plumping for the fare that threatened least heartburn.

"Better give that a warm through." Roland was quickly into the drawer and slicing at the shrink wrap. "See what I mean?" he said, flourishing the tinsnips again. "Wonderbra!"

"Got this for you," he said next, wafting a gaudy cuboid at Nelson. "Veggie lasagne. Lauren went through a stage a couple of years ago. Lasted about half an hour."

Pippa's pastry was popped into the microwave with a chivalrous "Ladies first!" then Roland eyed the pasta's fine print. "Are we 750-watt, 850-watt, or what?"

A procession of pings announced the first of the pirouettes was ended and in went the lasagne. While the contraption shuddered and grumbled Roland clunked a meteorite of cheddar onto a board and grated toenail slivers for his rashers. These disappeared under the hairpins of the grill just as the oven ran down to zero. The plastic tray was pulled from the spatter-flecked porthole. "Another two minutes." And back it went. *The un-ready meal.* Alerted by the spit and hiss of bacon, Roland was now across the lino deftly layering slabs of bloomer. Salt he would not be taking, he declared, on the grounds that 'it's bad for you'. Seconds later, he had settled the first of the plates and his sandwich stack at the breakfast bar where Pippa was sitting, waiting.

"It's hard work, this hosting lark, isn't it?" he puffed, wiping his brow. "Daddies?"

"No, thank you." She stared at the table, eyes following the length of her food.

"Would you like a knife and fork?"

A nod.

"You would!"

And he was off again, rattling through the drawer as the microwave sounded surrender. Still in its platter, the lasagne went straight onto a placemat that was deposited across from Pippa. Two sets of cutlery were produced and Roland re-claimed his seat, tucking a pennant of kitchen towel into his neckline. He exhaled at his sandwich then, at long last, pitched towards it.

"I've never seen a quadruple decker before," remarked Pippa.

He smiled on the swallow. "And I've never had guests to tea before, so I'm really pleased you could both make it."

And Roland had certainly made an effort. His usual hometime snack had been sacrificed, he had showered, deodourised, attempted his first-ever shave and gelled flat the commas and question marks that punctuated his hair.

"When's your mum home?" asked Nelson.

"About half nine on a Tuesday."

"What does she do?"

"She thinks she's a posturetrician or something, but she's really a lecturer at the college. Social studies, whatever that is. Messing, if you ask me. She takes the evening classes on Tuesdays and Thursdays."

"Sounds interesting," suggested Pippa.

A thunder of footsteps on the stairs suddenly cut short the chitchat. Lauren bounced rough into the kitchen, face temper-flushed. "A word! Now!"

The doorstop was unhanded. "If you'll just excuse me…"

A stool raked and reluctant legs dragged him to where big sister had set up ambush.

"Have you been using my Ladyshave?" The accusation rattled the hallway. "Don't deny it, it's written all over your face! Just look at you, covered in bits of toilet roll like return of the bleedin' mummy…"

"*Were you not in school this afternoon?*" Pippa whispered to Nelson. "*I was looking for you, to check you were still coming to tea.*"

"*Dental appointment.*" Straight-faced.

"*Is that why you were late getting here?*"

"*Bus didn't turn up.*"

A sudden surge in the disembodied voices turned them towards the door. "*I know he means well,*" Pippa went on, "*but he could talk a samurai into submission. I can tell you everything's he's done since his birthday. And I don't mean his birthday, I mean his birth day.*"

Nelson let go a grin.

"*I'm afraid I might have mentioned 4G,*" she continued. "*I hope you don't mind. It was the only way I could think to give my ears a minute.*"

"*It's all right,*" reassured Nelson. "*There are bigger secrets.*"

With the row in the hallway continuing one-sided, unabated, the pair at the table fell silent. As far as they could tell their host, in a departure from previous form, had hardly uttered a word. Striking an eavesdropping pose as a ploy to deter further inquisition, Nelson could have sworn he caught mention of missing underwear. Then the rant climaxed with a crack and a whoop of pain.

The romp of return up the stairs followed and Roland retreated to the table, rubbing the crown of his head. "Sorry about that." He grimaced.

Pippa had by now finished her meal and left most of her food, a grease-sodden playing card glued to the plate. Nelson, too, had abandoned his lasagne. Something about the phrase 'a couple of years ago' had blunted his appetite.

"Who's for fresh fruit?"

*

"Your grandad's a retard!" Roland failed hopelessly to contain the shock in his voice.

"No, *retard…*"

"I know. You just said."

"Not a retard… re-*tard*. He does not work anymore."

"Retard? Oh, retired!"

"That's what I saying, *retard.*"

Now Roland was unsure if Pippa was merely repeating 'retired', or outing him as a retard. He decided to let it go, for the sake of the party. "Very posh!" he offered, and a creamy trickle oozed down his choc ice. "Dad a financial adviser and Mum an accountant. They could pay for you to go to a proper school."

"They prefer to support the state system."

"Well, it's all right for them, *they* don't have to go."

"It's about mixing with people from all walks. You can learn lots of life skills—"

"…Intimidation, thuggery, theft, demanding money with menaces…"

Pippa smiled indulgently.

"So, what do you want to be when you grow up, Pippa?" Roland's mum had tipped him off to show an interest in his guests.

"Historian for me."

"That's nice," he replied, wearing a don't-forget-to-ask-me-face.

"And you, Roland?"

"Window cleaner, probably."

"Why?"

"No reason."

Nelson had been deliberately steering clear of this conversation. He could see where it was heading.

"And what do your mum and dad do?"

Knew it. "My mum stays at home knitting."

"And dad?" persisted Roland.

"Dad…" he said, eventually. "Dad…"

"Was that your dad this morning?" asked Pippa. "In that photograph you put in your rucksack?"

An involuntary: "Yes."

"Would you mind if I had another look? A proper look."

Nelson hesitated, fleetingly; he was enjoying her friendship. He took his rucksack and reached in, casually pushing its trifles aside. Yet within a breath the movements gained firmness, a haste that hinted all was not well. Suddenly his head was at the mouth and peering into the blue. *It's not there!* He upended the bag to spill its contents onto the breakfast bar. Clipboard, calculator, geometry set, sketch pad, ruler, pencil, pens here, pens there. A last, desperate rattle bought only crumbs and dust. He grabbed the pad and whirred crestfallen at its leaves.

"I had it. I had it!"

"Had what?"

"My photo!"

"Where did you have it last?" asked Pippa.

"This lunchtime, at Computer Club. I'd gone to print some copies. Then Norton came in – like he'd been stalking me or something – and shouted that I was looking at porn."

"You've never cracked the filters!" gasped Roland.

"Of course, I wasn't looking at porn, but the techie guy comes over anyway and everyone was crowding and I just needed to get out of the way. Next thing, Norton had me by the tie in the corridor and was swinging me around like a ruddy hammer thrower. I was spinning by the time he let go and then I couldn't see my bag and then I found it and then the bell went—"

"That's it then," said Pippa, "it'll still be on the scanner. We'll go and get it first thing."

"I hope you're right," replied Nelson, water from his tumbler defying gravity and heading eyeward.

"Yeah, I wouldn't worry, me," said Roland. "I bet you've got loads anyway."

"Not of my dad. They all vanished when he never came back."

"That's a strange turn of phrase," said Pippa.

"It's what happened. He went out to work and never came back. Then the day after, I got home from school and Mum was waiting to tell me we'd been broken into. She reckons she left the door unlocked. All the usual was taken. Money box, computer, stereo. The telly. We haven't had one since. We can't afford it and Mum says it's rubbish, anyway. We never had a microwave. It was only later I realised photos had been taken, too. Just the ones with Dad on. Not one left behind."

"So how come you had this one then, the one you've not got any more?"

"I found it at my aunty's on Sunday. And sort of borrowed it."

"But if you explain to her what happened, I'm sure she won't go mad." Roland was now fingering his ear. *Did he just say he did not have a telly?*

"But 'never came back'?" Pippa said again.

"He just didn't. He went out of the front door on May 4th 2000 and… and I don't know where he is."

"Did your mum call the police?"

"Before I got home, but they were taking ages so I reported it myself. She was amazed they actually turned up. I heard them telling her they would have to speak to their bosses about it. That would've been because of Dad's job. His other job."

"Other job?" asked Roland.

"He works for the government. Unofficially."

"And he's *unofficially* disappeared off the face of the earth? That doesn't sound good."

Pippa aimed daggers at Roland, but he was at the cupboard marshalling a terracotta army of gingerbread men and his back was not very much concerned.

"No. He's safe. I know it," said Nelson assuredly. "In fact, he's coming home soon. Definitely."

Nelson wanted to tell them more. So much more. He wanted to tell them how thoughts of his father brimmed the day, how he waited still by the bedroom window for that once-familiar silhouette, how he had forgotten the last time he had laughed, *really* laughed. And he was worried that if he got talking, he would run away with himself and break the pact they had made all those years ago and he was not one to take pledges lightly. Instead, he stared through out-of-focus knots in the grain of the cupboard opposite and said: "You'd like him, my dad. You'd like him." He repeated the coda under his breath. A warm blanket.

"Did they do a shit on the rug?"

"What?"

"The burglars. That's what they do," said Roland

"No."

"Oh."

*

"Mum kicked Dad out last Christmas." Roland cheerfully reclaimed the conversation as he began to pour the first foaming diet fizz, a haze of bubbles cresting each glass in turn.

"Did you see it coming?" Pippa asked.

"Not then. But looking back, the only time they spoke to each other was to have an argument."

"Do you still see your dad?" asked Nelson.

"I work for him Saturdays, we go round every other Sunday and sometimes I call on the way home from school. He's living above the shop."

"What shop?"

"We own Pikka Pet in town."

"Really?" Nelson was impressed.

"Mum says he wasn't exactly what she had in mind when she popped in for a dumb animal. Dad says he should have realised what he was letting himself in for when the piranhas hid behind their castle."

"At least they've kept their sense of humour," said Pippa

"They're not joking."

"Still, must be nice to see them both."

"So far I've had double birthday presents and double Easter eggs. Fingers crossed for Christmas!"

Pippa and Nelson offered uncertain smiles.

"Sometimes, if I time it right, I can get tea at Dad's and then have another tea when I come home. I'm like that cat, Six Dinners Sid."

Pippa was relieved to laugh as if she meant it. "I've got a cat. Bastet."

"Bastard?" said Roland. Nelson did not flinch, he had almost said the same yesterday.

"Bas*tet*. It's Egyptian. She looks just like my badge." And Pippa did the cardigan tug. "I bet you've had lots of pets."

"None, really," Roland replied. "But sometimes, on a Saturday night, when me and Lauren were little, Dad would bring us a kitten home and we'd play with it all Sunday. We'd always give them the same name. And then, on Monday, even though every time we secretly hoped, Kaboodle would go back to the shop."

He sipped his cola and replaced the glass in its ring.

"Now it feels like Dad's become of those kittens." His eyes picked out Nelson and Pippa and, despite the grin, they knew he was no longer smiling.

*

"I was having a look at 4G's journal at lunchtime. Absolutely fascinating. Like staring down a wormhole."

Roland sneaked Pippa the type of withering glance usually reserved for the more preposterous contributors to the bottom set.

"The writing's so vivid. It's as if a ghost has sought us out to share the life they once had. One last rage against the dying of the light."

"A ghost?"

"Yes. Do you believe in ghosts, Nelson?" asked Pippa.

"I think there are ghosts," he said, straightening himself, "but they don't let everyone see them."

"So how do they decide?" asked Roland.

"I'm not sure. I suppose they must want you to see them. They choose you."

"The ghost connects with you somehow?" suggested Pippa.

"I really don't know…" and he stopped himself adding '*yet*'.

"There's something else about the journal," continued Pippa. "Something troubling, counterintuitive even, about the handwriting."

"What do you mean?"

"The penultimate entry is dated Monday 26th October 1903. After that the journal jumps directly to the disorder and incomprehension of Saturday 31st. The logical conclusion surely is that 4G must have lost his arm between those two points. But if you look closely at the script there's an indefinable sense of deterioration leading up to that final page. It's as if his arm began to fail him before it was actually taken – almost like he was losing it by degrees. I can't figure it out."

"And I can't figure out how you never knew this 4G only had one arm," said Roland.

"I didn't even know he existed until Sunday," protested Nelson.

"He was your great-great-grandad, wasn't he?"

"Great-great-*great*-grandad, actually," interrupted Pippa. "And your great-grandad's *name* was?"

"Fair play," he conceded. "But how come we've never heard of these Vanishings?"

"Old narratives fade with each new generation," said Pippa. "These children are now lost to time, vanished in every sense."

"I think they were killed," Roland decided. "Can I have a look?"

"If Nelson doesn't mind. But I think we'd better wipe around a little before I put it on the table."

Roland pulled his hand into his cuff and windscreened a forearm across the cola drips. A follow-up swipe with his dry sleeve and he was pondering the open journal before him, toggling page to final page. "Some of that writing *is* bad, isn't it? I'd get detention for that."

Retreating into silence he began looking to and fro, scanning snippets, jaw chattering down and up.

Pippa turned to Nelson. "What does your mother say about all this, with your dad and everything?"

"Nothing. I think sometimes we would both like to talk about it. But we never do."

Before she could reply, the journal cover was extravagantly closed.

"That's it," Roland announced.

"That's what?"

"I can't believe you two are claiming this is some sort of mystery. I've just found your snatcher…"

Chapter Thirteen

The oiled clouds were black and blew horizontally across the stillness beneath. Trees, evergreen for eternity, hushed the breeze in respectful tones and at the roof of the underworld verges snuggled lush and trim against dense gravel walkways, swept mute lest they stir the inhabitants.

Towards the edge the chapel stood firm, proud glass stained and unmarked, and in the bruised sky, above towered clocks, a half-moon creamed the dark. Here and there stilettos of silver pierced the shroud, but the earth held a ghostly grey: the ashen parchment of the dead.

Not a sound.

But not only the silent: among the branches black-eyed Corvus crowed over the dead; Reynard stalked the cracking thicket, another day outfoxed.

And there. There. He stood.

Among soldier-straight headstones, blooms in mourning and tales of days that leeched away, he suffered.

Thoughts threaded back to *The Treachery of Images* in the top-set classroom (Pippa had translated the French and explained the significance of Magritte's pipe). What was before him now, reality or representation? The riddle was soon resolved.

"So, my fledgling, you've returned." He paused a whispery moment. "I have missed you."

Nelson spun about on the spot for, despite the thrill of it all, he still feared cackling ambuscade. Yet finding for company only the sun absent-mindedly mellowing the high, earthy windows, he mustered composure. On his way into the museum, Nelson had spied a neglected poster: a blue grinning hand with crossed fingers. 'It could be you', it read. But that was a lie; it never was you, or anyone you knew at all.

Until now.

"You said you could grant my heart's desire," he spluttered sharply.

"Patience, my boy. Are we to dispense so readily with the usual niceties?"

"I beg your pardon?"

"A good start, but my thoughts were more along the tracks of the 'pleased to meet you's and the 'likewise, I'm sure's. You know how it must be when two great friends meet."

"Great friends?" he stuttered.

"Just look at that beautiful face, carefree as mine is careworn. It is what we shall become, my dear, what we shall become."

The figure before him was no larger, he reckoned, than an Action Man, the acceptable face of boys' dollying. Nelson had heard tell – mostly during his aunty's photo perusals – of some mythical 'Sunday Best', and contemplating now his new friend seemed its head-to-heel embodiment. Moonlight spiked his top hat, spearing a shadow down his face that beaked the hook of a nose, dark at the end as if the blood would not quite reach; the glint of a gold tooth cornered a half-grimace; a collar glared as stiff and white as the neck it ringed; and above knotted silk, a chin to burst a balloon. A shaded waistcoat was interrupted by the precious grin of a pocket watch chain; a frockcoat (for journeying) descended to narrow-trousered knees; and at his feet, played by grave grass, a line of buttons ascended ankle-high boots.

There, watched over by the angels, he stood.

Black as a lion's lips and thin as the bars of a cage, he was his own prison. *An inaction man.*

"But you don't even know me."

"And yet I do. You'd be surprised at what I know. At what I have seen… Nelson Hitchcock."

The boy jolted backwards. "How do you…? This is a trick."

"This is no chicanery, and neither do you believe it so." A moment. "Else, why do you return?"

"But how do I know you're real?"

"Do you doubt the truth of you own senses? Can you not hear me? See me?"

"Yes, but—"

"Many things in this life appear fantastic; that does not mean they cannot be so. Is it not strange that light can radiate from Edison's orb on the whim of man? Is it not ridiculous to be told that, among millions, no two snowflakes, nor fingerprints, can *ever* be identical?"

Nelson stilled, mesmerised, willing the spell to hold, his own inhalations repeatedly startling him; lungs already working overtime in the tenacious grip of the tie at his throat.

"I have gazed in wonderment at Monsieur Lumiere's spirits caught upon a silver screen; I have held in these hands" – *how he yearned to reach out now!* – "photographs of long-abandoned manors where the dead peer from empty windows. Why not me, here, captive within this daub?"

"But how did you get in there?"

"How do the eight planets wander the night sky? It would take a greater mind than mine – yours, perhaps? – to comprehend my tragedy."

An incredulous smirk puffed Nelson's nostrils.

"You do not believe you possess such a mind, my young friend? Why do you think you are here now?"

Nelson wanted to say that… well, he had been asked. Though asked to do *what* exactly? Of course, he would save him, if he could; he was that type, his mum was always telling him. And promises had been made in return. And all he wanted was for things to be back as they were, that was all. And he began to wonder, now he considered it, if he was here for the man, or for himself. And his neck was chafing. And… and the last thing he wanted was to hurt anybody's feelings.

Finally, he lifted his gaze. "Because you asked for my help?"

"I see you gave your response some thought. Impressive in a boy – a man! – of such tender years."

Nelson rolled onto the balls of his feet.

"The moment I saw you I sensed that you were the one. I am never wrong when it comes to spotting those with the *gift*."

"You told me before I had a gift—"

"It is granted to but a select few." He lowered his voice and Nelson floated closer still. "Have you never wondered why you seem set apart from others?"

"I heard you when no one else could." He was practically en pointe now.

"Precisely. You are among the *optimi*, my friend." He teased out the words like candy from a crumpled bag. "It could only have been you. Such maturity. Such perception. Such sweet... sensitivity."

Is this what love feels like?

"I have searched across time for you, my boy," a resolute tone assumed. "Only you can achieve the task I must petition. I can trust no one else. There was never a choice, my dear. This... us... was always meant to be."

"*Who* are you?"

"Later. There is somebody here for you."

There was not. It was Tuesday afternoon in the worst museum in the world. Why would there be anyone else? There was no rain against those grimy panes. They had to be alone. Together alone.

"Hello, son."

Chapter Fourteen

"Hope I didn't make you jump, son, sneaking up like that. All part of the training, see? Comes second nature after all this time."

The soft-boiled figure of the security guard rolled into view like a raincloud, greedily hogging the panorama. *Training?*

"Straining?" enquired Nelson.

"That's right," confirmed the guard, evidently a martyr to battlefield tinnitus, "training, see. Military background. Aldershot." Another punter to 'impress' with tales of derring-do.

"You were shot?" came the unlikely reply. *He was not his 'son'.*

"No, it's a town. Like Hereford. Where the regiment is. The one" – *quick glance about with eagle eyes* – "we don't speak about. But keep that to yourself."

Nelson knew immediately he would have very little trouble keeping that revelation under wraps. For starters, he had not the foggiest idea what the nesbit was blathering on about and, for seconds, there was more pressing business to be attended.

"You've not found a jacket, have you? Chocolate brown." The guard tugged helpfully at his leg. "Matches the trousers?"

"No. Sorry."

"Mystery, that is," and he patted his pockets in turn as if the absent garment might be lurking miraculously within. "I've been through all the rungs."

"Rungs?"

"Rungs. The exhibitions. You must have noticed this place is set out like a ladder. Well, half a ladder. One long corridor linking everything, and *rungs* feeding off at ninety degrees." And he chopped horizontal palms to illustrate his point.

"I'm sorry, but I'm not really supposed to talk to strangers…" Nelson performed his best valedictory grin and waited for the none-too-fond farewell. When he eventually realised that goodbye was not arriving anytime soon (he had been holding his expression for so long he feared there was a danger of being mistaken for 'slow') he initiated a new pretence: the analysis of the triptych of paintings – graveyard dead centre – on parade before them.

"Do they teach you about the Falklands?"

The question was avoided on the grounds that a reply might constitute conversation. The truth was Nelson had no concern for what *this* grown-up thought of him. And, besides, it was not two minutes since the man distinctly said he did not want to speak about stuff.

"Tsk! Have you heard of Port Stanley?"

I've heard of Flat Stanley.

"What about Iraq, then?"

Nelson knew about that, all right. Mum never stopped going on about it. She had even wanted to join some big march, but the train is so expensive nowadays. "I think so," he said, non-committal.

"Oh, I give up." The guard surrendered in mock capitulation; yet his young visitor was taking no prisoners. "So, what's your game, then?" he went on, re-setting his shoulder holster (and line of interrogation). "Here on a Tuesday afternoon. No school today?"

Plan A. Nelson had arrived prepared for such a cross examination and dipped smoothly into the rucksack at his feet. Lying in wait was a green school clipboard biting hard on a pencil and pristine sheet of cartridge paper.

"Free period," he offered, nonchalantly as trepidation allowed, "for my art project." Settling into his mime, Nelson selected the scene to the left – a shortbread cottage pillowed in heather – and began doodling with his HB, hypodermic-sharp. Rectangle first, then the roof. If he had been sitting down this morning he would have fallen off his chair when Pippa suggested he could be a great artist. Still, so far so good.

Confidence waxing, he squeezed one eye and held the pencil vertically in front of him, cover for a furtive glance to his left: not to check *he* was still there – he was blowing like bagpipes – but to determine if he had been taken in by the sketching ruse.

"All the good drawers do that," agreed the blimp, pulling sagaciously at the liquorice of his peak.

Success, or disbelief, lifted Nelson's mood and for the first time he cast his artist's eye over his new shadow. How old was he? Fifty? Sixty? Seventy, perhaps? He sounded *old*. He moved *old*, and yet his face was spherical and shiny, like a hot-water bottle inflated by a strongman. His shovel feet, flattening cheap loafers that squealed '*squeaky when wet*', had come to rest at ten-to-two and his knees were hyperextended so he perched like an ostrich, pot belly counterbalanced by a spacehopper backside.

Nelson watched on as the guard wrestled with the toilsome process of tucking his cap under his arm, exposing a red ring where the headgear, fitted in fitter days, had rounded on flesh. His hair was hot and had recently opted to change shade, greasy mouse at the ends then peeping white where it disappeared within the flanks of his head. On top, a skim of longer strands swept like a punch-line over a plucked capon of mottled pate and, beneath this vanity, a dandruff cornice clung to Goodyear-grey shoulders.

"Are you not warm in that, erm… is it a jumper?"

"A bit."

"We used to have air conditioning in here, but they took it out. '*Rationalising*'. That's why we've started closing on a Monday, to save tuppence on the lighting. It'll be hotter than the Gulf come summer, if we're still open. No way to treat an old soldier."

"Mmm." And in went the downstairs windows, though Nelson's re-acquaintance with the art world was not to last.

All warmth and botheration, security suddenly began kneading at the doughy flesh of his chin. A groan and the top button was eased. "That's better!"

Nelson had never seen anything quite like it.

"It's a safety tie, see? In case anyone gets a bit *shirty*." He jabbed it at Nelson. "See the clips, see? They make a grab for it and off it pops, leaving you free for…" and he launched into a calamity of karate chops, tie flailing like gymnast's streamer.

On at least two of its passes Nelson felt certain it would have his eye out.

The demonstration was predictably brief, yet it took Nelson at least twice its duration to recover. Then, nerves barely eased, he leapt anew as the guard once more thrust out the neckwear, pincers like a stag beetle. "Do you like the colour?" he wheezed. "Biscuit, that is." And he scurried it into his pocket.

Biscuit? The man was food-mad.

"Hey, what do you reckon to this, son?"

An overly detailed letterbox was wilfully added before Nelson looked up. A golden palm was held out, examination urged. It resembled a credit card, but each time closer inspection was initiated, the hand was teased away.

"What is it?" Nelson enquired, soon weary of the rigmarole.

"Well, might you ask! What is it indeed? Read it! They do still teach you reading in school, don't they?"

"Military and Aviation Book Society," Nelson mumbled. The tip of a sausage finger helpfully underscored additional typeface. "Privileged Member. Micheal Picket."

"Oh yes!" confirmed the guard, polishing the solid gold plastic against the give of his breast. "They don't award these to just anyone, you know. '*Privileged Member*', it says."

He wriggled his wallet from a buttock cheek and pushed the card between a season's worth of used betting slips, all hopes of a startling number of stewards' enquiries fast fading.

"And for your information," he added, catching breath, "it's not Mykeel, it's 'My-cul'. As in, 'Row the boat ashore'."

"Oh…" said Nelson.

"And you are?"

Off guard. "…Norton," he gulped.

"Well, pleased to meet you… Norton." If the boy had been a few years older, and there had been corroborating witnesses, Nelson would have been treated to a firm bombardier's handshake, but you did not get to be a *Privileged Member* of the Military and Aviation Book Society without an eye on the perils of breaching exclusion zones. "Seen you here a few times lately."

Nelson was shocked. *Ruddy home knits!*

It was a fact that appearances at the museum were mounting up, but today was a first. Before today – before this afternoon – Nelson had been a truanting virgin. He had imagined slipping the school gates would have terrified him, but when the time came he simply strode out. Bold as brass. And he was only skipping PE so it barely counted anyway.

"You're from St John's, aren't you? Could tell by the tie. Just seen another one of your lot, as it happens. Where's your blazer, then?"

"At home." (The truth, *'the shop'*, did not quite have the same ring.)

"So, what's going on with yours?" He poked a frankfurter at Nelson's neck. "Is that the new style, that tiny knot?"

"It's called 'peanutting'. It's just a joke."

"Looks like someone's been swinging off it. Funny idea of a joke, son. You'll have a job untying that. You want to get one like mine – off it pops and kaboom! You need to get your dad to sort them out."

And all the while the pencil had scratched.

"Hey, Picasso, how do you like our latest addition?" Micheal pointed out the graveyard. "Cheery little number,

I don't think. Town cemetery, that is. Been here about a fortnight. Can't stand it myself."

Nelson regarded the scene he knew by heart.

"Still, it's a bit of local history, I suppose," the guard continued. "Did you not see it in the paper?" (Nelson had not. *The Respecter* was no longer welcome in the Hitchcock household following a fill-next-week's-letters-page editorial denouncing single mothers for a boom in shoplifting. "*If they're not at it themselves to feed their bingo habits, their feral runts are swarming through town like locusts, leaving pick 'n' mix pots as empty as their crania…*") "Made a right palaver of handing it over it, they did. All the bigwigs were here. Nice frame, mind. Gilt, I reckon."

They both turned again to the wall: Nelson to confirm a flurry of ticks for the birds winging over his cottage; Micheal to wonder if anyone would notice should the surround be swapped for a plastic lookalike in his garage.

"What do you think of him, then? There's something of the groom about him."

"What do you mean?"

"The way he's dressed, see. Till death us do part and all that."

"I like him," replied Nelson, truthfully.

"He looks creepy to me. Arrogant, too. Like he's saying, 'Look at me. I'm better than this lot here.' I suppose he's above ground at least."

"Do you know who it's by?"

"Unsigned. Can't be anyone famous, mind, or it wouldn't be here, would it? I wouldn't give it houseroom, personally. If you ask me, we've only put it up to get in the good books for the publicity campaign," and Micheal rolled his eyes to the canvas. "Who do you reckon he is?"

Nelson smiled. "If only he could tell us."

"Now, that I would like to see."

A mobile phone suddenly squirted into life. The guard flipped his wrist to check the watch strapped Marine-style against its underside. "We've been waiting for a delivery." His cap was dropped onto an anonymous bust and the handset clacked open.

"Is it here? Mike Papa, over…" He tilted his head to receive a squiggle of words. "Aah, Sierra Golf… Good news! Where, over? Really… well, that wasn't me, I can assure you of that. You know I can't entertain spicy food. Okay, roger that, Sierra Golf. Over and out."

The mobile was re-holstered.

"That was Simon in souvenirs. Found my jacket. In the toilet."

"Will you have to go and get it?" asked Nelson, hopefully not too hopefully.

"I'll pick it up on my way back," Micheal replied. "I'm warm enough yet. And I need to check the PIRs anyway."

"PIRs?"

"Passive Infra-Red sensors." Every syllable relished like covert ops. "See up there?"

Nelson looked to the corner of the room.

"System's been playing up. We were supposed to be getting CCTV, smoked glass domes, the lot, but that's been shelved. Too expensive. '*You're not guarding the crown jewels,*' finance director said, so we've had to make do with cheap domestic sensors. Tell you what, Norton," he said, "while you're here, would you just move about a bit so I can watch for it blinking?"

Nelson stepped sideways. "No, no… too slow. A bit faster. No… There! *No*. False alarm. Try over there. No? No. Forget it. Useless."

Micheal found a notebook in his shirt pocket, licked the tip of a bookmaker's pencil and made an important-looking scribble.

"If they ever were to detect anything," he continued, "a warning's supposed to go off at Central Watch and I'll be over like an exocet. I'm only five minutes away. And I'll bring my cobra, too, and you wouldn't want to be here then, see?"

The memo was popped away and Nelson had the uneasy inkling that Mykeel was building for another windmilling. Nervous knuckles had already tightened on his clipboard-cum-shield when the phone trilled again.

"Mika Papa, ovah…" Micheal listened for a sentence then cracked an eager grin, "'Bout bloomin' time, Sierra Golf. Be right over, over!" Communications were about to cease when the mood suddenly frosted. "Thin and crispy? I never have that and you know it, over!" Micheal made a horror gurn. "You lick anything before I get there… Well, you can foxtrot oscar yourself. Over! And out!" The mobile was snapped hard. "Got to go."

"What's happened?" enquired Nelson.

"Incoming."

The guard hitched his trousers, tucking the rolls of his belly into their waistband and its tug-of-war belt. "The pizza boy's just arrived and simple Simon's claiming *he* ordered the stuffed crust!"

A hastily re-attached tie bridged the gap where his collar should have fastened and his cap was forced back into its groove, peak centred. A foot slammed to the floor; fingertips were forehead-raised then sliced to thigh.

"Got to go," he repeated. And he scrambled away.

On a different day, perhaps, the well-delivered salute might have impressed. For now, there was merely a bemused stare to mark the send-off. Yet as security laboured out of sight, there was a moment's movement in the guard's shade.

And while Nelson's pencil played on a room away, Micheal halted and enquired in a hush, "Still here? You been eavesdropping?"

*

In The Gallery, the sketch was folded for the bin and the clipboard pushed to the rucksack. Checking right and left, Nelson addressed the cemetery. "Can you hear what other people are saying? If you can, I'm sorry about that. *I* don't think you're creepy. If anything, you're kind."

"It concerns me not. I have long endured the contempt of others; such discourtesies are of no consequence. Yet I admired your worthy defence of me, young Cicero. How I would have wished for counsel like you in my day!"

"What was it like, in your day?"

The reply was not immediate. "Lonely."

"Why?"

"I always felt distant from my contemporaries. I was *different* from them. I felt I perceived things they did not…"

Nelson's eyes grew.

"I was orphaned while barely eight years of age. My father had the good fortune to find work at the colliery and was unlucky enough to descend the day the shaft gave way. Then, one crimson dusk not much after, my mother left the house and had not returned when I awoke next morning. Expecting her home soon, I stayed within to welcome her. The following day the neighbours came. Mother had been ill before and they assumed she had been resting in bed, as was her habit, until the blacktime passed. I explained to the policeman I was waiting for her. She, said he, was not coming back."

"Why not?"

"They had discovered her face down in the canal."

"No…"

"With that I was sent away to my maternal uncle. There was another aunty and uncle, my father's side, but they already had a child – an imbecile, he was – and they would not entertain a second mouth to feed. My new guardian was a butcher: kindly in company, a devil in drink. He would leave me fearful and bloodied on a whim."

"What about his wife?"

"Wife?" A sneer of a syllable. "My uncle's ambitions lay far from marriage, which for years made the shadows my curse."

"Couldn't you tell your teacher?"

The voice sounded like a wry smile. "There was no schooling, my friend. My time had gone by the time Forster opened the gates to all. Not that I was without education, you understand. Memories of my mother are now as gossamer, yet her teaching me to read on her brighter days remains vivid. I fancy she picked it up in service before she met Father. In later years, when I could afford the volumes, I read hungrily. Are you familiar with Thomas Hood?"

Nelson shook his head.

"Mother's best-liked. She carried a Punch poem of his. Just one: she was not a woman given to ostentation. I ask of Hood merely to exemplify my uncle's parsimony. '*Oh! God! that bread should be so dear, And flesh and blood so cheap!*' His own flesh and blood at that."

"But you seem to have done well for yourself." Nelson had often heard his mum say much the same when she bumped into Jan, who ran the boutique. "Did he make you a partner?"

"Not quite. He died and the butchery passed to me. I stayed a while then left to make my way in the world. I was still a young man and sought many adventures in many places." A longing suffused his tone. "Every day presented new sensations. I gorged myself on the fruits of my ingenuity. Epicure himself would have blushed: meats young and tender, amusements ravishing and exotic. How the senses screamed in ecstasy! And now… now the least elemental tastes are denied."

Nelson fumbled guiltily for his Evian bottle, long since replenished by a reservoir's worth of tap water. There was so much still to ask.

"But *now*, how… how do you breathe?"

"I can, so I do. I give it no regard. *Dum spiro spero.* While I breathe, I hope."

"Is that Latin again? You said some before, didn't you? '*Now is not the time.*'"

"You understood? It was a reflex. The language of the Caesars, the greatest of men. I was never taught till latterly and in the end my tutoring ran tragically short. We used it as code so outsiders would not understand. I knew not a word at the outset, but others guided my clumsy tongue."

"Was it a test, to see if I could work it out?"

The man paused, assessing the merits of a new serendipity. "Were we to come to an arrangement my *bright* boy, I could hardly risk my fate – and my fortune – on a fool."

Nelson wondered briefly whether his friend needed to know about Aunty Thomasina and her schoolgirl Latin, then decided not. Instead, he scuffed his sleeve across his mouth and after re-wrapping the label around the slip of its torso, returned his drink to the rucksack. Fleetingly, amid the tick of the buckles, he imagined he caught another sound, a cough half-stifled. He gazed in turn at lifeless spectators. From their finger-smeared glasshouses, their shoddy, sagging plinths and their musted storeroom surrounds, they were watching every move, absorbing every word. He rose quietly from his haunches. "Is there anyone else here like you?"

"Like me?"

"You know… alive?"

"In here? I think not. Yet there will be some, somewhere. I cannot be unique. Their tragedy is not their incarceration, but that most will never meet someone like you."

By now the shadows across the walls were signalling hometime. Nelson tugged at the knot constricting his airway. He wanted to remind the man about the promise he had offered, but he was still not sure how he could possibly save him and it did not seem right to speak of favours until then.

"Your heart's desire?" suggested the voice.

"How did you kn—"

"Allow me credit for what I know, my friend. Of your great reward, we will converse further. It will come. But for now, I crave respite. I beg, leave me to rest."

"Can I visit again? Tomorrow?"

"I shall be distraught should you not."

Nelson smiled.

"Yet may I offer some counsel of my own? Let our friendship remain between us. Why invite the jealousy of others? I fear outsiders may judge harshly the bond we have formed. They may seek to break us, to divide our companionship. Should you and I both suffer merely because others do not – cannot – understand? Are we not men of the world? The situation in which I find myself brings many dreads, but my greatest anxiety is that exposure may risk our adventure."

Nelson was already nodding. Intrigue, secrets, adventures. He was his father's son.

A glance down at the timepiece he did not have. "I have to go now, anyway."

He and Pippa had finally relented in the face of unrelenting badgering and agreed to call to Roland's for tea that evening. What was it about this week? He had begun it without a friend in the world. Now they were everywhere.

Four o'clock, give or take a ten-minute margin for error, he estimated. Should have plenty of time, dependent on the Number 31.

Rounding up his belongings, a familiar question returned. "Why me?"

"Why…?" repeated the voice.

"Why are you doing this for me?" insisted Nelson.

"Surely, it is I who should be asking such of you."

"What do you mean?"

"Time will reveal all, my dear."

Nelson retrieved his pen for the petition – again! – on the way out, and started away. He halted almost immediately and, in his haste, failed to find the echo of footfalls not quite in step with his own. "Just one more thing."

"Yes, my dear?"

"I still don't know your name."

"My name?"

"Yes."

"Are you certain can you keep a confidence?"

"Certain."

"Then, it is Sheldan."

"Just Sheldan?"

"That will suffice, for friends."

And, for the first time (though Nelson *may* have imagined it) the face betrayed the merest breath of expression.

"Our little secret. Call me Sheldan."

Chapter Fifteen

Monday 12th October 1903

The windows were already bare to the first of the sun as we arrived at the house. The front door, a gate of fiery ochre, had been left ajar, presumably in expectation of our arrival, yet in conscience I rapped the tarnished knocker. A flutter of drapes.

– The bobbies! – came the cry and perhaps a dozen people streamed onto the street from within.

– A most lamentable event! – muttered one as she filed by. As soon as they had passed, I took a brief time to examine the latch. Not forced. As usual.

Across the red-painted threshold the gathering of neighbourly concern had warmed the vestibule to an uncommon degree. The heat and an accompaniment of unseen wails possessed me of the thought, as I wiped the street from my feet, that I was entering the very mouth of Hades.

Upon reaching the parlour I found the mother on

the largest chair, curled into a ball and rocking with grief. A husband's arm pulled her sorrow-soaked face towards him.

– I'll show you the room – said he, and as he let go she fell back into the seat and shook with a heartrending violence.

– The front door was open when we awoke – whispered he as we took the first of the stairs. – That was when I rushed back up...

I knew too well what to expect upon stepping inside the child's room: a vision of hollow normality. Where his toy soldier had guarded Christian's vacant bed, here a doll reposed for want of her owner's return. A pillow had been cast aside and blankets thrown clear. And there, faint as the draught from a moth, the foul bouquet. That sickly sweet, torporific stench.

I moved to the chair in the corner and was able to lift a single hair, blackest jet, from the antimacassar.

– Is that a clue? – pleaded the father.

– It is similar to one I found at my own home. I see it is not one of yours.

– No.

– Have you touched the broken window? – enquired I.

– How did you know? – and as he spoke his face betrayed the realisation of his worst fear.

We stood about the bed, I trance-like. I lifted a cross-stitch from the wall 'Home Sweet Home' – such irony! – but nothing lay behind. My breath on the window developed nothing. Where was it?

– You look confused, officer –

– There should be more – replied I – Is there a blackboard, or an easel?

– To what purpose? – asked he.

I had already sent Richards to check the back parlour and he returned presently with news of splintered glass.

– He has cut away at the putty before now – explained I.

– Yet I had nailed in each pane, to make it more secure.

– That I noted at the front – said I.

The father scrubbed fingernails at his orange locks – Our only child! She was nine yesterday – and he shrunk into her pillow and pulled its borders over his ears.

Making our way downwards, the man stumbled – I don't think the wife will be able to take this – said he – We only buried her dear mother a week past.

I rested my hand on his shoulder and urged him to speak of hope, for all their sakes; though, in truth, such a task was the only undertaking unshared with Ella that has ever gladdened me.

Upon our return Richards called for one of the women on the pavement to make tea while I offered condolences, as much for myself as for them, and spoke a few comforting words. Those I could not recall as soon as they departed my mouth so little confidence in them did I possess.

Taking leave, I went to close the front door behind me and it was then, as if I had been a blind man, I noticed a staining across its highest panel. I took my handkerchief and, with gentleness, rubbed its white cotton against the brown. Blood. Then, bringing the door back and forth against the sunlight, I was able to discern more. Letters. Six.

– What make you of this, Constable? – enquired I. Richards confirmed what was now as plain as day.

I ordered him back inside to look more closely at the entry window. He returned in haste to tell of spots beyond the sill and a whit of fibre upon a standing shard.

Ordering the door untouched for the pictures man, I carefully pulled it closed. Before walking away, something, though I could not say what, drew me to gaze again at the taunt daubed in the malevolent bile that coursed within him. The name I had heard before in the whispered distance. The cuckoo taunt I had found lodged in my own home.

The coming of nightmares.

CRI†CH

*

The journal was closed.

"So, after everything I've just read, you *still* think 4G was the killer?"

"All I'm saying, me, is that the disappearances *mysteriously* stopped around the time 4G died." He had tried not to pronounce 'mysteriously' in the tone of 'obviously', but could not help himself.

"True, but—"

"Thank you. Classic case of a murderer covering his own tracks."

"How?"

"By finding all the evidence."

"That's his *job*!" She had tried not to pronounce the exclamation in the tone of 'dimwit' but could not help herself.

"Okay, let's look at the clues. That hair 4G found on the antimatter. Of course it was similar to one at his home; it was probably one of his. He wasn't discovering it; he was disposing of it." Roland leaned away triumphantly. "Then he mentions being in Hell – *that's* because he knows he's headed below."

"Purely metaphorical."

Roland was clueless on that count so carried on digging. "And when he finally realises that his dopey assistant isn't going to spot the blood on the door he has to 'find' it for himself." The word 'find' gleefully bookended by air punctuation. "Invent a fake suspect, have everybody looking in the opposite direction, and in the end nobody's guilty." And the last of a chocolate muffin was popped into his cakehole.

A Stanislavsky yawn provided the cover for Pippa to assess her wristwatch. 1.20pm. Clearing-up time soon. She glanced over Roland's shoulder while he gnawed the prints from the ends of fingers. *Where is he?*

"Have you seen him today?"

"I'm not falling for that one," Roland announced.

"What one?"

"The old invisible man one. I use it all the time, me."

"I meant Nelson."

"Oh. No. Not today."

"What about Norton?"

"Oh God, I've seen *him* all right. Three days running now," he said. "I blame this Walk to School Week nonsense. I keep bumping into the maniac. It's more like Stalked to School Week. And he keeps asking me about Nelson."

"What kind of things?"

"Y'know, the usual stuff. Have you seen him? Where has he been? Has he said anything? Where do I reckon he gets those pullovers from?"

"Did he make any threats?"

"Sort of."

"What did he say?"

"Well, nothing specific. He just has this threatening way of being alive."

"So, that's all he said?"

"Do you know if it's possible to overdose on your inhaler?"

"He asked you that?"

"No, I was asking you. Mine's never out of my face at the moment."

Is he coming or not? Pippa sank back and reached absent-mindedly into her pocket. Onto the table she placed a pair of magnets that she began to cleave and cleave with an impatient click.

Another glance, but the doors refused to swing. In the foreground (mercifully out of focus) Roland was now sucking at the muffin cup.

Suddenly, the metal stuck tight. A saliva-dank hand pressed onto hers and a chocolatey throat readied.

"What are you doing?" she blurted.

"I was just thinking," Roland smiled, "how about I take us out for some tea tonight? Pizza'Ere has special offers on Wednesdays. It's all authentic Italian. They do kebabs, too."

"I'm not sure. I'll ask Nelson when he gets here."

"Nelson? No, I didn't... I was thinking just me and you, me. The two of us. On our own and that."

And that! Pippa did not even want to entertain the connotations of 'and that'.

"Look, Roland," she said, scrabbling for a placatory tone, "I really like you and everything, but, well, to be honest I'm not a big fan of olives and... I don't... I mean... I'm not... Oh look, *there's* Nelson!"

Roland's clammy palm had long retreated by the time Nelson had snaked his way through the maze of scattered chairs. Past the abandoned battlefield of cutlery; past the jilted blazer, pockets now cradling leftover sweetcorn and dollops of yoghurt; past the table with the tumescent erection etched delightfully in salt.

Jolly-jumpered, stern-faced, he arrived.

"Nelson! Where've you been all morning?"

"You're too late," added Roland, pointing across the hall, "the shutters are just dropping."

"I'm not hungry, thanks," he said, pulling out a chair.

*

At the serving hatch, the rattling roller shutter guillotined down as Sigsworth and Finch dashed their trays clear. Close call. At one point the grille had knocked the top storey of chips off his plate and Finch had almost surrendered a hand trying to scoop them back before the barrier clamped. The pair waddled contentedly away – half human, half buttocks – with the last of the not-quite leftovers. As their food had accrued, both had declared to anyone within earshot that they would be forgoing an evening meal tonight. That old fabrication. *The junkie's feint.*

The retreat to the staffroom had hardly begun before synchronised forks were launched. "Get in the hole!"

"So, what does Old Bridgey want to see you about?" A southern-fried breath.

"Swimming yesterday," Sigsworth sighed onto a chicken diplodocus, "and that Bentham lad half-drowning."

"What's that all about?"

"As you know, first time I've taken that bunch. So, I'm stood on the side and out pops our Bentham from the verruca pool and he's covered in badges – cross-Channel this, one hundred miles that. Looked like a veteran of Stalingrad. Next thing, he's heading for the shallow end and I says, 'Whoa! Hold it right there! Gifted and Talented, boy! We need to be *stretching* the likes of you.'"

"Brownie points."

"That's what I thought. So, off we toddle to the deep end and in he goes."

"Then what?"

"Sinks like a *bastard* brick." (Each was prepared to swear blind the word was 'blasted' should an over-zealous eavesdropper squawk.)

"You're joking. Did you go in after him?"

"Nearly did. Then I remembered my new Spotlights." They both glanced down at pristine Nikes.

"Furry muff."

"Fair enough, indeed. And, of course, the instructor – you know the one, *always* complaining – is at the other end with the paddlers and piddlers, so I seizes the long brush for pushing plasters about on the bottom and hauls him out coughing and spluttering."

"I bet you were," chuckled Finch as a stegosaurus was de-plated.

"Good one."

"No, seriously though, it sounds like a lucky escape."

"You're not wrong there. Cost a ton-forty, these. Chlorine would crucify the leather." And they dipped floorwards again.

"I'm on the baths run this afternoon. 9RR."

"In that case, my friend, a word to the wise. Just check none of the gormless sods turns up in their brother's trunks."

"Mmm." And Finch paused in grim contemplation. "Have you got more chips than me?"

*

Pippa beckoned to Nelson and patted the chair next to her. "I hadn't seen you this morning. I… we were worried about you. Are you okay?"

"I'm fine."

"Any luck finding your photograph?"

"Not yet. There are too many people about. Everyone's getting in the way."

Pippa held out the red case. "I brought the medal back. And the pipe's in my satchel."

Nelson said nothing.

"In other news, Roland here is sticking with his theory that 4G did it." Pippa had expected another robust defence of his forebear (there had been raised voices at the dinner party when the theory was premiered), but Nelson merely glared into space.

The stretching silence soon began to disturb Roland. "Where you off to now, Pippa?"

"Maths." And the magnets clicked together again.

"G and T?"

Pippa ignored the follow-up and returned Roland's opener.

"Me?" he said. "Should have been a free period." He meant PE – his canon of 'please excuse…' notes had long since been laminated and pinned to the staff noticeboard as a morale booster. "But I've got detention. Copying in my spelling test, can you believe? You should have seen the Ray Gun, all over me just because I got full marks for once. Some teachers don't want you succeed."

"Did you copy?"

"I'd rather not say."

"That's the thing about plagiarism, Roland: there's always someone, somewhere, with a big nose who knows, and who'll trip you up and laugh when you fall."

"I might not go, anyway."

"Just do your time, otherwise you'll get sent to Mr Bridge," she warned.

"Ooh, that reminds me, have you seen the skylight in the top corridor? Someone has gone on the roof and arranged gravel on the glass to say, ''Eff off, Big Bridgey'! Full word, as well. Now that *is* worth a detention."

Roland paused to confirm Pippa was still paying attention.

"It gets better. When the sun came out it beamed the message onto the floor. That was when we could read it properly because if you just looked up it was all back to front. Mind you, Pilchard in our class was claiming he could read it anyway because of his dyslexia. Probably the first thing he's ever been able to work out without his overlay, or something."

Mr Jones appeared from the margins. "Ready for maths, Phillipa?" He beamed, teeth tingle-white.

"Just finishing my lunch, Sir."

"Quick as you can then, please. Formulae, today. No pressure, but I'm relying on you to crack a few for me."

Did he have to talk so loudly? A glance through the crook of his arm as he fingered calculator cufflinks confirmed Deadly was indeed watching. Pippa looked up at him and strained a beam. Those in Young Jonesy's fan club – he was reigning playground pin-up – would no doubt have swooned at his black suit, black shirt, and silver and black-striped tie combination in the vogue of the pro footballer he had always hoped to be. They would have marvelled at a face full of angles; the trim, isosceles sideburns; the hacksaw stubble accentuating the vectors of his jawline; the scattergraph highlights spiking studiously unkempt hair. Instead, Pippa observed he was so richly tanned it was difficult to gauge where neck ended and collar began.

The deputy surveyed the hall, sponging up the adoration, twirling his wedding band, which spun so freely it seemed it might slip clean off (given half a chance).

"Afternoon, Sir." A pair of devotees from the school football team.

"Afternoon, boys. Big game tomorrow." He clapped hands together and the friendship beads around his wrist rattlesnaked. "Catch you in five, Phillipa." And he was off.

"Well, better get going," she said. "Baths for you this afternoon, Nelson?"

"Yep," he replied, miles away. "About the only place open Wednesday afternoons in this backward town."

The threesome, the last of the hall's nibblers, rose from their seats.

"This one of yours?" A cheerless lunchtime assistant, plastic-capped head peeping through a bright green tabard, held up the forgotten blazer. "No name in it," she added.

The trio shook heads in unison.

The dinner lady groaned. Another trip to Lost Property. As if she did not have enough to do. She tossed it onto a stack of chairs and returned to clear the adjacent table. A peeved flash of her dishcloth and the oversized penis was gone.

"Are you sure you're okay, Nelson? You seem a little preoccupied."

"Just thinking."

Nelson had spent the hours following morning registration at the museum. There, he had spoken of his father's disappearance, of the times they had spent together, of the ache that would not let him alone. Sketch pad in reserve, he had talked and talked of his heart's desire until ejected by half-day closing. He could not go home, where Mum would be waiting, and so had returned to school for the alibi of a dank swimming kit.

"Is it important?" She could tell by his face that it was. "A problem shared and all that."

"No. Not important."
Yet this morning he had been betrayed.
And Pippa could tell by his face that it was.

Chapter Sixteen

"Ever seen a leper's nob?"

The pale appendage was held aloft. Flaccid. Slumped. Yet still warm to the lip. Closer inspection revealed the skin had split and droplet of murky juice was leeching along the shaft to accumulate at the pinched tip, where it threatened like acid sundew.

A sharp suck through pursed lips ended the jaw-slacked silence then the room rang hard with the rattle of steel and the clatter of china: a muezzin cry to the pell mell of home cooking. She was not pleased.

At the edge of the slate floor, Heather – crammed against a velour leisuresuit – pushed a balled bundle across the concessionary marble, soaking up blooms of powdery gravy. Every swipe revealed a dark reflection of her future self. Still, she was not pleased.

If she had her way *her* kitchen would have been all clean lines and sheened faces. Heath disagreed. "Wouldn't reflect the character of The Cottage," he said. "More suited to a country style." And, while he was paying, this season's style was country.

So, there it was: pale grain panelling, nipple-knobbed doors, and, high above, untouchable cut glass behind unreachable panes. Sturdy oak girders beamed down from the ceiling, dustings of desiccated flowers slung beneath, and the olde-worlde look was completed by a boxy portable lashed into the vertex near the door, from where it was unveiling the woes of the world to itself at *The Respecter*'s expense.

The kitchen was barely a month old so Heath was not yet accustomed to the confidences of its nooks and crannies. At least that was his excuse for never brewing tea or filling the dishwasher. It had been the penultimate job on his retirement masterplan, sandwiched between the new bathroom and the attic conversion. This past few months had felt as if the builders had taken up residence – squatters from the Land of Yob – but he would rather have the hammering and whistling and clanking of oversized mugs now than when he was savouring the hard-earned fruits of his career.

Heath was rather pleased with the kitchen (all except the worktops, so he steered clear of those) and, as usual, it had not cost as much as it might. He had worked out a cosy deal with Central Eating Ltd: they would advertise their bespoke wares with *The Respecter* and, in return, Heath would receive a healthy discount on the design of his choice and free fitting thrown in. To the untrained eye it appeared the kitchen outfit was paying both ways on the transaction, but Heath had relished raising merry hell with his advertising department for a dreadful run of errors on the firm's double-page spreads – minor speeling mistakes, incorrect colour schemes – and, week after week, Central Eating Ltd was given a credit note for a re-run in the following edition.

He had kept it up as long as he dared. When *The Respecter*'s ad manager was eventually dispatched under threat of the push to personally oversee the proofs, Heath finally had to stop tampering with the artwork at the printers. The kitchen company received eight weeks' centre-spread publicity for the price of one, as well as a couple of prominent puff pieces thrown in – a ten-a-penny Investors in People plaque and a shortlisting for an entirely fictitious national good service award.

All told, the enterprise amounted to a fifty-fifty split between editor and advertiser. The oldest trick in the book and regional had still not cottoned on. *Deserved everything they got.*

Heather's sole contribution to the refurbishment was the black marble worktop. He had wanted oak, but she had cajoled and promised and sulked and schemed and there it lay, solid as rock and gleaming like a mirage under secret spotlights. Yet even that success had proved pyrrhic as anyone daring to plunge headlong into its mirrored plane appeared instantly aged. The ghost of tinned mints to come. In its malicious jet she was shown lines she was certain could not exist in the present, saw eyes heavy and hooded, found frowns mined into flesh.

Some people – she recalled the book she often carried as a student, and almost wished she had bothered to read it – had the picture in the attic to find the face of their future. Heather had the gloom of her marble worktop. She did not want to look and found it impossible to desist. She was grimacing at it now and, more than ever, she was not pleased.

"If you let that drip onto the tablecloth!" she warned.

Back at the dining table, Heath was mid-examination. "What?"

"I said stop messing with that sausage," and she wrung the dishcloth (if only it was his neck!) into the sink, pocking the white stone with bursts of grey.

"Oh, is that what it is?"

"I spent all afternoon making that casserole." She was watching herself in the tiled splashback and, despite the blur of her own reflection, she could clearly see its look of disgust as she stooped for the sympathy card.

"Really? Well, can I suggest that next time you spend an extra five minutes browning the bloody sausages under the grill instead of putting them straight into the pot. Just look at it!" Heath slowly rotated his fork, affording a 360-degree panorama of finest pork and leek. The greasy dangle of sauce at the end shuddered precariously as he brought it to a halt.

"Doesn't even *look* cooked," he added. "Probably give us the raging trots. In fact, I said to Norton it resembles a leper's—"

"I heard," Heather replied, still talking to the wall.

"There's no happy medium around here. It's either burnt to a bloody crisp, or half raw."

Norton was keeping his head down… it *did* resemble a leper's nob, or how he imagined one might look, but now was not the time to be taking sides. He would soon be in need of all the grown-up allies he could muster with Little Heath's change of heart about his weekend visit and sixteen jokes yet to conjure.

*

This evening had been a new dining experience for the Edwards. Heath had for years fended for himself on a Wednesday ('fended' as in mixed meat satay, egg fried rice, spring rolls and a complementary cloud of prawn crackers). *The Respecter's* deadline was traditionally eleven that morning and his window at the printers 6pm till nine-ish, notwithstanding a major story breaking or, more likely, a minor machine malfunctioning. The straddling warehouse, one half all QuarkXPress and flatscreen jiggery-pokery and the other prostrate redwoods and ear defenders, was only five miles distant – or twenty, using the arcane measuring system known in the trade as 'expense mileage' – so Heath was usually back on his patch for 10.00pm. It was his habit to catch the last thirty minutes with the chaps from the Local History Society, drag the chosen few for a wind-down pint and then make for the takeaway.

However, the myopic management at the printers had treacherously succumbed to a better offer: some upstart midweek football rag that Heath was confident would not see out the season. But these Johnny-come-latelys paid better – and more readily – than *The Respecter*, so that was that. Shunted to the late slot. *There's loyalty for you.* Starting last week, Heath had not been putting the paper, or himself, to bed until the early hours.

There were bound to be mistakes. He had already received a jokey missive from the vicar chiding him for permitting 'Brianteaser' to slip through on the quiz page. The Rev Brian Drian had written, only half-mockingly, that he hoped this was not the start of a campaign of torment and taunt against the Brians of the world. The letter had even included a suggested headline, a weedy 'Strife of Brian' pun. Heath accepted the criticism with his usual grace; he just hoped the holier-than-thou smartarse was still chuckling when the editor's apology was published this week in place of the usual free plug for the church fete.

Heather's reaction to this shift in home circumstances had been to invoke a little Dunkirk spirit. "A good old family meal," she had declared ('good' being her interpretation, rather than the dictionary's). Most other nights, she reasoned, Heath was still at his desk when Norton loafed down to eat. Now, her husband could come home instead of heading directly for the printers and they could all enjoy some quality time together. Like the stars do.

Heather would never come clean, of course, but her dusting off the Delias was not founded entirely on altruism. On the first occasion of the new arrangement, Heath had found *Wok This Way* shuttered so headed instead for the late-night elephant leg emporium. Stomach first, and fearfully running the gauntlet of the midweek wastrels, he had demanded a Dynamite Donner. *You wouldn't mess with someone who ordered a Dynamite Donner.* Back at The Cottage, he horsed it down while scouring Sky for exorbitant cheap thrills before creeping stiffly disappointed to bed. The next morning brought Heather one of her rancid migraines – an event not entirely unrelated, she later deduced, to the lack of breathable air in the bedroom. She would have been better off on Venus.

*

"Are you not finishing that?" asked Heather.

"What are you, a dinner lady?" Heath's retort.

"Only asking, darling. Are you full?" She hoped he was. "Mmm…"

"Bet you could squeeze in some apple pie and cream?" *Too full for the kebab house.*

"Where's it from?" he enquired nonchalantly.

He's bloody well checking it's not home-made, she thought. "Marks."

"Go on then."

Heath returned the cold sausage to his plate – *save a little corner for a Dynamite later* – glanced at his watch and sighed. Off out again soon. The graveyard shift. Still, not long now, and he consoled himself with thoughts of a heart's desire to come.

The hiss of cream announced pudding was served and the three of them decanted, bowls in hand, to the sitting room. Heath shuffled to *his* chair where *his* dailies waited freshly uncreased on the occasional table that accompanied it. Sometimes, when Dad was at work and Mum was having one of her facials, Norton would hover trembling, like rain on a car window, in Heath's seat. He would caress the cool of the leather, finger the space-time of its blunderbuss buttons and sniffle his inquisitive head into the depths of its flanks. Orders were barked out to family members yet to be (in his vision of the future, he had become the chair's rightful owner following the tragic death of Little Heath in an accident with a threshing machine, or some such mangling equipment). And then, with thighs singing, he would retreat to the rug before hitching his sleeve over his palm and polishing away his prints.

Heath was first to finish eating despite squandering several seconds pursuing a splinter of pie crust. Heather would usually have collected his dish as soon as the spoon had stilled, but she had been a late starter herself today on account of forgetting her husband's slippers. In the interests of fairness, he *had* held out his empty bowl for several moments to give her a chance to catch up. *Useless.* Instead, he was forced to balance the dish on the chair's arm while he reached across to reel in the slab of newsprint, a manoeuvre that ended predictably with the crockery spinning to the floor.

"Norton!" he bellowed, and the clatter was retrieved in a heartbeat while he fired a 'see what you made me do?' glare at Idleweiss.

Heath regarded reading the papers at breakfast as 'work'. Perusing them in the evening, in the comfort of his Chesterfield, was 'pleasure'. Notwithstanding that, should the opportunity have presented itself for an easy lift, he would have selflessly demanded the phone and, after first complaining that 'he obviously had to do everything and they'd soon have him delivering the bloody thing as well', set a teatime minion to task. But those were different days. The days before head office's perfidy.

His pleasure this evening began before he had peeled back the first cover. "Look at this!" and his audience did as summoned. "It reads," he continued, flaring nostrils to catch his spectacles, "'Learn Italian in a week with our one-a-day CDs'. And what does it say under that?" He did not wait for any guesses. "Nine to collect... Bloody nine! A *week*! Ha!"

Then followed a minor fluster as Heath chanced across a story concerning a well-women's clinic – "Why do they need their own bloody clinic if there's nothing up with them?" – and next, in the television listings, he spotted '*Horizon*: current affairs programme dealing with a topical issue (rpt)'. "Topical... *repeat*... bloody laughable..." he muttered over and over again, crossing his ankles so his feet almost toed Norton in the face.

"I don't know why you read those things," Heather mumbled between crumbled mouthfuls. "They only make you angry."

"You don't know why I read them?"

Norton glanced up from his position next to the stain that betrayed last week's calamity with the full coffee cup – his legs still carried the tracks of Heath's retribution for that slip – and moved ever so slightly away. From this new perspective he had clear view of the contrary soles of Dad's footwear, and the still-to-scrub-clean *HEAD* and *DICK* that Little Heath had surreptitiously penned in turn across right and left on his previous visit home. Little gleefully informed Norton that he had chosen the terms on the grounds that the construct applied whichever way Dad's feet were set. And then he departed for the clear water of Newcastle upon Tyne.

"Don't know why I read them? It's my job! I have to work to get pennies to keep you in the lap of luxury. Have you seen the cost of calories these days?"

"But you keep saying you're not bothered anymore," Heather replied. "The way you'd been treated in summer over the group editor's job."

"Well, that was in summer, wasn't it?" And the ramping menace in his voice signalled the conversation was at an end.

She was right, of course. *Bastards! Never even offered me an interview!* Yet the evening ritual went on. Perhaps he felt he had to maintain a pretence of appearances if only for his own self-respect, or his sense of duty as the head of the household, or out of habit, or something. She *was* right, of course, but that was scant reason for him to pass up the opportunity for a needless argument with the other half(wit).

Heather fed the last of the pie into her mouth then rose, still chewing, to round up the dishes.

"Tea or coffee?"

"Tea, please," said Norton.

"That's two teas and…?"

Heath ordered coffee, just to be awkward. "And get me the post on the way back."

As soon as he heard the clap of clogs on the slate, Heath ditched his newspaper to the rug and hunched forward.

"Thought she was here all the way up to the bloody soaps," he said, twisting his head towards the kitchen. "Did you go on that errand today?"

Norton dropped his pen onto his joke pad. "Yes. This morning."

"Did you show it to him?"

"Just as you said, same as yesterday afternoon. That's two times now I've put it right in front of him."

"So, you'd rather be in school, would you?"

"But why does he want to see it?"

"What's with all the bleedin' questions? Anything *personal* was the request."

"Oh, right."

"Don't suppose he said…"

"No."

"Did he do *anything*?"

"No."

"Then how do you know he saw it?"

"It was right there." He held his palm across his eyes. "Just like you told me."

"Anyone see you?"

"Nope." (Norton assumed people working there did not count.) "But *he* turned up again just as I was leaving."

"Interesting. Did he see you?"

"No. I hung around, but I couldn't make anything out."

"Okay."

"Hey, Dad, on the way out I swiped a pile of petitions from the front counter. Dumped them in a stream on the way home."

At the rise of footsteps and the dull click of filled of cups, Heath sat back in his chair so its wings funnelled the sound of his mutterings. "Remember," he mouthed while his eyes daggered towards the doorway, "not a fucking word!"

Heather was now back at the room balancing, with a funambulist's devotion, a weighty tea tray. She shuffled unsteadily towards Norton, who curled into a ball as she teetered by – he did not want another stumble over a sprawled limb. After using the tray's edge to ease aside a battery of remotes, the refreshments were unhanded to the coffee table.

"Tea up," Heather announced, only part-feigning breathlessness, "come and get it."

Norton reached for his cup and helped himself to a couple of biscuits. Heath declined the invitation and instead waited for his drink to be passed over, as was right and proper, along with a wad of envelopes secured by elastic.

"Did you remember the sugars?" he asked in a tone that was one lump enquiry, one lump accusation. He brought the cup to his lips then paused, permitting senses to brood on the aroma. *Has she used those bastard Hermasetas again?* "I don't want any of that sweetener shite you poison yourself with." His nose dipped to the swirling meniscus, milky vapour threaded its way up his nostrils and, mostly satisfied, he claimed a sip.

Heather smiled condescendingly. *Once.* Once in twenty years had she run out of sugar. And anyway, he should have been more concerned that she had just spent the last five minutes wiping his cup with the Marigolds she saved for cleaning the toilet.

*

The band that had encircled the envelopes cracked painfully against Norton's cheek. "Bullseye!" and Heath congratulated himself on his marksmanship.

While Norton massaged stinging flesh Heather collected Penny Lancaster from the magazine rack, along with the plate sheltering on the tea tray. "Jaffa Cake?" she asked.

"Have we not eaten already?"

Heath's barb was ignored and she flopped into the cuddle of the couch, one leg folded beneath her. With a Jaffa half-protruding so she resembled a novitiate to a lost tribe, she caressed this week's *Hello*. It had arrived yesterday – October 28th, 2003, Issue 788, the cover declared – but she had not yet settled down to look at it properly. Her habit was to spend the first day scanning the pictures, gorge on its juicy titbits over the next few evenings then tackle some of the three-course writing over the weekend. 'HelloWorld' was a golden, sunlit place where Heather sensed (no, *knew*) she belonged. There was nothing better than teasing open those glossy doors and falling headlong through its Cartier furs.

Before diving in she reached for a second nibble and checked over at Heath, still muttering and moaning his way through the papers and now fingering his nose. *Oh no. Nothing better.*

Heather's head spun with the narratives of her famous friends: No Posh on the front this week. Shame. Still, Penny looks nice, relaxing on her couch in that white dress. 'Why I'm happy not to be Mrs Rod Stewart'. Good for you. Why I'd be delighted not to be Mrs Heath Edward. She's reading a book, too. Beauty and brains. Must find a book to read. There's got to be an update on Gwynnie. Hope she's still not feeling low. Mind you, I'm not surprised after playing that miserable poet lady: felt like ending it all myself. Wouldn't it be nice if she marries that Chris Coldplay? Will Carling and his new baby. Gone off him since the business with Lady Di. Do we think those are real, Caprice? Who's Princess Olga Romanoff? Oh look! Martine! This *is* her moment...

Heather counted back. Eleven *EXCLUSIVE!* pages on Penny and Rod and the 'fabulous home they share in LA'. Plucking the hat-trick Jaffa, shared unawares with the family fly, she settled down to find out more. For good measure she studiously adopted Penny's front-page pose: elbow resting on sofa arm, knees proprietarily teased together, perfectly manicured nails clawing at reading material, carefree tresses flicked oh-so-carefully about the shoulders, bronzed thighs... second thoughts, keep the thighs under wraps, at least until the thread veins have been lasered. Well, what a lovely home, Penny! One to be proud of and no mistake.

Unlike Rod the Mod's, Heather's living room screamed *history*, more was the pity. 'Character features', the home-improvement gurus might have gushed. 'Old-fashioned', she would have countered. Of course, the restrictions that accompanied the kudos of listed status, coupled with Heath's aversion to expenditure, did present certain restrictions on the renovation front. But there must be ways and means. How else would Heath have gained consent for his loft conversion? Then a fleeting moment of clarity: Heath actually wanted a loft conversion.

Where to start? The grandfather clock with its fustian beat, lurking hideously in the corner like a child's coffin, would be first out of the door. She could live with the three-piece suite *tick*, and the parquet floorboards *tick*, but that big bloody beam like a weal across the ceiling *tock*, and the 'English Manor' rug with its hideous green Aubusson florals *tock*, the Edwardian fireplace with the William Morris doodles and the hearth that bit at your toes as you edged past *tock*. And the too-tiny windows that kept in the heat a million years ago and now just held back the daylight *tock*. They would all have to go.

Yet what annoyed her most was that chair and all it represented *tock*. Heath's do-not-bloody-touch arse-palace chair. *Tock!*

"A timeless classic." *She knew the speech by heart.* "Queen Anne in oxblood red. Instantly recognisable as a Chesterfield, simply perfect for that cosy corner next to the fireplace. Hand-stuffed cushions as standard. High leg, high back with all-the-way studded wings and hand-studded facings."

Loved his chair, Heath. Loved running his fingers about the rollercoaster of its hollows and highs. In yesterdays, his father and grandfather had sat in it and righted the world. One day, too – though certainly not any time soon – his rightful heir might be allowed to settle proud among its creases and folds. Of course, they would have to fight for it: Cain and Abel. Romulus and Remus. *Little and Norton.* No gift wrap here.

Oh yes, needs a makeover, this place, Heather thought to herself. *Time for a revamp. Penny wouldn't put up with living in a museum. Ooh!* That reminded her…

"There was a call today, from that chap at the museum. The manager, Mr Billinge."

"What's he doing, ringing here?" snapped Heath, as if the man had personally taken a nap in his bed after emptying the house of Coco Pops or, worse still, buttocked his chair.

"He wanted to know when you're going to run with that campaign you promised, saving the museum from closure. Apparently, he thinks things need a boost."

"I'll bet he bloody well does. I ask you, how can a town – a village! – this size justify its own museum? They'll be wanting a bloody superclub next. Arse!"

"He did mention an angle for a potential story. His petition has gone missing."

"Well, hold the bastard front page!"

"I was only relaying—"

"No, no, he's got a point. I could tie it in with news of

that paper clip I mislaid yesterday. Tell him he can piss off with his bloody pointless crusade. You can't halt progress."

"But you promised him in return for exhibiting the pai—"

"Bloody pillock! I hope they do convert that place into executive apartments. Might attract some intellectual types."

"Isn't that what a museum's for?"

Answering back?

Without the bother of re-folding the uppermost tabloid, Heath placed his relaxation stack at his feet. While he was down there, he flipped off his slipper and brushed it upturned under the Chesterfield. Everyone knew what he would find.

"Don't tell me the Dyson's broken again," he sighed, rising rubicund.

As a rule, only Heather referred to the vacuum as 'the Dyson'. Not everybody had one. She stared hard at Penny. *Perfect Penny.* What would she say to Rod in a tense situation like this? It was an age before the mumbled, "I don't want to talk about it."

"You don't want to talk about it?" Heath held an accusatory finger at blue tartan. "Let's talk about *this* then, shall we?" To his delight, the slipper was now fur-lined on its outside, too. It spun with a slap into her midriff. "Just look at it! If I ran that Hoover around this place it would pick up more muck than a Dutch satellite."

Heather resisted a suicidal jibe about her husband running anywhere and instead replied, "I can't do it tonight. I've got yoga."

Heath let out a snort like a dog licking beer. "It'll take more than nodding off on a mat to shift that lot!"

"It's not like that. Everyone's doing it. See for yourself!"

And wriggling free from the couch Heather dropped her magazine – and the proof within – onto the newspaper tower.

"Do you seriously believe I'm interested in that celebrity shite? Don't leave it there."

The slipper was returned to Heath's gravity and Heather filled her hands with a mug and a plate while her feet recovered their clogs. Her offer of an empty armpit for *Hello* rebuffed, she was away clacking like joke shop dentures about to run down.

"And you can turn that bloody telly off in there while you're at it," he boomed. "Nothing but doom and gloom on the news channels these days!"

Out of sight, Heather again stared grimly into her worktop. *Quality time?* She could not wait for that football rag to go to the wall.

*

With Mum retreated to the sanctuary of the kitchen (Heath only ventured in when *absolutely* necessary: the slow shuffle for snacks, or – more often – to mount a chair and stab a fuming finger into the smoke alarm) Norton resolved to retire to his own room to attend to his jokes compilation.

"Where you off to?"

"Nowhere." And he lay back.

"Good." Heath poked an eye around the wing of his chair. *All clear. She'll be finishing off the Jaffas, stocking up on energy for unrolling her mat.* "Listen, I want you to start taking things a little more seriously at school. Tighten the rack. Make him feel desperate, like he's got no choice."

"I know, Dad."

"Well, make sure you do. You wouldn't want to let me down, would you?"

"Never, Dad. You know that."

"Good. You can start by sorting that out."

The slipper brushed Norton's chin as it landed across his writing pad, heat rising from its trampled depths.

"Course, Dad."

Industrious plucks were employed at the down of dust and hairs, and the plaid began to re-emerge.

"You sure you got it all off?"

"I think it's done, Dad." He scrabbled onto his knees to slide the slipper back over Heath's three-day sock. While he was there the curve of Heath's shins, he noticed, mirrored exactly the roll of the Chesterfield's. Both hairless, too. Funny, that.

"Heath!" A call from the kitchen

"What?"

"Ask Norton to set the machine for *Corrie*."

"Ask him yourself, lazyarse!"

"Norton!"

"I heard!" and Norton let out an indignant tut, echoing 'lazyarse' under his breath.

He was about to bellycrawl to the remote when he detected new movement that caused him to stall. In his periphery he spied his father making acquaintance with *Hello*. And Heath, after briefly checking out the blonde piece on the cover, had begun to twist the magazine into a cosh.

Now, if Norton had dared tut at his father the least he would have expected was a clout around the head with the back of a hand. Well-deserved, too. But, ordinarily, Heath did not concern himself with stuff directed at Mum.

"What are you going to do with that, Dad?"

Hello was wrung tighter.

"Dad?"

Heath's face was screwed the colour of fury as he took to his feet, club raised over his head. Norton flinched.

"Little fucker!" he growled.

And off he set in pursuit of the fly.

Chapter Seventeen

"Do we have a note explaining your absence yesterday morning?"

The yellow sun cowered behind the nearest cloud and gloom happily claimed the early corridor. To the right, a wall of grimed window looked out on indifferent pupils awaiting the summons of the morning bell. To the left, the Swap Shop noticeboard with its jumble of junk for sale or exchange. And up to the front, escape now barred, the safety of the swing doors and the staffroom beyond.

A second glance at the Swap Shop, a porcupine of pin and poster parading a farrago of dusty goods and services. Many of the items had once been second-hand before being upgraded, just prior to Ofsted's last swoop, to 'pre-owned'. Pre-*loved* had been deemed a little too un-British.

Start at the periphery and work in. Orders for home-burned CDs and DVDs were being invited by Roger Jolley in Year Eleven. He had left and was last seen doing car boots on Sunday mornings. Also up for grabs were boyband tickets, the gig long since played and creative differences at large, size five ladies' sprint shoes with the spikes withheld on health and safety grounds (Gemma's dad was a personal injuries lawyer), school trip 'souvenirs', receipts unavailable, sundry spectacles, unwanted Christmas gifts, ill-chosen clothes, homemade cards for every occasion, seaside tat, and soppy verse for a sweetheart – this latter service a front for plagiarised essays and homework.

It was a standing joke among pupils and staff that the Swap Shop was never cleared. Doc White had been handed ownership and had proved too forgetful or too unwell. Mr Bridge occasionally ordered spot checks, yet this corridor was dead-ended by the caretaker's room and the headteacher passed only rarely. In truth, he was all for getting rid, but the inspectors liked it and that sealed its survival. There *had* been close calls. Scurrilous sales had twice put the enterprise in jeopardy. In its first week, a collection of missing school microscopes had been advertised. Then last summer a bidding war had developed over nude pictures of Miss Lyttle – rumour had it somebody knew somebody whose elder brother had a Saturday job at '*SunnySnaps*'. It was all a hoax, of course, but she had been secretly thrilled anyway. Well, she reasoned, everybody wants to be someone's fantasy.

So, the posters and postcards and post-its built up and up like silt deposits. The entire confection would plunge off the wall before long. And if it happened to land on someone's head, or near enough to make them quail slightly, it would only be a matter of time before Gemma's dad was citing emotional anguish at the other end of the Batphone.

"Are you listening to me, sunshine?"

"What? Pardon? Yes!"

"So, *do* we have a note explaining your absence yesterday morning?"

"How do you know?"

"I'm the one asking the questions. Note?"

"No."

"'No' what!"

"No... no, Sir?"

"That's better. I don't think you realise how serious this is."

Nelson realised all right, and he was more than keen to send out the right signals. He understood the conventions these situations demanded. Everybody did. Listen closely, speak only when spoken to, due deference and all that. Unfortunately, the diversion sought in the Swap Shop appeared only to have inflamed his inquisitor. *Pay attention! That Great Pyramid snowdome can wait.* Yet he was desperate, still, to avoid eye contact and so now sought out the floor. There, the feet opposite appeared cocked, all side on and planted in anticipation. His own? A flimsy cat's cradle of knots and polished scuff. And in-between, varnished concrete. No soft landings there.

There was a silence, but Nelson was reasonably certain it was not his turn to speak. He ran his eyes down the blunt creases of his greying trousers and on to the rings circling the bottom where his mum had let out some length for the new year. He would be as tall as his dad if he carried on like this. For a moment he considered putting his hands in his pockets, where his own hastily scribbled advertisement waited, then thought not; it seemed a little *too* casual, and what if he could not release them and cracked his head?

"Are you going to look at me when I'm talking to you, boy?"

Dipped nostrils caught the breath that trailed the enquiry and drew its smoky staleness into the parch of his mouth.

The hush was at an end. Now it *was* his turn, but the tobacco fumes had caught on his throat and, with nothing to rinse away their choking film, he began a retch that moistened his eyes. In involuntary spasms he held his knuckles to his mouth then raised his face in the gasp for breath. And for the first time he was looking straight ahead. Not at his interrogator, but past those grinning, grimming features; down the corridor and through the wondrous windows of the double doors.

These had recently been upgraded to portholes of head-height safety gauge, concentrically ringed like glass onions, after an inquisitive Year Ten had emptied her BB gun at their predecessors. The surrounding timber had been re-painted school green, but the doors had been glossed over so many times – so many colours! – edges had been lost, and where they swung together they had to be planed down so the layers could be counted like the rings of a rainbow tree.

Nelson's best hope was that the corridor beyond the doors would be congested at any moment, yet the blurry view remained frustratingly bleak. Until now.

In and out of teary focus, Mr Reagan emerged from the staffroom beyond. Through the bubbled glass he paused in profile and raised a steaming cup to his lips, the bare putty that held the pane encircling his form like a creamy aureole. Nelson quickly weighed alternate futures: a saintly face hastening towards them to enquire of their presence and escort him gratefully to shelter; or a tonsure of receding grey and the mayhem likely to follow.

Please, Mr Reagan, walk this way!

Before the distant head had chosen which way to turn Nelson was off his feet. He knew where he was destined. As he was lifted about the chest and levered backwards, the Swap Shop spun again into his compass. Could he advertise his next ten minutes up there? Any takers? *Thought not.*

Bundled away, tiptoes pawing at the teasing floor, Nelson's back slammed flat against a familiar image, trousered-legs wide and arms open. '*Hands up*' would have been more appropriate, like someone facing a firing squad.

Once across the threshold, Sir marched him backwards and into the eerie echo of the boys' toilets.

"So, why weren't you in school yesterday morning like all the other good boys and girls?"

"I wasn't feeling well… Sir."

"Oh, yes?"

"Yes, Sir."

"Let's get something straight, you were seen out and about, so I think the lies need to *fucking* stop now!"

Nelson might have yelled if his vocal cords had not been knotted, might have roared the house down like King ruddy Kong until people arrived from far and near to investigate the commotion, but he was choking soundless. He turned an ear for rescuers' footsteps, yet the sound of the civilised world was gone, drowned out by the drip, drip, drip of a hidden cistern, one deafening plink every second or so – the duration of ten clattering heartbeats. Clamped by the throat, Nelson glanced into the aluminium trough and its rubble of germ cubes. There were green arches where the sluice hissed too infrequently down the brushed metal, and someone had left a five pence coin among the lemonade shades: a bait too inexpensive to be missed; perhaps just enough to tempt the desperate.

And up above, etched across the spume-spatted brickwork, all manner of boast and libel: 'my nobs as long as my leg; free blow jobs in the end trap; Big Bridgey shag's his teddy; theres a kink in my cock; Call Ryan 222222 for a good bum; count my THREE balls …'

The whole cell hummed with the waft of a can't-be-arsed mop and the first dump of the day, though Sydney had been told on countless occasions he must make his way to the *staff* toilets should he be caught short on his rounds.

What was Nelson doing here, like this?

*

It had been another sleep-free night, yet tiredness was nowhere to be found this morning. Tiredness had done a runner. Nelson had come to school early this Thursday because he guessed Norton would not, to search again for his missing photograph. He had saved a splodge of breakfast porridge in an old Tupperware cube dug from the back of a cupboard and smeared it around his chin and jumper just before activating the office buzzer. It was a risky ploy as he could have been quarantined on the spot and turned away at the foyer door. In the end, the mess on his pullover and the palpable desperation in his voice secured safe passage inside.

As pupils were not ordinarily allowed in before opening bell, Nelson had briefly enjoyed the free run of St John's. He had lucklessly re-traced his steps through empty corridors and classrooms and checked everywhere except the ICT suite, which had yet to be unlocked for the day. He was just about to pin a 'REWARD!!!!!!!! Lost Photograph!!! Sentamental Value!!'

poster on the Swap Shop when he had been disturbed. And though it did not seem so for the moment, he had probably been saved some little ignominy as a part-used pocket diary was the best he could muster by way of inducement.

*

"There is no absence note, is there?"

"How did you get in?" Nelson croaked.

"I'm the one asking the questions." But then he could not resist. "I spotted you wandering about inside."

"But how did you get in?"

"I just knocked and said, 'Please, Miss, please, I really, really need to go to the toilet right now, Miss, and if you don't let me, I'll just have to flop it out and do it right here, Miss' and… and," he glanced around at the four walls of their blind-eyed crypt, "and here I am. And, so are you."

"Look, we both know you're not interested in any absence note. The bell's about to go and the place will be crowded in two minutes flat."

"You're right. I'll tell you what. You'll have to pay a fine and we'll say no more about it."

"I haven't got any money. I'm on packed lunches."

"No money? But there's five pee in there." And he motioned at the urinal and its primordial broth.

"I'm not doing it."

"Not doing it? Say you didn't have a choice."

"Say I did."

There was an impatient exhalation. "Put your paw in the piss."

What would his dad have done now? Nelson pulled his shaking palms into the sleeves of his pullover. He wanted to make a fist of it but feared the holes in the weave would show his hand.

"In the friggin' piss. *Or else!*"

Chapter Eighteen

The closed fist landed with a satisfying slap against its target, drowning out the half-hissed

'KAPOW!'

that soundtracked the blow. He had always secretly fancied himself as Adam West, had Mr Bridge. His hapless victim was still rocking back and forth like a metronome when the knock hit the door. Her other hand simultaneously opened it.

Miss Lyttle strode in, all executive blouse and strawberry-blonde sheen slipped from its tethers. "How are you getting on with your new plaything?" mouthed deep-red glossies.

Mr Bridge, warm-faced, gurned like a schoolboy caught fiddling down his trousers. "Erm… not bad, thank you… it was very kind, I must say."

"Not at all. I saw it and I thought, *Just the thing to help the hard-working headmaster* stroke *executive de-stress when the need arises.*"

"Thank you." He smiled. "Yes, it is a good way to let off a bit of steam. I must admit, I've never seen a desktop version before."

They both watched as the red leatherette orb settled upright at last with an orgasmic shudder. The silence sparked.

"I'm led to believe that it's very good in the suction stakes," she eventually said.

Do not think he had not imagined.

"Yes, well, I've not managed to knock it off yet," he replied deliberately.

"So, are you ready for me now?" she enquired. Double deliberate.

Miss Lyttle settled down for the Thursday morning ritual: the briefing session (or *de*-briefing, as the voice within referred to it – do not think *she* had not imagined). While the office manager worked for too many seconds at making herself comfortable, Mr Bridge peeked at the reddened knuckles of his right hand and sprang his fingers out and back. If only some of St John's whining parents *stroke* carers had just witnessed that swingeing hook. They would not be so keen to come knocking on his door shouting the odds then, would they?

"Now then, April!" A sense of first-name mastery swashed through him. "What've we got for the day?" and he brought his hands together, fingers knitted at his chin, and tried hard not to stare at the ghost of her bra as she sat across the desk, notebook erect.

"A few bits and bobs and a run through the diary, if that's okay."

"Fire away." And he determined to take his mind off that ivoried, soft-focus lace by pat-a-caking a pile of newly arrived envelopes into an orderly stack.

Mr Bridge's office was barely recognisable from the bombsite of last week. Miss Lyttle was a tidy person, he not. Yet today the files on his shelves stood straight as dominoes. The scatter of papers had been swept away. The outdated diaries had disappeared. The rash of post-its, taunting him with impossible deadlines, improbably cured. And the catch of cups with their Petri-dish bottoms herded into the steam-cycle. She had playfully teased him about the clutter and now, miraculously, all seemed shipshapely. His office archaeology had even unearthed a previously unseen section of desk to make way, she fondly surmised, for her little gift.

He hoped she had noticed.

"First things first, then," Miss Lyttle began, "Doc, erm, *Mr* Whyte has just called in sick."

"Again! What's the matter this time? He's only just back from two days off with a twenty-four-hour bug."

"Says he's got a bit of a stomach upset."

"Again! He's making me bloody upset!"

(Mr Whyte was not for broadcasting the information, but he was almost certain the gurgles were not entirely unrelated to sucking on Norman's dad's pile pipe.)

"He says he'll try some eggy bread then see how he feels for this afternoon," Miss Lyttle went on.

"Oooh, Captain Oates lives!"

"Shall I call the agency?"

"Better had. And better get supply for all day. Can't see eggy bread bringing him around."

"He said they were free range."

"Cock-a-doodle doo!" and Mr Bridge slumped angrily back in his chair then – *You idiot!* – remembered, and immediately flashed his palms. "I'm sorry, Miss Lyttle. It's not your fault, is it? Don't shoot the messenger and all that. Shouldn't be allowing my ire to bubble to the surface. Most unprofessional."

"Not at all, Mr Bridge." But in that micro-moment she loved him just a little less.

Content that alarm had been avoided, Mr Bridge permitted himself a rock backwards and sleeked his famous right hook through a treasury of silver hair. '*Arctic Sunrise*', Miss Lyttle had impishly rendered it. Side parting, swept over and back from the front. Maintained the sheen with a pea of Brylcreem. Not too much, mind. Made it greasy. His late wife Judith – she was not dead, just never on time – had not once made even passing mention, yet he regarded it as his crowning glory, especially as most of his contemporaries had long since thinned. He perhaps kept it lengthier than a man burdened with his authority should, but his sister-in-law, Dell, had remarked at a party that it reminded her of Roxy Music. That, all too predictably, caused a scene. Judith had not heard the comment first hand (the traffic was terrible!) but was not best pleased on its report back. He had grimly taken a crew cut the following day – death by a thousand holiday queries – and relations between wife and brother's side irrevocably soured. There was nothing going on. *Of course, there was nothing going on.* In hindsight, he was sorry he had told Judith, and even sorrier that family parties where one might receive the most exhilarating compliments had come to an end. Charles regretted, too, the fall-out with brother and sister-in-law, and had since gone out on a limb to make amends. To build Bridges.

Foundering in the wake of the 'Ferry disaster', as he had solemnly labelled it, he had initially accepted that his childish excitement may have unnerved his wife. Perhaps he should have sat her down, had a word. "Let's stick together," he might even have said. But the more he recalled, the more he recanted. What had she expected? It was hardly his fault he had spent an entire married life starved of approval. They never discussed it now, but twelve months on the locks were back, and he and Judith living like train tracks.

"While we're on the subject, Miss Lyttle, could you get me the latest on our supply budget, please? Must be heading for the troposphere."

"Oh, I meant to have a word with you about that new lady we've got covering for Miss Ffortune," she replied.

"All taken care of. I introduced her in assembly this morning."

"That's what I wanted to speak to you about. Her name's Miss Cox."

"I know it is."

"But you kept referring to her as Miss Nobbs."

"I didn't." He was adamant. "Did I?"

Miss Lyttle nodded and they both smiled easily.

"Fancy her not mentioning it."

"She might have been embarrassed."

"I'm not surprised with a name like Nobbs."

"Cox!" and they both laughed again.

"Well, I lay the blame squarely at the feet of Miss Ffortune," decided Mr Bridge.

"How long's she off for?"

"Six weeks at the earliest."

"Six weeks…" he muttered. "How can you break your wrist like that? And at all places!"

"That's the thing about cocktail sausages. Very prone to roll."

"Really?" He was not sure if he was being set up.

"And those paper plates are so flimsy. If you don't happen to be looking at the floor as you're walking past…" and she mimed a misadventure with the flat of her hand.

"I suppose you're right," he conceded, "but you'd have to admit the woman's a Jonah. Remember that time she fell over the wet floor sign? And I'll tell you another thing: over my dead body am I sending her to next year's conference. She'll probably get run over before then, anyway."

"I'd better make a note in the diary."

"Excellent." *Completely trustworthy, our Miss Lyttle*, he had long since concluded. "Now," he went on, "I believe Mr Jones failed to get on his training course? Anger Management in the Classroom?"

"Full up, apparently."

"How did he take it?"

"Went absolutely ballistic. I overheard him on the phone to the teachers' centre. He was giving someone a fearful rocket. I imagine he was quite puce… under that tan." And they shared a conspiratorial pout.

"Did you get chance to ask Miss Anderson if she fancied the assertiveness training?"

"She said it was up to you."

Mr Bridge sunk to his desk and caught his to-and-fro-ing head. He washed his hands around his face then made a blowhole. Once the exasperated air had escaped all that remained was the slow whisper of thigh drawing soft beneath pencil skirt.

"What have you got next?" he said, features surfacing. "Cheer me up."

"Have you seen the gravel on the skylight?" she asked.

"I have." And he sighed again.

"No respect, some of these youngsters today. I've spoken to Sydney and asked him to get rid of it."

"Thank you, Miss Lyttle. It's a parlous state of affairs, but, unfortunately, this kind of thing comes with the territory. When you're the one making the big decisions, the alpha male, so to speak, you're bound to upset the disgruntled few. Truth is, I'll bet it's no worse than some of the comments made about me in the staffroom." And he permitted himself a dry chuckle his own absurdity.

"Well, I can say now, hand on heart," and her palm pressed her breast pushing, he could not help noticing, a crease of tanned cleavage into the vee of her blouse, "that if I was to hear any such sentiments, Mr Bridge, I'd have no hesitation in putting them straight."

"Really, Miss Lyttle?" he replied, finding himself off-puttingly straight. "It's nice to know one can count on some people around here." She could do his cock-a-doodle any day of the week.

*

She had not always been Miss Lyttle. For a time, seventeen reclusive years, all told, April had been Mrs May, who had mistaken bullying for love. On their wedding day he had called her his calendar girl, then watched her round the clock as the days and months and years leafed by. On the advent of her fortieth birthday, she bumped into an old friend at the supermarket and attracted an invitation to a girls' night out. She did not go, of course: he would not have stood for that. But the following week she bypassed the cottage pies, fish paste, corned dog, best butter, tomato bloody ketchup on everything, and the Keep Britain Tidy cans of Skol, and walked instead to the letting agents to rent their cheapest shopping money bedsit. Closing a new door behind her for the first time, and checking and re-checking its bank of locks, she realised she now possessed nothing. And had all she needed.

It took a while; she was lost in the only place she had ever known. In those first dry-mouthed days she saw him in the face of every approaching figure, heard him in the thump of every footstep, smelled him in the doorways of passing pubs. Her gaze grew the turning circle of a barn owl and her thumb locked arthritically so that she had to prise the rape alarm from its whitened grasp at bedtime. He came looking – they always do – and wept like an ulcer as soon he realised the threats would no longer work. But the police were true to their word and the burly sergeant's quiet advice was received loud and clear.

With little money of her own (the housekeeping had been handed over with great ritual every week to be weighed against receipts) she managed to negotiate a few meagre hundreds for her wedding and engagement rings, and told him they were at the bottom of the canal. Leaving nothing to chance she transferred across town to a flat she named No Forwarding

Address and, shackles removed at last, the calendar began to turn more easily. She bobbed her hair because he liked it long, wore lipstick outside the house, dressed in trousers because she could, and visited her parents and sister on just-passing whims.

But the freedom fund and paltry benefits were never going to sustain her for long so the search for employment became a full-time occupation. It was a novel experience – *no wife of his was going out to work* – and at first she took a masochistic pride in scraping a minimum-wage existence in a succession of bars and after-hours offices. And then one dreary bin-tipping evening she found, scrunched among the browning apple cores and crinkle crisp bags, a temping agency flyer. Frustration and confidence fermenting symbiotically, she applied some half-remembered keyboard skills and was thrown in at the deep end of the typing pool. The extra income that two jobs afforded secured driving lessons and she celebrated a first time pass with banger Bessie. Her new-found mobility brought a twelve-month clerical contract at insurance towers; she made new friends on the eleventh floor and, after scrubbing the cleaning job, more at evening classes where she mastered Teeline, Excel and occasional dating.

Then Mrs Pfyle took maternity leave from school, fell hopelessly in love with her first-born and could not let go. Mr Bridge advertised for a replacement; Miss Lyttle emptied her account for an interview suit and started the following week. She liked the place, the place liked her and the one-month trial was a hoopla formality. Full-time permanent appointment, improved salary, designated workstation, team of three: St John's High School Administration Assistant.

That was five years ago. She was office manager now with a room of her own.

What could she have been if she had been allowed her wings? Wasted days. She was never loved, nor cherished, just someone to have and to hold too tight. She was not even his fantasy. Never had been. All he ever wanted was a caterpillar in a matchbox. Funny thing is, even now, she was still not sure if it was bravery that drove her escape or the embarrassment of facing that classmate at the following week's checkout.

He? The husband. The *jailer*. She had not heard. She did not hate him now. It was more visceral than that. She pitied him.

Those memories had been sealed core-deep until a fortnight ago. Mr Bridge had asked her to take the minutes at a child protection meeting where the boom and bust of domestic violence rattled the walls and, as the Family Circle were returned to the right angles of their tub, the past was poured out. He listened with increasing admiration and made a mental jotting to avoid truculence in her presence. That conversation opened eyes for both. They had entered it colleagues, ended it confidants.

"Now, really. Is there any good news?" he pleaded.

"You've had your invite to the annual Littlewoods Ball."

"I have not. Should have had it weeks ago, but it never turned up. This is getting ridiculous with my personal mail going walkabouts."

"I always pass on what Sydney leaves on my desk."

"Oh, I'm not saying that, April. Not at all."

"Well, a reminder's arrived."

"How much this year?"

216

"£35 a ticket."

"That's a little steep."

"They're doing a deal this time. One pound a week for thirty-eight weeks."

"That's more like it," Mr Bridge said. "The thing is…" he began absent-mindedly, "The thing is, it's not really Mrs Bridge's thing, her scene, if you see what I mean. I mean, I don't know… I'm not sure if she would be able to get home from work on time."

Miss Lyttle watched his face eagerly. "Why don't you ask me, Charles?" And her Papermate tapped out a rising heartbeat against her lower teeth. "I'd love to go. I could buy a new gown, I have a little savings, and I'd skip Legs, Bums and Tums for once. I would be on time – early, even – and I'd make you laugh and we could dance, you could hold me and…" she wanted to say.

Now, she was softly nibbling the end of her ballpoint. He wished she would not.

At last he scooped a deep breath. "Would *you* care to accompany me, Miss Lyttle? It will soon be out in the open that Judith has asked for a divorce. It won't stay this little secret forever. The ball isn't until summer anyway so we'll both be free agents, so to speak, and you needn't feel inhibited by what other people might say. Of course, I wouldn't want you to think that you were being invited as some sort of stop gap – far from it. I mean, the more I have thought about the situation, the more I have come to understand that, well, I… I… not that it would be any of their business anyway, I mean, you have always behaved with the utmost propriety, anyone can see that…" and when the voice in his head finished he sat, mute, staring through her.

"Are you all right, Mr Bridge? You're looking tired."

"Pard... yes. Yes. I've had a lot on my mind, Miss Lyttle, that's all, as I'm sure you understand. And I was up all night wrestling with that report for the work-life balance accreditation."

"Oh yes, I saw that on my desk this morning."

"Do you think you will have time to type it up today? Make it look more presentable? I'd have done it myself, but I needed a couple of hours' sleep."

"I have rather a lot on, Mr Bridge."

"I see."

"How about I skip lunch and do it then?"

"Thank you, Miss Lyttle."

"So, Mr Bridge. The ball?"

"Oh yes. I... erm... I think I'll have a think."

"Of course."

"Right then. Was there anything else? I do believe we both deserve a coffee." He found a relieved smile and glanced at the clock on the opposite wall. Ten past nine. "The staffroom should be clear by now."

"Just one more thing, Mr Bridge. We had a call from that chap who did the staff training on recall strategies."

"Ah yes, the memory man. Very good, wasn't he? What did he want?"

"He wanted..." Miss Lyttle closed her eyes (the man said that helped), and the headteacher failed to resist the opportunity for another furtive peep at the wisps of scallopy silk beneath. "No, it's gone. Don't worry, I've written it down somewhere."

"Tell me later," he said, rising from his seat, the rush of starchy blood subsided. "Let's get that drink."

218

He reached out to the mahogany-effect hatstand bequeathed by his predecessor and collected from one of its horns the jacket of his new suit. He slid inside, hitched his tie and tugged at the cuffs of his shirt, all the while sucking at his stomach.

"Are you ready?"

There was a knock at the door.

"Come in!" he beckoned.

It was one of the office underlings. "Can I have a word, please, Mr Bridge?" She stepped from the doorway in case Miss Lyttle had to leave.

"Fire away, then... erm..." he said. "Fire away..." Her name would not come, and he did not want to risk another Miss Nobbs palaver.

"It's Hitchcock," the underling continued. "He's been beaten up in the toilets before school."

The midriff fell. "Who by? By whom? And what's he doing in at that time anyway?"

"He'd been sick outside apparently and needed to clean up. Mr Reagan found him. Arrived just too late by all accounts."

"And did he say who'd done it?"

"I believe Mr Reagan saw the culprit."

"Bring Hitchcock in, then. Let's have a word with him." The coffee with Miss Lyttle would have to wait.

"He's fled the premises, Mr Bridge."

"He's what?"

"Just ran past and burst out of the door. There was nothing we could do."

"Marvellous." And the jacket leapt back onto the Batstand. "Miss Lyttle? Will you initiate the protocols, please, and could *you*" – her name was not going to come: waste of money, that bloody memory chap – "ask Mr Reagan to find me during assembly?"

A nod and the mystery woman was gone.

"Leave it to me, Mr Bridge. I'll get in touch with home." Miss Lyttle made for the door then stopped and turned, her hand – he noticed – hanging on to the knob. "Shall I just bring a warm drink through?"

"Thank you, Miss Lyttle. That would be lovely."

The door clicked shut and Mr Bridge returned to the spruce of his Batdesk. Miss Lyttle was a conundrum all right. She despised aggression, and with good reason, he conceded, yet had bought him a punch ball; she recoiled at raised voices and yet he had heard the way she occasionally spoke to the children. *Women.* Another thing he had in common with Bryan. Slaves to love, both.

He fell into his chair and eyed the top drawer where a Wispa had been stashed last week. Caffeine was all well and good, but this situation demanded a sugar rush. Finding the compartment snagged tight, he wedged his fingers deep into the shallowed-out hold and leaned. On the first attempt his grip gave way, leaving him wafting hands into a hot blur. After briefly inspecting the groove for detached fingernails he re-set. *The Caped Crusader would not give this up…*

A second attempt prised a slice of darkness from the drawer's depths, and a third a little more. How he wished now he had not crammed all that junk in there during his tidying session, but

HOLY COW!

he was not giving in. There had to be a way…

Another cursory knock at the door and Miss Lyttle was again inside, morseing a cup and saucer. "I've been down to see Mr Reagan – he was just drying off. Says he'll be up at 10.30," she explained. "Says the other boy was the Edward lad. Norton Edward. Apparently, he's left the premises, too."

"Thank you, Miss Lyttle," he sighed, and he wearily pictured the extra hours on the desktop thumper before he invited that one's dad in.

"Not at all." She shifted to go then hesitated. "Mr Bridge?" An added afterthought.

"Yes, Miss Lyttle?"

"You do realise there's a hatstand wedged upside down in your desk?"

Chapter Nineteen

"You remind me of someone I knew. Once upon a time."

Nelson stood before him. Both eyes swollen and scarlet, though it was the left that had felt the flashbulb of Norton's knuckles. He had not gone down without a fight, but the welter of blows was beginning to take its toll when Mr Reagan bounced into the washroom. A bitter slurp of his coffee in the corridor had caused the teacher to turn tail and, through the blurry portholes, he had caught glimpse of the back of a blazer taking to the toilets at the Swap Shop. Returned to the staffroom, he popped a sweetener into his palm before releasing it *precisely* this time into the swirl of his mug. Now running late, and keen not to be further delayed by having to dispense one of his 'It says '*Smoking Kills*' for a reason' lectures, he determined to pretend he had not witnessed what he had just witnessed and trundle his unsuspecting way to class. Yet out in the corridor the poke of his conscience diverted him. Reaching the door, he paused and rapped accusatorily; it was never done to enter pupils' lavatories without a warning cry, though this was the usual precursor to a mass flushing as dog-ends were dumped. No cisternic cascade greeted him now.

Instead, ear pressed to the veneer, he found the grunt and thud of scuffle.

Although he could not see faces, Mr Reagan realised immediately that Hitchcock was involved: there was an arm trapped tight beneath the assailant's knee and only one boy in school wore a pullover like that. He boomed at the brawl and the punches grudgingly ceased. Howling frustration the aggressor leapt up, raised his blazer dockrat-fashion and barged towards the exit. Mr Reagan stepped instinctively to block the escape then retreated too slowly once he understood the boy was not stopping. The teacher's sharp intake as piping coffee spilled out across his polo shirt attracted enough of a look-see for a positive identification, and Norton was gone. Kneeling scalded to the groaning heap, Mr Reagan instructed Nelson to stay put while he repaired to the staffroom to insert a pad of tissues between stain and skin.

With only echoes for company the wounded sailor climbed upright to find his teary doppelganger in a mottled wall mirror. He pinched the end of his nose, where a bloodsnot ball had collected then watched part-fascinated, part-appalled, as the bubble fell down and popped against the distressed porcelain of the sink. Satisfied the worst had passed he gingerly released his grip, swilled his face and screwed at his skin with a paper towel. The blood had stemmed, but the tears were not yet ready to dry. What was that for? What had he done? How was it going to end? Mr Reagan would be back any minute for an explanation Nelson did not possess.

There was only one place he wanted to be. And only one person who could help him now.

*

"His face used to flush like that. When the tears came."

"Who was it?" asked Nelson, thrilled that all – whatever 'all' had been – appeared forgiven from yesterday morning.

"It was my boy."

"You had a son?" He commandeered a sleeve to soak a pink droplet from his nose.

"I did. For a while." And there was a weight in the words. "Too short a while."

"What happened to him?"

"He was taken from me at a much younger age than you are now. So, you see, we both understand loss."

"Taken?"

"There was a woman," the voice continued, "older, who came to my uncle's shop. Her husband was a cruel man and thus we shared a bond of unhappiness. We met once by chance on a summer's evening, and after that we chanced again. There was nowhere to run, but we escaped in each other's company among the tall grasses, or her home if the brute was at drink in town. Months later her round belly told the tale of our assignations, yet she convinced her husband of the child's provenance. What was I to do? Heap disgrace upon her? How could I, penniless and pitiful, do justice by her and our child? She continued to visit the shop and, though outwardly incurious for all our sakes, I marvelled at my boy with pained pride.

"Then one morning she failed to arrive for her usual order and I overheard a neighbour relate that the boy, still not three years, had developed a raging fever. I was convulsed with anxiety but had to go about my business as if the world owed me not a care."

"Was that the day he died?"

"The following night. When the news spilled from the queue my legs buckled and I dropped all I was carrying, for which I received a beating when the doors were closed. I was eighteen by then and could have taken my uncle's air if I so desired, yet I begged for more. I demanded pain. But even those spiteful blows could not overcome the numbness."

"Did you see the woman again?"

"She left and I did not seek her out. When the boy died my instinct was to blame. First her for not preventing the death, then myself for having neither the fortitude nor the funds to do right by both. Never again, I swore."

Nelson pocketed his hands and studied the space below the frame.

"But, please, let that be enough of my own woes. You have come again and I see the wars have found you."

"Sort of. A one-man war."

"And who is to defend you from this nemesis?"

"That's why I'm here."

"A son needs his father." The words grew softer now. "I have seen him."

"Where?" Nelson leapt to the wall.

"His hair rolls in waves, like yours, but he wears his parted, to the right. And his eyes burn azure. His jaw is strong, his nose straight and narrow, and creases line the side of his face when he laughs, though for the moment he has little to cheer him. Most of all, he is a powerful man, a fine specimen. A father who could protect a son."

"Is there anything else?"

"In what regard, my young friend?"

"His arm? The right?"

The voice closed its eyes, and the drone of that fluorescent tube surged into the void.

"Nothing of the extraordinary," came the reply. "Intact, if that is your point."

Nelson sank.

"Wait, I see it now. A mark on the forearm. A tattoo. '*England Forever*', does it read?" *Dad's Sean Connery homage.*

"It's him! Where did you see him, please? Is he all right? Can you talk to him? Can *I* talk to him?"

"What if I could reunite you?"

"Yes!"

"We may yet have time."

"What do you mean?"

"What is today's date?"

"Thursday 30th October. 2003." The morning radio had told him enough times.

"So soon," said the voice, at last.

"What do you mean?"

"Too soon," it resumed. "It seems my final pleasure is that I made the acquaintance of such a brave and noble ally. You have a brilliance, young Osiris, an artistry that courses through you. You could ride the unicorn, tame the sphinx. You could be King of Phrygia, Ozymandias—"

"What are you talking about, Sheldan?"

"We are all prisoners of the clock. The difference between we two, my friend, is that I know the exact hour my blood runs to dust."

"You're going to die?"

"A grim anniversary falls."

"But what about my da… no, that can't be right! You said I could help you."

"And you alone could. But by midnight tomorrow my place among the shadows is sealed."

Chapter Twenty

"So, you really don't have a telly!"

Roland stared open-mouthed at the void filling the corner of the room. Everything about the layout was set up for a magic box: the leather-look sofa and accompanying armchairs angled in its direction; the pouffe within easy reach of restawhile feet; and, across an alcove, the underused wall shelf that could have accommodated maybe three-dozen video cases. Even Nelson's school photograph, which Mum went without two balls of wool and five lunches to buy, gazed optimistically sidelong from the fireplace.

The inquisitor shuffled over, removed his hand from crinkled pocket and anchored it to his knee for support. He stared hard at the aerial socket that he half expected to have healed over. "Nope," he confirmed, "there's definitely no telly."

From the close-up of his crouch Roland noted a change in the fade of the anaglypta where some long-forgotten object had checked the sun, and he could still make out telltale ridges in the carpet, though these were being gradually eroded like dinosaur tracks as the surrounding nylon yielded underfoot.

"I reckon you had one," he concluded, rising in segments, "but it's not there now."

"You don't say," said Pippa, increasingly embarrassed by the whole carry-on.

"That's what I told you," said Nelson

"I know what you *said*, but it was too unbelievable to believe."

"I thought I heard voices!" The malarkey was brought to a hasty conclusion with the arrival of Nelson's mum at the lounge door. Ruddy-flushed and hair wild as wire, she padded excitedly in. "I was upstairs, Hoovering," she thrilled, puffing upwards at the dew on her brow. "Well, this is a very pleasant surprise!"

Roland and Pippa froze dumbstruck as the slender, luminous-legginged figure – a dizzying jumble of cast-offs and cast-ons – skipped towards them. On top, she was wearing one of her own creations, possibly a shawl, which was hung together tight-woven as a cargo net. Underneath, her blushes were spared by a sky-blue T-shirt that had caught dark beads of sweat in a sprinkle down her chest. In the moment it took her to scoop at the nape of her neck then let the frizz fall refreshingly back she was holding out a hand, swiped dry against her thigh.

"Hello, you two! I'm Mrs... I'm Nelson's mum. Don't tell me, you must be Pippa. And no doubt you are Roland." Roland was unsure whether the 'no doubt' was a good thing or bad. "Nelson has told me so much about you both. It's a pleasure to meet you at last. Won't you have a seat?"

Mum made a pleased face as she gestured towards the settee, though Nelson considered the naming of his friends hardly the toughest of guessing games. He was also concerned about the peculiar intonation she appeared to have adopted. He need not have worried. As Roland was about to find the welcome of the leather-look she suddenly yelped, "Not there!" and scrabbled behind his cushion to retrieve a paper bag spiked with knitting needles and the embryonic knot of a Christmas pullover. "I'm sorry about that," she said, the tips of her plastic double-ohs, and affectation of plumminess, exposed. "Tools of the trade. I do a lot of knitting."

Roland smiled tactfully. And privately wondered why she was owning up.

The paraphernalia was pouffed and, for the first time since entering the room, Nelson's mum looked properly at her son. A mother's gaze. He was sitting where he usually sat, lounging soft in the armchair, but something was different. A nostril betrayed a ring of red crust.

"What's happened to you, Nelse? Have you had a nosebleed?" She moved towards him. "And your eye! Has someone hit you?"

"No-o," he replied with a nonchalance he hoped did not suggest over-rehearsal. "A football caught me smack on the face in the playground."

"But you don't like football." There was doubt in her voice.

"I wasn't playing, Mum. I was walking past and bang!" And he pushed his hand at his cheekbone, stopping just short of a direct hit between nose and eye. "That's all."

She barefooted over for a closer inspection. It looked sore. The skin was grazed: an Ishihara scrape of red and blue dots that promised a black eye come morning. She wanted to give him a kiss, tell him she loved him and reassure him it would be all right. Instead, she ruffled his hair then turned to their guests as Nelson rested back, relieved.

"Did you make that yourself, your... smock?" asked Pippa. "I do like it."

"Why, thank you, Pippa. I did."

"Reminds me of a dreamcatcher."

"Really?"

"Oh yes. It's very individualistic. I like that."

"How lovely," Mum replied, and she (and Nelson, too) warmed against the countering cool. "Well, this *is* very nice," she announced as smiles levelled out. "I didn't know we were having company. Had an after-school club?"

"No, Mum."

"It better not be detention!" she growled, half-joking.

"We've just been up to the mooseum," Roland joined in.

"Have you now? Well, I'm very impressed," said Mum. "I must say Nelson seems to be taking quite an interest in that place."

"Nelson said it would be all right if we called here on the way home. I hope that's okay with you, Mrs Hitchcock?" said Pippa.

"Couldn't be more delighted. Do you live nearby?"

"Not really," Pippa replied. "I live near school. I don't often come to this side of town."

"What about you, Roland?"

Roland was back staring into the gap, watching the television set that was not there.

"Roland?"

"Pardon? Oh, sorry... live nearby? Me? No. Live miles away, me. My mum won't be home till late so I thought I'd come here rather than put up with my sister."

"And have you walked all the way from the museum?"

"We have," said Nelson. "Fancied a stroll."

In truth, he would have preferred the privacy of one of his friends' houses when they were emptied onto the street at closing time, but he had already exhausted this week's bus fund on jaunts across town and his was the only place remotely within walking distance. And he was desperate for the three of them to stick together: there were things he had to say he did not want the pavements to hear.

"You must be peckish," suggested Mum. "How about I put the kettle on and bring you some biscuits?"

Mum wished they could have stopped for tea, but the week ahead had already been planned and, even if she ate nothing herself, two veggie burgers would not go into three. "Let me take your jackets." And, laden, she left the room revising the sugars order.

At the flush of the tap, Nelson edged to the brink of his seat. "Thanks for coming with me today," he said.

"You were upset. What are friends for?" said Pippa.

"Twice in one day. Your mum's right, you might as well move into that mooseum."

"I know, but still, I'm really grateful that you both came back with me."

"I didn't know what to think when I found you hanging around after school. I was concerned."

"Well, I would have come *during* school if you'd wanted," Roland offered. "I've always got a ready note about my gran dying."

"I might need one of those tomorrow," said Nelson. "They'll wonder where I'd got to this morning."

"I wouldn't bother going in, me," Roland added. "They're not going to miss you on a Friday."

"I can't do that. There are things I need."

After waiting in vain for Nelson to detail what 'things', Roland finally edged around to articulating what both he and Pippa had been thinking.

"Look, Nelson. I'm not being harsh, but… he didn't say much, did he?"

The scepticism came as no surprise. All three had skirted embarrassed around the subject on the walk home. Pippa was not sure what to make of any of it, while Roland had been more interested in the chronology and choreography of the ding-dong in the toilet. But now there were things that needed saying and plans that had to be made.

"I know he didn't talk, or answer your questions about the Victorians, Pippa, but not everyone can hear him anyway. Otherwise, there would have been a roomful of people searching around the museum during our trip. You have to be…" and he barely checked the word 'special' escaping. "You have to be *lucky*, I suppose."

"So, was he saying things to you back there and we simply couldn't hear?" asked Pippa.

"No, he didn't say anything then."

"The old 'treat 'em mean' trick," said Roland.

"No. He always speaks when it's just me and him."

But Nelson had already buried his visit the morning before when he had talked and talked about his father and Sheldan had said nothing. No acknowledgement of his presence. Not a word. *Not a breath*. He had brooded over any offence he may have caused but could find none and had returned to school that lunchtime feeling bereft and rejected, and resolved to do whatever it took to repair their friendship.

"Listen, Nelson, let's just think rationally about what you are saying: you can converse with a man miraculously trapped in an old painting, and he can tell you – though he has neglected yet to do so – where your father, vanished while working for the government, is being held?"

"I think he was annoyed at me for bringing you along. He's told me often enough."

"Told you what?"

Nelson fired eyes at the doorway and dropped his voice lower still. "Told me that all this was our secret. Just him and me. But I had to tell someone, I couldn't keep it in any longer."

"He told you that?"

"There's something else, too."

"Go on," she said.

"He's dying."

Pippa abandoned all pretence as her expression crashed.

"Look, I'm not making this up, you know."

"How can he know where your dad is?" asked Roland. "And how can he be dying when he's not even alive?"

"So how can two snowflakes never, ever be the same?"

"What's that supposed to mean?"

"Look, it doesn't matter. I don't care what it all looks like, how it all *seems*. All I'm interested in is how it *is*. And he's alive for me. For now—"

"There's something else, isn't there?" said Pippa.

Nelson scouted the door a second time. "There *is* another thing," he confessed. "And if I tell you, you must swear to tell no one."

"Okaay," said Pippa.

"It's just that I've made a promise to save him. And the more I think about it the more I don't think I'll be able to do it on my own. That's why I came back to school for you."

"Go on." Roland was intrigued.

"Look," said Nelson, and he let out a cough that he caught in a grab at his lips, "there's something *slightly* illegal I have to do."

*

In the kitchen Mum emptied the kettle's seething innards into the teapot, clamped on the lid and swaddled the brew in a hopeless home-knit cosy. While the potion matured she rifled, with wanton disregard for the calendar insisting 'Thursday', the *weekend* biscuit stash: a handful of own-brand custard creams perilously close to best before and a single homemade flapjack that might be halved into matching fingers. She selected a plate, spun the china's murk then began the arduous process of spooning sugar into Roland's mug.

*

The lounge was home to mute disbelief when Nelson's mum reappeared, cups in hand. "Tea up!" she trilled as the delivery touched safely down. Speedy seconds later she was back again, this time accompanying the biscuit plate. The goodies had been arranged in a ring around the rim, six creams padded out by alternate trios of morning coffees. Roland avoided the flapjack fingers crossed like HARMFUL in the centre and circled the outer loop. A final review to check there were no partially obscured bourbons and he plumped for a custard and the three closest coffees, the stash shuffled and stacked croupier slick.

"Well, you three sounded like you were having a good old chat."

"What do you mean?" asked Nelson.

"What do you mean, what do I mean? Are you all right? I think that ball in the face might have rattled your brain."

No one spoke.

"Discussing anything interesting?" Mum continued.

Nelson hoped this was not a double bluff. "Not really, just a bit of school gossip."

And he waited. If Mum was going to announce that she had heard it all, every word of the scheme that had stunned the friends she now found dumbfound, this was the time.

"Here, let me pass you your teas." Coasters were positioned at the foot of each chair then the operation repeated with warming mugs lifted from the coffee table. Nelson reached for a custard cream, an opportunity too good to miss on a weeknight.

"More biscuits?"

Pippa shook her head, smiling. "No, thank you, Mrs Hitchcock."

"Mrs Hit... oh, please, call me Harry."

"Okay, thanks, Harry," she said without blinking.

"Thanks, Carrie," repeated Roland.

"It's *Harry*, Roland. *Harry* with a 'Huh'."

"Oh! Sorry! I wasn't being... sometimes I have a bit of glue ear." And he helpfully pointed to the side of his head. He briefly considered repeating his 'Thanks...' but decided against on the grounds that could not bring himself to call Nelson's mum a boy's name.

Harry selected a morning coffee missing a corner and was now safely ensconced in the armchair nearest the window, looking more at home by the minute. The cleaning, it seemed, could wait. Nelson was quietly delighted that she had not so far embarrassed him and took further comfort in the knowledge that any evidence of him wearing a dress was not within a three-mile radius.

"So, Pippa, Nelson tells me you're gifted and talented?"

What did she say that for? thought Nelson.

What did he say that for? thought Pippa.

"It sounds very impressive."

"Not really, Harry, it's only for English, maths and science. I get to do a bit of extra work at lunch. Investigations stuff, really, and it's better than being on the playground." She could have added 'where there's no one to talk to' or 'where Deadly NightJade lurks', but she sipped at tea instead.

"Investigations?"

"The maths is mostly theoretical, but I'm building some loudspeakers in science at the moment. In English we're studying Dylan Thomas for rhythm and cadence, though my real love is wordplay: designing crosswords, anagrams, inventing neologisms and such like."

The sweat of the walk returned to Roland as he began to wonder just what Mrs Harry had in store for him. What had Nelson been playing at, speaking to a parent about his friends? He need not have worried. Pippa watched her wrist. "Is that the time!" she announced. "I've got drama class at seven. I'm really sorry, I've got to go."

"Oh, that's a shame. How will you get home?" Harry asked. "We've no car, I'm afraid."

"I'm sure Dad'll pick me up. Do you mind if I give him a call?"

There was a moment's concern as Mum faced the prospect of admitting they did not possess a usable phone, as well. It would probably be best to be candid and confess the landline had been cut by the telecoms privateers. Or she could claim it was broken.

She need not have worried. Pippa delved into her blazer to retrieve a mobile that flipped open to a fanfare. "Would you like a lift, Roland?"

"Please." He nodded eagerly as the song of connection played.

"Hi, Dad…"

Everyone stilled for the duration of the call, playing out the pretence of not listening. At the handset's close the room eased back to life.

"Doesn't your dad mind coming for you?" asked Nelson.

"No, he's really good at stuff like that. Says he'd much rather a little inconvenience so he knows I'm all right."

"That's a nice phone," said Harry.

"I got it for my birthday. Do you have one?"

"Sort of. We use it as a house phone. It's only pay as you go so it probably can't do all the fancy things I imagine yours can. The battery's dead at the moment." Mum was always lax about recharging when its credit was out.

"I've got a new ringtone on mine," said Roland. "*Monty Python* theme. I love them, me. Hey, did you put my number in, Pippa?"

"I think I lost the paper."

"Lost it?" and he exhaled wearily. "You wouldn't have lost it if I'd written it on a ten spot. Go on then, I'll give it you again."

Drama class began early as Pippa beamed a 'Thanks!' then played the keypad under Roland's scrutiny. "Would you mind, Harry, if I took your number, too, in case I needed to speak to Nelson about school, or something?"

"Of course, though I can never remember it. Give me a second, I'll check the box."

More minutes than expected passed before Mum returned; she had been waylaid removing a parade of Scoobys 'drying' on a disconsolate radiator (two more sleeps to switch on!) just in case Pippa's dad accepted convention's invitation to step inside. As she handed over a tear of notepad and a pair of coats, there came a polite, melodic knock.

"That'll be Dad," said Pippa, and she was gracefully into her duffel, lifting anthracite hair into the hopper of the hood. "Are you ready, Roland?"

Harry had already made her way to the frosted glass of the front door, primping hair and pulling at her T-shirt along the length of the hallway.

"It's your father, Pippa," she called.

Crocodiling silently past the disrobed heater the trio found her post-handshake, filling the inner airlock while Pippa's dad bounced back pleasantries from the porch, the offer of entrance declined on the grounds of dirty soles and an uneaten dinner.

"Hi, Dad."

"Hello, love. Had a good time?"

"Yes, thanks."

Pippa introduced her friends in turn and confirmed that Roland could be dropped off.

"No problem, love, you know that. Are we all ready, then?"

Nods all around so Mr Hill reiterated his appreciation and retreated through the outer hatch.

"It has been really nice to meet you," said Pippa as she made her way out to the dark.

"Yes, thanks, Mrs... Thanks!" added Roland.

The group made its way down the four-flagged path, past the snarling dandelions to the undulation of the wall running the length of the terrace. Leaving Mum in the forty-watt porch, Nelson tagged along as his friends ducked into the royal-blue A4.

"Seatbelts on." The cry from the wheel.

The silky slice of the engine, waking blink of headlights and then an electric window whirred at the rear.

Roland leaned out from the back seat while Pippa buckled up. "I'll have a think about what you said before. Y'know..."

"Thanks," said Nelson, now alongside on the icy pavement.

Pippa stared straight ahead. "I won't," she said. And there was a chill in her breath.

Chapter Twenty-One

The kitchen snapped and crackled as Heath's happy spoon broke the surface of his Coco Pops. Norton was sitting uniformly across the oak table having the same – not too many, mind, the next weekly shop was not till Tuesday. And Heather was at the working tops in baggies and kitten heels, stripping a banana to accompany her cereal while waiting for the DeLonghi to whistle.

The Cottage was residence to a freak hat-trick of good moods.

Freshly perked from admiring a downy pair of ski-jump breasts – his very favourite – on Page Three, Heath had this morning picked up two cracking tales vying for the coming week's splash. There had been a tip-off from his contact at Accident and Emergency about a teacher from St John's breaking her wrist after slithering on a cocktail sausage at – *'wait for it, Mr Edward, Sir'* – a health and safety conference, plus routine police calls reported that Welephant had been involved in a fight with a drunk at a bonfire safety demonstration. *The Respecter*'s chief reporter had already been dispatched to school for a dig-around – name, address, head's comment, etc. – and a message left for Derek at the fire station. The picture would be the clincher. In the teacher's case one at either end of the career spectrum would work best: young stunna or osteo-elderly, preferably sporting a sling and a wince, and perhaps holding a cocktail sausage on a stick with their good hand. A genuine photograph was not so crucial for Welephant. Of course, an image of the actual fireman (it would be fire*fighter* over his twitching corpse), red pachyderm head slung pugnaciously under his arm, would be ideal. But if push came to punch he could always use a stock picture; no one was going to know it was not *the* Welephant. He could even Photoshop a shiner for comedic effect.

Heath was already running headlines across imaginary front pages:

YOU SILLY SAUSAGE!	PUNCH TRUNK!	JUMBO THUMPS DUMBO!	BANGER AND SMASH!	MEET WELE THUMP!

At least two decks, block caps, seventy-two point, maybe even a WOB, and dog's dick obligatory.

At any rate, he planned to sell both stories to the tabloids, adding a little exclusivity premium on top for each. There may be up to a grand in it, all told. And if it all went tits up, they were worth a couple of Sun Spots at the very least. It was days like this that made him think he might miss it all.

But most of all – most of all – happy Heath was another morning closer to the gold rushing his way.

Heather's cheerfulness on this occasion was not founded on material advantage, but on Little Heath's impending return for the weekend. It would be nice to catch up with their eldest. Any news on his *Big Brother* application? Had he thought about the extras for the short he was planning (she was prepared to travel for a breakthrough part)? Was there a girlfriend yet? How was the weather up there in the tundra? Was that tutor still picking on him?

His train was arriving tomorrow and she had selflessly agreed to collect him from the station at two, which allowed a couple of clear hours for a spot of lunch and boutiquery.

Any pangs of trepidation that Norton had fomented at his sibling's imminent reappearance were easily offset by the thought of the day's – and night's – pleasure to come. He would face the weekend from two o'clock tomorrow. Until then, and he looked up across the table to check, it was just the two of them. He was going to make him proud.

He knew what would happen if he did not.

And he was pleased, too, that Little Heath knew nothing of it all. *That wanksock would have done it for free.*

Heather was hacking raggedly at the fruit with her spoon. The last of the knives was in the dishwasher and, she reasoned, you do not get a dog and scrub your own pots. She was not banana's biggest fan, but the odds and clods dumped onto her Frosties were a minor sacrifice for a sugar-free breakfast.

The smoking kettle had calmed and, quietly mapping her day ahead, she fizzed hot water onto a sand of flavour-free decaf. It was not as if there was no alternative; just by the sink the new Gaggia was hiding shamefaced under dust. Quite the thing for the upwardly mobile homemaker, especially when impressionable friends visited, she had told Heath in not as many words. Yet on arrival it had all looked so disconcerting, with its flight deck of dials and handles and rounds and grounds, that no one had bothered to tackle the instructions. On reflection – she informed her husband when he offered a legitimate enquiry in light of his outlay – she was worried about the effect of all those espressos on his precarious blood pressure. And then, unspoken, was the faffery of it all. It was only a bloody cuppa after all. She simply did not have the time.

Today, too, was looking like a busy one. There would be the breakfast dishes to load *milk*, the washing machine to empty *sweetener for me*, catch a few minutes of *This Morning* and elevenses *the boys' sugar*, call Augusta for an update on her divorce *stir*, Marks' salad for lunch *grab a couple of pittas from the freezer*, toning tables at two *coasters*, back for a quick shower *coffees to the table*, and on top of all that…

"What do you want me to make for your tea, Norton love?"

Norton paused between spoonfuls and scribblings. "Don't need any. I'm going to McDonald's with some friends then straight back to school for the Halloween Disco."

Halloween! She had forgotten about that. *The day just gets busier!*

"A disco. That's nice," she said, pairing off Heath's mug with a mat, "Are these friends boys or girls?"

"Boys."

"Do they have names?"

"Everyone has a name."

Heather was not going to give Norton the satisfaction of pique, and instead burned her glare into the back of his head.

"You'll have to invite them here some time."

"Mm."

"Have you got a costume sorted?"

"Someone's got a spare *Scream* mask that fills with blood if you squeeze a squirter in your hand."

"Sounds lovely. Have you got your ticket, then?"

"Obviously."

"And how are you getting home?"

"His dad said he'll give me a lift. God! It's like a friggin' police interrogation!"

"That'll do, Norton," Heath interjected. "Don't speak to your mother like that." That was a privilege reserved for him.

"Why, thank you, Heath. And what about you?"

"Me?"

"What do you fancy for tea?"

"Nothing. I've got a council meeting at six."

"On a Friday?"

"I don't set the soddin' meetings, I just report on them."

"Can't you send someone else?"

"There are a couple of people on Planning I need to speak to about the conversion," a finger pointed loftily, "and I think a face-to-face might be best."

"Oh. And will the councillors be discussing the museum?"

"It's on the list."

"Very interesting." One of the *few* perks of marriage to the editor of the local newspaper was the chance to circulate reliable gossip days before anyone else. "You'll have to let me know."

"There's a lot to get through tonight," now finger and thumb held an imaginary agenda between an inch of a gap, "and I'll probably nip for a pint afterwards so there's no need to wait up."

Council meeting on a Friday? Not coming home for tea? No need to wait up? Returning to the marble to retrieve her Frosties, an insidious scenario wormed its way into Heather's head. *He's planning a bloody kebab!*

"What have you got on, today?" Feigned interest.

"Quite busy, actually, Heath," she said, joining them at the table, "I'll hardly be drawing breath. Now you two are not coming home I'll at least have time to nip into town get some chocolates for trick or treaters."

"Chocolates for trick or treaters? Bloody American crap! They'd get a treat boot up the arse if I answered the door. And don't be bloody well scoffing those chocolates yourself!"

Heather wondered briefly about initiating a discussion on the nutritional merits of a couple of funsize Milky Ways versus a Dynamite Donner, but decided not. Instead, she daintily scooped her breakfast while beginning her brain gym, which consisted today of mentally totting the limits on tomorrow's credit cards.

The table had found a near silence, disturbed only by the occasional clink of spoon, the waft and sigh of newsprint, and the rolling scratch of Norton's ballpoint. She liked it like this, Heather. Family time. Mum, Dad, offspring. Like a television advert for a microwave feast, or funeral cover, or something. All that was missing was Little Heath. Perhaps when he was a film director he could make a commercial and they would all be in it. She would suggest that, tomorrow.

"Could you do us a favour, love?"

Love? He *was* planning a bloody kebab! Even Norton raised his head.

"Would you just nip to the study while I'm working on these headers and get my contacts book? I think I'll give Dick at the council a call, see if they can give us an ID with this teacher. There might be a bit of extra mileage if we can wheedle some puns from her name."

"Sure. Won't be a sec." Heather pushed back her chair, grating its legs at the stone floor.

"For Christ's sake!" snarled Heath, and he swiped a fisty arm in her direction.

She jerked backwards, jellying joggers and barely clinging to her kittens. "What?"

"That *bastard* fly again," he muttered, unconcerned at the near miss he had just inflicted.

"Where?"

"There! That big brazen bugger," and he outed a prune of an individual buzzing into the sanctuary of the dried flowers. "Been following me all week. I'll flatten the fucker yet!"

Heather was gone, and Heath knew she would be a while: his contacts book was not there. The kitchen to themselves, father and son mirrored each other across the table. Heath pushed aside his empty bowl and the notepad riddled with its amalgam of short and longhand. Norton, too, rested his pen and began to finger the outsized knot of his school tie.

"You ready? For today?"

"Yes, Dad."

Heath stared out at his son.

"What, Dad?"

"You know, I envy you."

Norton shifted in his seat.

"You lot don't know how lucky you are. Things I do for you, the sacrifices."

"I know, Dad." Norton knew what he was expected to say.

"There were days when I detested *my* father, and days when I would have done anything – anything – for that split-second nod of recognition, that affirmation he knew I existed. The point is… it made me strong. And you'll thank me one day. There's no patron saint of gift wrap."

Norton sat back. Sure and unsure. *Patron saint of gift wrap?* Still, this was going to be a grand day. And there was the money, too. A straight ton simply for enjoying himself.

"Do you still want me to take those… relics, Dad, the… y'know?"

"Better had. I'm in and out of the office and I don't want to leave them in the car. Bastard town centre's a den of thieves. It would be just my luck. Have you got everything? Both halves and the book?"

"Yes, I checked—"

"Good. Don't let them out of your sight. Or else."

Slow, slatey footsteps announced Heather's predictably empty-handed return from the study.

"I couldn't find it," she apologised, hugging the worktops.

"Couldn't find it? Bloody hell, if you want something doing, eh? I'll get it myself in a bit."

"Look at the time, Norton," Heather trumpeted as the big hand reached half past. "You'll be late if you don't get a wriggle on."

"I'm going, I'm going. Keep your hair on." Norton pulled his blazer from the back of his chair and confirmed the loose cigarettes smuggled to the bottom of the lining. Once within, he popped the collar to his shaven nape and checked his shirt was hanging out. The writing pad he had been working on over breakfast was retrieved – the quota of jokes he knew would not be enough to save him from a brotherly bruising over the weekend – and he was ready.

"You got plenty of charge on your phone?"

"Yes."

"Good." And fleetingly (though it may have been indigestion), Heath seemed to tip his head in his son's direction.

"I'll keep in touch, Dad. Don't worry."

The schoolboy heaved the straps of his Timberland at his feet and marched to the Rockports at the door. Heather began to corral the breakfast crockery for the dishwasher and Heath settled down to knock off a Jeremiah editorial on the perils of health and safety gone mad.

And all the while, from a watchful crack in the beam, the fly rubbed a thousand eyes.

Soundless, the door clapped closed and Norton leaned out into the day, rucksack hoisted slow, and fast, against his back: for, today, it was heavier than usual.

Much, much heavier.

Chapter Twenty-Two

"Has that woman from *The Respecter* gone yet?"

"Just, but she's at the school entrance now asking parents and pupils what they know."

"Can't we move her on?"

"Not as long as she's stood off the premises."

"She's persistent, I'll give her that." Mr Bridge got up from his castored chair (if he had been alone in the office, he would have propelled himself over with rounded heels to save the bother of walking) and peered through the misty grime at the tittlers and tattlers gathering by the gates.

"She said she was in for a fearful rollicking if she didn't get Miss Ffortune's name and address."

"So, what did we tell her?"

"Nothing. I just gave her Dick's number at the press office."

"Good work, Miss Lyttle. We can't be seen to be giving out employees' personal details to all and sundry. Did you mention data protection? Always a good standby."

"I did. She said to expect a call from her editor sometime this morning. He wouldn't be pleased, apparently."

"That's fine. I'll be more than happy to explain school's position to these people. I wonder who they think they are, demanding this and that when we've got a school to run."

"You are aware that the editor is Mr Edward, Norton's father?"

"The brawl-with-Hitchcock Norton?" Thank heavens the film of filth clinging to the glass prevented his reflection finding Miss Lyttle. "Oh right. No. Well. Perhaps I'll be able to kill two birds with one stone when the call arrives." And, watching at the window, he made a mental note to be too busy to answer the phone all day. He did not need that on a Friday.

"That reminds me," Miss Lyttle continued, "we've only got a mobile contact for Mrs Hitchcock and her phone was switched off every time I called. When Nelson arrives today I'll give him a message for his mum to get in touch."

"That's *if* he turns up. I'd say there's more going on here than meets the eye. We need to nip it in the bud."

"I agree, Mr Bridge. And that being the case, I have taken the liberty of posting a letter to the home address. It should arrive today."

"Good work, Miss Lyttle. Efficient as ever." His back still facing her, he wet a hidden finger in the condensation puddled on the windowsill and then drew the digit corner to corner across the dirt-thickened pane. Next, he added the opposite diagonal to complete the kiss. Had he been alone he would have added a child's loveheart, arrowed and initialled CB + AL.

Rubbing his handiwork clean, Mr Bridge returned to his day. "Is there anything else, Miss Lyttle, before the meeting?"

"Not much," she replied. "There's been a stack of *Recycle News* hanging around the staffroom for a week. What do you want me to do with them?"

"Stick them with the wood for the next week's bonfire," he said, drying wet tips around the folds of his handkerchief.

"Will do."

"Oh, I forgot to ask yesterday when we were discussing training at the briefing: did you give Mr Rowse those details for the self-motivation course?"

"I did, seemed very interested."

"Good." He posted the hankie into his pocket. "Has he booked on?"

"Not yet."

A knock at the door. A heavy knock. A knock menace-laced.

"I wonder if that's *him*. Shall I check?"

"May as well, though I'm not looking forward to this, I can tell you."

Miss Lyttle shimmied across the room (she hoped he would be watching from the window), twisted the knob and eyed the slot. "He's here," she said.

Her speed of turn caught Mr Bridge by surprise and his eyes darted, too late, from backside to clock. "Show him in please, then flick the Do Not Disturb across."

"I'll stay if you like," she offered. "For support."

"No, thank you, Miss Lyttle," he said, drawing his jacket from the hatstand. "This needs to be sorted mano a mano." He paused, then added: "I'll tell you what, though, give it fifteen minutes then ring me on the Batphone," and he pointed to the direct line on his desk reserved for calls of vital

252

importance – Ofsted, Legal Department, Chair of Governors, School Advisors, Judith… April, "and tell me I've got to drop everything."

Do not think for a moment she had not…

The door was eased and her head slid momentarily out of sight. "If you'd like to follow me," the timbre of her voice deadened by timber, "Mr Bridge is ready to see you now."

Miss Lyttle led the way. Collecting her clipboard from the desk, she offered a smile of encouragement unseen by the visitor and then made back for the door. They crossed as he entered and she exited, and he could not resist glancing back while her grey trouser suit walked tight-fitting, yet unshimmied, by. As she shrunk around the door he looked ahead to the head and made an 'Oooh!' with his lips.

"Come in," said Mr Bridge, finding cuffs up his sleeves then, with a wary sweep, designating a chair. "Have a seat, Sydney."

*

Another knock at the door.

"Come in!"

"I'm really sorry to interrupt. I *have* moved the Do Not Disturb, but I was hoping you hadn't started yet and if I don't tell you now, I'm concerned I may forget. I've just spotted the reminder on my clipboard."

"That's fine, Miss Lyttle."

"Remember yesterday, when I said the memory man had called?"

"Oh yes…"

"Apparently he's mislaid his diary."

"And?"

"He wondered if he'd left it in the staffroom."

Mr Bridge ruckled his brow.

"I'm terribly sorry to interrupt," she repeated, and she was gone.

Sydney had slouched askance in his chair, legs crossed and an oily forearm seesawing insouciantly at the top of the backrest. He was split-shifted – contracted 6.00am until 10.00am then returning two till sixish to repair the aftermath of the school day – and Mr Bridge had purposely summoned the meeting during working hours. He had also asked Miss Lyttle to photocopy the relevant entry in the school diary: more evidence for the work-life balance scrutineers. The caretaker was dressed in his St John's uniform. Pea-green polo shirt hanging loose, easy-care trousers – dark blue polyester bobble magnets with sewn-in crease and anti-vandal smears – and paint-freckled work boots. He had thought about making an effort, shirt and tie and whatnot, but that all seemed too much of an effort.

"It's tidy in here."

Surprised? I've done it myself. It should be your *job.*

"Thank you, Sydney. Just the windows to do now. Thought it was about time the place had a makeover, a spring clean."

"It's Halloween."

"Indeed it is. *Late* spring, shall we say?" and Mr Bridge squeezed his features into a smile. Sydney made a show of contemplating his watch. If they did not get a move on he would be here in his own time. And don't think those scrutineers would not get to hear of it.

"Now, *Sydney*…"

Referring to the other person by name is an effective way of opening up a rapport and circumventing any thoughts of potential confrontation. What came next? Oh yes.

"Now, *Syd*ney, I don't want to be having this conversation *personally*, but *professionally* I feel I must." The training consultant further recommended adopting a wind-like expression of pained concern at this point (cue laughter among the assembled heads).

Charles paused and Sydney waited.

"The thing is… The thing *is*, Sydney, I have been in receipt of a telephone call from a neighbour. Not a neighbour at home, you understand, a neighbour of the school. Now, it is not important for you to know the identity of that neighbour, but this person felt a duty to inform me that they had seen someone on the school roof the night before. Near the skylight in the Year Nine block, they estimated."

Sydney waited.

"The very same skylight where an insulting, not to say obscene, message regarding my own person was discovered the very next morning."

Sydney *waited*.

"Their first thought was to contact the police – and as we speak I am awaiting a follow-up call from our community officer – but then, Sydney, they realised the person, the one on the roof, Sydney, that *crepuscular* silhouette… well, they thought – nay *knew*, Sydeney – that that person was you, *Sydney*."

The wait was over.

Mr Bridge braced himself. This was it. This was the moment when Sydney leapt up, fist-fought the desk, knocked the punch ball into the middle of next week, kick-tipped a chair or two and generally reversed the much-admired tidy-up.

Instead, narrow-eyed, he murmured, "Crepuscular silhouette? Where do you get off using words like that?"

"So, it's true, Sydney."

"That and more." He shifted in his seat, legs now splayed, searching for the right position. This could take a while. Then, off he set. 'Coughing', was how the constabulary would have referred to it. 'Full and frank', *The Respecter* may have permitted. He owned to everything – the skylight, the BA*D* MA*D* additions to the school sign, the Hitler moustache, the misplaced ball invitations, the chaotic fire alarms during Charles's assemblies, the five litres of PVA glue sloshed onto his windscreen during the governors' AGM, the head's missing training shoes that reappeared dangling out of reach from the dining-hall lights, and plenty, a whole cream horn of plenty, more besides. Even the defamatory graffiti he had just left in the staff toilets.

And when he had finished, he sat back and shook with grins.

"But why, Sydney?" Charles had resorted to thinking on the hoof as the consultant had completely overlooked this scenario.

"Why? Why? Are you having a laugh? I'm a forty-five-year-old man who's a school caretaker. How shit is that? The children treat me like shit. You treat me like shit. I *am* shit!"

"You are not *shit*, Sydney."

"So how come you got it all?"

"I resent that! Do you think it's pure fluke that I'm sitting here? *I* did the studying, *I* got the qualifications. I've worked damned hard to get where I am today. *Equality of opportunity, Sydney.* You can't deny that."

The headteacher had been pondering the best time to air his second grievance, and now seemed as good as any.

"Furthermore, Sydney, while cards are on the table, there's been a complaint from a member of staff about you harassing them, encroaching, shall we say, their personal space."

"April?"

"I'm not at liberty to name names at this point in the proceedings."

"Proceedings? So, it's going to be like that is it? Proceedings? Your problem is *you* want her all to yourself!"

"I beg your pardon?"

"You've always had a thing for my girlfriends."

"Now, you know that's not true, Sydney. For a start, Miss Lyttle is not your girlfriend. You seem to forget you are a married man."

"So are you."

"We are not here to discuss me, Sydney."

"So, what exactly are we here to discuss? Some sort of warning? A *written* warning?" No reply was forthcoming. "Are you going to fire me?"

"I didn't say that. In fact, your services are very much required for this evening's Halloween Disco."

"To lock up?"

"Well, yes... and I wondered if you'd take on the role of Mongo again. You know how the children drop their crisp bags and stuff."

That was it! Locking up, fair enough; he could nip across from the Tooth and be back at the bar before the head had gone flat. But the thought of being paraded like last year as some beast-in-the-cellar type litter picker was too much.

"You know what? You can stuff off," and a flat palm saluted his receding hairline. "I quit! And I don't care if I never see you again!"

"Why, Sydney, *harbour* this resentment?" He was embarrassed as soon as he had said that.

"Do you know what I've just realised?"

"Go on."

"That all this is really about you. Mid. Life. Cry. Sis."

"What makes you say that?"

"Throwing your weight around, for one. The sudden interest in tidying. *Nesting.* The way you are with April. The constant fussing with your hair. You'll be crotching a Harley next. And a little birdie has told me about a certain sponsor form doing the rounds. Aren't we suddenly the daredevil?"

"Now that is quite enough, Sydney."

"It's more than enough! I shall be having words about the way I've been treated."

"Words? Who with? With whom?" There was a tremor in Charles's voice.

"Oh, I think you know!"

"Now, wait just a minute. There's no need… I'm sure we can resolve this little misunderstanding."

"Too late."

"But why cause upset?"

"Because big brothers are supposed to look out for little brothers. She'll have something to say about this, don't you worry."

Charles leaned back, casting around for any suitable role play he may have been coerced into on training days that he could now employ. Recalling none where the aggrieved party was threatening to report management to their mother, he determined attack to be his only credible defence.

"You've got a nerve, Sydney Bridge, a damned nerve! You didn't have a job! You hurt your back, remember? The bankrupt builder. I went out on a limb for you. I could have been an adviser by now. HMI, even. Can you imagine the whispers at the authority? 'Strange that his own brother should secure the caretaker's post. What a happy coincidence!' Internal Audit could've crawled all over this place."

"You've always looked down on me."

"All I wanted was to help out, try to put things right."

"Is that so?"

"Look, how many times do you want me to apologise for what happened between Dell and Judith? You know what she's like: headstrong, impetuous, wilful. *Jealous*. She treated you both shabbily and I told her so at the time. And all over an innocent compliment about a hairstyle."

"So, I'm just a sop to your conscience. Thanks, brother."

A welcome interruption at the door.

"Come in."

Miss Lyttle. He could not fault her timing, though he distinctly remembered booking a call to the Batphone. She was accompanied by a Year Nine errand boy.

"There's been another fight."

Good one.

"No, there really has, Mr Bridge," she continued. "Mr Ingram's biology."

The boy could contain his news no longer. "Kitt's been stabbed in the eye!" he interrupted. "By Fry, Sir."

"Any idea why?"

"They were falling out over that damned stuffed duck on display in there," said Miss Lyttle, pulling rank. "Apparently, Kitt kept pecking him with the beak, there was a pencil within reach and… the ambulance should be five minutes, that's the reckoning."

"Is it that bad?"

"Bill."

"Pardon?"

"Bill," Sydney repeated. "Ducks have a *bill*."

"Semantics, Sydney, semantics. I'm on my way, Miss Lyttle."

The secretary withdrew and the caretaker, could not care less, followed her out.

The room to himself, Charles spied grim-faced through his newly wiped window. Had *she* gone yet? The last thing he needed was that *Respecter* snoop dodging a paramedic wah-wah steaming through the gates.

Halloween.

Day of horrors. A resignation, though he had received nothing in writing, yet. A ride in an ambulance. Norton's father on the horizon.

How could Sydney say those things? Would he really speak to mother about him?

Night of demons. Oh God! That reminded him, school sodding disco tonight. Roll on midnight. Roll on November.

All the same, he could not hang around all day fretting. There was a student to see about a missing pencil.

The skylight. Deep down, he knew. Growing up, he had always been 'Big Bridgey'.

The headteacher absorbed the pane, then retreated into an outraged clench.

How *could* he say those things?

The door slammed behind Charles as he gingerly sprang digits out and back. Soundless was the corridor, but in his wash the office was rattling yet while the red leatherette orb ticked its last, off its anchor, off the desk, on the floor.

Chapter Twenty-Three

"How was drama class?"

*

Today was not usually a popular day for school dinners. Friday chippy run was the traditional herald of the weekend's beginning, but cook's initiative had been amply repaid with an almost full house. Boring old spaghetti had become 'bloodworm's'; garlic bread – 'vampire repealent'; potato wedges – 'zombie's toe's'; and meatballs – 'ghoulie's' (she had expected Mr Bridge to pull her up on this one, but he appeared to have enough on his plate at the moment). Rotting intestine's' was an arterial-hued casserole starring value sausages, which made the concoction taste even more gruesome than it sounded and, for dessert, there was oversized chocolate biscuit – 'mad cow's-pat's', or a pus-spattered spotted dick – a fiendish moniker for the latter considered an irrelevance.

The hall was abuzz, a jackhammering house of horror. Screams stilettoed the din as a beaker of 'rat's' blood' tumbled onto a crowded table, blackcurranting blouses and shirts; and boys, babycarrot-fanged, lurched childishly after wish-list sweethearts, who fought them off squealing and cruciform-fingered. One Year Eleven had modified a climbing rope into a noose and was cheerfully dangling, eyes rolling, tongue lolling, and feet safe and sound on Sydney's upturned mop bucket. Another – a prefect – sweater and blazer pulled over his head, galloped blind circuits slapping his own backside. By the time he was reined in, the headless horseman had routed a rump of Year Sevens and four-faulted a trestle of orange juice set aside for the evening's entertainment.

And there, cringing behind a parapet of double-deckered gym benches, were the decorations for the Halloween disco – Jack o'Lantern pumpkins and dread streamers: dangling bats, dismembered limbs, Frankenstein faces and hounds of hell – ready to spew forth once the brushes and mops had come to rest. (A hit squad of teaching assistants armed with sticky tape and staple guns had been put on standby and charged with – "*No word of a lie,*" recounted an incredulous Doc White to staffroom colleagues – making the dining hall more frightening.)

Service now at its peak, the racket within was satanic. Yet, indifferent in the corner, Sigsworth and Finch were on the lurk. The exceptional turnout had caught them on the hop; leftovers giveaway would be at least fifteen minutes delayed. Still, their wait would not have been in vain. Staff's extended attendance in the hall at lunchtime was rewarded with a free school meal, so today's bonanza would be on the house. They had gone out of their way to wish Mr Jones – the nominated sentinel and now their unsuspecting witness

– a 'good afternoon', but decided against asking him the time even though Finch was adamant that usually worked a treat in the films. Teachers were officially expected to carry out foot patrols in return for their crust, but the pair had been temporarily waylaid at the periphery by an alimentary debate. Their tentative conclusion was that a Terry's Chocolate Orange did, in all probability, constitute one of your five a day. ("Get in the bastard hole!")

*

"Drama class? There wasn't one. I was acting."

"But you said—" protested Roland.

"I had to get away and it was the first thing that sprung to mind," said Pippa, scanning about. "I couldn't think straight after Nelson's little announcement. And I wasn't at all comfortable with the Gifted and Talented stuff, either. Too much pressure!"

"Oh… Hey, your dad didn't mind taking me home, did he? He seemed quiet in the car."

"Don't take that to heart. He was just a bit miffed that I hadn't checked in sooner. They like to know where I am. What he won't admit, though, is that he secretly relished the opportunity to weigh up my new friends."

"I never get it when grown-ups are over-protective like that. That's not the real world."

"It's *my* real world."

And, amid his own chaos, Roland secretly wished it was his too.

*

"Mr Jones!" Sigsworth's best sportsfield roar part-hushed the hall and his outstretched index pointed the deputy to an emerging fracas that Finch had artfully spotted. In all likelihood they could have reached the mêlée first, what with their sprinting backgrounds, but from their vantage point they could spy several trays of 'S'not s'tew' in the vicinity, and everyone knew the potential havoc that presented for shellsuit linings.

They need not have concerned themselves: the deputy had their backs. He smoothly withdrew his trusty Thunderer and blew it tinnitus-hard. Even the climbing frame, which had refused to budge all year, hummed harmonically. By the time the entire building had stopped resonating he was between the combatants and signposting them in opposite directions. The tallest of the girls took the upbraiding in good heart, merely promising to cut the '*tiny* tits' off her opponent at some future encounter, but her adversary was far less amicable and only withdrew – with sensible haste, most witnesses later agreed – after slamming a petulant parting shot onto the dining table. The hall held its breath.

"The next person…" it was Mr Jones's mouth that was moving, but the voice was a monstrous imposter, "to speak above a whisper will be stood out and banned from the *disco!*"

Everyone knew the usual MO when Jonesy was suffering one of his arch tempers. Orders would be given, everyone got a five count to acclimatise, and then he would set about looking to make an example. *All the best teachers made examples.*

From the Year Sevens, wildly anticipating their first unparented school soirée, to the Year Elevens, who had already put down deposits with the bum-fluffed alcopop smugglers via the miracle of the Swap Shop, all fell hushed. Some who did not trust themselves golloped final mouthfuls then marched solemnly back to the serving counter to dispatch utensils and leave through swing doors they nursed back into place. And all the while the bin lid clock far up the wall, purchased expressly for the *Silence! Exams in Progress!* GCSEs, pounded out the seconds louder than ever.

All eyes on Mr Jones. He stood swelled and locked, lips grimly puckered, nostrils hunched and eyebrows gathered, watching from the shadows, mousetrap-primed.

And yet, in the absence of an early scapegoat, muted murmur began to emerge and a few nervous conversations resumed, sideways on.

Movement!

All eyes on Mr Jones.

They watched as he pulled an origamied tissue, whipped it undone and held a corner against his tongue. He dabbed seething at the spatter of green curry drying crisp against his face. More saliva and he moved on to the lapel of his grey Hugo Boss.

"Young Jonesy'll never get that out," Finch predicted. Quietly.

"Shall we?" Sigsworth nodded towards the serving hatch.

By now, the diners had thinned out to re-enact The Splattering in the hideyholes of the playground, leaving the pair, at long last, to bisto their way to the counter.

*

Although Mr Jones had expressly sanctioned whispering, Roland was worried about breaking his silence on the grounds that it is difficult to gauge volume when a martyr to the Atlantis of glue ear. His first attempt left little to chance.

"Do you believe him?"

"Pardon?"

His next braver, though still with a nod to caution: "I said, 'Do you believe him? Nelson?'"

*

Raised voices suddenly threatened the peace.

"What do you mean, you old hag, 'There's nothing left'?"

"I'm sorry, dearie, we're sold out."

"Well, sorry just won't cut it. We've been doing dinner duty. Dinner. Duty. Check with Mr Jones if you like. We've done the duty and now we want some dinner."

"You should have told us, love. We could have put something aside."

Finch was finding this setback hard to stomach. "Surely there's something we could have. What's that wizened crone got there?" and he fingered a second assistant clearing away in the rear.

"Congealed Vomit."

"What's that?"

"Carrot and broccoli pizza."

"I think I preferred 'Congealed Vomit'. Right. We'll have that lot, then."

"They're a bit burnt."

"Look, just hand them ove…" *Too late.* The crone pressed into her clog and the foot-pedal bin gulped them greedily down.

"I don't believe this!" Sigsworth chipped in. "Is the boss about? Can I speak to her, please?"

"She'll be back in a minute. Just nipped to the stock cupboard," and she turned to the crone. "Norma?"

"Yes, Adele?"

"Will you tell Sandra there's a couple of gentlemen would like a word."

*

With the stain removal at an end until he could clap eyes on a mirror, Mr Jones was back on the ball and computing his next move. That younger one, the one who thumped the edge of her plate in temper (was it Jade something or other?), he would be seeing a representative from home about her, threaten them with the dry-cleaning bill. Hit them in the pockets – all they understand, their type. And there would be a week's worth of detentions to contemplate, beginning Monday. He would spread the word as well. Put down a marker, let the others see he meant business. Just look at his results. The hall was library-quiet, especially now that a smattering of ticketless show-offs had been stood firing squad against the wall. They had briefly entertained defiance – gurning class-clown at his turned back – but wearily capitulated with the audience too cowed to smirk at their histrionics. *Clink and conversation.* Just how it should be. If only Old Bridgey, or the Chair of

Governors, or even Ofsted would walk through now. They would see he meant business, all right.

*

Pippa quietly resealed her Tupperware lunchbox, gathering her thoughts; Roland picked at his spotted dick.

"I can't think what to believe," she whispered. "I do know one thing: he looks terrible. I thought at first it was the aftermath of the fight – who wouldn't be shaken after that? – but he doesn't look like he has been sleeping. He looks dishevelled."

Roland thought Nelson always looked like that, his hair anyway, but was not sure if saying so would help.

"I couldn't believe it when he dragged us to see that painting," she went on. "I mean, I was happy to go for his sake, but—"

"I'm getting to know that mooseum like the back of my hand, me," Roland agreed.

"He was staring at that hopeless smudge job last Saturday when I was with Mum and Dad. I assumed he was mumbling to *himself* at the time. Little did I realise he actually believes he was having a dialogue. I've tried telling him we all have a voice in our head, but we don't converse out loud with it. And his dad, too. A secret agent?"

"I know."

"And to top it all we now have this harebrained – not to say criminal – enterprise for saving the life of a figure in a painting! Do *you* believe him?"

"I'm not sure…" Roland's head was spinning so he returned to his pudding; it helped him think. "Not as bad as it sounds, this dick stuff," he said, comforted. "What do you reckon its real name is?"

*

Negotiations at the serving hatch were crawling to a conclusion. Cook had been summoned and had located a couple of lukewarm baked potatoes (there were always a handful set aside for calorie counters and faddy eaters). Spectacularly overcooked, they resembled fossilised testes. Opinion from the ovens, however, was resistant to any thoughts of a grisly alias, lest it put off the fusspots. The potatoes were stuffed with scrapings from the cheese tub but cook stood firm in the face of a good cop, great cop routine alternating grovelling with flattery, and refused to open a catering tin of beans. In retribution, her counter-offer of a side salad was rebuffed out of hand.

The last remaining slice of vampire repellent went to Finch on a best-of-three paper-scissors-stone, and pudding was to consist of the two mad cow-pats that cook had intended for herself and her husband as reward for taking the grandchildren trick or treating. Scratched white plates were loaded onto teak-effect trays and dinner was served.

"Enjoy, gents."

"Thanks, you wart-riddled old witch. Much appreciated." It took a monumental feat of self-restraint on Sigsworth's part not to add a valedictory 'For shit's sake!' aside as the pair turned away.

Putting on a brave face – they were role models, after all – Sigsworth and Finch headed for the staffroom reciting a lexicon of expletives under their breath and vowing never again to volunteer for dinner duty. Not only that, once they had settled at their usual seats (those with the hollows) they determined to warn off every other prospective do-gooder within earshot.

*

"One thing is for certain, we need to stop him before he gets into real trouble. And I'm talking police record here. We've got to make him see sense with his ridiculous plan."

"He's definitely in. He walked past the window with Miss Lyttle before morning break."

"But you've not seen him since?" Roland shook his head and Pippa rolled her eyes. "We need to find him this afternoon, talk him out of it."

Roland's spoon scooped a last mouthful of custard. "I bet he's in The Dungeon. Miss Lyttle will know," he said. "And when we find him, leave it to me."

*

Almost 1.30pm. Almost bell-time. At the counter, the last of the blood, sweat and Sigsworth's tears had been wiped away and Sandra cook was re-acquainting herself with next week's menu. Today's success had made a change of plan a formality for Wednesday. Early menu thoughts included 'Guy's Gizzard's' (usual spaghetti bolognese), 'Gunpowder Pot' (spicy vegetarian option with a side scoop of baked beans), and 'For Fawke's' Sake!' (sausage and two dumplings).

Dessert would be 'To the Tower Chocolate Log' (that one *had* to be run past the headteacher).

While Sandra set about locating ingredients in the fresh calm of the kitchen, beyond its shuttered grille the clean-up was underway. Clawing into yesterday-damp rubber gloves Norma and Adele ventured towards the hall furniture. Buckaroo tables, sticky traystacks and vagabond chairs. Dishcloths were perfunctorily circled, crumbs spun to the floor then surfaces upended and danced to the edge of the room. Chairs were piled into risk-assessed sixes and hitched onto a trolley that sped them for the weekend behind a concertinaed curtain. Next, the duo swept back to the hatch and made for the industrial brooms: giant straggle-shagged pincers that gathered the dirt then refused to give it up, like some Rasta dog defending its bone. Mowing methodically up and down, they cut satisfying swaths through the morass before herding the findings sharp-eyed – there was occasionally coinage lurking – onto a wide blade shovel, and from there to a basking shark of a bin. And all before the disco decorators' 1.45pm appointment.

Cook had just returned from checking stocks of HP sauce when Mr Jones, freshened from the staff washroom, moved in to collect the salad and low-fat strawberry yoghurt ordered at the start of service.

"Busy one, ladies?" He knew all right. Just had to look at them.

"Rushed off our feet."

"Never mind, think of your bonuses!" And they snorted as one at the lampoonery. Mr Jones plucked pleased at the cutlery and turned for the staffroom. He was about to exit when he checked mid-step.

"By the way, ladies…" They paused to peer down the hall as, for dramatic effect, he crescented a cucumber slice and let go a wink. "*Love* the face paint."

And the old crone grinned.

Chapter Twenty-Four

'*Climb ev'ry mountain…*'

Yet poor Mother Abbess had barely scaled the foothills before an impatient thumb was at the green receiver icon.

"Yes?"

"It's me."

"I know it's you, tit! Your name comes up on the screen."

"Course…"

"Well?"

"He's just gone in."

"You sure it's him? It's pitch-dark out."

"Certain."

"I'll be right over. Wait around the corner."

"Will do."

"And switch it off now!"

"Will do, Dad."

Chapter Twenty-Five

Much more of this and he would be a dried-out husk, like one of those spiders that does not know it is dead and still clings to once-murderous finery, trapping only dust. There was doubtless a specimen just like that here now. He hoped it was not in his corner. Probably was, given his luck. Still, could be worse: offered a choice, dead or alive, he would take deceased and desiccated any day of the week. Yet the longer the blindfolding isolation played him, the greater his dread that even a *live* Incey Wincey – even a salivating, head-biting toupee of a brute, a cock-of-the-jungle horse-eating job – might be the least of his worries in this cave. How could a room dedicated to bleaches and foams and lemon-fresh potions *feel* so dirty?

The pitch dark had overshadowed his view, but his palm on the floor had felt pins of grit and gatherings of fluff that peaked between his fingers. There was also something mysteriously moist that he could not put his finger on, though his hand had jumpily caressed it several times. And beneath the rise, rise, rise then soft snuffle fall of his chest, was that a scurrying?

He had taken to squatting on his feet, soles flat to the floor, knees steadied by a wrap of teary arms, and backside resting against heels. That way nothing was likely to crawl up his trouser leg or, worse still, through the hole in his pocket.

And these were just the fears *within*.

He had not been in there long enough to venture out just yet. *Do not move.*

It had been a terrible day…

*

"Seems to be a pattern developing," Mr Bridge had said, thrusting the printout across his desk. "Unauthorised absences. Unlike you, Hitchcock."

Nelson nodded and pretended to study Exhibit A.

"Sessions unaccounted for. Need to nip it in the bud."

While the headteacher inwardly commended himself on his authoritative brevity, Nelson wondered if Mr Bridge was saving words for a big chat with someone else later on.

"Upset?"

"Pardon, Sir?"

"Anything upsetting you?"

Nelson invented a thinking face.

"Fight!"

"Sir?"

"The fight yesterday. *Edward.* Care to tell me about it?"

Nelson unlocked his features, though lips remained bolted. May as well ask if he had grown weary of his kneecaps.

"Can see you don't want to say, Hitchcock. In that case, you can spend today's breaks in the Nurture Room until I have chance to speak to Mum or Dad. Miss Lyttle will check you arrive. No smart aleckery."

"No, Sir," said Nelson at the doorway, and he began his exploration of the path that led to The Dungeon.

*

Sit tight.

*

The end-of-afternoon-break bell was at full rattle when Nelson emerged squinting from Nurture's mollifying glow. He had passed the last fifteen minutes serenaded by orcas while gawking hypnotically at a floor-to-ceiling bubble tube. His retinas were still cascading vents of multicoloured spheres as the pair found him.

"Nelson, thank goodness! How are you?"

"Oh hello, pretty relaxed after all that," and he hooked a thumb over his shoulder and tried to focus on Pippa while prismatic effervescence rose mesmerically over her face.

"Miss Lyttle said you'd be here," Roland explained.

"What did Germ Bird have to say?"

"Who?"

"Mr Bridge," said Pippa. "Or 'Dolby Dirge', if you prefer Old Bridgey."

"Oh. He was asking about the fight, but I didn't tell him anything, which goes without saying. He had my attendance for the week. I've missed quite a bit, apparently."

"Have you been wagging it?" There was a barely disguised admiration in Roland's voice.

"So, what is he going to do about it?" Pippa persisted.

"Said he's going to tell my dad."

"And what did you say?" There was a barely disguised concern in hers.

"I said I'd tell Dad myself, face to face," and his voice almost buckled, "once tonight is done."

"I see…" *This had already gone too far.* "Actually, that was one of the things we wanted to talk to you about. Roland…" and she stepped back.

The soothing fizz had practically dissipated to reveal Roland staring hard at his feet, the lower half of his face pushed into the horseshoe rolls of his chin.

"Go on, Roly," Pippa urged.

'*Roly*', was it now? "It's about later, Nelson. I can't make it. At all. I know I said I probably could, but Mum's booked us both in for aquarobics and I can't get out of it."

"Aquarobics?" Nelson waited for a pay-off that was not arriving. "You know I can't do it on my own. I explained all that at my house. It will take at least two of us, even you agreed about that."

"I did, but—"

"Well, thanks a lot!"

"Look—"

"No, no… that's fine," and Nelson raked the back of his head. "I understand you need to get your priorities right and… well, both *your* dads will be sleeping in their own beds tonight."

"It's not that, Nelson. It's because we care," Pippa began.

"Oh, I can see that," he snorted.

"We don't want you to get into trouble, that's all."

"More like *you* don't want to get into trouble. Can't even

borrow *his* sister's bloody tie, can we, Miss Goody bloody Twoshoes." He suspected he might regret the words the instant they slipped his mouth – and knew with absolute certainty in the aftershock that trailed their wake.

"Well, that's settled then, isn't it?" he eventually muttered.

"What do you mean?"

"I mean it's all over. Finished. I just hope you'll both be happy when I can't find my dad and when *he*... when *my friend* is dead!"

Nelson turned on his heels, head shaking, lips murmuring.

"What was he saying?" asked Roland, trying to catch receding sound in a turned ear.

"He said..." Pippa relayed, aching. "He said... 'Do something. My advice, always, is do something.'" Words she had said before.

And they watched in silence as his form was absorbed again by The Dungeon's depths. And there, tears rinsed away the last of the lingering bubbles.

*

Aquarobics? Since when?

Now? *Five minutes more, just to be on the safe side.*

*

Mum? He would prove her wrong as well. He was sorry now he had called home, but he needed food and did not want to arrive too early: more chance of being noticed, he reasoned. Why had she said those things? Out of spite, obviously. He knew the truth. And not just the-truth-according-to-Nelson truth, either. The real truth. The *true* truth.

*

What time is it?

No point looking at a watch he did not own, though Dad's timepiece could have illuminated the entire room with its digital fluorescence. *Spotlight the spider.* Alarms, time zones, fastest laps, a blur of milliseconds and backlight for signalling. Dot-dot-dot, Dad would announce at the end of bedtime story then say, "Got to dash-dash-dash!" Lying in his bed, Nelson would hear the kissless click of the front door, and the sigh of Mum's iron in the living room.

Nelson had been promised that watch when he was older. Mum had something to say about that, too. But she did not know. Dad had told him lots of things he had not told her.

*

Alone in the dark for the third time today, Nelson sensed his legs beginning to sear; pins and needles jabbing relentlessly from below.

Surely be safe, now.

Fumbling tenderly outwards, he found a makeshift crutch angled at his side and began to heave himself upright along its timber shaft. As he rose, thighs bristling while the blood rushed back, the cold grey tendrils that had earlier tormented his hand oozed dark against the floor and damp began to seep at the split in his shoe.

He was at full height now and weeping no longer, but he was not yet ready to move. He shook legs in turn to recover lost feeling then, arms out front, stepped forward until fingertips found the crusted paint of the door. Chest drumming, he creepy-crawled to the handle and closed his grip around its metallic chill.

Now or never.

He rubbed around the last of his watery face with a sleeve no longer there; lungs gulped a final interpretation of Forest Pine. Slowly, slowly, he twisted at the doorknob and was out into the Fire Exit glow of the corridor. No alarm. No hoot and whine of intrusion. *Still not fixed.* Left and right then a last squint back into the hideyhole he had stumbled across last Saturday while looking in on the cleaner. He was hoping he would spy a torch or a box of matches, but a mini cityscape of bottles and tubs and tins was all he could make out. That and a mop-minus-a-bucket leaning out of a puddle, low-tide anemone drooped at its base.

He pulled the door behind him and edged away, wallpaper-tight.

Up ahead, through the easing murk, he could see where the corridor opened out into the room, that room, *his* room. At its entrance, a cast of forged Greek warriors awaited. His plan was to merge with the phalanx, move invisibly to its head and from there he was within striking distance. Scuttling across open ground, he made the rearguard and began his weave between shield and cuirass and greave.

One pace from the front rank, a thread caught his face. Nelson pulled it away as he ducked carelessly past another figure. A figure that did not belong. An imposter that spasmed dark into life.

Nelson had not witnessed its convulsion.

But he knew it was there when a hand landed hard and heavy on his shoulder.

Chapter Twenty-Six

"What do you think you're doing here?" The hand tightened around the nape and held firm. "What exactly is it you're playing at?"

There was no reply, not that one was expected, so the chastisement continued uninterrupted. "You're going to cause a terrible mess. And who'll be left to clear it all up? Not you, that's for sure."

Unwilling to risk a wriggled escape, Pippa scooped her free hand under stiffened legs and pulled the catch into the comforting snuggle of her cardigan.

"Becoming a little fatty, too," she teased, exerted. "Now, do you want to tell me exactly what your little game is?"

The eyes looked up at her, searching for clues in her tone. Was it all right?

Those eyes. Those kitten peepers. Who could stay angry at those?

"Oh, come on then, you little scamp. Give me a cuddle and we'll say no more about it."

Bastet settled down in nestling arms and began to rev while Pippa itched reassuringly at the soft drum that spanned the mandible. She could have stayed there for ever – they both could – but tonight there was work to be done, so the cat was eased forgiven to the bedroom carpet and sent on its way, Pippa's hand tracing its outline to the tip of its erect tail. She followed as it sprung, soft as a bird, onto her quilt, then turned back to re-place the coffee mug partially dislodged by the cat's surprise lunge onto her desk. Her tissue soaked a tilt of milky spill. A lucky escape: firmer contact and 4G's precious journal would have been awash.

There was, of course, the usual homework to tackle, but that would have to wait. This Friday evening had been set aside for The Vanishings; she felt she owed Nelson after their words outside the Nurture Room that afternoon.

Draining the remains of her drink, she returned to the leaves of October 1903. Since arriving home from school, pausing only for untidy forkfuls of linguine carbonara, Pippa had pored over the months from Christian's loss in June towards the hieroglyphs of the one-armed entry to come. Once she had become attuned to the calligraphy the earlier passages had been an absorbing diversion (mother had become audibly vexed by the *third* reminder that dinner was on the table). The more she read, the more she delighted at the journal's tangle of police business, case records, observations, digest and underlines. Even the mundanities of the days seemed extraordinary to her: a constabulary fuelled by cheese and pickle sandwiches; the saga of the leaking station roof; a harridan's weekly complaint about the failure to locate her lost purse and its farthings, and the whip-round that followed to 'Make Mrs Hector a Far-Thing!'; the forced march to Croasdale's Hat Shop to support the display of police helmets;

and the throwaway asides on the working-man's perennial distractions: Wednesday reigning champions and Rock Sand uncatchable over middle distances.

There were the quotidian court summonses, all duly noted. A six-shilling fine for allowing pigs to stray, a 5s 6d fine for being drunk in charge of a mare, an identical forfeit for riding a bicycle on the footpath, and a woman prosecuted for swilling paving stones – another 5s 6d. Pippa began to wonder if there was any offence, other than those involving the porcine, that did not carry this penalty.

Disgruntlement among the rank and file was manifest in myriad mutterings about the temperamental tea urn, the rainy-day bucket rota and the superintendent's miserly edict that stamps were to be used sparingly on account of their 5d cost.

Yet it seemed to Pippa that 4G remained apart. He chronicled the grumbles and carps around him, but never once contributed his own. And Pippa's best explanation – one that caused her to admire him all the more – was that all these quibbles were ash. Christian's return was his only care. The name did not appear on every page; there were the occasional 'my son', 'my darling' and 'my precious' to relieve the repetition, but the missing boy was omnipresent. Every moment, every breath devoted to his return.

The sergeant's investigations, official and otherwise, strung together days and weeks. Pages were given over to nascent forensic science: trace evidence, entomology, toxicology, dynamometry, blood grouping, dactyloscopy. A theft involving billiards balls and the conviction by fingerprint that followed became the catalyst for home-spun experiments with soot and starch, then graphite and brushes and blows. Superiors were urged without success to embrace the new. Yet 4G was not easily deterred – '*In times to come forensics will be the greatest of detectives*' – and he worked unseen at honing his skills, collecting from colleagues surreptitious tips and palms to decipher their loops and whorls.

But 'times to come' would not arrive soon enough and by late September 1903, with reckless disregard for his personal and professional reputation, 4G had recorded his first impressions of those Pippa took to be the Spiritualists.

She reckoned them a dozenish group, all ears and tiptoes, that doubtlessly knew who – and what – 4G was, and were sceptical of his unannounced appearance at their meeting house. Crowded out, he stood firm on the doorstep to render his motives and ambitions. They listened politely then withdrew in silence to re-emerge minutes later, spearing him with vestibule light. One more stride, they warned, would put him at odds not just with his earthly superior. Pippa's stiffened index followed his response: "'*The saints have turned their backs on me,*' said I."

Arms reached into the darkness and bore him down the hallway to a sitting room, 'lace-furnished and dimly lit, and at its centre a large table to which an extra chair was hastily presented'. The sergeant was discreet enough avoid names for prying eyes, and buried notes of subsequent meeting as a nondescript PS at the end of respective entries. Over the following weeks the postscripts appeared with increasing frequency.

Upon reaching Saturday 24th October 1903, Pippa located reference to preparations for that evening's public meeting at the town hall – the same gathering mentioned among the funeral cuttings exhumed by Harry. *What was the vicar's phrase again, 'unearthly petition'?*

*

Sunday 25th October 1903

As last night's occurrence will most certainly be common knowledge by now, I see little reason to re-tread each sordid detail. In consequence of the invective to which I was unjustly subject, and some little interval now having passed, I wish merely the opportunity to state my own interpretation of events at the town hall.

At the outset I relayed to the assembled audience, with certain ongoing threads purposely omitted, the unresolved state of 'The Vanishings' inquiry. The news was not well-received. This was both my expectation and opportunity, for it was then that I offered my proposition.

My address was well-practised and I began by talking of my original reservations in pursuing more unorthodox approaches to the case. I followed by relaying earnestly the revelations recently wrought upon me: the visiting trance lecturer, the automatic writing that I, wide-eyed, had witnessed, the exudation of ectoplasm, communication via the Ouija board, and all possibilities beyond mortal conceit presented therein. It was at that moment I made my appeal for the strength of the many to come to the aid of the few.

I had expected, perhaps, a handful of dissenters, but the howls of derision that rang off the walls showed I had foolishly underestimated their readiness for such an enterprise.

The Supt immediately called for a recess and I was dispatched to the tea urn (once more mended). Donning white cotton gloves, as if to accept my degradation, I joined Richards, similarly attired upon my instruction, in proffering cup and saucer to all. As drinks were finished and the crockery returned, my unwitting accomplice was to waylay with brief conversation, just enough time for me to deposit the used china at my feet in receptacles alphabetically marked.

The great and good began to drift away, but the Rev Brody remained to converse. A dear friend and an amiable fellow, I did not need his words to tell me he was horrified by what I had suggested; his countenance relayed all. We talked around awhile and then, fearing plainly for my eternal soul, he asked me to reconsider my absence from mass. He said it was not too late. I replied assuredly that it was. He is without doubt a good man – yet a deluded one.

Sunday 25th October 1903 11.24pm

PS Visited this eveningas arranged and sat again. Desperate nevelation...

The following day's entry, Monday 26th October 1903, recorded that 4G had been summoned to meet the chief inspector that afternoon. The rest of the leaf remained blank, except for a single bisecting line that read:

Ordened homeforthwith to rest.How can i?

One more page. Pippa stretched away and picked up her phone. 8.11pm. Time enough. Hunched under a hot Anglepoise cone, spectacles hidden among her curls, she decoded the date – Saturday 31st October 1903 – then puffed cheeks in contemplation of the horror scrawl to follow: a grotesque of lines and rings and jabs scattered in all directions, barely recognisable as handwriting at all. Margins had been pressed for a tower of mangled abstraction, footnotes sharp-lefted at the paper's edge then darted vertically before the nib halted, half-buried, or the thoughts ran out. Despite earlier misgivings, it now seemed to Pippa the only possible explanation for the dissonance before her, and the silence from the 26th, was the loss of 4G's arm.

With scowled squint she began to painstakingly transcribe any words she felt she could interpret. Towards the upper third, a scribbled 'den test', or 'dentist', seemed a possibility and, further down, 'testis be foneme!!!', each exclamation more subterranean than its predecessor. 'Testis… *Testis*'.

The state-sector diktats to which St John's was subject had rendered Latin a foreign language to Pippa, but her dad had a reference book for dealing with solicitors and crosswords and some of those phrases, she half-recalled, shared similar construction.

The bookcase in the dining room was arranged in a repeated ABC sequence with qualifying family members allocated two shelves from six, according to seniority. Pippa held bottom and third up. Mum came next at five and two, with Dad – the tallest and *the man* – pulling rank for fourth and top. Baby brother's books, a library of Thomas Tanks and crayon-whirled colourers, were stored in the nursery room upstairs. There were two bookcase rules – one official, the other a convention that had taken on quasi-legal status: paperbacks at the top and each shelf arranged alphabetically by author.

Latin Phrases and Quotations was on the top shelf, left-hand side. Pippa reached up and tipped it out. Flicking, she passed slipper-soft the couch bookended by parents, heads down in novels.

"T… T… Tes-tis. Testis. *Witness*."

She remained buried in Branyon for the return upstairs, floating diagonally towards the back bedroom. Her room.

Yet on the landing, among the shadows at the door, she paused.

Darker than I had left it.

Racing sharp into the blot-black she rounded the bed for her desk. "What have you done now, you daft cat!" she barked.

There were enough clues in the tone this time for Bastet to bolt. Ducking the Latin lobbed aimlessly onto the bed and zipping contrary to a blur of feet, the pet swiped the door frame and was gone.

Pippa tore through the gloom for the halo of smoky light at her desk. *Dad will go mad if the varnish has been marked!*

She was in luck. The metal hood had tipped onto the blanket of notes and papers where she had been stationed. The lamp was jerked up by its crane and the light raced outwards like oil on water. It was then she realised exactly what had absorbed the scorching heat.

"Oh, dear God!"

With the Anglepoise righted she saw – and smelled – the journal, still open at that final page. A page now browned. Branded.

Pippa patted the scribblings to gauge the warmth, and to seek reassurance that the entire volume was not about to combust. Returning to the door to confirm the commotion had not disturbed the readers, or stirred baby James, she lit the room and glowered after the cat. "Goddess of the family, my foot. Could've burned the house down."

In the pearly glow, she stared down at the aftermath. A singeing bruise eyed back from the top of the page.

How was she going to explain this to Nelson and Harry? A century without blemish. Less than a week with her, and this. Better to be honest. "My idiot pet, *Bastard*, jumped onto my desk and knocked over my reading lamp while I was out of the room." Sounded slightly implausible, but the truth sometimes does. *Only a lie*, she speculated, inappropriately pleased, *leaves no room for doubt*.

Pippa crouched at the desk's edge and began to peel back the corner of the paper. She was still not convinced the whole thing would not shatter like a jigsaw puzzle. The page creaked. What if it had fused with the sheets beneath? What kind of historian ruins history?

What if Nelson never forgave her?

Head at a tilt, she peered into the sloping gap held by forefinger and thumb. Making her mouth into a kiss, she blew a stream of air and the pages separated with a sigh. The uppermost held momentarily at its apogee then eased gently to rest. Scarred, but intact. A sort of success.

The plan now was to call it a day before anything else could go wrong. She would close the door behind her, curl up in the reading lounge with Fitzwilliam Darcy while cold shouldering the cat, then check again in the morning in the vague hope that it had all been a bad dream.

Just one final task. But as she reached for a pencil to jot down her 'truth, lies and doubt' aphorism (they were always useful for impressing examiners) a flashback leapt at her. An image of two pages floating briefly apart. An image in the oblique. An image that did not exist when last she rolled the pages cover to cover.

An image of writing on an empty page.

She stared out to the distance and played it over. Then, crouched once more, lids jammed unshut as though to blink would wipe those words, finger and thumb picked again at the corner of the day. She breathed, and lifted...

In a spotlight the dimensions of the lampshade, within the exact diameter of an Anglepoise hood, was the faintest blush of pen work. She switched repeatedly between the old and the new, thoughts of splintering paper fleetingly forgotten. Her first theory was 'strike-through': ink leaching from the upper page. But no, the text did not align and, in any case, the new hand appeared evenly presented, not the hammer and hatchets of the final entry. On nose-to-paper inspection the lines, though hazy, bore comparison with 4G's in earlier days. *Think*. Perhaps he had somehow written secret notes at the back when he had begun the journal. Somehow? Secret? What was she thinking? *Think*. More likely he had made jottings at the back and inferior ink had gradually faded to nothing. Why swap inks? Why start at the end? *Think*. Whatever she had found it certainly pre-dated 31st October: the handwriting alone was proof of that; this was no wrong-armed hotchpotch. *Think!* It was difficult to be certain because the spotlight had fallen on so few words. If she deserved any luck today the lamp would at least have hit the centre of the page, where there may have been more to read. *Think!* It is only a riddle. Be methodical. Logical. Start at the top and work down. The top.

At the perimeter of the heat, Pippa found the lower edge of what may have been a dateline. She grabbed her pencil and sketched in mid-air the missing upper portion, adding probable peaks to numbers and letters. Snatching a scrap of paper, she gently traced the half-lettering she could see then committed to the upper blanks she could not. Her handiwork was held alongside the journal for comparison. *A match*. Her focus darted left to right to right to left. The copy she had conjured perfectly married the fragment of date on the page.

But… but that could not be possible.

Chapter Twenty-Seven

"What do you think you're doing here?" The hand tightened around the nape and held firm. "What exactly is it you're playing at?"

Nelson's shoulders rose instinctively and loosened the grab enough for him to half-face his assailant. One of the Hoplites had sprung to life from the shadows and was digging fingernails into the flesh of his neck.

"Ruddy hell! You nearly gave me a heart attack! What are *you* doing here?"

The grip was released with a grin.

"Thought I'd find out what you were up to."

"You said you weren't coming."

"I did. But you're my friend and, ridiculously enough, I haven't got that many to lose. And who wants to go to shitty Aquarobics anyway?"

The pair exchanged stifled smirks that grew into hissing wriggles of relief. As the paroxysms subsided, Nelson held out a grateful hand that Roland took and shook. Before these silent witnesses they were now officially brothers in arms, comrades among the phalanx.

"What's happened to your sleeve?" asked Roland, pointing.

"Long story."

Nelson leaned in at the contact, concerned. "Never mind that. What's happened to your eye?" he asked, voice a natural whisper in the espresso air.

"A souvenir of a little disagreement with a certain pupil at the end of school."

"Norton?"

"You get the goldfish! He bumped into me in the corridor near the tuck shop. I need to start varying my routine, me." Roland eased back onto a warrior's cocked knee and brushed a spitter of shiny spats from his jacket.

"What did he say?"

"He wanted to know where you were."

"Why?"

"Don't know, but he didn't look happy."

Nelson caught a corresponding perch on one of the tableau's fibreglass boulders. "How could you tell?"

"Nice one. Anyway, I said I hadn't seen you, because I hadn't, so he pulls my arm right up my back, like this, and asks if it's true that fat lads have little nobs."

"And?"

"I said it was most probably a matter of proportion, but he was welcome to help me find mine. I should have said, 'Yes,' and not tried to be smart. And then he smacked me in the eye just as everyone was looking the other way."

Nelson made a wry smile. "Bit unlucky that, about the bystanders."

"Can't say I blame them. I wish I'd hit him back now – I should have bloody bodysplashed him – but while it's happening you just want it over with. I'm not as brave as you."

"I wasn't brave. I just didn't want my hand in a load of old pee, that's all." Nelson took a closer view as he spoke. "It looks sore, though." And in the dark he pushed out a clumsy finger to trace the yolk of swollen flesh.

"Ow! That's because it is, you idiot!" and both smirks returned.

"Who said you're not brave, anyway? You're here."

"But this is different. This is *adventuring*. You know Noah's the Newsagents?"

"Yeah."

"Swindling him royally, me, till he banned everyone else from the shop. Had to ease off then because it might have been a bit obvious, what with me being his only customer. I never even needed to take stuff. I just enjoyed the adventure. The entertainment."

"This isn't entertainment."

"No, I wasn't suggesting—"

"I know, I'm sorry. I'm just a bit scared. Well, a lot scared, actually."

"Concentrate on the prize, not the punishment. Usually works for me. Besides, I reckon you're a bit of a dark horse. Wagging it, brawling with the cock of the school, breaking and entering. We'll have you swearing properly next."

"I'm scared for my dad, too."

"You're going to save him."

"Hope so."

Nelson scanned the gloom to the rear of their staging post. The corridor tunnelled out like a gullet. The longer he looked, the more it danced hungrily, ready to swallow them down. Their exit was waiting down there. And the path to his dad. He knew it.

"I really hope so…"

"You will."

"How did you get in here, anyway?"

"During the trip last week, I noticed a window with a broken latch," replied Roland. "Well, I say *noticed* – it was actually me who broke it. I was just messing and it snapped. I've always been clumsy, me."

"What if it had been fixed?"

"It was still broken when you brought us yesterday. And if the worst had happened I've brought a tile cutter from home."

"Would that work?"

"Tied to a brick it would."

Nelson shook his head in wonder. "Pippa's right, you know. You could get into lots of trouble here."

"So could you."

"I've got no choice: two lives are relying on me tonight. And, for your information, *I'm* not the one who's vandalised museum property." A smile broke. "*I've* been shockingly locked in by dopey staff." It broadened.

"Incredible!" Roland leapt in. "That happened to me, too. You'd think they'd check. We could sue."

Nelson pulled at his remaining sleeve and examined his wrist. "It's time."

"How do you know? You haven't got a watch."

"True, but I've got this intuition thing where I can sort of sense time."

"Really? Go on then…" And Roland's forefinger tapped at his Casio.

Nelson closed eyes for accuracy as his friend's hand shaded the face. "About eight."

"I don't believe it! Absolutely incredible! Want to check?"

"Go on then."

Roland thrust out an arm.

"6.56," said Nelson, grin gone.

"Yep."

"Oh."

"What time do we have to be *there* again?"

"Midnight."

"I knew it. It had to be bloody midnight, didn't it?"

"I can't help that. I'm only following instructions."

"I've heard that one before. That's what the prefects say when they're reporting you for next to nothing." And Roland's head replayed a litany of half-trots down the corridor, shortcuts across the courtyard, picnics in assembly, armpit farts in chapel…

"I think we should do it now," said Nelson. "We can always kill a bit of time at the other end."

"I'm not stepping foot in that place till the last possible moment, and don't even use the word 'kill', tonight of all nights. *And* it had just started to rain. That would have been about 6.10, by the way." He tapped a tease at his watch. "What time did you get here?"

"I called home first and saw Mum," Nelson recalled, though that was an encounter he was desperately trying to forget, "so just before half-five closing."

The chatter lulled momentarily while a yellow comet slid

across the ceiling. The car droned by, wheels slurping at the wet on the road.

"Come on, I'm off for a nosey." Roland was tugging at his laces like a starling at a lawn. He horned off his boots and peeled away polyester blend, airing velociraptor toenails.

"What are you doing?" hissed Nelson.

"Fingerprints, of course," he replied, slipping hands to the tips of the moist tubes.

"What about toeprints?"

"Do they even exist?" Roland levered himself up, jigging briefly on the cold floor. "I'll chance it." Upending his boots, he pushed each into jacket pockets then scampered a talking sock around his friend's shoulder. "Come on," he wheedled, "it's too early to leave and we can't sit here for four hours. What harm could it do?"

"Unbelievable. The whole day here last Friday and you hardly moved from one spot. Now, in the dark – after breaking in! – you want a tour."

"Ah, but last week was different. Last week I had to be here. Tonight is a choice. Matter of principle."

*

They had been in retreat for ages, though time evidently operated to different parameters in this place. Nelson had come to rest in the flush of an aquarium casting toothy shadows at Animal Magic. He had never made it back here on the day of the trip. Then it had been mobbed by eager pupils – "*Have you seen all those skeletons? Awesome!*" – and a minion had to be summoned to operate a strict five-out, none-in policy. Yet now he was actually within, in sight of its perimeter sideshows and the circus parade bones marching the heart of the room, even in this soft-focus drizzle, it was the last place he wanted to be.

Where has he got to?

Up ahead, Roland had trilled unseen past a xylophone of elephant ribs and hopped a for-display-purposes-only barrier. Planting his feet in the greengrocer grass of a North American forest he squared up to a frightful alopeciac grizzly; a sparring-sock jab knuckled the bare bear and he was off.

By the time his friend had hunted him down, Roland had alighted on an Asian jungle and was astride a big cat.

"What are you doing?"

"Climb on!"

"This isn't why I'm here."

Roland dismounted and patted back the handful of stripe he had unexpectedly taken with him. "I'm sorry," he said, stepping over. "But have you never wondered what it might be like to ride a tiger?"

Nelson turned to retrace his steps to the corridor.

"Wait for me! Hey, here's one. If you could be any animal in the world, *any animal*, what would you be?"

"Erm…" Nelson was not at all bothered, but the longer he bothered to feign interest the further they were travelling in the right direction. "Erm…" he said again after remaining hushed as long as decently possible. "A dolphin. They're intelligent. They're free. They stick together."

The questioner pulled a face.

"Not convinced?"

"Wouldn't fancy holding my breath all day, me," said Roland. "Mind you, they're always smiling."

On they walked.

"Go on then."

"Go on what?"

"Ask me!"

"All right. If you could be—"

"A *giraffe*," said Roland. "No reason."

*

"What's next?"

Peering leftwards Nelson read, 'Land of the Pharaohs'. The final rung on the climb back to The Gallery.

"Can we have quick look? Please."

*

Ancient Egypt, with its model village re-imagining of the Karnak Temple, Anubis guardians and gauze-wrapped mummies, had been fanfared as the museum's renaissance. Tie-in paraphernalia flooded the souvenir shop, flyers were dispatched to schools and residential homes, a pedestrian-luring *full-colour* banner had been strung across the main entrance, and a deal thrashed out with Carter's Photographers for visitor portraits, heads poked inscrutably through a hole in a plywood sphinx.

The grand opening ceremony, now two months ago, had been overseen by Micheal. Orders were distributed, troops mobilised and bleary-eyed manoeuvres rehearsed. Staff were cajoled into traditional Nile garb for the big day and the local press invited. The culmination of Operation Sandman would see the mayor snip the ribbon (in a neat touch, a length of elasticated bandage dunked in tea) and then Round Tablers, Rotarians, Soroptimists, Cats Protectioners and various pillars of the community would grab a vol-au-vent and step back through the ages.

Unhappily, the exhibition was jinxed from the off.

Within minutes the fire brigade had been summoned to extricate the Lady Mayoress snagged watch-the-birdie fast, and a wine-fuelled Pensioners' Link *Wilson, Keppel and Betty* reboot was brought to an abrupt close by a dislocated hip.

The ill fortune was not to end there, as the media coverage that followed was hardly encouraging. *The Respecter* gleefully declared the venture the latest victim of Tutankhamun's curse: a front-page teaser was illustrated by a picture of a fireman hacksawing a tearful mayoress from the sphinx, while page three featured the sand dancer's stretchered removal. To supplement this dire catalogue, a quarter-page panel, watched over by a stock shot of blind Boris Karloff as The Mummy, detailed the terrible fate of Carnarvon's crew and grimly pondered, 'Could you be next?' And set alongside, lost among the doom and the gloom, the £300 overpriced advertisement from the last of the museum's budget.

And just when the losing streak seemed ended, the first spot of rain began to wash the paint from the banner outside.

Once the dust had settled, the most high-profile victim of the pestilence was the mayor. In what at the time was considered a winning photo-opportunity, he had donned a pharaoh's headdress and posed magisterially. Readily available from *Respecter Reprints*, the snap was immediately seized on by political adversaries as proof of the old buffer living in the past. Even the paper got in act after unqualified support for Heath's loft conversion failed to materialise. 'Tut tut! "Giza" job, say council workers!' went the headline on a piece that recycled the headshot and fingered the mayor for a mythical round of town-hall redundancies.

*

Roland gawked down into the glass case, hands pressed either side of the Do Not Lean warning. Inside lay an identity parade of remarkably well-preserved figurines and, beneath, a label that read, 'Ashabti workers – believed to carry out the pharaoh's bidding in the afterlife. These Ashabti are replicas of those found in the tomb of Tutankhamun'.

"How bad's that?"

"What?" asked Nelson, arriving to look.

"These. Bloody *models* of models. How cheap is this place? Worst mooseum in the world."

Nelson reached across and turned his friend's wrist. It was too dark to see, but he was ready anyhow. "Come on," he said. "It must be time."

*

Once more they stood at the entrance to the room. *The* room. Beyond the phalanx crouched Talos, dominating the midpoint amid smatterings of Greek statuary. Windowing the glassless side of The Gallery were the paintings. It was impossible to make out the detail of their landscapes and portraits, but Nelson knew exactly where his prize hung.

He moved cautiously, tracking the cool of the wall, fingering the screwdriver missing since this morning from Sydney the caretaker's toolbox. Reaching his destination, he stepped out and gazed in. Now cast before him in the milky glow of the high panes to his rear stood the figure. Skin scuta scuffed, eyes sunset blazed. The frozen lean into cold stone. The defiance.

"You have come." The voice clearer than ever in the pitch night.

The accomplice came into view and, had it been in his gift, Sheldan would have grimaced.

"Is he ready then?"

"He's been ready for a hundred years. Are you ready?"

"Why not, while we're here? You hold that side."

The pair halved and Nelson, to the left, ran his hand down the fingerholds of the picture frame until he came to the brass lug fixed at the plaster. He pulled the screwdriver and began to twist. Slowly, the portrait was guided through its capsize until it found equilibrium. "Swap sides."

Nelson lengthened the partner screw. "Get your hands underneath." A last turn and the scene tipped free. The heft of its squared awkwardness fell at them, taking them by surprise, and they staggered quasi-comically, belt-bound Olympians.

"It's heavier than it looks, this," panted Nelson.

"I'm taking these off, me," wheezed Roland. "I can't get a proper grip. If anyone was coming for us they would have been here by now." And he mopped the blisters off his brow before dragging each sock from his hands, puffs of lunar-sparked flakes rising.

They stood looking down on the cemetery, hands at hips.

"Why don't we rip it out of the frame? It'll be miles easier to carry."

"No, we can't," said Nelson. "He was very specific. We need to take everything."

"Bit of a diva, isn't he? Give us a sec, then…" Roland withdrew to his backside and replaced his boots, stuffing the excess of their laces within. Rising, he brought his hands to a clap before swirling them together in expectation. "Shall we?"

The pair moved off, Nelson walking backwards at the front, Roland steering from the rear and the figure bobbing horizontally between.

"Where are we going?"

"The gift shop."

"Now's not the time for mementoes."

"That's where the biggest ground-floor windows are," said Nelson.

"And what do we do when we get there?"

"I'll climb out and you pass Sheldan to me."

"Not that. I mean when we get *there*."

"Oh that! I don't know. He hasn't said yet."

"Hasn't said yet…"

"He said we would get further instructions when we arrive."

"Who from?"

"I don't know."

"Do you think it might be your dad?"

Please let it be Dad. More than anything else in the world, please… "I don't know."

"Can we stop just a minute?"

Nelson waited while Roland eased his corner onto the cap of his toes and rolled a clacking palm around the rubber tip of his nose.

"Hey, Nelson, you know who I think this is?" he said, eyes on the oils.

"Go on."

"Your guardian angel. My nan says we all have one."

The painting was raised once more and, strides and smiles in synchronicity, they headed from The Gallery into the corridor leading to the main entrance.

They were on their way at last. Now *was* the tempus and nothing was going to stop them.

Yet high above, courtesy of the technician's handiwork that afternoon, a peering, peeping Polyphemus blinked red-eyed awake…

Chapter Twenty-Eight

Tuesday 3rd November 1903

She re-read the dateline. Again. Three days after the final entry? The calligraphy was virtually recovered. Gone was the horror scrawl and back was the lucid nib of earlier months.

What should she do? She held the new page to the light to check for traces of additional lettering. Nothing. If there was more to be uncovered the paper would require heat. What should she do?

Pippa crept to the bedroom door. "Well, look who it is."

Bastet, encouraged by the returned calm, looked up fawn-cute.

"Come to see what a fuss you've caused? You'd better come in, then." Pardoned, it brushed past and found the recumbence of the quilt. She was dogged, that cat.

The latch was homed and Pippa returned to her desk, insides writhing, for the scorching to begin…

Despite the dreadful pain, the worst of which, I fear, is yet to be endured, it is with a sense of release that these words are written. For until that night the state of my mind had not been even. Now my meditations have taken shape.

The opening paragraph was recited dry-mouthed. Pippa had been judicious in her approach, holding down the bulb a few seconds longer each time until the words began to surface; the risk taken in pursuing her goddess's clumsiwork justified.

Just wait until Nelson saw this.

For now, I must keep my investigation from all. This malaise runs deeper and yet higher than I could have imagined.

I am ever mindful of the risk I run in leading its agents to the noose. Should my campaign be cut short, I leave this veiled record of horrors already uncovered. I implore whosoever shall discover it to make the knowledge of their eyes known...

The words could not come quickly enough. Pippa was a rhythm of lower and lift, lower and lift, gaze hunched impatiently under dipped hood then upright eyes rubbed furiously until the blindness went.

What is scribed below is a true and faithful record of the events of Saturday 31st October 1903. On the morning of the aforementioned, two components of my investigation fell together. The first related to the public meeting at the town hall. That brought me to the second: an appointment at the dentist.

*

"Why, hallo, Sergeant Fitzgerald. What an unexpected appearance at so late an hour. I do hope I have done nothing wrong," and there was the evanescent glint of smile.

Arms were spread to display, beneath police-issue overcoat, civilian attire. "Just passing."

"Are you well? You look frightful, if you'll forgive my candour. You're not here to make a reservation, I hope!"

"As I said, just a social call."

"In that case, shall we dispense with the formalities? Please, step inside, Caleb." He abandoned the buttoning of his waistcoat and offered a curve of arm.

"Septimus."

Beyond the threshold, feet were scraped and the cap and outercoat taken and hung. The tweed jacket and neckerchief remained despite the welcoming dance of the coal in the sitting room beyond.

"Come into my parlour." He pointed the way. "Can I offer you a taste, while you are out of hours?"

"Tea will be fine, thank you. Two sugars."

"Tea it is, then. Please, make yourself comfortable."

The sergeant passed the staircase – narrowly eluding the trip of a travel bag at his feet – to enter as directed and, standing within licking distance, sandpapered the last of the outdoors from his hands. Turning to warm his back, fingers crossed behind, he listened intently to the clank of the kitchen then, an interlude upon him, surveyed his surroundings. The darkened sitting room was pleasant enough. Up above he followed a barrelling beam, knotted and gnarled and wavering in the fireshadow, from the picture rail opposite a pair of framed landscapes were chained, a fruitbowled sideboard ran the length of a wall to his right, crystal decanter glowing upon and, at his feet, a tasselled Turkish weave partially concealed the herringbone floor. It lacked a woman's touch, but there was no obvious trace of the profession.

Caleb's gaze was attracted to movement through the doorway.

"I've put the water to boil." The parlour was entered and a gas lamp intensified. "It's just a matter of time."

Caleb fixed on the glowing orb. "Fiat lux," he mumbled.

A gilt case was flashed. "Cigarette?"

"I don't smoke."

"I must say," the host continued theatrically, "with the knock at the door this late on Halloween I thought it might be the devil himself come calling!"

"Indeed," said Caleb, declining the invitation to sport.

"Please, have a seat while you are waiting."

Caleb made for the nearest chair.

"Not that one, if you don't mind, that's mine. Take the armchair over there."

Trousers were hitched at knees and legs lay crossed as both men faced each other, separated by flames.

"You know, my memory must be playing tricks."

"How so?" asked Caleb.

"Well, I'm sure you must have visited previously, but I've been struggling to recall when. I know I wasn't here when your dear wife passed on."

"Quite." It was a fact so obvious that deliberate provocation could be its only intent. "It was Mr Mort who honoured her," Caleb recalled, "but he departed quite suddenly. And you arrived."

"I did, didn't I? So, to what do I owe this... delight?"

"I have been to the dentist today."

"You have my sympathies, my dear Sergeant, but toothache is rarely fatal."

"Oh, I don't know." And the officer let go wry nostrils.

"Is that a riddle, Sergeant? I do so enjoy riddles."

Septimus sat back, shielded. The voices quietened, leaving only the cracking bones of the dying fire and the slow knock of skeleton hands, slashed diagonally across a heedless face, to fill the room.

Two wordless minutes later – the hands deformed to 11.27 – Septimus climbed to his feet. Yet before he could utter a sound, before he could make his move, his eyes were found and Caleb whispered, "I miss my boy so much..."

"I shall see where the tea's got to." And the host was gone.

He reappeared in moments, bearing clinking china that was handed over with a stifled rattle. "Two sugars?" he confirmed.

A criss-crossed beaker followed behind. "I'll have a whiskey, if you've no objection." The decanter was tipped and a couple of fingers flowed into the cylinder. Septimus stood tall to suck in the liquid then inhaled deeply, chest filled, as the warmth trickled down. "Single malt. I do like the occasional drop," he said, flourishing his glass. "One should always have a vice."

"I have none."

"Really, Caleb? Why, a man lacking vice is in grave danger of presenting himself as a bore."

"Is that my situation, Sir?"

"A tedium, you mean?"

"One of *grave* danger?"

"That is a word, I shall admit, I tend to overuse. Comes with the position," and he smiled alone at his quip. "In any event, I am almost ashamed to report that I have enough vices for the both of us."

"That I doubt not."

A second amber sip was taken. "My dear officer, I detect a note of hostility has entered our discourse. Have I done something to upset you?"

Septimus edged closer to his guest and, beaker pressed to lapel, reached down for the fireiron that had etched its own hollow into the Morris hearth. He lifted the brass spike and began to stab at the embers, flighting a surge of sparks.

"So," said Septimus, the digging now deeper and harder, "tell me more about this visit to the dental surgeon."

"Why don't you tell me?" Legs were uncrossed. "You were there."

The pokery stopped. "As a matter of fact," said Septimus, rising, "I did have occasion, by happy coincidence, or not, to attend the dentist today. There was an extraction required." The dulled shaft was aimed at Caleb's eyes. "But I didn't see you."

"My intention entirely. I required Ratchett to provide his personal appointments. You seem to have been spending a good deal of time there."

"I was not aware that dental care had become a police matter."

"Nor was I aware that dental care required such frequency of visitation. Unless, of course, your care was for certain narcotic substances."

"Narcotic substances? How terribly grand."

"Nitrous oxide? Laughing gas. *Seeing God*, some name it."

"I like to inhale, if that is your meaning and, as far as I am aware, it is a perfectly legitimate pursuit. And for your illumination, the only deity likely to welcome me open-armed is Morpheus." The last of the whiskey was drained. "This may surprise you, Sergeant, but one occasionally – not least in my profession – requires a little distraction. It renders the pursuit of vice quite vital."

"Mr Ratchett informs me you have been working together on a portable contraption for your nitrous oxide."

"The euphoria that my little recreation affords can be somewhat diminished by the visits to his base surgery with its ragamuffin trade. Gas is, after all, an anaesthetic, and if I am to be dead to the world I would prefer my own universe beyond the reach of prying eyes. And hands. As for our Ratchett, I deal with him simply because dentists have the purest and most readily available supply. I pay, he provides. The transaction profits both."

Caleb reached out for his tea – the host's attention suddenly fixed! – and raised the cup to his mouth.

"Oh dear," he said, sipless, and holding its bowl to the light, "I seem to have smudged your china."

"It is of no consequence."

"If you but knew."

"Are you not to drink, Sergeant? You'll have it cold."

"I'm not sure. Its scent is a little… peculiar."

"I'm afraid I can't help you there. One's olfactory perception, you understand," he wafted circling fingers under his nose by way of explanation, "the gas."

"It smells uncommonly sweet." The cup and saucer were returned to the balance of the chair's armrest.

"You asked for sugar."

"My son has been taken," he said.

"It is a terrible thing."

"I doubt you could begin to imagine."

"And how is the investigation progressing?"

"I know who took him, if that is your meaning."

"Really?" Septimus looked back from the business of a refill. "That is quite singular news."

"Do you know maestro Keats?"

"You suspect a dead poet?" Contents downed in a swallow.

"I greatly admire his work, and philosophy. And if I may paraphrase," Caleb paused to stare lost into the whitening coals, "he invites us to act upon the truth of our pulses."

The china separated into a thousand sharps and shards as it crashed against the hearth. Its liquid, rejected and vital, threw itself clear of the impact and slipped for safety to the gutters gridding the tiles. From there, the slow drip of evidence soaked under the fender and away into the rug, to the thirsty crannies of the cellar below.

This damage was irreversible.

The cup's plunge was precipitated by Caleb's abrupt hand as it snatched for leverage against the armrest. That same hand was now one of a pair crushing Septimus's throat.

"Where have you put him?"

"I have no idea what you are talking about…" was what only the host heard as reply.

Contorted backwards over the sideboard, the full weight of his assailant pressing down on him, stoppering his lungs, Septimus had been reduced to conversing in primal grunts and groans, and a frenzied code thudded out with thrashing heels against the furniture.

"That tea smells of abductions!"

And then, swift as it began, it was over.

Only the fight for air remained. Septimus the undertaker, face scarlet-blue, slumped racked to the floor and whooped in crashing, spluttering lungfuls.

Across the room, Caleb had staggered clear and was doubled over, deprived, hands clinging to knees, cheeks flushed and wet where streams had washed at the quills of his moustache.

Slowly, achingly, his opponent scaled the sideboard and lay hot across its mahogany length. Face pressed flat, his gasping grew fleeting clouds against the varnish, the scope of each diminishing in turn; his bloodshot, doused landscape oscillating as he alternated cheeks to make the most of the cooler degrees.

By the third turn Caleb was glowering black-eyed over him, invading his sphere, his living room. The shock jolted Septimus to his feet. Risen, yet unready. "Enough…" Hands held in submission.

Recognising his plea had been accepted, he wiped the froth from his mouth and perfunctorily brushed down his dusted front. "I think you have made a terrible mistake," he heaved.

"And I think not." Caleb retorted.

With what remained of his strength Caleb seized his opponent and shouldered him hard into the armchair. Fixing his glare, he slipped out of his jacket, halved it with a forearm and rested it on his seatback. Then he took his place, to no protest, in the mighty Queen Anne.

"Let me tell you what I know."

It was then I relayed, breath by scouring breath, my painstaking research of the previous weeks.

– We live in days of discovery – said I.

He languished unimpressed, soaked in whiskey sweat, as I told how I had enlisted a new partner in my enterprise: forensics.

– Are you aware of the minor case of Harry Jackson and the stolen billiards balls? – asked I.

Of course, he was not. That was why he had never worn gloves. Why solicit attention on a warm evening?

I described the individuality of fingerprints and how I had painstakingly collected examples from every surface of Christian's room, left untouched for his return. There were but two sets that could not be confirmed. A child's – clearly those of my son – and an adult, then unknown. An adult who steadied himself with a palm as he signed himself 'Critch' on the wall above Christian's bed.

Then appeared the bloody clue on the door at the girl's home. I took its timber and balanced its stains of fingers and thumbs against those in my own house. Identical! I returned one late night to dab the father and confirm what I already knew – Critch was not he.

But now some progress had been made. I had proof the same individual had snatched our children.

Accounting for his continued presence, and the fact that the girl was taken on a Sunday when a stranger would have little business in town and none such was reported, I surmised Critch most likely lived among us. Yet despite my exhortations, my superiors stubbornly turned their ears to my scheme to fingerprint the populace.

It was then I formed the scheme of the meeting in the town hall. I reminded Septimus, lest the evening not mean as much to him as to me, that he declined a biscuit – on account of a toothache, I now deduce – but happily accepted a cup of tea.

– You read the leaves, did you? – asked he, insouciant like.

– No – says I – I read the china.

In the coming days I worked sleeplessly through that stack of used crockery diverted to my home. And then came the breakthrough for which my prayers had passed unheeded.

– A beautiful impression, most likely the left hand, on the underside of a saucer from the receptacle labelled 'E' – said I.

There were five sets of crockery contained within that division and, of those, two, I realised immediately, belonged to the aged and infirm.

Just three remained who could be responsible for the matching fingerprint and, given I had their initial, I knew exactly who they were. But, which of the three?

It was then I addressed the issue of the blood, chancing that some little bluster would remain undetected.

I told him how the intruder at the girl's house had suffered a nip from the jagged pane, sufficient for a trail of spotlets to map the route through the home.

– Correct me if I go wrong – said I – but entry is always taken in the solitude of the rear, whereupon the back door is unlocked from within. But what had escaped me, even in my own home, was that the front is also unlatched to provide alternative flight should circumstances necessitate. It is only then the stairs are climbed.

He turned from me as I maintained my rumination.

– Little could Critch know it, but that last taunt on the sunlit door was a calling card as likely as leaving a name and address.

I paused for this information to take hold then précised, to blank visage, the excellent blood typing work of Landsteiner.

– That blood could belong to any creature, to a rat trying to escape that filthy little hovel for a better life in the sewers, said he...

"...And I suppose this blood will tell you who did it and why and when," said Septimus. "The blood is of the type AB, isolated only last year by Decastrello and Sturli. I have made it my business to know these things."

"And?"

"It belongs to just three per cent of the population."

Septimus snorted "There must be ten thousand people in this town, that's still hundreds. Hardly conclusive."

"What I required was a sample of an individual's own blood. Having such would enable me to make an exact correlation." And the sergeant held back a blush.

"In that case, you cannot claim the blood matches mine. I have given you none."

"True enough…" Caleb, fixed on his opponent, dug blindly into his waistcoat. A hand reached out. On the palm rested a slip of paper. "But you left this behind this morning."

The red-rooted molar was re-wrapped in silence, and the package returned to the safe keeping of the waistcoat's innards.

"The blood on your tooth – and Ratchett will give testament it is yours – is the blood on the door. My tests prove it beyond misgiving."

Septimus rolled his tongue into the fresh, tell-tale hollow in the maxilla. "Bravo, my dear Sergeant! Evangelised with the missionary's zeal."

"Doubt it not, science shall one day make gods of us all."

The face opposite was a study in emptiness: no shock, no fear, nor the sudden realisation that all was over. Instead, he spoke calmly. "If you are so convinced of your science why did you not end me just now?"

"You have something I want. You have my son."

*

There was a gentle tapataptap at the door.

"One second!"

The shower of scribbles swamping the desk was hastily

rearranged to resemble order and the Anglepoise returned to perpendicular.

"Come in!"

A head appeared around the door. "Still working, love?"

Pippa nodded. "History project."

"Something burning in here?"

"Bastet," said Pippa, glancing in the curled cat's direction. "Knocked over the lamp while I was downstairs and scorched some paper."

"Really? I'll check the smoke alarms in the morning. I'm doing hot chocolate?"

"Yes please, Dad."

"I'll get changed then bring it up. Another hour and lights out?"

"Okay."

The door was almost closed.

"Dad?"

The head popped back.

"Yes, love?"

"Love you."

Chapter Twenty-Nine

"Hold on, hold on. Let's have a minute."

The carriers made a scalene of the wall, floor and picture then slid down either side, the sweat pressed startlingly cold against their backs.

"It's heavier than it looks this. What's it painted on, lead?" Roland was in his pocket for his inhaler. "I'm perspiring like a pig, me."

By a margin of two to nil (it would have been three had *he* been asked) they had voted to take the most direct means of escape and were now halfway along the single corridor that edged the length of the building. Down there – in the hunkering dark – was the entrance, the souvenir shop with its come-hither windows, and the first of their freedoms.

Nelson, knees up and arms rested on top, spoke first. "You all right?"

There was a pause: he was holding his breath while the Salbutamol mined his lungs. "Nothing a lifetime of aquarobics wouldn't cure."

"I couldn't have done this without you, you know. I'm sure Sheldan will understand."

"I hope so. I could be waist-deep in my surfies now, me, surrounded by head-turners from the pie fanciers' association." And he let out a puff of disbelief.

"I didn't think you'd come."

"I almost didn't then this happened…" he pointed to his big eye, "and I thought in for a penny, in for a pounding…"

Scrunched into the wall, each receded into a moment's reflection.

"On the other hand, I knew *you'd* be here," Roland restarted. "That was a pretty determined face you were wearing this afternoon."

"What did Pippa say? After I'd gone, I mean?"

"She won't think for a minute you've gone through with it. She seemed pretty convinced she'd put an end to it. And, to be fair, I may have given the slight impression that I was backing out, too. She'll think I'm tucked up in bed now with a milkshake and Benjamin Zephaniah. I love saying that name, me."

"You think so?"

"Oh yeah. She might be clever, but I wouldn't say she was *streetwise*."

"How do you mean?"

"You know the type. Probably puts her middle initial on her schoolbooks. And on her diary, too. She's a cert to keep a diary." Roland made an air label with his hand, "Pippa *M* Hill," he boomed like a newsreel. "Pippa *Margery* Hill."

"Is that her middle name?"

"I don't know, but sounds like it should be."

"She's grandmaster bright though, isn't she?"

"It's all from books." Roland made it sound like cheating. "She reads all these facts and then she knows about stuff. It's not rocket science. Ask yourself the following: would she be able to break in here after closing? I'm not sure which encyclopaedia she'll find that in."

"She *will* be furious about this," said Nelson, shifting position.

"You like her, don't you?"

"She's all right. Don't you?"

"I think she's the poshest person in the world. Have you ever seen anyone want a knife and fork to eat a sausage roll? She'll not be mixing with the likes of us when she's older, that's for sure. It'll be brainiacs and billionaires…"

Though the gloom had taken some of the margin's finer detail, had Roland been entombed in blindfolds he still could have made out the disconsolate wilt next door.

"She likes you, though," he added, quickly, comfortingly, despite his suspicion that Pippa was most likely a lesbian (and his inner eye flashed to a deserted table *per due* at Pizza'Ere).

"You reckon?"

"Course she does. Whenever I see her, she's always looking for you, or asking about you."

"Really?

"Yes, really."

"Oh." And Nelson briefly took to a cosy silence. "Are we ready, then?" he asked, revived.

"One last puff." A quick shake and icy white was inhaled. A ten-second breath was released through a wobble of lips and Roland was on all fours to lever himself up. Both back on feet, the watery wood of the frame was seized, and fingers found purchase among its ripples and eddies.

"Bend knees," counselled Master Grange, a veteran of fish tanks and sawdusty hutches in Pikka Pet's plate glass.

"Is he the right way round?"

"Are you having me on?"

Heads leaned in.

He was not.

"How would you like to be bounced around on your side?"

The painting was downed then re-hoisted after a quarter-turn tip.

"Ready now?"

"This way," and Nelson led the stuttery march backwards, glancing over his shoulder every few steps.

"Cap approaching!"

A giant flat cap – an art college tribute to the trade union movement – lurked ahead. Circumference of a minor roundabout, the headgear had gained legendary status on the day of the school trip as the refuge for a furtive heavy petting session. The culprits, shamefaced, sore-lipped and half-dressed, were detained by security until personally collected by Mr Bridge and Miss Lyttle. *You have to admire their imagination!* Now, rounding its metres of tent pole and tweed – 'take the *first* exit' – the trio edged beyond, and the home run beckoned.

"Nearly there," stuttered Roland.

"And then the marathon begins."

"How long do you think it will take, once we're out?"

"About an hour, I reckon."

"Will that give us enough time?"

"What time is it now?" asked Nelson.

"If I take my hand away, I'll drop the picture. You'll have to use your superpower."

"I'd say it's about nine o'clock."

"Righ… t."

Up ahead, only fifty metres separated them from liberation. The cloak of the darkened streets, the darts between doorways, the tin can sneak of cobbled ginnels, the fondling mist of kiss-me-quick car parks and the offhand stares of grille-blinked stores, all tease and no touch. All that. Waiting for them. Just down there.

But down there, also – muffled by the grim and cryptic gloom – outside was wanting in. Keys were rattling hard and anxious and *furious* in a lock.

Chapter Thirty

His first instinct was to leap to his feet and bound the staircase screaming out rescue, yet he remained unnervingly still, turned to the fire. Locked.

"I know what you are thinking, Sergeant." Though, in truth, Septimus had anticipated much more than this stage fright.

"You are thinking," the undertaker presumed to go on, *"I will chase up there this minute and charge every door until I find him and then never let him from my sight so long as I live."*

Caleb offered no sound.

"My dear Sergeant, it was never going to be as easy as that."

Will he not reply?

"You have to understand my position. I cannot be too careful. People could turn up here... *unannounced*... at all hours, strewing all manner of accusations. There has to be an insurance."

Septimus searched in vain for an intimation, a clue to his own future. The wet, blinkless eyes. The arrow of their empty gaze.

Is it the poker on which he is meditating?

The host pointedly scoured the splashing dagger of its tip; weighed the possibility of its shaft, flames wrapping shadows around its worn edges, crashing fierce across skullbone. "You are not scheming anything foolish, are you? Only I know the where and how of safe passage. Hurting me will mean he is lost."

Nothing. *Nothing?*

"I shall require an accommodation. You'll have to let me away, of course. Or my mind may change."

"Four returned is a fair exchange for one let go."

At last!

"Is that a proposition?"

"I must have all four."

"Then it is agreed?"

"I am a man of my word."

"I believe you are, Caleb."

Septimus raised himself pained for the climb, Caleb following close.

There was a moment at the sideboard. "I'm going to have a reviver. I don't suppose I can tempt you?" A companion beaker was held up in emboldened jest.

"I think I might take a small one."

Septimus let go a crooked smile. "I do hope I have not lured you into sin, Sergeant. That would not do."

The tot, fingers clawed about the rim, was handed over. Caleb swirled and sniffed at the amber then it was gone, sluiced hard past virgin tastebuds.

"You have me, Sergeant. I accept that." He trusted Caleb was listening, despite the faceful of aftertaste. "But," he added, "I should like to be sure that we are settled."

"We have agreed terms," the hoarse reply.

"I rather hoped we had."

"Then, shall we go?" Caleb was distractedly balling shirt sleeves at his elbows.

"As you wish," though there was a new trepidation in Septimus's voice as the curtain was raised on those marbled arms of the law. "Can I interest you in fruit, Sergeant?" Caleb shook his head, but the undertaker's own hand dipped into the passing bowl as he edged towards the darkened hallway. "This way."

"Wait!"

Septimus stopped dead in his stride.

Was this it? Fight? He had waltzed enough for one night. The alternative? His legs would never carry the door.

Edging slowly around – and expecting the worst of those hewn limbs – the undertaker found a glass thrust swift at his throat. Hands were raised in surrender and the echo began, "Hurting me will—"

"I should like another one of these, *please*."

"Certainly, Sergeant! I think I shall join you."

Both draughts replenished, they moved tenderly away. At the exit to the sitting room Caleb lagged momentarily to take in the landscapes on the wall. Buckling strides later he was back in tandem, foot for foot, whiskey leaping rhythmically from its glass to burnish the toes of his shoes, and desperately wishing his eyes had just deceived him.

To the staircase, each step groaning as it was pressed from its drowse, and they found the waiting summit.

A ladder!

Heads looked to the hatch in the ceiling.

"There," Septimus whispered, jabbing heavenwards. "They are there."

Caleb jolted to rush past but was blocked before the first rung. "Be warned," Septimus hissed, "there is a mechanism guarding the entrance that I alone can negotiate. Intruders will find only mute witnesses. I will pull you up. Presently. But first I need you to see this."

"That can wait!"

"And hazard the diminution of your full regard? No, it will not do."

Caleb was directed left into a room of shrouds. Pallid linen cloths shawled the furniture like ghouls and heavy bloomed curtains were drawn tight together so their flare overlapped and gathered on the floor. The door clicked behind and Septimus was in, swiping at the material like an illusionist at tablecloths. A chair materialised. "Take a seat, Sergeant." Then a desk was conjured and Septimus rested into it, half perched, arms folded, glass glowing wordless on a writing pad.

Caleb took his place tardily. "If we don't get to, I am likely to change my mind."

"I shouldn't do that if I were you."

"So, what is it you required me to see?"

"What are your thoughts, Sergeant, on forbidden fruit?"

"What?"

Septimus put his hand into the bulge of his pocket and pulled. "Do you know what this is?"

"It is an orange."

"Almost. It's a *Maltese* orange. Have you ever tasted one? Delicious. Shipped from the heat of southern Europe and scandalously expensive. You should have taken one when it was proffered."

"You waylay me to boast of fruit?"

"Not quite." Taloned fingernails picked at sovereigns of peel and, sparkled against the black of his suit, bursts of exotic oil began to perfume the room. "Do you not wonder how a lowly undertaker can indulge in such extravagance? You are a solver: in that is the motivation."

"Money—"

"Bravo! Yet another of my vices. I must be quite the disappointment."

Septimus bit hard into the wet flesh and his grinning chin trickled ruddy juice, dabbed dry with the tip of crisp white handkerchief. "'*Much have I travell'd in the realms of gold / And many goodly states and kingdoms seen'*. You see I, too, know your poet. Yet unlike him I have no intention of passing in penury. I have become a man of certain means over the years."

"Over the years?"

"Oh yes, please don't take me for a neophyte at this caper."

Caleb fleetingly eyed the door yet remained seated.

"A wise decision. Do not forget, I am the spider here." There was a deliberate, teasing, tormenting wait as Septimus slurped noisily at the segment dregs. The fruit finally parched, he rolled his tongue around his lips and rocked upright. The handkerchief was pincered again and rubbed around sticky fingers. "I brought you in here to gather your thoughts on…"

In two strides the undertaker was at the three-legged phantom in the corner, its linen raked away.

"…this!"

"What has that to do with our arrangement?" asked Caleb.

"Take a closer look." Septimus had now shifted viper-fast to thrash open the curtains. There was no light to come rushing through, just the glassy reflection of the glow within. He nuzzled the bare window, hands blinkering his face to shade the room, breath misting the cold glass: searching, expectant. "You won't be able to fully appreciate it in this light," the distracting pane was informed. "And it is still to be inscribed, but I cannot deny it as one of my best."

With no one yet to see outside, Septimus wheeled to face the noiseless room. "Oh, there you are. I thought for a moment I was talking alone. What do you think?" and he nodded gravely in the direction of the tripod.

Caleb, gone from his seat, stepped closer.

"There is craft in all, would you not agree?"

The voice was so near in his ear, so heavy with menace, that the officer was not sure if he had uttered the words himself. He scanned the oiled canvas, a futile search for a name – *his name* – among lifeless rows of unreadable grey.

"It is fixed exactly from a viewpoint down there…" Septimus had slipped back to the window. "Please, come see for yourself."

Caleb knew the location well enough; he did not need the window to tell him.

On the tremulous walk to the pane, he resolved the choreography of how this charade would be played out. And he was glad now for the destiny he had just administered.

Taking his turn to peer through a tunnel of fingers, Caleb gazed heartbroken into the night, out to the mourning moon and its ashen caul, down to the veil of methane wisp and the soiled earth, dark as death, beneath. Crouching somewhere in that distance, plain as day, the painting's wretched reality.

*

It was then he felt the wind rush from his body, learned the splintering of rib, burned with the searing heat of ferocity. He dropped to his knees and caught fleetingly the reflection of his assailant, standing roar behind. Rolling lungless from the black glass, Caleb crumpled to the skirting board. Now, Septimus was towering over him, polished boot pinning writhing trousers; a walking stick, dull and heavy-sphered at the top, swaying upturned from his whitened grip. With a sneer, the leadened orb swung pitilessly high. A futile arm was raised instinctively as the cudgel whispered harshly down. Then, the rifling snap of impact…

The strangest thing was the lack of blood. His face was a drench of panting pain and eyes rimmed red – whenever were they otherwise? – but not a drop of blood. At last, Caleb gathered himself to look at his bare wound. The brunt had been borne just below the roll of his sleeve. Porcelain bone was through like the last of a Sunday carcass and the peeping giblets pulsed yellow, grey and blue. As he reached to bring the elbow to the comfort of his body, what he had once claimed as his forearm danced like a wrung neck at a gundog's mouth. All this, and yet not a drop.

Then the room trembled as he bit down on his lip and growled as hard and low as his shattered ribs would tolerate.

*

332

Peering down curiously at his handiwork, Septimus bounced the inverted walking cane into the cup of his palm. "A little advice, Sergeant," he said, matter of fact, "never turn your back on a man with everything to lose."

The club was returned to the lean of the desk, and Caleb's chair – so accommodatingly warmed – was dragged close to the squirming heap. Septimus eyed his glinting pocket watch then made himself comfortable.

"Slight change of plan," he began. "As I have you, and a little time, this would seem an apposite juncture to divulge a little of the splendour of my industry. I am not entirely certain you will want to hear of it, but I could endure a telling; there are so few opportunities in polite company. And I shall play fair. Should I begin to bore" – a smirk at his own finger-wriggling exemplum – "simply raise your right hand."

An agonied grunt from the floor.

"Oh, do indulge me, Sergeant. I should very much like to tell, for I was not always the gentleman of refinement now before you."

Septimus cleared his throat to the tips of his fingers. "To the outset then. When I was a young man I had no money and fewer possessions. All that you see here today would have been as alien to me as the canals of Mars.

"And yet the catalyst for my climb, or – as you may have it – my descent, was not the finance. My initiation was a gratis performance. Close to home. *Very* close to home. They say you never forget your first, and even now the abject terror on his crapulent face seldom fails to provoke a smile." And he drifted momentarily, lost in a bludgeoning rhapsody. "A grand pleasure that was, after all those years. The provocation was revenge, but I found to my delight that there was, indeed, some little money in it and I was quickly – and willingly – seduced by a world of rare amusements."

Without warning, Septimus suddenly lashed forward in the chair, face beating down on his quarry, teeth gritted, flecks of spittle pocking the sergeant's features. "Do you know what I detest above all? Snobbery." Syllables extruded through lupine snarl. "I shall be frank, I was not born with a silver spoon, far from it. But no matter how hard you work, how hard you strive, there are those to wilfully exclude you upon some spurious reckoning or other. '*Know your place, boy!*'" he howled.

Septimus eased back, leg returned over knee, casually picking at a stray weave on his trousers. "So," he went on, "I was now my own man with income from my uncle's premises, and I took my rightful place at the functions to which my new position entitled me. However, my welcome from the snobs of provincial society proved somewhat chill. To them, I was yet the delivery boy. At every turn I saw their looks, suffered their insinuations. I realised then that what I needed was more – enough to buy and sell the lot of them. That would command their respect.

"Serendipity came calling one evening when I chanced upon a conversation between two of the town's more refined gentlemen. Their discourse was, shall we say, of an earthy piquancy. Perhaps I should have been repulsed, but my initial thought was of advantage. From their lordly references I made note of higher connections and saw a course to more well-fed fish.

"I let it be known I was on to their entertainment, upon which they had the temerity to threaten my person! Well,

I became all working class and told them instead I would be willing to supply their particular wants in return for remittance from their betters. And I sealed the contract by offering the pair a skim of my fee in gratitude for sparing my ''*umble neck, gentlemen*'.

"Outwardly, they played suspicious, but I gleaned they were not displeased to hear this. After some little shallying an instruction was placed on behalf of an organisation they named The Orbis. That night I walked over the fields clutching the phial of chloroform provided and took the first. There was no plan, an unlocked door deserves all the trouble it invites. And, apart from the late hours, the work did not bother me. This was my opportunity to accrue some handsome funds.

"Recompense from The Orbis arrived as promised. These were, after all, men of honour, and once the neighbouring hue and cry died away I was engaged again to sate their appetite for tender meats. Of course, mistakes were inevitable while I learned my trade – overdoses, sightings in the shadows, bothersome struggles, flights from wakened households. And my two blood-sucking lampreys still demanding their slice!

"Before long one of them disappeared and other, fearing the same, swam away to his masters. The Orbis was persuaded it was time for me to move on and I found myself rent to the highest bidder.

"Moving from town to town I quickly and – permit me this little boast, Sergeant – deservedly made a reputation among certain underground fellowships, all coils within The Orbis. This brotherhood exists, Sergeant. Do not console yourself this is all myth and mirrors. There is fundamental truth here.

"And what of the goods I collected? Let us say they were spirited abroad to new lives with the wealthy childless, or are waiting yet inside a mountain, or beneath a castle. The Orbis was glad to pay and what did I care? Their business was none of my business. If someone had offered more to keep me warm by the fire, that's what I would have done."

Septimus lifted his gaze.

"You seem vexed, Sergeant. Does the nakedness of my enterprise unsettle? You should be proud: just look at what you have made." And he held arms wide as Caleb spat froth to the floor.

"Perhaps I should have furnished you, rather, with a tale of the loss of some child of my own, 'If I can't have mine, why should you have yours?' and so forth, but an infamous deception that would be." He paused a moment, becalmed. "There are more than enough anyway. And if *I* may paraphrase a favourite, a little culling decreases the surplus population."

"*Goods?*" A groan from the heap.

Septimus again leaned in, his ear at Caleb's contorted face. "Goods? Did you say? Really, you must try to speak up. That's right, '*goods*'. I fail to see that I am different from any purveyor of wares. Are we not all capitalists?"

"They are our children."

"Well, you should have a care with them!"

Septimus returned to seated and fixed an icy glare at Caleb. "Please refrain from these melodramatics, Sergeant. You disturb my train of thought." Flat hands were brought together and eyes closed, as if in prayer. "...And so, I was brought here last year. I was not initially aware there was a vacancy for an undertaker. Neither was he. But what better occupation for burying secrets? Splendid accommodation, too. Worth a good deal, wouldn't you say? It was signed over to me as soon as Mr Mort *relinquished* his position."

"This shall all be evidence," Caleb whispered.

"Evidence indeed of wanton injustice. It pains me greatly that my genius receives such little accolade. The indifference troubles me."

"What?"

"You are familiar with the work of Miss Mary Ann Cotton?"

"What man in my line would not be?"

"Of course you are, as is the entire country. Took twenty at least. Adults, children, her own babies."

"A vile individual."

Septimus distractedly rhymed off the ditty, a waving hand to conduct the beat:

> *Mary Ann Cotton,*
> *She's dead and she's rotten,*
> *She lies in her bed*
> *With her eyes wide open.*

"She is remembered! The entire population could recite that!" Harmony abandoned his voice as quickly as it appeared. "She gets immortality, yet that slut is no more worthy than me. Where is my jaunty little verse? Where are the faces cowering in their beds at the mention of my name? After all that I've achieved! *That's* why I leave my calling card."

"Never before on the door."

"Ah, that last episode was among my foremost. She was

very young to attend a funeral, do you not think? Imagine she had not been permitted to go, not been *noticed*. Is it not a curiosity how great consequences hinge upon trifles?

"Anyway, to the scene. I'd sliced my arm, the goods had begun to revive, the house to stir. What a squeal from the staircase! In all haste I thought I would have to leave unheralded. Then, at the threshold, I felt my own wet blood on my fingertips…

"The odds must have been one hundred to one against that night, yet I succeeded. Why shouldn't people eulogise, gape their mouths in admiration? It deserved – *I deserve* – better."

"And the pain of those left behind?"

"Pain was my bedfellow for years! Life *is* pain."

"So, who is your Critch?" The voice clearer now.

"I note you are a little recovered, Sergeant. Try to remain unstirred. In my experience, shock is a marvel at the suppression of suffering. It is, however, an ephemeral. The agony will return, mark my words. And I fear" – and he brushed the length of his own jacketed forearm – "*that* will have to come off."

Septimus left his chair to pace the room, a hand on his chin playing at the sticky tale of fruit. "To answer your query," he continued. "At first I left nothing; I was meticulous in avoiding intimations. But after a while, I began to comprehend the impotency of any pursuers, present company excepted, of course. Then I happened across a group singing Cotton's rhyme in the street and felt a pang that was both provocation and envy. Returned to my lodgings, I recalled a previous caper in a pleasant little house in a hovel of a town. In the playroom,

I'd spotted a rudimentary paint set and easel, and it caused me thought of how to claim some glory for my exertions. I could not give my own name, evidently, for the crafting would be quickly doomed, even the dullards of the constabulary would have had my collar before long. So, I meditated on the nature of the role I had taken in order to accumulate my funds. And there and then, with a little clever letterplay on my part, *Critch* was born. When the opportunity was next presented, the artist in me could not resist and I boldly daubed the new moniker for all to wonder. A number of towns, each unaware of their singular connection, have since made acquaintance with my darling Critch. Once I am satisfied, the dots will be joined and all will be out. I mean to outdo Mrs Cotton, so help me. And I shan't desist until my fame eclipses the best of hers."

"It that all? Just *Critch*?"

"There is more: a forename. But I find we are no longer on those terms, are we, Sergeant?"

Septimus's wandering had brought him to rest at the tripod in the corner. He seized the canvas by its frame and carried it to the window, where the diminished form of Caleb had now stilled, arm cradled, eyelids squeezing out the gathering hurt.

"You failed to offer an opinion earlier: what make you of this?"

The eyes slitted wearily. "I know where it is."

"But *what* is it?"

"A daub. A souvenir."

"Almost again, Sergeant, but I do consider 'souvenir' rather tawdry. Puts me in mind of those hideous seaside cards of which the numbed masses are so fond. This..." and he pushed it forward so Caleb's contours could almost touch the rise and fall of the oils. "This is a map. A treasure map." The relish reflex flushed his voice. "An aide memoire for my return."

"Return?"

"In these uncertain times I have made gold the preferred reward from my sponsors. I keep some at hand for expenses" – and he pulled at his mouth to reveal three molared nuggets – "but I required somewhere safe to store my fortune. *This* is the tale of where that fortune is located. I have made others, too, illustrating my ports of call, but what is interred there is of value only to the worms."

"If you have this fortune, why continue?"

"Why indeed! I have enough to outbid any of those petty bourgeoisies who thought me beneath them. I could go back tomorrow, demolish their ten-a-penny establishments and pitch them onto the streets."

And he waited a while to watch over those weeping evictions, their bundles of rags, the wretched pleas for forgiveness.

"But not just yet. My sights have raised since the outset. I intend to purchase an estate and inherit the title it confers. Only then I shall return, like Augustus into Rome."

"Unless there is a second, better estate to be had?"

"Finding a penurious aristocrat is hardly the quest for the Holy Grail."

"And The Orbis?" Caleb had levered himself against the wall, legs outstretched.

"What of it?"

"Will they let you retire as you please?"

"Why not? Are we all not in thrall to money and repute?"

Caleb began to laugh: an amalgam of anger, agony, loathing.

"An amusement, Sergeant?"

"It is nothing, really." Caleb snorted softly. "I was merely contemplating the pristine gold in your mouth, and the irony that it will be a rotten tooth that has you dangling."

Septimus played a smirk, lips tight.

"Have you forgotten the rest of Cotton's rhyme?" the officer went on.

"Certainly not. Shall we?"

Discordant voices railed:

> *Sing, sing, oh what can I sing*
> *Mary Ann Cotton is tied up with string*
> *Where? Where? Up in the air*
> *Selling black puddings a penny a pair…*

"She hangs," said Caleb as the ditty faded. "As will you."

"They knew you were close."

"*They?*"

"You don't know? How delightful! The watcher watched. Podmore Street and all that. They told me it was time to leave, found me a new destination with fellow pilgrims. I have already sold all I hold here to an idiot cousin. So, my dear Caleb, what are you to do? Arrest me? Take me into custody, make me your honoured guest, but they will not let me fall. Their own necks depend on it. Even an idealist such as you can see that every path leads me away."

"And what of our bargain?"

"Oh yes, I almost forgot. The four." Septimus had ambled across to the writing desk and the detritus of the fruit eaten earlier. "Would now be the time?"

Without pausing for reply, he spread his handkerchief across his palm and corralled to the edge of the desk the molehill of peel, where it tipped into the silk. The cloth was bundled up and returned to his trousers. "I do so hate mess, Sergeant, don't you? You strike me as a man who prefers the neat and tidy."

He returned to the window and dropped to his haunches, straddling splayed legs. Caleb leaned about him, hoping to catch sight of the door closed on the attic beyond.

"I have a confession to make," Septimus whispered, "I needed the ladder merely to retrieve a few items. There is no one there. And so, despite all your science – your *forensics* – your case is considerably weakened. You have no body. And *nobody*. If you want to see them, you would be better served looking through the window."

Septimus waited, disappointed, for outrage. Instead, there was laughter. "And now?" he sneered.

"You cannot see it, can you?" said Caleb.

"See what?"

"Your boasts of wealth, connection, claims to better station. They are all veneer. They will never regard you as equal. You have been used and when your time arrives, they will deny you." He grabbed at Septimus's lapel and pulled him close. "The clothes may be finer, you may dowse yourself in expensive scent, but you remain their delivery boy."

"That we shall see," he replied, rising. "My employers are above such middle-class pettifoggery. And more, they are commendably catholic in all outlook and tastes. And in their requests. Male, female, any colour, any creed. Godless, pious, Jewish…" He looked hard into Caleb's eyes. "…*Christian.*"

Outrage now arrived. A swiping leg whipped the undertaker to the floor and two sharp body blows hit home before Septimus climbed back astride to grip bronco tight. Pressing hard into the crooks of Caleb's elbows, he dipped beyond the woodpeckering headbutts and bites that ended, all too soon, with his opponent slumped exhausted, a rocking lather of tears and snot and drool.

"Well, this has been so very entertaining," said Septimus in a voice bubbling fury. "I think an ovation is in order, don't you?"

In one movement, he had slipped his hands from elbows to wrists and enforced a macabre round of applause: one wearied hand offering minimal resistance; the right, none at all.

Caleb contorted his face into an empty scream and slumped over to the floor, racked. Septimus returned to his feet. "Really, this will not do," His rightside ribs took an exploratory rub then he recovered his hair to its point. "Just look at you. Sobbing and blubbering. Pitiful."

A drawer in the desk was released and a nest of tubes and cylinders gathered. "Would you take some of this? Nitrous oxide, the portable device of which Ratchett spoke. And don't believe for an instant his petitions of innocence. That's the trouble with chloroform. So difficult to administer the optimum dose. Not enough and the goods resist; too much and my evening has been a waste. *This* should make my work so much easier."

The mouthpiece was offered at arm's length. "Try a little science, Sergeant. It will take away the pain. You may even die laughing."

The pocket watch was studied. "I'll take your lack of response as a 'No'. Your funeral," he said, distracted.

Septimus took his frockcoat from a wardrobe and pulled it on. "Freedom is a wonderful thing, is it not, Sergeant?" A hat was selected from a shelf. "My escort to the train will be here presently."

Eyes on Caleb, he reached behind for his whiskey and necked the beaker in a single swallow. Then he strode over, fixing sleeves, to crouch again across the deformed figure. Inquisitive hands stroked the drench of Caleb's face. "I could tell you that I hate to do this." *Searching*. "But neither of us…" *Caressing*. "…believes that to be the truth." Suddenly a clench, mantis quick. Caleb's legs began to rattle convulsively, more in gesture than expectation. The grip whitened about the throat and all that remained was a final show of enmity. With the last of his breath Caleb raised the spike of his shattered arm, pulled aside the dead hand and forced a stab of exposed bone into Septimus's gaping mouth. Splinters clattered among the bite and slashed at the inner cheeks, yet still the strangle held. And soon the jabbing slowed, and jaws closed tight and firm for Septimus to suck dreamily at the creamy marrow, that salted ooze.

The stump slipped free. He was tired now. Too tired.

"*Fetch me, boy. Fetch…*" Caleb shrunk and sagged, dead air clamped within a lifeless body. Where once he would have hoped for the brilliance of salvation, gloom was all he found. And the gloom deepened. And deepened…

knock…

Knock, knock…

Caleb widened his eyes to blinding light.

Heaven? Only if earthly hell was part of the bargain. He was flat on his back blinking up at the ceiling rose.

Knock, knock, knock!

Outside.

He made to move, but his legs were paralysed under dead weight. He raised his aching head and found Septimus, face flat to the floor, slumped deep over his lower half.

KNOCKNOCKNOCK.

He peeled the body aside and a freed foot, fizzing paraesthesia, pushed it drunkenly clear. A confusion of limbs schemed to draw Caleb grimacing up the wall where, flat against the flock, he peered around the rise of the window frame. In the dark below, two hatted figures waited for response at the rear door. Lips spoke together – the words too far away – then the callers, attracted by the light at the open curtains, arched upwards. Caleb ducked away and hoped they had not seen him, though in that split second he had sighted them. He suppressed the urge to look again, to make certain. That would have been a redundant risk: he knew those faces well enough.

He waited, pressed.

Moments later, the swing of a gate excited a second glimpse. The two figures were swallowed up. A snap of leather and their carriage wheeled away.

They would be back, they could not live with the uncertainty. It was twenty minutes to the railway station and return.

Caleb staggered over to Septimus's limp form and resisted the urge to scuff it black and blue. "A little advice," he wheezed. "Never turn your back on a man with *nothing* to lose."

Kneeling alongside, he allowed sour breath to rise and fall lightly against his own cheek. A wrist was raised to confirm a pulse and, as he did so, its shirt sleeve fell back to reveal a ragged-red scar, the wound from the rear window.

Arrest him? Caleb was in no state to shift the body from the house. And, even if he made it to the cells, what he had just seen assured him the door would not stay locked for long.

Finish him? He had once vowed to tear the fiend limb from limb, but now – now – he found that cold-blood was not in him.

Instead, his sound arm reached to his back pocket (he always knew it would) and retrieved a slim, hide-bound volume. He placed it carefully onto the floor and flicked at that precious parchment until the Book of Shadows butterflied out at the spot brooded over a thousand times.

"You crave immortality? Then you shall have it."

He fumbled for his penknife and, with his teeth, drew out its blade.

And in the room below, the grandfather clock began its chime of twelve.

*

Caleb steadied himself against the banister as he retreated the stairs, though they were easier to negotiate than the ladders moments earlier. There would be less than five minutes before the carriage returned frustrated, and on the chance the two visitors waylaid him on his journey home, he had determined to leave empty-handed.

What has been done will do for now.

At the foot of the steps, he turned to the parlour to retrieve his jacket. There was no need for anyone to know of his presence this evening. When the tweed was lifted from the back of the chair, he watched a dark hair, stiletto straight – one of the monster's – drift against the lace of the antimacassar, as it must have done that night in the girl's bedroom. Grimacing, Caleb slung the garment over his shoulder then found the fruit bowl to pocket the three lemons he had earlier noted. A last cast about and he made for his overcoat and cap.

Reaching the margin of the room, he halted once more at the landscapes on the wall. There had been another, a fog-bound morass, passed on the stairs. These two were side by side. The first, an unknown copse in an unfamiliar wood; the other, a nameless, hope-less moor. Searching their oils, his thoughts plunged sheer and sharp to Podmore Street the evening after his town hall appeal. Those lost souls the medium had channelled. The desperate revelation they had shared…

Squeezing firm at the sticky neckerchief covering the newly opened slash across his palm, Caleb edged closer, eyes drawn to the lower corners.

It was in those corners the artist had left his name. The mark of the beast who had taken his son.

'*Septimus Edward*'.

Chapter Thirty-One

"Hello?"

"Is that... Harry?"

"It is, Pippa."

"How did you know?"

"My friends sound a lot older than you." She laughed. "Did you want Nelson?"

"Yes, please. I've got some amazing news for him."

"I'm afraid he's not here."

"Oh."

"He's at the Halloween Disco. At school."

"Disco?"

"I thought he might have been meeting you there."

"Not tonight, I had homework. Do you know what time he'll be back?"

"First thing tomorrow."

"Tomorrow?"

"Yes. He's stopping at Roland's. I wasn't going to let him, but then we had... words, and I suppose I wanted to show him that I trusted him." At least that was Harry's reading.

"Oh."

"While you're on, you've not got Roland's home number, have you, love? I'll give his mum a call, check they got away all right."

"I haven't. I'm sorry. I've got his mobile…" And the digits were relayed.

A hush filled the line.

"Is everything all right, Pippa?"

"Yes, fine. Are you okay?"

"Fine…"

"This amazing news then? Would you like me to take a message?"

"No thanks, Harry. I'd prefer to tell him myself, if you don't mind."

"I don't mind at all. Okay then, love, I'll let you get off, save your credit."

"Harry?"

"Yes?"

"What did he go as?"

"Go as?"

"To the disco. You do realise it was fancy dress?"

"Oh…"

"You know, I'll bet he got changed at Roland's," said Pippa, recovering. "He's bound to have lots of that scary stuff hanging around."

"That's it… of course. He strikes me as the fancy-dress type, Roland," and Harry chuckled, relieved. "I'll tell him you called the minute he walks through the door."

"Thank you. I'll get my supper then and call it a night. Sorry for disturbing you."

"You haven't."

"I'm glad."

"You do think he'll be okay?" Harry asked.

"Nelson? At a school disco? What could possibly go wrong?"

"You're right."

"Well, goodnight then."

"Goodnight, Pippa."

The call was ended, but the phone lingered in Harry's grip. She should have asked if Pippa knew anything about a man who had been helping Nelson find his dad. But she had not.

The call was ended, but the phone lingered in Pippa's grip. "*Halloween Disco*," she fumed as her thumb worked blurred through mobile's address book. "*After all that's been said.*"

Down the alphabet: a hammer of names, crescendo of notes.

Then the chimes of connection.

Chapter Thirty-Two

The frame jabbed into Roland's chest as it slammed to a halt.

"Oww!"

"Shh!"

The pair were at last in sight of the souvenir shop. A bank of glowing, slowing glass was all that separated them from the treats within.

First inside, housed against these lamppost-yellowed panes – Nelson knew the layout by heart – were the dead shelves: the showpiece zones reserved for the museum's history bestsellers. Here winked a one-eyed Nefertiti, reduced to £9.99 after customers complained about the wear and tear. There were dinky dinosaurs, locked in mortal combat for your viewing pleasure (or mating each other, once the school parties had swept through to dispose of their spends) £4.99, and gladiators, duelling to the death (or mating each other...) £2.99 each, £5.00 a happy couple. Cash-carrying passers-by heading innocently in or out of the museum were tractor-beamed by this treasury of tat, and it was where Nelson and Roland needed to be next.

Across the walkway, up ahead and to the left as they squinted, was the security den. And between the two narrowing sheers the floor fell away in a fan of steps that led to the imposing timber entrance doors.

"I think my nipple's bleeding. It's all wet."

"That'll be sweat."

"Char-*ming*."

"Did you hear that?"

"What?"

"Keep still! I thought I heard a noise."

The boys froze fast, breath stayed, heads still, eyes scanning for sound.

"I can't hear anything," exhaled Roland, incredulous.

"There!"

They paused again as a second squeak split the silence.

"I heard that one!" hissed Roland. "Do you think it's a rat? A huge bastard rat!"

"Don't be daft!"

There was a supplementary disturbance – a rattle of iron – then the squeaking eased into a rhythm.

Eek, eeek, oof, eek, eeek, oof...

"It's coming from up there," said Nelson, jogging his head in the direction of the entrance.

Stares were fixed on the strait ahead, watching where the shadows closed. Still. Still. Then a bobbing of movement...

An ellipse of flattened headwear rolled heavy up the wheelchair ramp.

"Bloody shittery! It's Mykeel!" yelped Roland.

The boys crabbed against the wall, the picture rocking between, then shuffled chain-gang to curl around the first gap that dashed their way.

"Did he see us?"

"Don't know," said Nelson. "He kept looking back."

"What's he doing here?"

Among the rising squeaks came a wheeze from the top of steps, a steely command to the darkness behind: "Cobra!"

"Oh my God," Roland wobbled, "he's brought the snake!"

The pair listened as keys poked impatiently at the security office door. Micheal was spitting. The useless thing had only been fixed about five minutes and already he was getting dragged out on false alarms. *Not that one.* He removed his cap with a pop and squeezed it under his arm. *Where is the bloody key! Do they think I have nothing better to do on a Friday night?* His shoe was on the backswing... *I'll put my bloody foot through this door in a min...* when the match was located and pushed snugly into the slot. And his triumph was topped when he suddenly recalled the engineer's contact number scribbled on a scrap and waiting by the office landline. *Let's hope his missus drags him to the phone when he's halfway through Soldier Soldier.*

The lock negotiated, Micheal was in. First things first and he wriggled his hand into the half-bag of Pickled Onion Monster Munch that Sierra Golf had foolishly set aside that afternoon. Head full of crunch, he snatched up the numbered fragment and rehearsed his battleplan. *The alarm's on the blink, blah blah blah, no, you need to come now, blah blah blah, look, I've just had to set the video too, blah blah blah...*

The last of the digits had just been dialled when a fat finger cut the call.

Micheal eyed curious the PIR control panel set on the wall opposite his desk: the spaghetti-filled pizza box where the engineer had spent the morning digging and doodling, dissecting and deliberating. They had not had a peep out of that thing for weeks and now it was flickering like cheap Christmas lights, itching to tell its tale of sensors tripped.

"Well, well, well," Micheal muttered as he made his way over. "Perhaps we have a situation here," and he knuckled the box several times just to make certain. A trail of LEDs, Zone This and Zone That, blinked out from Animal Magic, Ancient Egypt, The Gallery and Flat Cap Corridor. *Hansel and Gretel for the new millennium.* Then, as Micheal watched, the bulb headlined Stone Age Man quivered apologetically into life.

"It appears the compound has been breached!" He grinned to himself, and how he wished he had a cigar to chew. All those bench-press blockbusters, the Military and Aviation Privileged Membership, that summer camp in the cadets before flat feet trampled his dreams – his entire existence – had been leading to this moment. Just wait till those dolts in army recruitment got to hear about this.

First things first: what would Arnie do? "Lockdowwn. Securre der perrimeter," a gruff Austro-American voice growled in his head. *Securre der perrimeter.* It was true that Micheal had left the front entrance on the latch (he had been convinced he would be out again in minutes), but that wicket door was back down all those steps, and he had never been a fan of steps. And anyway, better to leave an emergency escape in case he came face to face with a gang of bloodlusting heistmeisters.

He ruthlessly rationed out the rest of the Monster Munch – one for now, one for later – re-placed his hat, patted the eBay handcuffs hanging from his belt then checked his watch. Nine o'clock.

"Twenty-one hundred hours."

Keys were gathered, torch beamed, a distracting blob of maize-based snack tongued from his bridgework, and it was action stations.

His head emerged from the office to squint both ways. All quiet. "Come on, Cobra," he beckoned. "Intruders. We'll engage them at the War Zone." Then, barely resisting the temptation to perform a parachute roll, he squeezed out into the corridor and moved off.

*

The crescendo of enemy approach played like a funeral march in their ears. If they stayed rooted, they would be shared equally between security and snake.

"Come on, we can't hang around here," said Roland, tugging at the give in Nelson's torso.

"What about Sheldan? We can't just leave him."

"We'll have to. How can we run heaving that – him – about? Rest him there and tell him we'll be back once we've given Mykeel the slip. No one'll spot him against the wall."

The squeal of stealth footsteps was almost at the other side of their divide. Nelson bent, hurried out the scheme and jumped to his feet. Roland was already on his way through the gloom – the asthmatic's head start – and the pair dived for cover behind the shag of a speared mammoth. Through the polyester tangle a huge, horror-film shadow loomed, an ovoid of silhouette against the fire regulations glow. Micheal, arms akimbo, stared in from the doorway. Then a halting hand was held out to the darkness behind, and he creaked by, his only trace the glistening footprints rent from the puddles outside.

"He hasn't seen us. Let's go," said Roland, rattled.

"Wait."

"What?"

"Sit tight a minute. In case he doubles back."

The eavesdrop ritual began anew, each hugging the mammoth as the huff and puff of search receded.

"Now," said Nelson.

Raising themselves, they moved away, each step weight upon a winter pond. Yet they were scarcely halfway to the painting when the stabs in the silence resumed, gathering substance.

"He's coming back!"

The boys spun, darting beyond the cast of the Ethiopian hammerstone, past the Paleolithic art display and around the giant sloth to dip, terrified, into the sanctum of *The Flintstones*' video cave.

Seconds later, security's backside eclipsed their vista. By the rotation of greedy cheeks, the pair could tell Micheal was scanning the room. At last, he stilled and about-turned, stomach stoppering the cave entrance ball-and-socket. Then a face descended sideways on, left jowl hanging, right lolling against the nose, long strands of comb-over dangling. Stone-still beneath fake fur, the boys narrowed against the fibreglass. A cone of torchlight poked within, yet fanciful contemplation of a squeeze inside was cut short when Micheal suddenly snapped upright, a circle of white bobbing against the floor as he arched and kneaded the sting of sciatica. *Perhaps not. There's no one in there.*

Instead, he returned for the rendezvous with Cobra. There had been no commotion from the corridor so the intruder must have moved deeper into the museum before their trap had been set. No panic. Famous Faces next. They would outflank them there.

*

Nelson inched forward and peered out. "He's gone."

The pair slithered from the dome and lay against the floor, all eyes on Micheal's route.

"Listen," said Nelson. "You leave if you want. I'll manage with Sheldan."

"I'm not coming all this way to go home empty-handed."

"I can't help thinking, y'know: what if someone had been with my dad and they left him just to save their own skin?"

"Well, you don't need to worry about that tonight." *If only he had known.* "You ready?"

Nelson nodded. "Come on then. Quietly does it."

The Liberty Bell abruptly clanged, loud and clear. Roland launched into a flurry of fumbling; patting blurry pockets, ferreting wild until at last he plucked it out. "I could have sworn I turned it off, me," he was murmuring to himself. He squinted at the screen, goblin features lit from below. "Hey, it was Pippa," he said, pleased. "That's the first time she's ever called. Wonder what she wants at this time of night?" Then he caught Nelson's glower and his face fell back to gloom as the phone was switched off and stuffed away.

Faraway footsteps were becoming less distant by the stride. The pair did not exchange a word, they knew what must happen next. Crouching either side of the painting they heaved it to hip height. In the panic, Roland broke one of his cardinal rules and assumed the lead. Grip to his back, convict chic, he cupped the frame and stepped out, escape ahead. Out and away. Beckoning. Like a sweet shop. Under the lintel. Out. Out into the corridor.

The frame jabbed into Nelson's chest as it slammed to a halt.

"Oww!"

Up front, Roland was going nowhere. With squeaks rising and jabbing, Roland was going nowhere.

There it was, directly in front of him. Head swaying, mouth gaped, fangs bared, at least six feet from tip to tail.

"Good cobra," said Roland. "No biting…"

Chapter Thirty-Three

Pippa listened to the whirr of disconnect then immediately hit redial.

"Sorry, it has not been possible to connect you," said the well-spoken voice. "Please try again later…"

He's switched it off, she thought. *And so would I, if I was breaking and entering.*

Pippa tried again, and on the inevitable 'Sorry…' (was it her imagination, or did the lady sound a little more impatient this time?) she weighed her options.

She could call Harry, but Nelson's mum had no transport and could do nothing except worry. She could go to the museum and head them off, but how would she get there? It would not be fair to ask Dad at this time of night. She could call the police and explain there had been a terrible misunderstanding, once she had outlined the mitigating circumstances only a swinging brick would fail to let the boys off with a stern warning.

Or she could keep her mouth closed and fingers crossed, and hope they got away with it.

Whatever tomorrow morning brought she would, undoubtedly, tell both – well, Roland primarily – that she wanted nothing more to do with them. And despite being usually of a half-full disposition, in her mind's eye she played out this scene in a custody suite with Harry signing release forms and wailing like a babushka while father drummed his steering wheel outside.

And then? Following a suitable period of ostracisation she might strike up a pen friendship with Nelson, just to keep him company among the young offenders. Later, she would perhaps visit him and, later still, rehabilitation, release and who could tell? So that was the next five years mapped out.

But what for now? She sipped her hot chocolate. There was little point sitting about waiting for the sirens. Best to keep busy.

Pippa padded to her bedroom door. "Dad, please can I go on the internet?"

Permission granted, she grabbed at a garble of cable under her desk and jerked roughly at each end until she had just enough slack either side of a central Gordian Knot. One length was clipped into her computer and the other, following a low-level scramble, to the telephone extension point beneath her bed. She brushed herself down, stepped across the newly strung tangle and double-clicked the screen's oversized 'e'.

As the burps and beeps of dial-up began, Pippa resolved to distract herself from the deceit of so-called friends by filling in the backstory to the hidden diary's revelations.

"Septimus Edward. Septimus *Edward…*"

Not the most commonplace name. She scrolled mentally through all the people she knew and half-knew, then all her parents' friends and acquaintances, then the neighbours, and then all the friends of friends she could recall.

The Phone Book was retrieved. Dozens of Edwards, but only one entry for *Edward*. 'J Edward, 5 Gilda Road'. Never heard of him. Or her.

Yet she knew there was another, the one her first instinct had thrown up. And it was near-certain he would be ex-directory – *he* would not want the hoi polloi pestering.

There would be a lot to tell Nelson before she was no longer speaking to him.

*

Pippa held the few remaining empty pages up to the light in the hope of finding the indent of handwriting, but there was none. The revelations they may contain would have to wait for the heat of the Anglepoise. That took time and for now she had a name, a prime suspect and a net to snare an Edwardian devil.

Her theory was that the mystery men had returned after 4G had fled, discovered Septimus unconscious, gathered the narrative of the evening and sent him on his way. What happened after that was anybody's guess. Perhaps he wrought his terror on other towns, maybe he returned to exact revenge on 4G, or perhaps the law elsewhere, or the surviving lamprey, had finally caught up with him.

What was undeniably – and uneasily – thrilling was that she had succeeded in bringing to light the madman's identity. Thanks to her, the world would soon know his name.

*

At last, Google Search appeared. 'Septimus Edward' was crashed across the keyboard. *Feeling lucky?* Probably not.

Seconds of delay until the results flashed bare and white.

Septimus Edward. Nothing.

Caleb Fitzgerald. Nothing.

Pippa located *The Respecter*'s online archive, only to find it awaiting content. She rolled back in her chair. What she really craved was photographs – faces for names, the chance to stare these ghosts in the eye.

One final look. Before unplugging, Pippa decided to check the borough council's website. She found, as hoped, a heritage section and was briefly lost in sepia oblongs of local landmarks, sod cutting at the infirmary, theatres and pubs in their pomp, the unveiling of the obelisk, end of the shift at the pit…

And then she saw the tab 'Town Mayors' – *Past to Present*, parentheses promised – and pressed. She scanned the dates and names columned top to bottom. *1903–1904: Mr Jos Thomas esq.* The mayor from one of Nelson's newspaper cuttings. An icon alongside, a miniscule camera, indicated photographic media was available. She clicked, and the official portrait – stern seated to the left, tight-lipped and loose-chinned, clean-shaven and burry-browed, chest puffed and chain slung – grew slowly down the screen. The vignette was of little use to her investigation, but she counted it as a minor victory. As Pippa reached in to navigate away, the image suddenly jumped upwards and fresh white claimed the screen. A rectangular border gave notice of a second picture downloading. From its uppermost a background of ornate panelling emerged, warmed by blossoms of gas lamps. Then, line by dialled-up line, the crowns of bobbing heads began to appear, like bathers slowly surfacing. A crowd scene with the mayor, swamped in full regalia and smiling avuncular, holding centre stage and surrounded by perhaps half a dozen comradely grins. A scene of celebration.

*

In the bedroom next door, Pippa's dad whipped off his slacks. He had attempted to put them over his pyjamas to save time, but the paisley cotton had runkled to the top of his legs and there was no way he could contemplate any journey in that discomfort.

Primrose, pulling her dressing gown tight, was a rat-a-tat of enquiry: "Are you sure, Solsbury? Surely it can keep till morning? How much have you had to drink?"

"Only a couple of sherries. I'll be fine. You've seen how upset she is."

Underpanted and over-trousered, Solsbury dragged an argyle sweater over his head, pulled the collar of his pyjama jacket into place and flattened it around the crew neck. Behind him, just beyond the doorway, Pippa paced and wiped at her tears. Fear and frustration. Hitting Roland's dead number over and over again.

"We won't be long," and Solsbury leaned across to peck his wife's puckered forehead. He raised his voice, "Will you get my shoes please, love?"

Pippa headed downstairs to the rack. *Redial.* She was distraught. *Dead.* And not even certain why. *Redial.* Switch it on, Roland!

Dead.

*

Pippa had torn out of her room in such a hurry, she had neglected to log off. The screen glowed bright and burned into the dark, like the approach of a tunnelled train. The 3D Pipes would activate shortly, but for now the monitor was frozen on that sepia gathering and its accompanying caption, that bold lettering she had first scanned so casually. Those wicked words that dragged her drowning to the screen.

Our new Mayor, Mr Jos. Thomas esq. officially takes office surrounded by well-wishers (from left) Sir Wm. Josephs esq., Mr Thos. Williams esq., Mr Geo. Will...

And the list played out as she married and tallied.

And there, in the back rank, half-hidden, a face in the crowd. A name in a list. Cold-eyed. Smirk-smiled.

Sptms. Edward esq.

Or as Pippa knew him, Sheldan.

Chapter Thirty-Four

"That's not a snake," announced Roland, apparently honing ventriloquistic skills.

"Really, Sherlock?" replied Nelson in kind (Malcolm the Dummy *would* be proud). "Just don't look it in the eye."

Roland had no intention. His gaze was elsewhere.

"What are you doing?" asked Nelson. "How can you think of food now?"

For the first time in the conversation, Roland's lips did not move. He was into a secret pocket – for a mountaineer's pencil, the shop assistant had speculated – and had extracted a length of Peperami. "A last supper," he whispered, sniffing along its cellophane shaft, anticipating the meaty goodness within. The wrapper was stripped away and the innards raised longingly to Roland's mouth, the tease heightened with a sensual, 'Mmmmmm…'. But he did not bite (oh, how he wanted!) and instead held out the goodied hand, wafting it just beyond strike. Then, assured of undivided attention, he drew deftly overarm to launch the turdy wand as hard as he could into the dark of the corridors.

There was a skitter of claws on polish as the German Shepherd turned tail and hounded after the treat, mirrored in a kerfuffle of feet as the boys bolted in the opposite direction.

"Seize, Cobra!" Micheal had finally arrived at Stone Age Man but the quarry, along with his guard dog, was long gone. "Cobra!" he barked again, gasping in the murk, palms pressed high into the crutch of the wall.

*

At the scratch and slide of jaunty approach, Micheal peered under an armpit to spy the dog on its lip-licking return. "Heel!" he panted. "You bloody heel." The mutt was cuffed across the head, then waistband hitched to stomach. "Two of them, weren't there?" he enquired, looking down. But Cobra was saying nothing.

"You stay with me this time. And try to keep your mind off food for at least thirty seconds."

The dog peered up. He was saying nothing. Though, secretly, he *was* thinking about the fish supper that had been mooted on the drive over.

*

"I should have known better."

"What?"

"If I'd thrown the Peperami the other way we could have made a dash for the souvenir shop," George hissed in the quiet.

"We can work it out," urged Ringo. "When Mykeel heads back this way, we slip past him and grab Sheldan. Then it's hello, goodbye and stopping for no one."

"Just say the word then run for your life."

"I will."

"All together now."

Stepping from the shield of the Ludwig drum kit, Nelson beatled to the edge of the Famous Faces zone.

*

"Go, Cobra, fetch!"

Micheal watched the dog disappear into the deep of the first zone. Sniffing, scenting, snaffling, *searching*. Cold wet blackness up front, impatient tearers next and a sierra of molars aired, ready. Someone was keeping him from his share of a jumbo battered cod.

Security knew every step of this terrain. They were on his turf. Parallel rooms, loose-themed crosspieces, climbing in a rise of one-ways and no entries from War nearest the entrance to The Gallery at the top. Then, along the edge, Flat Cap Corridor passing the length of the building, the sole access to the exit. Each zone was dead ended at its rear. *One way in, same way out.* Micheal's team had reassembled at the start. Now, his plan was to transit the entire building, rung by rung; send Cobra to flush them out while he waited, silent assassin, at the corridor's interface. There was only one path away from those expectant jaws, and Micheal had it covered.

*

Cobra rushed back. No bloodied fangs. No howls of pain from within.

"Clear!"

*

"What did he say?" Roland whispered, joining Nelson to peer into the penumbra of the corridor.

"Sounded like '*clear*'."

"What do you reckon that means?"

"Beats me." Nelson half-turned and a glint met his eye. "What are you doing with that?" he rasped.

"I've got a plan."

"Really?"

"Oh yes. You take this," and he handed Nelson the diadem he had just borrowed from Her Majesty, "to The Gallery's toilets. Throw the crown so it makes just enough racket in the cubicles and Mykeel will go charging after it, into an empty room. You just have to make sure you're out of the way before he gets there."

"Great idea. And I suppose while he's in there having a look around with the dog, he'll be unable to resist a sit down and a read of his paper."

"Erm…"

"Thought not."

It was then that Roland came up with an instant embellishment that made, he considered, a mockery of his bottom-set status. "What do you know about the toilets in this place?" he asked.

"What kind of a question is that?"

"How do you get in them?"

"Have we got all night? Oh, all right, through the door?"

"You *push* the door." He regarded himself an expert on account of having spent a good chunk of the school trip within, eating several of his packed lunches.

"And?"

"But on both sides of the door there's that vertical rod that you grab hold of. Stainless steel. Easier to clean. Germs, and all that."

"So?"

"So, as soon as he's gone *inside* you get a long pole, or something, and push it behind the rod on the *outside*. As he pulls from the *inside*, the pole will jam against the frame *outside* trapping poor old Mykeel till morning. And we'll be home free."

"Clear!"

"Just one drawback," Roland continued, "where will we get a pole at this time of night?"

"I know just the place."

*

Back at the main entrance, away from ears and eyes, the unlocked wicket door – that overgrown cat flap – eased open. And two more stepped inside.

*

Nelson thrust the crown back into Roland's grip. "Are you sure you'll be all right?"

Roland nodded, unconvinced.

"I'll get going, then."

"Make sure you are there on time," Roland gulped.

"Will do."

Nelson edged away.

"Wait!" A whisper into the enveloping cloak.

"What now?"

"Maybe we should stick together?" said Roland.

"We agreed. You sort the diversion, I'll sort the pole."

"All right."

"It was *your* plan."

That was the problem. It had begun as Roland's plan, but had morphed into something little resembling his first notion:

> "*As soon as he's searching inside the toilets you double back and meet me.*"
>
> "*Meet you?*"
>
> "*That's right. I'll stay here while you're being the bait. As soon as he rushes past, I'll sneak off and be waiting at souvenirs with Sheldan.*"
>
> "*How come I'm the bait?*"
>
> "*You're faster than me. And, anyway, it was my idea. And my Peperami.*"

Instead, inexplicably, it was him now risking a tetanus jab into the shredded flesh of his backside.

Roland padded tarantula-soft into the corridor. He glanced behind, still puzzling at his starring role, especially when the original version had him minutes away from those memento dung beetles and attached chocolate ball.

Up ahead, the museum's limit lay in wait. Here, The Gallery – inventory update: *plus* one white space, *minus* one framed painting – covered the back of the building. Ending where it had all begun. Its extremities housed the public toilets: recessed and sunken, gurgling hidey-holes of Formica and fumes. And it was against these screens and cisterns that the royal headgear was to rattle and roust.

Roland, breathless with anxiety, halted outside the door, its matronly silhouette daring entry.

Where has Nelson got to?

"Clear!"

Roland sensed movement at his back, air being pushed towards him.

He said he would be here.

The blackness began to shift with life. If he did not do it now, it would be too late anyway. He stared at the door in front of him. The ladies. He had often wondered what it must be like, 'the ladies'.

Please don't let me get caught in the ladies.

One push and he was half-in. Motion-sensored lights began to flutter welcome, threatening to beam his profile down the encroaching corridor. In panic, the crown was heaved blindly inside; it missed the thrones and instead sprang timidly off the mirror (*look at the size of that mirror!*) where it rolled, whirring and hopping, across the tiled floor. Just enough noise for someone hoping to make no sound.

On the same breath he was back out and packed terrified against the wall.

He said he would be here!

Roland found the shadows just in time. A clatter of feet and paws careered by in a jumble of perimeters. The skirted lady was thrown into reverse and, though Roland heard the first ping of fluorescents, the door slammed return faster than the speed of light.

An eerie quiet.

Then began a rise of bangs, a crescendo of temper as successive doors were thrown around their hinges to reveal no culprits pleading upon toilet seats.

Next move? They would check the windows and be out in seconds.

Nelson said he would be here!

Roland peeled himself away and was almost run through by a mop. "Where have you been?"

"Are they in?"

"Can't you frigging well hear them?!"

Nelson jousted by and swerved into the recess. The mop's wooden stale, now heavy as iron, swayed like a polygraph as he aimed it at the smattering of centimetres separating the door and its rod. Inside, the climax of the search was a frustrated hoof against the gable of the hollow terrace. They had been in here. Micheal, all puff and pant, knew it. And he would crown the bastards all right when he got his hands on them.

There was the lightest scrape across the grain as the tip of the pole found its slot. The dog's ears pricked, but it was too late. The odds were with Nelson; all he had to do was push the mop home and the trap was sprung.

Blithely ignorant of the rules of probability (what *did* he get out of all those shared hours in front of the racing?) Cobra, hackled and barking blue murder, skimmed past security and threw himself at the exit.

Why?

Won't?

It?

Slide?

Back on the *outside*, in the cramp of the alcove, the mop's dank, dangled fronds had wedged fast. Nelson leaned, straining and pointless, into the shaft, but the angle of entry was too tight, the geometry askew. The tip alone was never going to hold.

Back on the *inside*, the dog bounced hard off the flat of the door. In all the excitement he had forgotten it opened inwards.

Back on the *outside*, the mop sprang loose as the timber shuddered and yelped. Think fast! "Give it here!" Roland grabbed its length and raised it almost vertical. *One chance.* The only way (back on the *inside*, Micheal *had* recalled the details of push and pull) was to dagger it acute between frame and rod then level it out like giant needlepoint...

*

The door shuddered and recoiled then scratched and rasped with a furious stamina, but the mop held firm.

Chance taken.

The boys shook hands and hugged awkwardly at each other.

"Thanks, pal."

"Let's get our backsides out of here."

They were about to set off when Nelson halted. "What's that?"

"What's what?"

"Over there." A finger pointed. "Won't be a minute. You go. I'll catch up."

"Can we just leave? I think we've pushed enough luck for one night."

"Get Sheldan. I'll catch you up."

Roland, alternate forearms swiping at the sweat on his forehead, embarked on a lone shuffle-skip routine along the corridor. The door was rattling yet, and he resolved to put as much distance as he could between it and him. He glanced sideways at each passing rung, counting down to escape. Motionless figures (though he was moving only marginally quicker) watched him as he went. Almost at Stone Age Man. Almost at the painting.

Then, from the rear, came the splintering of wood and bounce of steel. Next, the unmistakable roar of unconfined beast. The mop had done its best, but it was never built to withstand Micheal's draught.

Roland turned to face the toilets and waited for Cobra, and the inky brute of its outline, to arrive like an avalanche.

Nothing.

It must have gone into The Gallery. Why hadn't Nelson come straight away? There was nothing to do now but wait for the screams.

*

"Roland? Roland!"

"Over here."

"Where?"

"Here."

The peak of the giant cap tipped inches and Roland, flattened, peered out, anticipating a figure from an apocalyptic picaresque: all tattered clothes, misaligned limbs and face falling off.

"You're alive!"

"Just about."

Roland climbed out from under the tweed, pulling the painting with him. "Didn't Cobra get you? At all?" he asked, dusting himself down.

"I heard the toilet door about to give so I took off towards the corridor. I was convinced he would be on me in seconds."

"So how did you get away?"

"Not sure."

"Not sure?"

"It was really strange. There was all this mad dog palaver and I was running, really running, and I could sense him getting closer…"

"And?"

"And then there was a horrible yelp from behind. And everything just stopped."

"That's it?"

"Yes."

"I told you, didn't I?"

"Told me what?"

"Sheldan." He gestured. "Guardian angel, this one."

"I hope you're right. Has Mykeel been this way?"

"Not heard him," said Roland.

"Then let's get a move on before he turns up."

*

He pitter-patted, stocking-footed, big toe peeping, along the corridor. Rage had focused his thoughts. He knew they were down there.

From the ladies, he had followed Cobra's lead, though was too far behind to see what had brought the pain. And there had been tears in his eyes as the dog hobbled whimpering back to him. *No one hurts my family and gets away with it.*

Moments before, he had been a commando. Now? Now, he was The Terminator.

Sticking close to the wall and the plaster casts of the Ancient Romans, though their Mediterranean diet offered precious little cover, he silently progressed towards the exit, gaining ground.

There! Rolling in the mist, two of them. Carrying their swag. Thieving swines.

How to bring them down? From his experience – a savant's recall of the Steven Seagal Gold Collection – surprise was the key.

The assault to come ran through his head. A little closer and then rush them. They would ditch whatever it was they were stealing (they may even throw it at him, so evasive action could be required), the furthest thief would have to go first – a punch to the solar plexus, or chop to the back of the neck – and then his accomplice would get what's coming, even if he surrendered. No quarter offered today.

Blurs were beginning to firm. Up front, they had not heard.

Micheal filled his chest and tightened both fists. *Say 'Hello' to the Ouch Twins.*

Suddenly, his tie was raised up and he instinctively recoiled. Proximity was upon him. The clip clicked away from his collar and a shadow full of hurt reached out across his face. He felt the wind, but no knuckles on flesh. It was not to last.

"Wha?" Bemusement half-articulated, then security dropped to the floor in a flail of fists and swings.

*

"What was that?" Roland stalled.

"Keep moving."

By now, they had reached the streetlight-washed sheers at the corridor's end. Roland, to the fore, found the entrance to souvenirs.

"Put him down a minute," he said. Sheldan was propped in the doorway and they ducked within.

"Which window do you reckon?" asked Nelson.

"Try a few."

There was a tug of latches until one frame gave way. They heaved the sash and another light blabbed frantic at the pizza box.

"It's a bit of a drop."

"If you climb out and hang by your hands it won't be so bad," said Roland. "I'll go first then you pass him down."

"You'll drop him. The frame'll smash and he said he needed the frame."

"All right. I'll find something to lower him down with." And Roland was gone, searching. He was not away long. "Nelson, here!"

"What?"

"Here!"

"What?!"

Returned to his friend, Roland was pointing down the fan of the steps. "Why don't we go that way?"

Nelson leaned in and followed the straightened arm to the wicket door, swinging wide open.

*

Out into the drizzled streets they went, the frame bobbing awkwardly between them. They planned to take the quiet routes: best not to attract attention, especially at this time on a Friday night. Reaching the last of the museum's shelter, Nelson eyed his friend's jacket. It was slipped off. "Here, you have it."

"Thanks."

Then Roland watched slack-jawed as it was wrapped snug around the painting. "Keep him dry."

They crossed the main road to waddle out of view. At their backs, the museum's pediment displayed 9.35pm – more than enough for the hour's walk ahead. But beneath that mooning clock, and half-hidden by lead-tainted dorics, the door they had not bothered to shut behind them nosed open.

They were not going to hurt him and his daddy like that and get away with it.

Cold wet blackness up front, enamelled tearers next and a sierra of molars aired, ready; Cobra stole out into the street, bent on revenge.

Chapter Thirty-Five

The Audi groaned, impatient. He had resorted to counting the seconds between intermittent sweeps of the wipers.

...four... five... swooosh!
...four... five... swooosh!
...four... five... swooosh!

Solsbury checked the time on the dash: 9.35pm. Virtually bedtime. He looked across at the passenger seat. "I must say, I find this tale of yours more than a little fantastical."

"Me, too."

"You don't really believe that this Nelson is capable of looting the museum, do you? He's a schoolboy, for goodness' sake."

"I think 'looting' is a bit of an exaggeration, Dad."

"Let's not quibble, darling."

How long are we going to be made to wait?

"And what is he planning to do with his booty, this painting? Sell it through his network of underworld fences? Put an advert in the newsagent's window?"

"Don't make fun, Dad. It's complicated. And preposterous. But I think he's in danger."

"Okay… okay," and he gazed into the crimson bloom.

The damn thing's stuck!

"You like this boy, don't you?"

"He's a good friend."

"Well, your mother and I are very pleased that you seem to have made a friend. But he's not in your class, is he?"

"Please don't start with all that. Is it the knitwear?"

"No, in school, he doesn't do lessons with you?"

"Oh, right. No, he's not. But we all have different talents; he strikes me as rather bohemian. I shouldn't be surprised if art is quite his thing. You'd like him."

"Good."

"And he's had a tough time at home with his dad and everything."

"This isn't one of your sympathy projects, is it, Pippa? Remember all that 'Home a Newt' stuff?"

"Dad!"

For the next few hours (it was that at least) there was just the moan of the engine and the occasional twitch-footed whine of displeasure. Solsbury inclined out over the steering wheel.

Is anything coming the other way?

"Not a soul on the road."

But Pippa was not getting involved: she was at the keypad in her hand. Redial. Disconnect. Redial. Disconnect. Redi…

Faces finally glowed emerald – *it can't only be nine thirty-seven!* – and the car escaped before the traffic lights changed their mind.

Solsbury found fourth and turned to his daughter. She was entranced, curled over, index finger playing and replaying a robotic rhythm on the buttons. Perhaps he should have said, "No." He should have said, "Wait till morning. Everything seems better in the morning."

Things you do for those you love.

"Just round this corner…" he said now.

Pippa raised herself from the phone. "Look out!"

*

They swerved to leap sideways onto the pavement, buffeted and bounced in their rodeo seats. A thud of airless rubber. Shocks startled. From this altered night a dark mass lurched up towards them, heading for their personal space. The bonnet thumped and jumped as the figure spiralled up like a roller in a carwash then wheeled out of sight. The windscreen emptied just in time for a best-seats-in-the-house extravaganza as the last of their momentum found a dithering lamppost (it really *had* to work on that sidestep). Then the whiteout as heads were buried in hissing marshmallow.

*

The stillness that followed was broken by a shuffling on the street and the pop of re-forming panels. The figure groaned heavy and windless on the tarmac, and then arduously unfurled. Raised almost upright, it paused to roar instruction into the night and, not glancing back, crashed away.

Solsbury, hands rounded hard to the wheel, lifted his face

out of the airbag and gingerly tracked the ratcheting orbit of his neck. "Are you all right, darling?"

*

"We were driving home when a dog, an Alsatian, a German Shepherd-type, I think it was, came from nowhere, right in front of us. We didn't stand a chance. I swerved to avoid it. I don't think we hit it. But then again, it might have been limping when it ran off. I couldn't swear… anyway, I swerved to avoid the silly thing and we mounted the kerb. Accidentally, of course. Pure instinct. And there was… well, he was right in front of us. I slammed on, but we couldn't stop and we just hit the poor man. He came over the bonnet, onto the roof and then fell off.

"It all happened so quickly so no, I didn't get a good look at him. After a moment or two he got up, he had his back to me, and started yelling something about, 'You carry on,' or something, and then he hobbled away. I shouted after him to see if he was all right, but he just ignored me. I wondered at the time if he was being sarcastic. I mean, surely he would have seen the front end wrapped around the lamppost. We were going nowhere.

"I'll try. I would say he wasn't particularly tall, and he was wearing a three-quarter overcoat. I can't really be any more specific than that as he had come and gone in a flash.

"We were on our way to pick up my daughter's friend, weren't we, Pippa? To be honest I probably need to speak to you abou…

"Pardon? Well, I did have a small sherry earlier.

"Do you think that's really necessary? One sweet sherry?"

Downcast in the oblique light of the stooped lamppost, Solsbury began to empty his lungs into the box of tricks, waiting for the chemistry to begin.

"There it is! The dog! It's back, over there! Heading for the museum!

"Sorry. Sorry. Of course. I just… Do you want me to do it again, Officer?"

Chapter Thirty-Six

Stark and hateful, it watched.

Judith's cotton wool pad accumulated the last of the greasepaint plastering his cheeks then swiped flesh-coloured stripes down his neck. He bent into the sink and cupped clouded water to his face. Fumbling blind to the towel already piled atop the cistern, he shook loose its dizzied folds and flattened it over his head.

And though *he* did not want to look, the bathroom mirror, stark and hateful, watched.

*

"Would like to give me one?"

How many times had they both imagined?

"I would love to, Miss Lyttle."

"How does first thing Monday morning sound?"

"Perfect."

"In that case just leave it on my chair and I'll see if I can get a few of the neighbours signed up. I'll explain it's for a good cause."

"That's very kind, Miss Lyttle. Very kind."

"My pleasure, Charles."

The keypad algorithm was fingered and the pair made for the door as the countdown's pulse initiated.

"I do appreciate you stopping tonight. We were a smidge short-handed, what with Sydney abandoning his post."

"I quite enjoyed it," she said, walking on. "It's nice to have some company on a Friday evening. I'm only sorry I didn't have something suitable to wear."

The conversation found a premature end and April turned to discover she was talking to herself. "Charles? Charles?"

"Here, Miss Lyttle." He jugged up, ruddy flushed. "Sorry about that. Shut the door on my cape," he panted.

They laughed together. And he held out a hand, its umbrella ramrod-pert, to shelter her from the rain.

"Have you any plans for what remains of the evening?"

"Not much. Glass of red," he said, "while Judith gives chapter and verse on the nightmare day she's no doubt had. Come to think of it, might need two. What about you?"

"A warm bath then straight between the sheets for me."

And the brolly shuddered a creamy sprinkling down her back.

Their side-by-side passage to the far end of St John's car park was illuminated by glowing plates set into the high exterior of the school hall. The timer had been adjusted to 11.00pm, offering fifteen minutes more before a blanketing dark embraced them.

"Will you be wearing your outfit on the big day?" She eyed him up and down.

"I don't think so, Miss Lyttle. I'll feel foolish enough as it is without standing up there in this garb."

"Oh, I think you'll look marvellous. Heroic, even."

"Well, I'm certain I won't feel it," he said. "I don't even like heights. It was one of those mad moments at the rotary club when everyone was signing up and one sort of feels obliged. I suppose it gets one like that, Children in Need."

Too soon they reached their cars, nuzzled adjacent in the mute shadows. He turned to face her within the umbrella's enclosure.

Where to start?

"Well, I admire you for it," she said, overcoming the pittering riff about their heads.

"Sometimes in life, Charles, there are risks are worth taking…"

Where to start?

With his free hand he peeled a festering scab from his cheek.

*

"Charles! Charles! Have you finished up there? I'm waiting to get to the denouement of the missing herbal teas and you've disappeared."

Never mind his pending trial by bungee, he would give every penny he possessed to underwrite *her* for a sponsored silence.

Mr Bridge drew deep and dread at the towel's camomile musk.

She had already chided him for taking the trouble to wear fancy dress to the disco ("*Who's ever heard of a Zombie*

Batman?") and now she was in his ear about tea bags. Bloody bastard bollocky tea bags.

He dragged the feathery white cotton from his head to face his own cadaver. The horror look was clean away, yet in this moment he felt more than ever one of the walking dead.

Was it only forty minutes earlier that April had told him he was a hero? Neither of them now believed that to be the truth.

"Are you coming down, or not?"

"Yes, dear."

He was no marvel at all. The facts of his existence were undeniable: Charles Aloysius Bridge was a coward.

*

He looked on, hand too limp against the inner door release, while she drove away. As she passed, she had turned, raised a sideways palm and smiled. But that smile – her smile – lied. And he, voiceless, fell wretched to his steering wheel.

The car park lights clicked out and in his dry grief he thought he heard a vehicle's return. *A second chance.* He raised himself to re-write his future, but there was no one. He was alone.

Through the dolorous gloom, the trapezium of the rear-view mirror met his gaze. He tried to look away, but it held him, transfixed.

All this while it had been watching. Stark. And hateful.

Chapter Thirty-Seven

The gates were locked. *Good. Keep them in.* There was a half-hearted railing, all bubble and rust and not a spike in sight, set on a three-course wall with lofty ambitions of dry stone. That would be no problem. They could hop over and slide the painting through.

"I'll go first."

"If you insist," said Roland, hoping that would be exactly the case.

Of all the horrors of their journey – the leery Jack o'Lanterns, the cackling, tippytoed witches, and the ten-pint zombies – none threatened the febrile fear, and thrill, of now.

A quick check down the friendless road and Nelson was over and beckoning with wet palms. Roland, straining, posted the frame then heave-hoed breathless behind, size tens squeezing what little remained of the mortar from the crannies between bricks.

"Took your time."

"Weighs a bloody ton that thing," he replied, sucking on his puffer.

"How long have we got?" asked Nelson, re-jacketing the picture.

"Thirteen minutes."

"Let's keep moving."

The load was raised once more and they staggered inside.

Within sight of the pavement, feet milled in the crunch gravel, but as they moved on, beyond the glare of complainers and correspondents, the pathways began to lose their form, their investment. Out-of-view verges, too – alternately matted and bald, like the contours of a stray's back – lay unkempt and unkept; haphazard edges stooped in shame, or snagged with tumbles of high-tide leaves.

"Which way?"

"Wait." Nelson bent his head into the canvas. "This way."

On they went. Hidden away from the kerbside burial grounds, headstones had been sapped of their sheen and their axis. Tributes abraded, they leaned grey and green and ramshackle as teeth, clinging desperate to the gummy earth. Some had given up the ghost and lay exhausted, to be interred by nature's creep. Others were sheared in two, upper halves stubbed crooked in front of their base: toast racks of forgotten lives.

"Further."

"Had to be."

They shuffled on. Past a sooted cross losing its remembrance of subterranean catastrophe; past Bakelite blooms spilled from wind-worried pots; past a fossilised sea urchin of petalless stems; past a booby-trapped bench, last resting place of a colony of woodworm; and past an empty bin, a cube of mesh, legs buckling gently under the weight of nothing but time.

Further still.

The owl watched their side-stepping advance and hooted out hilarity.

"Can we have a rest? My arms are killing me."

"We'll have a quick time check."

The painting was unhanded...

"Eight minutes."

"Let's keep going. Not far now."

"I've heard that one before, me."

...briefly.

Ahead now was the profile of the old chapel, darker against the dark. They approached via the dishevelled cul-de-sac that curved directly to the porch at its front entrance. *Keep the tear-soaked dry.* Up close, fierce iron rails barred the jutting shelter and, beyond that, the gothic doorway had been bricked tight. Lying between was a checkerboard of red and white tiles, where hunched lager tins played demented chess among the swirl of carrier bags. Above as they went, a tree sprouted from a wooden-paned window; higher still, clumps of look-out grass cressed the gutters and weary cherubs retreated within blackened puffs of stone. Between finials and foundations paint flakes the size of dragon scales hung from lintels; smut walls were dotted with fresh orange where the frost had been; a fading dash of lime proclaimed 'Tessa 4 Jack'; and level with scraping feet a ventilation grid, big as a bible, had been stoved in.

Nelson paused, listening. "Just behind here, he says. Let's go."

They made the corner, to be greeted by an angel.

*

"This is the place in the painting!"

They took a moment to orientate, to gain a sense of place. In the distance to their rear, a smattering of lights dotted the night. Across a newly consecrated expanse, that barren patch patiently awaiting its first incumbents (*people are dying much more reluctantly these days*), lay the constellation of The Cottage.

To their fore, a dartboard stump, upon which the painting was rested and unveiled to the night as Roland's waterproof was flipped away. Then they stooped, hands to knees, contemplating in turn the oils and their new environment. A toggle of Spot the Difference.

The passing years had impaired the likeness. This destination had, for a time, been the most desirable part of the graveyard, the dead had been falling over themselves to get in. But as soon as *No Vacancies* was posted, once room service was withdrawn – the grievers who had lovingly tended the plots laid out, supplanted by the forgetful and the feckless – life had returned. Trees were thicker, lawns run wild, and the undergrowth teemed. Nature was back in business.

"Use the angel as a marker."

"Which one?"

"What do you mean?" Nelson asked, incredulous. "The one that's in the painting."

"But there are two here."

"Where's the other?"

"Over there, in the grass. You can just see its hand." Roland pointed and Nelson stood to check. *There.*

393

It was not easy to locate, midnight-stained and supine among a grapple of vegetation; the tip of an arm, raised accusatorily to the heavens, only just visible. Nelson strode across in high, exaggerated steps. He leaned over and pulled at a blanket of ferns, blindly catching a sting of fingers against solidity. He tried again, gingerly parting the green to bare a cage of risen tree roots and, trapped helplessly behind, the tumbled statue. He knew instantly this was not the painting's angel. That had a beautiful face, feminine and serene. This was twisted, unknown. And although darker, more polluted than the first, this angel's omission from the painting meant it could only have been sited after the last of the brush strokes.

"That's not the one," he shouted on his return journey. "Good spot, though."

"Thanks." And Roland quickly followed up his observational success. "Hurt your hand?"

"There must have been some nettles among that lot. Just stinging a bit."

"I'll find a dock leaf. Do you know what one looks like?"

"No time." *And no point.* Nelson knew that sharper pain was to follow. "So," he continued, squatting back at the painting, "if we line up our angel *there* directly facing us, move forward two rows, across three headstones, providing none have tipped over…" He counted them out, Roland nodding along. "That must be it! That's the one he is standing against!" They lugged the frame to the place they had pinpointed. "Has to be."

Cold, defiant among the dead, there it stood.

The headstone, like its semblance in the painting, was blank, storyless. Only the rounding of its edges told of the century passed. Nelson stepped before it, sweeping his palms over its outline, hoping to interpret the cracks and nibs. "How long?" he said, urgency returning.

Roland knew the question would come and had snatched a glance while propping the painting against this slab. It had been two minutes then. "One minute."

"Now or never." Nelson reached into his back pocket and pulled out his penknife, unpeeling its gleam to the hideaway moon.

"What are you going to do?"

Now he knelt before the canvas, lower half swallowed by grass. Hand hardened around the handle, he mumbled an incantation (or prayer – Roland could not tell, he simply watched on, impotent).

"You're not going to hurt yourself?"

Nelson dropped his gaze and corkscrewed the tip of the blade into his thumb. When he could take it no more, he withdrew, wincing, then watched fascinated as a ladybird of blood rose from the wound.

Roland was numbed. He wanted to help – that was what the entirety of the night had been about – but, once more, he had no idea what help looked like.

Far into the night, across the turned-away town, the church clock began its ritual of chime. Without warning, Nelson lurched forward and pressed his bloody thumb against the face in the painting. He held it there, a reckoning of eleven, then drew it sticky away.

As he rose to his feet the bells made twelve. A new day. *Day of the Saints.*

Standing astride the rectangle of grave, Nelson raised his

head and braced himself. Roland, meanwhile, looked lost to his feet to find he had somehow – despite his best intentions – retreated from the epicentre.

And amid the oils of green and grey, Sheldan was now gorged in scarlet.

Where was the thunder? The lightning?

There was none. Only the rising purr on encroaching foliage.

They waited.

At last, Roland found his stride and reached an arm around his friend.

"Is that it?" asked Nelson. "All this. Everything? For nothing?"

He slammed the painting face down in frustration and moved to storm away but managed only a few steps before knees buckled and he fell to the seat of the stump, catching his head, and its briny rain, in his palms.

"I'm sorry, Nelson. I know how much you wanted it to be true." Roland collected his jacket and spread it across his friend's undersized back. "Keep you warm," he said. "Move over."

They both stared unblinking at the floor, nothing to say.

"Should we go? I could make us some chips."

A nod.

"Let's get the painting at least." Roland returned to where it had been left flattened and reached to its headstone for leverage. "Aargh!" he yelped, bolting upright.

"What's up?"

"The stone! It's red hot!"

They watched on as the slab began to fire and bruise. Pocks of hissing rain danced across the hob of its flats and bubbled into the night. The grass skirting its base curled and shrunk in crackles and pops, and the masonry began to jolt against the drying earth. With a rush of air, it suddenly raged smithy-bright and its face, now viewed through masks of fingers, came alive with a scurry of scarlet leeches whirring wild below the surface.

"My God! Look at that!"

The creatures, barrelling in all directions, etched rows of symbols and ciphers that burned raw like fresh cattle brands.

"What is it?" Roland gasped.

"Get the painting!"

Cringing at the searing heat they stretched out for the frame, but before groping fingers found contact the headstone surged supernova-white to force a skittling retreat. Then, just as swiftly, the light died and the marble, foundry-hot yet, stilled. Half-blind and squirming, new-born pups, they inched forward again. Now their grasp stayed, and they scrambled reverse on wet stomachs.

"Let's have a look," said Roland as soon as they were clear.

The frame was still warm, and the edge closest to the slab had blackened. With juddering hands, they started to angle it upwards, anxious to check the oils on the underside. They had barely raised the canvas off the grass when Nelson sensed it had gone far enough. *They* had gone far enough.

It was then they heard the snap of a twig at their backs.

The heat deserted them. A look across to each other, heads fixed, neither daring to be the first to follow. At last, in fearful unison, they turned towards the source.

"Good evening, gentlemen…" came the voice.

Chapter Thirty-Eight

"Am I not to be welcomed?"

The words came unseen from the circumference of their vision. Crouched – make yourself *very* small! – they lashed about their centre, hoping to locate the origin.

A second twig, over there this time. They wheeled around and back. No one.

"No way…" said Roland.

Nelson did not respond. He had heard those tones before. And the drops began to tip more heavily.

"I owe you gentlemen a gratitude."

The voice was suddenly upon them and they spun again, knees scrabbling after hands. Thoughts whiplash-fast; motion treacle-slow.

The boots now before them had not suffered for the rain: hopeless spheres found no purchase on their sheen. Bubbles of burnished jet stood their ground and, above those boot buttons, fine pinstriped cashmere creeping darker where the grass had licked. Eyes rose to the splay of a frockcoat beginning cobwebby-wet. Within, a sparkle of chain grinned from a sombre waistcoat and, higher still, a bundle of crimson split the throat of a moonlight-grey collar. The stack of a top hat was tilted in full silhouette at their cowed bodies and, beneath its rim, a mystery face enveloped by out-of-sight shadow.

But, ducked at those feet, Nelson knew. He had heard these tones before.

There, found among the lost, he stood.

Unnerved and unsure, the boys remained on fours to back away beyond arms' reach.

"Sheldan?" Nelson croaked, rising.

"At your service," came the reply, though the hat remained untipped, features hidden.

"P-pleased to meet you," Roland spoke up. "We thought you wouldn't be able to make it for a minute there, me."

The figure was untroubled, uninterested. "Come, young apprentice," the voice hoarse and rasp, "I have secrets to impart."

Roland instinctively gripped a shoulder, yet Nelson broke free and stepped out. "My dad," he whispered.

A hand, small and sallow, and with bones too big for its flesh, reached into the diminishing void, beckoning. The boy was soon before him. "My dad..." he said again.

"Well, well..." Kneebone knuckles caressed Nelson's face and a hammered-out thumb pushed the wet from the boy's firm cheek. "How well made," said the voice. "Are you not a work of art?" The fingers dropped from milky skin and the figure moved off, orbiting, taking the darkness with it. Nelson waited, cadaver-still, as if sound would break the spell. He stared, listening into space then, behind, sensed the halt of whispered footsteps. "So like him..." came the voice through the night. "There is fire in you. And yet I..."

Nelson made to turn…

"…yet I feel like *death*."

The figure held out its arms, inviting faceless embrace. "I have grieved for human touch."

Nelson moved closer. From the margins of his gaze he saw that Roland, too, had limbs outstretched: a palindrome played out. "Let's go," his friend mouthed.

"*I need to ask about my dad.*"

Nelson slid wordless into the waiting arms and was swallowed up by the bat wings of the coat. Hugged. Squeezed. He was not certain before – his face was already numb – but now he realised that Sheldan was vacuum-cold. And inside that icy shawl, a scent sickly-sweet soused his nostrils. An arm pulled Nelson's head against the chest, where he could discern the glacial pucker of a heartbeat, interminable interlude bringing fear that each pulse would be the last. *Not before I know!*

Never mind what Mum had told him those grieving hours past. Her version was not the answer. That could not be the answer. He would find his answer now.

Tight. Then tighter.

Tighter yet.

Too tight!

Suddenly, Nelson was fighting desperately to wriggle jacking arms between their clamped bodies, but he was too weak, too dizzied. His head danced a pirouette and there came a riotous pounding against the back of his skull. He opened his eyes to find, through a waterfall haze, he had been twisted around and was now facing Roland – his friend, arms still outstretched, face full of horror.

The captive began to run, but he was held hard. It was then Nelson understood, lungs stoppered, that he was choking. The forearm locked across his throat was killing him.

"Get off him!" Roland screamed. But he had been ignored before.

Quickly enough the struggle subsided (the years had not dulled his touch), and with his thrilled heart no longer racing and Nelson still in his grip, Sheldan reached his free arm into the air to pinch at the glossy brim. Bowing forward, quarry limp in his clutches, he elegantly raised his hat to reveal the top of his head, neatly slicked save for the kink where the band had sat. Next, the devil's peak from the portrait rose into view as slowly, oh, so slowly, he lifted his face to the moon.

It was the kind of shock that loosens legs, that screams for the shelter of insensibility but, somehow, Roland – *somehow* – held his ground. As Sheldan's features were brought at last from shadow it became shudderingly clear that every crease, every indent, was steeped in deepest scarlet. *A face-pack of human blood.* Only the eyes and the grinning teeth, exaggerated against their background, escaped the horror. A string of congealed gore swung from the end of the pointed nose, and around the deep-drenched ruffles of the forehead blackened scabs were crisping.

Roland opened his mouth but spoke only silence.

Then, erect and unflinching, staring straight through the appalled figure ahead, Sheldan parted his lips and slipped out his tongue. It was difficult to tell at first (what with the dark and the downpour and the prancing shadows), but then Roland's terror became absolute...

The tongue kept emerging, like a parasitic worm extricating from its host. When it began to flick at the air, to taste the liberated rain, he knew it was not human. *That* could not be human. Blue and cleft at the tip, it was the tongue of a *lizard*.

It swept and stroked around its own face, erotic and dread, slurping at the blood then drawing it back to the mouth to be savoured. Its fork claimed the dangle from the nose and pulled it within where – eyes gathered tight – it was chewed and swallowed.

*

Why did he do it? Why did he run? Faster than he had ever run before. He could have stayed. He could have tried to talk him into releasing Nelson and letting them both go. Put it all behind them, say no more about it. But he did not. He chose to run.

Why did he do it?

*

Roland raced as hard as he could at the shoulder of Sheldan, skittling into him. The bodysplash he had been hoarding. The bone-juddering collision was more keenly felt by the less cushioned, and narrow Edwardian finery was bounced backwards, releasing Nelson to the gasping ground. Despite the stagger of exertion, Roland had suddenly found his voice: "Get off my friend, you fucking bastard!"

But he was berating no one. His opponent had vanished.

Once the last of his momentum had dissipated, Roland reached down to the woollen heap: coughing, howling and newly conscious on all fours. He grabbed a handful and pulled upwards; the knitwear yielded willingly but continued to give as he ran out of reach. "Come on," he gasped, gripping under arms. "Time for those chips."

Roland heaved them both upright with Nelson – rubber hinged – supported in front. Conjoined in a curve of belly and back they faced the pathway home, yet only one was ready to race.

"Take some deep breaths, pal, we need to get going."

It was then, amid the urging and the whispering, that the night was filled by a visceral howl. The song of the slaughterhouse.

Roland chilled. *Two were now three.* His ear burned momentarily with acrid breath then his skull was snapped back by its curls and, for the second time, Nelson crashed to earth. Sheldan was back to claim his dues.

Seized by the hair, Roland was lifted shrieking off his feet, like Perseus parading Medusa's head, except this body and legs were intact and kicking at the night. Floundering wildly at arm's length, the boy began to seep under the weight of his own gravity. Bulging eyes wept murder, sweat surfaced in his face's blueberry blush and spittle foamed through the grimace to collect in a dead man's gurgle at his chin. Down below there was wet, and worse. Roland blindly juggled spasm hands, searching for purchase to ease the inferno in his scalp, but the moment the clench was located he was let loose to the jarring grass. And before the boy's arms had slumped from overhead, Sheldan slipped creamily behind to truss him like a wrestler.

*

As soon as he felt its wet warmth, the scratch of its teal caress, the squirming and backheeling ceased. It began as a damp fingertip in his ear (that old classroom joke), then traversed his clammy cheek to probe his nose, both nostrils simultaneously. Testing. Tasting. Next, it found his mouth. He could tighten the teeth, gladly, but pain had drawn the lips apart. In it slid, dripping slime in its wake. Penetrating. Brushing against enamel, sampling the detritus of the day, groping in the gap the sugars had made, leaving the boy's own cowering in the dark.

Satiated, it withdrew and went.

"Get off you dirty fuckhead!" Roland's tongue, now emboldened by the retreat. "We did what you wanted so let us go."

He listened for a response, but he had been ignored before.

"Nelson, get up! Get up!" he urged the twitching bundle below. "Get some help."

Beneath, Nelson was rising dazed, senses too slowly repairing.

"Aargh!" Roland's cry was an amalgam, a guttural swirl of terror and disgust. "My dad will fucking kill you for this!"

The lizard lick had returned, crackle and moist, and slipped around Roland's throat like a boa. Sinews hardened within a fleshy fold and the clamp was closed. A living garrotte. The squirming and heeling resumed, but with arms held hard behind his head Roland's jolts and jerks could never be enough.

*

Amid the long grass, the darkness shifted. Shushing overgrowth rose and fell, puffing misty wraiths in its wake. Wetness gathered in the scented air; the pitter-pat of stride gathered pace.

The vigilant were wise to the approach. Night-time watchers retreated to holes, divots and dens, or curled jagged as the shadow lashed by.

They knew.

Black was moving. Low and lithe.

Locked on, black was moving.

*

Bouncing out of the cover it sprang at the fight. It came from the side, jaws snapping at the space between the two bodies, where the enticement was strongest.

Four had become eight.

The first thrust found the frockcoat and it held with a low growl, front legs planted, head tugging in time. An instinctive boot flicked out to connect just below the eye, its jolt causing the muzzle to release. Now Sheldan, captive still fastened full nelson, shied away from the interloper, protection from a second offensive. The muscular tourniquet tightened, squeezed. He needed to finish this.

But black was on the move again, driven by instinct, atavistic urges. The next lunge came under the coat and pierced the flesh at the top of the thigh. *Priorities revised.* The tongue recoiled from Roland's neck and whipped home. As the jaws anchored, Sheldan rent a frustrated cry and slammed his choking blue boy to the ground.

Though arms were now unburdened, he held his riposte. Instead, he savoured this moment, absorbing the ecstasy of his agony: the pain of life returned. He glared dismissively down at his attacker, watched curious the scragging of teeth, marvelled at the pulsing synchronisation of their bodies, and then slammed the heel of a fist onto the snarling head.

Assault had been anticipated and the grip held. Again and again the mantrap bite stayed. He reached down to probe the eyes and the jaws retaliated, drawing more blood. *The soft underbelly*. Sheldan swung his free leg, yet the contact merely drove the beast deeper in, causing the two – locked like lovers – to topple. Flat on his back with the rest of the dead, Sheldan was now hammering impressionless at the scuffling skull.

Abruptly, black froze, ears cocked, listening beyond the body on which it was mounted. *Another presence.* Sheldan heard it, too, and in the lull he lashed a swingeing, swiping blow against the nose. Fleshy lips rose to the tops of teeth, their invisible tips still embedded in finery, and the night of its eyes flared angry white. Now, the listening was over. In it went again. A frenzy of searching, sniffing, biting. Unable to surface, a drowning desperation gripped Sheldan. Limbs blended, a blur of kicking and gouging, pulling and pushing, but the beast would not release.

*

Nelson had dragged himself upright and, ignoring the tryst on the grass, headed towards his friend. Roland sat buckled, hunched, rubbing the saliva-slicked rolls of his neck.

"Are you okay?" Nelson asked.

"Been better, me," he spluttered. "Are you?"

"Think so. We need to get out of here. Can you walk?"

Without looking back the pair were away, embraced, hacking across the graves.

*

They were out of sight when the yowl found them, though the crack of impact had not carried. Once again this evening it had swung into canine flesh. Wounded, the beast had skimmed away, carrying in its mouth a bundle of white: the prize it had sought.

Breathing hard, Sheldan pressed his hand to his wound then raised a palm, patterned red. His wipe taken, he rubbed the blood across the wet grass and pushed himself up. Recovering his top hat, he brushed it around with his sleeve and, swiping back his hair, returned it to his head. He examined the bite holes at the skirts of his coat, plucked away cottons of grass, then dusted both shoulders. Doused in fight, he dragged his fingertips across his forehead and irritably flicked the moisture, melting with leftover scabs, into the dark. Now he was ready to speak.

"A timely intervention, I am in your debt." The hat was doffed. "Do you have all I requested?"

The wares were handed over, wordless.

"You have done well."

An uncertain smile found the lips of the deliverer.

"Now, it is time for your reward, is it not?" The heavier of the two was placed on the ground and the free hand, bones too big for its flesh, held out. "Come with me."

*

Away in the chapel the pain of the blow was subsiding, replaced by euphoria, a remembrance of days passed. Safe in that abandoned sanctuary, bedded beneath a pew fogged with panting breath and laced with the stench of wet dog, Jasper had pulled apart a knot of silk and was feasting on its tumble of blood orange peel.

*

The rain was daggering down as Sheldan rose to face the world. He had outrun the sun. And there was no going back, not while the key was his. From prisoner to warder.

For the first time in a century, he had sense of his own weight, his own flesh. Surveying his realm, he freed his birth tongue and tasted the storm. He ran fingertips around the flesh of his face, pushed his hand down his waistband and cupped and coddled, delighting in the course of blood. He was alive. Arms wide, he grinned the victor's grin. Then into the terrified night he roared his success to the dead and the dying, "Sheldan Critch is reborn!"

Amid lightning and thunder, the leeches resurrected their death whirr in the tombstone. Eyeing their work, he collected up the painting and tucked it inside his coat. He had been able to keep the brushwork dry as he followed instruction, yet now it went away a single drop dashed against the oiled face of its seraph.

He retrieved his stick from the ground and turned to watch, fascinated, as the tombstone cooled. Something new, a sly amendment to his original blank marble. Something Fitzgerald must have added to the artwork that night as a warning to all.

The script, that pentameter, flashed and burned. And the artist smiled, satisfied at the epitaph bestowed:

> *Here lies one*
> *whose name is writ*
> *in slaughter*

Then the words faded to nothing on the sibilant stone and he stepped on, out once more into the waiting world.

What a wonder his Critch would be!

*

And behind, among the consecrated reeds and weeds, in that patch of root and cloaking fern, there was a new hollow.

Where once it had lain, the fallen angel was no longer snared.

Chapter Thirty-Nine

How long had it been, since he had eaten? An eternity. He could not even recall the last thing to pass his lips – not that it was of any importance.

He was hungry now.

The streets, his streets, were unrecognisable. At this time in the dusky morning the day did not know if it was coming or going. There had been a chilly, sunless dawn and – though he was wrapped enough – the tingle air loitered, dragging its heels. The last of the rain had pressed on, but its washed-out canopy lingered and leap-me puddles were bouncing monochrome off the sky.

Yet the palette of the new world had no designs on surrender. He had tapped tenderly within the amber blush of streetlamps; watched his shadow shuffle by spark-white windows. And now he marvelled above at the lurid Perspex – all names and doodles and brighter than anything he had ever seen – radiating the length of the street like a crystal seam in a crag.

At each step, resurrected senses were in overload. Sights, sounds, smells rushed at him in freefall. He had jolted at the savannah growl of a motorbike, stalled crane-necked at a traffic light until the sequence ran looped behind closed eyes, caressed the dewy glutes of overnight cars, and scanned the sheltering horizon at the siren whine of distant palaver. And that was not all. Leaving the cemetery, he had stared high (drawn by the low roar) to follow a blink of red and white traversing the sky. He had returned to a land of *dragons*.

Hunger.

These cold, peaty hours he had wandered. As the evening's ghosts and ghouls sought out resting places, he was lured to their abandoned food. Among the late and early pavements he had found a polystyrene tray, its fries waterlogged and floating like fingers, he had poked at the roadkill of a shish supper, and circled a sector of plastinated Hawaiian. He had not been *that* hungry.

He was hungry now.

With 9.00am meandering its weekend way, a scattering of bodies began to emerge. Older and Younger. He did not need to see their faces, he could sort them by the way they moved: the weary and the spring-stepped, that irretrievable bounce of youth. Up closer, both wrinkled and unlined were wrapped in smocks and uniforms of varying shades, and they busied – winding, wiping, directing, inspecting – in and out of doorways like a weather house. The shuffling streets were waking. The day, it seemed, had decided to come.

Critch moved aching by, dragged by the nose to a plate window and its ovenly glow. He stared in at glistening pies dotting trays like double nines; eyed bread rolls cobble-crammed; and craved, wet-mouthed, a gambrel roof of pastry tiles. Further along, he digested toothrot pumpkins, absurd chocolate bats and icing-boned gingerbreads, all headed limp for the bargain bin. Decay was everywhere this morning. Following the warm air to the threshold, where fresh loaves secreted their pheromones, he reached dishonestly inside. Here, he met the untimely smile of a Younger – Gregg, he thought his name – arranging phials of black gloop in the nip of a humming cabinet. Spotted, Critch retreated and shuffled empty-handed away to search for a crowd, the pilferer's accomplice.

Clipping gingerly down the next sidestreet he found a wheeled box the size of a house, park-anywheres winking knowingly at its corners. From a jutting shelf, blocks of brown were being disgorged into the arms of Youngers stamping impatiently at the stirring road. Around the leviathan's head a gruff man, head bowed, was shouting into space, one hand squeezing a cigarette, the other pressed to his cheek, words clouding about him. Critch moved closer and leaned into the orb of his walking cane, inhaling passively, drawing in. How he could enjoy a cigarette. Suddenly, the gruff man sensed adjacency. He halted mid-sentence – some tirade about missing *fucking* boxes – and eyed menacingly up and down.

The encroacher was unmoved. Did this fool not know who he was? He was Sheldan Critch, the man who bowed to no one. *Time itself was his.*

"Are you perturbed?"

"Perturbed?" The gruff man echoed, the choice of adjective serving only to reinforce the probability of homosexual proposition (at this time of day!). "If you don't fuck off, I'll *perturb* your fucking block off!"

Critch said nothing, but sucked deeply again, holding his ground.

"I'll call you back." The stand-off was at an end. The mobile phone was tucked away, his smoke discarded to the pavement, and the gruff man stepped up, raising hands for the protocol of pushing, that precursor to an exhibition of streetwar.

Critch exhaled through parted lips, yet still said nothing. There was no need. Instead, a flicker of glistening blue cowed the aggressor into withering retreat. By the time the man returned with an incredulous posse, his lizard manmonster had departed, and a day of ridicule arrived.

Back at the main thoroughfare, Critch passed the clang and clank of portcullis shutters ascending for business, watched skeletons returned to closets for another year, was momentarily caught in the bee dance of men delivering high-stacked trolleys, then gazed in longingly at the Phoenix Café – risen in triumph from the ashes of a flood – where Breakfast Bin Lids were happily occluding arteries.

Moving on, searching, he dipped in and out of conversations: half-heard tales of laughter and lament, the vernacular of a new world. '*Round the block with Josh being Freddy, egg all over the four by four; quiet night inski, out on the razz; goggle-box, Xbox, inbox; upload, download, mother-lode; happy-hour hero, bouncing bonce; cock like a French stick, knockers like naan beads; steaming down the curry house, ring of fire; tight as a fish's, green round the gills, blue in the face, happy as Larry and sick as a bastard dog*'.

What could it all mean?

Critch traversed the pedestrianised zone for an oasis of street furniture. He had barely arrived at the opposite pavement when a skitter of clicks – unseen, yet getting louder – waylaid him.

They appeared from around the corner, heading his way. His back straightened and he played with the hang of his coat. Pulling on the last of the gruff man's cigarette, he set himself for the approach of the giggling half-dressed. Closer they came. Vertiginous heels, deep blue skirt and jacket, white blouse beneath. All conker knees and clavicles. Extremities had accumulated jewellery like a scrapyard magnet and, down at their feet, a tattooed bloom rose and fell with every step. He would have doffed his topper had he kept it. Instead, a forelock was tipped. "Ladies…" He grinned.

"Oh my God! A pervert tramp!" and they skidded by to Sunseekers, laughing louder as the margin grew.

"Lousy whores," Critch muttered, and turned away.

He dipped hopelessly into a bin he had spotted from across the cobbles then came to rest at a bench. Jasper's handiwork resuming its sting, he settled onto the etched timbers. Though he was not cold he blanketed his overcoat around his bones, until the escape of a muffled clink triggered an instant freeze. *A new hiding place must be sought for those.* He studied downcast the length of his body and flattened, Canute-like, a torn pocket flap. Those bitches were probably right (he regarded himself as knowledgeable of threads and this was without doubt a desperate garment), but he had seen enough from the shadows to realise he would be too conspicuous in his professional garb.

Unable to orientate at eye-level, Critch searched for a sense of place to the street's upper strata. He marked smog-stained bricks lacking all sense of discipline, black-out windows with peeled-away peep holes, long unused crests championed by lions and lambs, and – three storeys high – '1874 AD'. Good

Lord. Landmarks he wanted to remember, but could not. He had never needed to look before.

Back to the ground he looked on as an early-start family, a cringe of shellsuits, stopped enthralled to watch a pigeon pecking at a pie crust. It was that kind of family. It was that kind of town. It had not always been. And he knew if they had not been there, he may have had that crust himself.

Leaning forward, he used the shining tip of his stick between mossy blooms to rap out a ditty:

I'm a little messenger summoned by a call,
I should very much prefer to be big and tall,
I would be a bobby then, very great and grand,
Stopping all the traffic when I held up my hand.

The tapping beat was joined in duet by a rubber-tipped claw. Critch gazed up to find a tumbledown man in a fluorescent jacket, face stained as a walnut and doubly furrowed, grinning over him. Eye contact brought a momentary pause then the standing man struck up again, keeping beat with a booted foot while strumming the claw with a comic-strip glove. His musicianship was accompanied by a tuneless howl that fell into wheezing laughter after just a few bars.

"Only a bit of fun, Catweasel," said the man, slapping Critch on the shoulder (no fear of germs penetrating those deep-sea gauntlets). He reeled around chuckling and pushed away his handcart, stopping – when someone was looking – to snaffle a tossed wrapper and poke it at his bin liner. This exertion released a tarry cough that shuddered his trundler and tipped, unnoticed, a folded newspaper from the broom holder. *Litterbug*. Critch, initially taken aback that his duettist might be able to read, idled over to recover it. Returned to the bench, he skimmed his find. Conundrum solved. It was a picture paper. The front page was re-examined: Saturday 1st November 2003. *One hundred years.* A dirt-runnelled palm (last night's excavating) was pressed against the slim, hidebound volume secured in his inside pocket.

Just as the book had predicted.

*

I had him as a table tipper, a mere toe popper. Sitting in the dark with his Podmore fools reeling bogus incantations, chasing a glass better employed for whiskey. "Yes, no, and three bags full, Sir." And that night at the town hall of which he is so fond, well… when he implored all present to form a circle around the room holding hands – holding hands! – to call upon the dead for assistance, I expected him chased from the county.

And yet he secured some wild sorcery on me.

I was away to new adventures when he came knocking. Thirty more minutes and he would have found a hollow house. But there he arrives, all social and 'Septimus'-like. Of course, I could decipher his purpose like a child reads ABC and I was happy to indulge him at first – what proof could he have? Then followed his tale of fingerprints and the tooth with its Judas smear.

My chance was to lower his guard, take him by surprise and leave him shrouded for the others to tip. So, I gave him hope. I know human nature; none of us is so different. Desire drives us all and the hook will be bitten if the bait tempts – the boy and the adoration of his father, the greedy fool and his lust for gold. Fitzgerald and his love for his son.

"Follow me, if you must. He waits upstairs." *As does my stick. Offer their heart and they run like puppies.*

Fitzgerald must have contaminated my tot when I bid him join me at the window. "As though of hemlock I had drunk…" *His odious invalid.*

And then… and then, for all his bold talk of science, he resorted to hocus pocus.

I should have stayed my counsel once I had bested him. I was a fool to talk of connections, of walking away, yet he had me all puffed up and boastful. Was he really to arrest me once my escape was laid out? The law he may have been, but he was a father, too.

What life did he have, I wonder? In his years ahead would he think of me, as I think of him now? He probably imagined no one else each time he made to stroke his face with a hand no longer there.

Did he perform his necromancy again, on those from The Orbis? The book is testament I cannot be one of a kind. (He was looking even now at others, trapped – yet moving – in the frames of the shop window opposite.) *Prisoners like me have slept across time, most never to find their means of release. But we are known. We are the watchers. The unseen and unheard. We lurk in whispered conversations and the nightmares of children.*

My own century was almost closed out, upon which my cell would have been forever barred, yet I am renewed, transformed. And ready to resume my calling.

First, one task awaits. My work in the cemetery shall stand for now, but the bargain must be met in full.

Blood will take its rightful place. This prophesy shall out.

*

A slow, hypnotic beat had wormed its way into his subconscious. Critch opened his eyes to a different day.

Moustachioed men, arms tucked about waistcoats and floor-length aprons, idled against tunnel-of-love doorways. Daylight windows, split like noughts and crosses, offered Cadbury's Cocoa, Maypole Tea at One and Ten, and Fry's Delights. Painted signs presented the Botanic Beer and Porter Stores, the Friendly Co-Operative Society and, adjacent, Croasdale's Hat Emporium. And through each dark and comely entrance, he glimpsed the bustle of women tenderly straightening coconut-shy tins.

People walked briskly by. Working men in quickstep clogs and caps to cover the years; mothers patrolling in shawls, clinging grim to pennies and creaking wicker baskets; and children and dogs chasing from store to store gobbling up – only in their imaginations – the treats within.

A world recognisable.

Critch burned with nostalgia. He knew what he would do. A citizen of note in his exquisite veneer, he would amble these familiar streets: accept the respectful nods of contemporaries, a smile for half-recalled faces, inhale the sweet and the spice and the must, feed till he could take no more.

But he found himself powerless to join the day. He was hardened, unable to move, to touch, to make himself heard. *They don't know I'm here.* The ghost in the window.

And the beat grew inexorably louder.

While he watched helpless his day began to turn, to rotate; slow at first, as hour hands, then quick as a fairground.

Circle and chase. Awnings opened and shut like eyelids in hail, sounds zipped and babbled, moments of rain and shine brought instant damp and dry, and the browns and whites of leaves and snow smattered and went.

Carefree customers disappeared upright into shop doors to be spat out, enervated and hunched. From the corner of his eye a short-trousered boy grew soldier-strong parading by, only to collapse in a shrunken bundle at the opposite side, medals chiming as he hit the stones.

This waltzer gathered pace. In the core of the vortex he watched cars arrive like the head of a great migration, saw red-alert trams jump their grooves to rove at will, sat pained through a crescendo of horns, and sucked in air grey and heavy. Before saucer gaze, fashions thinned and flapped, flared and drained. Hats vanished, and the brilliantined hair beneath ducked and tailed, rainbowed, rolled, spiked and bristled. Shoes gleamed then crept and winkled and stabbed, then propped up giants to fall flat and rise again.

While the century burned, the sun shone less and the flurries came no more. And all the while the dark was in retreat. Electricity blurred night and day, spots of light – signs and streetlamps – streaked around his head, faster and faster, centrifugal scars that beamed and burned and clung, layer on layer, lightning-hot, spinning, spiralling. A cocoon of roaring white. And then, with a visceral jolt, it stopped.

The corner of his newspaper lifted gently.

He was released. Back where his day had begun. Back to denim blue and polyester crinkle, to November trousers and occasional hemlines, to Youngers in caps (though not to be doffed), to anoraks zipped high, to the early-poppied clinging at frames or astride whining trikes, to the leap of a ringtone and to muted shows in the television shop opposite.

Time.

The beat, the rhythm – the hooves – had stopped.

"You're a new one, aren't you?" said the constable, leaning down from his indifferent mount. Critch looked up startled from the bench and instinctively pulled the walking cane to his chest.

"No mutt?" and two pairs of eyes (the horse was not in the least interested) scanned the floor in vain for an absent assistant. "Nice bootees. Fancy dress?"

Critch made no reply, just eased his feet out of view.

"Listen, I don't want to see you begging around here, goddit?" *Now* the horse snorted its approval. "'Cos if you do, you'll have me to deal with." The officer sat hard and sturdy in the saddle, looking dead ahead. "And do you know what I'll do?" A gloved fist closed around the ribbed handle of his bruised truncheon. "I'll throw a bucket of soapy water on you, and we both know you won't like that!" The horse rocked its head up and down, tusky teeth bared, bit rattling like a dungeon. *Good one, Boss. Good one.*

A flick of stirrups, but Dobbin had his own ideas. Dobbin had *business*. The tail was casually hitched, and a loose-green turd poured insouciant and wet at Critch's feet. Now it was the constable's turn to air equine chompers. And still there was business. A heroic squeeze, and a long-forgotten ball of dung – a strawy alien's head – began to emerge from the ragged sphincter. It teased its way out, wiping its feet, and spattered heavy into the pile. *Almost there, Boss.* One last heave, but all that escaped was a whoopee-cushion fart to rattle the retiring, puckering folds of chestnut skin.

Job done. *Job* done.

A click of tongue and they idled away, snorting.

Critch stilled as the clopping diminished then rubbed together his shins to smear flecks of manure into cloth. He absent-mindedly slapped his walking cane into his cupped palm (*that nag would be the first for the glue pot!*) as, in his memory, he re-traced the whirlwind's forgotten streets. He heaved himself up, absorbed, and half-slid as he broke the steaming crust at his feet. Recovered, he rasped his foot bullfight-fashion in radiating lines along the paving stones: sunbeams of shit. He brushed at his grassy knees, drew the overcoat back across the gash at the crotch of his trousers and ran fingers through his hair. Stick firmly gripped and the route now mapped in his mind, he was ready at last for his destination.

Making his way, he loitered behind a shopper pulling fresh notes from a slot in the wall. Left alone, he too poked at the keypad but found the largesse exhausted. He rapped on the darkened window and shouted for the clerk within to pass out funds. Ignored, he sought consolation in a reminder of the currency he carried. First scouting for the idiot with the claw, he plucked stealthily at his cane's stitching and prised back a little of the black leather that snuggled its orb. As he brought it near a flash of golden sphere glowed warm against his face, like a child's buttercup.

Closer towards his goal, he came to a butcher's window and stopped to admire its cuts (and slashes). His appreciation of the handiwork was interrupted by a scream and Critch turned to see a snarling young woman wrenching a handbag from an elderly lady, twiglet fingers no match for the teenage heft on display. He did not go to help; no one went to help. Instead, he returned to the shop with its enticements of flesh and blood. Except, he was now not alone in his approving glances. There was a skip of pads and Critch, not yet ready to look, sensed the stench of damp fur. It waited, in reach, tormenting, clacking licked lips. As it moved to his other flank the walking stick was subtly inverted in his grip, ready to renew acquaintance.

The shriek of a sudden whistle caused both to flinch. Each turned instinctively towards the call. A distant, "Here, boy!" and it was away, back to the man rattling the flaccid lead. *Not the same beast.*

Stick righted, he focused on the reflection in the glass as, behind him, people rushed in – too late – to lift the whimpering victim from the ground. A chair was produced, and the scrum narrated the appropriate accompaniments: "It'll be drugs. No respect these days. Where are the police when you need them?"

I know what Fitzgerald would make of this. He would shake his prissy head and bewail a new Gomorrah. But he is wrong. Here is milk and honey. This new world shall suit, after all.

He moved away at the clip of returning hooves into a tangle of sidestreet and corner. From there, he emptied out onto a small square, what had once been an open-air market now paved, planted and pewed, and enclosed by squat office blocks. At its centre stood an obelisk, plated bronze with the glorious fallen. There was time for a moment's pause. 1914–18: some of its register familiar, the disaster not.

The adjacent surface, and that behind, alphabetised the zesty youth of 1939–45. And the fourth face was blank, awaiting the next in line for their sweet and decorous end.

Finally out of distractions, he looked at last beyond the needle, as though he had been purposely holding back the thrill. There it was: the Town Hall.

The Town Hall. Just as stained and grubby as the last time.

There is work to be done. I shall find The Orbis and reclaim what I am due. And then…

Critch cast the tabloid he had been carrying back to the street, where it was seized by the damp.

…And then I shall have my revenge.

Chapter Forty

"What took you so long? Getting dressed?"

Heath was simmering. One final inspection left and right of the patrol car for I-spy neighbours and sprint-home joggers, and the net curtain crashed back.

"We've had a busy night, Sir. Trick or Treaters terrifying the old folk, and then an emergency shout at the museum. Break-in. Security guard knocked unconscious. Clip-off tie on the floor. Only came round with his dog licking his face. I think it was wanting its breakfast. Limping, it was, Sir. Poor thing. Vet thinks it's been struck with some heavy implement."

"So a wobble-arse sleeping on the job gets priority over a missing boy, does he?"

"We're not saying that, Sir…" and the officer, seated at the kitchen table, drummed a nervy riff on the roof of his cap.

"Well, it sounds like it to me," and Heath unveiled his own fingerwork. "Now *I* want to know what *you* are going to do to find Norton."

"We'll be doing everything we possibly can, Sir, you can rest assured of that." A pocketbook was flipped open to prove his point. "Now, when did you realise what had happened, Sir?"

"This morning," Heather called over from the range. "I popped into his room to borrow the portable for our other son – he's on his way back from university today, BA Media Studies – and the bed was untouched."

"And you say Norton had been to the school disco. Was he with friends?"

"Was he with friends? No, he was on his own, Columbo. Just him and the DJ. Got plenty of requests played, though."

"What I meant, Sir, was did anyone accompany him? Someone we could talk to, try to formulate a timeline."

"Formulate a timeline?" Heath's Newspeak senses were tingling.

The officer stuck to his drill. "We are just trying to establish the events leading up to you reporting your son missing, Mr Edward."

"He left here about 8.30 yesterday morning," offered Heather, seizing the opportunity to defuse the tension while her husband popped more paracetamol. "He was going into town with some friends after school for something to eat then on to the disco."

"Friends?"

"He didn't say. He never really talked about friends, did he, Heath?"

"Did Norton have a mobile phone, Mrs Edward?"

"Nokia."

"And have you called it?"

"Bloody hell! I can see you running Scotland Yard!" spluttered Heath, his tumbler somersaulting about the sink.

"Why didn't we think of that?" and he hammered a cylinder of fist into his forehead.

"There was no reply," Heather said quietly.

Heath yanked a surprised chair across genuine Yorkshire Stone and pounced down, eyeing the uniform opposite. "Formulate a bloody timeline…"

"Do you have a recent photograph of Norton, Sir?" The officer was going to add, 'To assist with the FRIP', but thought wiser of it. There was no need to bore Mr Edward with the intricacies of the Facial Recognition and Identification Protocol.

Do not let him foolz you. Hee'z actingz all conzerned, but it'z only becoz hee thinkz if hee findz ze boy, hee will find allz heez promized.

"I'll go." Heather temporarily abandoned the eggs slapping the frying pan – now was not the time for calorie counting – and headed in search of a likeness. Heath watched her round the door and listened for feet on the stairs. He knew she would not be long; she preferred her yolks soft.

"Any clues about the break-in, Constable?" His tone now disconcertingly matey. "One of our scribes picked it up from morning calls."

"It's sergeant, Sir."

Heath declined the briefest nod at the trio of digits tapping the chevrons on the officer's arm and arrowed, instead, his gaze directly at plod's face.

"You know how it is, Sir. I leave all that to the press office."

"I see. What's your name, Constable?"

"Duff, Sir," the murmured reply. He had told him once, and was unnerved to be asked again.

426

"I see. How's the super, by the way? *Frank*. I suppose he's mentioned his stint working undercover. Must have."

The sergeant tried not to blink.

"Knew it! Is there anyone in the force he hasn't told? Undercover my swinging sack. Couldn't pull the wool over a child's eyes, that one." Heath leaned back, smirking. "Anyway, I was just on the phone to *Deepthroat*," he continued, "arranging our taxi for the Law Society dinner."

It was a fact the annual shindig had been mentioned in passing, but of more immediate concern during the conversation with Frank was that a plain-clothed officer in an unmarked car be sent to The Cottage. A jam butty would only alert the locals, and caring less than little for the privacy of others did not warrant his own being fair game. He had also requested that Frank sent the best man available though he, evidently, was not available.

In truth, the super did not share Heath's alarm for the boy. He had seen it all before: young lad – turned fourteen, did he say? – sloshed on White Lightning, bunks down at a mate's for the night, slopes home late afternoon nursing a faceful of pillow scars, tuft on his head that refuses to play ball and a Frankenstein-sized hangover. If it had been anyone else ringing him at home first thing on a Saturday morning, he would have fobbed them off until teatime at least, but Heath being Heat…

*

Unfailingly amenable in his dealings with the editor, Frank the dissembler kept great secret – '*it never leaves you*' – of the fact that he did not at all like Heath, and detested intensely the little twerp ordering him around. Hence the insistence this morning that his sergeant don full ceremonial regalia before venturing out in the most conspicuous vehicle in the lock-up. He would have had him blaring the theme from Z-Cars all the way down the road if he could have got away with it.

*

That sergeant now eyed the cauldron of testosterone bubbling across the antique oak. Even seated – even uncapped – he dwarfed Heath by a good twelve inches. Little with large. Paunch versus pecs. Visitors from outer space peering through the nets would have no trouble. They would know what's what, who's who. *Make no mistake, it is a jungle out there on Mars.* But here on Earth, once elevation up the social ladder had been factored in, Heath towered head and shoulders over the officer. Among the beasts whose favour was required to enjoy success in this town, the editor was a silverback

"Not that much to say at the moment, Sir," the sergeant mumbled at last. "Seems a painting's been taken; well, there's a gap on one of the walls, which is highly suggestive, and a number of screws have been located in the near vicinity. We don't know if it was valuable. May have been stolen to order. And there's a Peperami wrapper that may or may not prove significant."

"So, it would be fair to say you don't know much at the moment."

"Well, Sir, enquiries are ongoing, shall we say?"

Heather reappeared breezily – had she brushed her hair? – and handed over a four by three. The sergeant inspected the snap at focal length. It was not, as is usual in cases of this nature, a school photograph. Heather always maintained those were never worth the expense. On most occasions they had no sooner received approval copies (though how anyone could approve of those gurning abominations…) than Norton's uniform – and educational facility, for that matter – was out of date.

"I see he has a scar," said the officer. "That's good.

"That's good? I fail to see what's *good* about that."

"What I mean, Mr Edward, is it gives people something to look out for, something distinctive."

"He got that playing football when he was younger." Heather had her back to the table, cajoling sunny-side-ups onto a spatula. "He was wearing his glasses at the time. Blind as a rat without them. Anyway, the ball hits him in the face and the lens pops through, digging right into the side of his eye. Blood everywhere. Quite shocking, really. Ketchup?"

"Oh, yes please."

"He was lucky. Sounds silly, but he was. Of course, they patched him up with butterfly stitches, but it left scarring – and not just the one in that photograph." Doughy lids of thick sliced white were plopped in place. "Became very *sensitive*. Refuses to wear his glasses now. We've tried, haven't we, Heath? And he's quite protective of anyone else who wears them. It's as if he doesn't want others to go through the same torment, to share his pain. *Very* sensitive."

"I'm sorry to hear that."

"Here's your sandwich, Officer. Take care with that *splendid* uniform."

"Thank you." Her smile was reciprocated. "Missed breakfast this morning. Coming straight here and everything." He bit away an oozy arc then took up his pen. "Now, Mr Edward, if I can just confirm a few more details…"

*

Don't liztenz to him, zergeant. Don't believz a word heez tellz you. Miez knowzez ze truthz. Miez witnezz to everythingz.

With elephantine effort, memory was scoured for the testimony to be whispered into the investigator's ear.

It all ztartedz whenz miez waz juzt a babzie…

And closer she sidled.

One dayz, miez followz himz into loftzez. Miez never beenz beforz and miez waz curiouz, likez. What therz waz up? What doingz waz hee? Leavz hee hatch awidz and miez zneakzez inz unnotized. Miez waz little nervezz at firzt. Miez alwayz been prettie jumpiez. But zen hee zwitched ze lyght and miez zeez plaze waz filthiez. Warmz it waz, too. Miez likez warmzez. And filthiez.

Boxez and cazez and papziez waz ztacked az far az allz eyez couldz zee. Zoon miez zitz wiz him dayz, ztaying lotz aroundz bulbzie. It pazzez timzez, juzt watchingz. And it gavz miez buzzez to knowz hee waz unawarz of miez prezenz.

Miez hearz him zay heez waz clearingz loftzez, for buildiez or zomezingz, and fillz didz heez lotz of bagz blackz zat alwayz attractz crowdz. Hee alzo zneakz upz foodzez – bizcuitz and cakzez – which miez likez to zharez.

Zen, it happenzez.

One dayz, miez knowz whenz notz exactliez – miez notz zo goodz wiz datez – hee movez a zhackilie old trunkz, all emptiz and itz lidz agonz. Wherz it ztoodz, a knotz iz dropzez out of floorzieboard, leavingz a holez, a temptationz. Miez watchez az hee putz in ze fingie and pullz. Wiz a creakzez, ze boardie comz looz in heez handz. Hee popppzez eyez into ze gapzez and whatevez hee zeez muzt haz big intereztz becoz hee wentz ztraight down laddiez and zoon backz wiz torchzez. Miez wentz zeez for miezelf, whilez awayz he waz, but zpiderz iz everywherz. Don't likez zpiderz.

On kneezez, hee liftzez next floorzieboard, zen anozerz and anozerz. Zen hee reachez inzidz, ryght up to ziz partz (the sergeant was tapped hard on the shoulder) *and pullz outz a flatz. Heaviez muzt it be becoz onze hee outez it hee ztoppzez to wipez wetz off hiz head. Zen hee lookz again and ziz timez hee pullz out two pointiez zat hee fixez togezzie to makez 'walkingz ztickz', hee zayz itz. Heaviez iz zat, tooz, wiz a ballz on ze endz.*

Ze flatz waz all wrappzez aroundz in zheetz and whenz heez openz it miez zeez it waz colourz. And ztored on topz oz zee colourz waz a readie littlez.

Hee ztartzez doingz ze readingz of zhadowz and next timz too, and next timz more readingz and miez iz zinking miez of oldz agez diezez unlezz zoon zomezingz happenz. And zen ze chatteringz ztartz.

Firzt miez iz zinking heez zayz allz to zelfhimz, but zen hee zeemz to be givz lotz of anzweringz. Miez won'tz pretendz miez underztandz allz, becoz zometimz miez getz upzidz down, but miez hearz zay, "Weez iz familiz after allz," and, "Yez, miez heart'z dezirez iz goldzez." Zhrough miez bodyie, undeztandz youz, miez hearz all ziz.

"And what was Norton wearing last night?"

She was not sure the officer was taking it all in, so edged closer still.

Zen getz hee bookz of hiztoriez and regiztriez, and makz hee treez of familliz – zo hee callz themz – and hee findz ziz namezie and knowz hee ze age and whenz hee goez for more cakez hee zayz namezie 'Nelzonz Hitchcockz' to hiz boy and hiz boy findz of himz at zchool. Now all zmilzez and handiez rubbingz and next givz hee ze colourz to muzeum and heez own faze iz in heez newzpapiez wiz hiz colourz on wallzie and ozzer colourz nextez. And hee zayz to hiz boy, "Zhout him outz at zchool vizit zen our colourz willz knowz 'Nelzonz Hitchcockz'."

Zen, after nuzzer darkzez, hee zayz fryght 'Nelzonz Hitchcockz' for heez dad. And duz it hiz boy. And likzez it hiz boy.

Yezter mornz, hiz boy takz zhadowz readie littlez and partz of walkingz ztickz, and zneakzez allz in hiz zchool zack. Laterz, talkie ringz and ze man zayz 'Titzez' and outz hee leavez to hiz boy to acquaintz wiz hiz kinz from ze colourz. Hee duz not zpeak wherz he goez, but beforz – whilz miez waz quietz havingz babeziez meiz own – miez heardz himz tellz hiz boy, "We muzt be zure hee ztealz it outz, and takz to place byz willz free. Zemz iz ze rulez. We followz and watchiez untilz freee our kinz duz walkz. Zen we zwapzez all for goldz."

Yetz, comez back hee all alonz and ouchez and zlant! Hiz boy iz all awayz and hee zitz in darkz waitingz. Zen thiz day hee goz outz earliez, ztill all zlant and limpzez, and miez followz notz, becoz not inz zat cold. Zen hee getz backz and waitzez morez untilz ze mum wakeyz and shoutzie, "No, boy!" And zen youz comzez.

"Height? How would I describe yours, Mr Edward? Well… erm, av… just above average? Yes? Shall we put average for Norton, then?"

Notz youz takzez himz awayz? Allz iz zpokzez truez!

The last set-square of crust was popped and the pocketbook realigned.

"So, what happens next?"

"I think I've heard enough, Mr Edward."

At laztzez! Thankzez youz, zergeantz.

"I'll be on my way, Sir."

Whatz?!

"I'll have the team check last night's CCTV between here and school, and I'll get in touch with the headteacher, see what time Norton left the disco."

"And to contact you?"

"Just call the station, Sir. They'll pass the message on."

Heath said nothing. It was all he needed to say.

"*Or* I could give you my personal number. That way you can keep up to date directly."

"That's a very kind gesture, Sergeant," said Heather. "Isn't it, Heath?"

It'z notz rightz. Takzez himz wiz youz. Hee knowz morz zan hee zpeakzez. Have youz no earzez beenz?

*

Sergeant Duff was back on his feet and rolling his shoulders, newly aware of having acquired a minor stoop. Heather flattened his details beneath a Slimming World fridge magnet – wait till she pointed that out to Augusta, a real policeman's phone number – and, while she was at it, discreetly removed Heath's motivational epigram especially for her, 'Keep Back Crumper!' and screwed it for the bin.

"Right! Well, thank you very much, Mr Edward. Mrs Edward." The peak was played. "Rest assured, this will be our number-one priority."

"Oh, I know that it will, Constable. Give my regards to Frank."

"Sir."

The two men made their way to the vestibule with Heath at the rear, hands in pockets, fingering the folded photograph of a boy and his father and a kite retrieved from Norton's room that morning.

At the front door, the sergeant crouched to slip his feet back into mirrored shoes then reached for the Yale to let himself out.

Waitzez!

The policeman paused, rotating to face a scatter of frames. "I see you have some old photos of the place, Sir. Is that our cemetery?"

Zemmietreez! Miez hearedz zat wordz beforz! Miez comz lookzez.

Sergeant Duff leaned towards the print, almost nosing the wall.

Miez juzt catchz miez breathz. Miez notz az youngz az miez waz... howz timzez fli...

Without warning Heath's arm speared over Duff's shoulder, furious fast. There was a crash against the plaster and within – to his core – the officer leapt. Deliberately, he turned, fingering the shackles at his waist.

"What was that all about, Sir?"

"Sorry, Constable, I didn't mean to startle you. *That's* been annoying me all week and I was just about ready for it today."

Heath retracted his arm to explore the smeared palm of his hand. The officer returned to the revised paintwork. There was blood and he was quite certain it was not human (he had always fancied a stint with scenes of crime). There was black, as well, and a smattering of yellow and gossamer.

Heath, too, had spun. He was shouting through to Heather. "You might want to bring a cloth to wipe this up."

"What is it now?"

"What *was* it, more like. Got the little bastard!" he yelled.

"Got what, Heath?"

"Here. A fly on the wall."

Chapter Forty-One

Thursday 5th November 1903

It was not within me to kill. Nor would I see him free. My deed could not be abandoned for others to discover and yet, with the carriage likely to be searching, neither could I hazard carrying the evidence away. Thinking fast, I heaved all up the ladder into the attic, that lightless prism, and concealed the items within.

It was later that I felt regret: regret at my stupidity in leaving both prisoner and key together. Of itself the book could not provide means of escape, but the path to deliverance would surely be illuminated.

Now this day has brought grave news. 'They' require resolution. His house is to be searched from bottom to top. It is a risk too great to countenance. The clarity I have recovered of late shines a light on what must next be done. Tonight, I shall bear cleansing flames to where he lies dormant, for while the painting exists my lineage will never be safe. Does not the book forewarn:

"The blood of jailer and liberator must course as one."

*

He had never held a girl by the hand before. Not like that. Not like *this*. He alternated cupping her Play-Doh palm, kneading its soft falls and plumps, with interlocking fingers in hers to share the moist warmth of the tightrope skin at their base. They had each been clumsy at first: they could not work out which side to stand – the briefcase was not helping – and then he had squeezed too hard. "I'm not bubble wrap!" she had told him gently. But the awkwardness had left them now. They fitted. And Nelson liked it.

On quieter parts of the pavement, arms swung carefree in step with their pace. In the single-file zones (outside McDonald's and the bike shop, where a pile-up of deserted two-wheelers chicaned the pavement), he had zigged and zagged her manfully through, determined to hold the link.

Making at last the pedestrianised zone, the blackened roofs of Town Hall Square now cresting the horizon, they resisted the opportunity to spread wide across the avenue of cobbles. Instead, they edged closer still. Leaning in, bumping shoulders and hips; savouring each sweet collision. Towards the rendezvous they strolled, serenaded by a garden-chaired pensioner pumping the world's most beautiful love song from his accordion, past the hinnying hawker with his psychedelic inflatables and Day-Glo worms ferreting about splinter sticks, and beyond a trinket seller where Nelson had clung on tight as he fished a pound from a pocket to exchange for sweetheart beads.

Further along, even the baying wolves of the personal accident pack brought an intimacy. Here was shared giddy an incident that had already been inducted into family folklore. She and her mum had been accosted the week before. "Quick question, madam?" pounced the thrusting buck, all go-getter hair and slickbacked suit. "Certainly, young man," Primrose had replied without adjusting stride, "what's the capital of Peru?" And mother and daughter were off, all gapes at their own temerity.

She was smiling again today as cobbles ducked beneath tarmac and the vista opened out before them.

"There's Roland!" she said. Hands instinctively separated. "Is he smoking a cheroot?"

They crossed the road at twelve exactly, the distant peel of bells saluting their punctuality. The meet-up had been arranged for the dead men's needle on the square. Pippa had telephoned first thing to say – somewhat ominously, both boys thought – that there were things all three needed to discuss. Roland cited his shift at Pikka Pet to buy time until lunch hour, but over the toast course Nelson had asked him to return the call so he could see her straight away. He could not face home just yet.

As the couple landed, Roland was leaning against the cenotaph, killing time watching the crossing and uncrossing of Sunseeker legs on the bench opposite, and searching for famous faces in the thumbprints of discarded chewing gum at his feet. "I'm not sure you should be touching the monument," said Pippa. "It's sacrilegious."

Roland lurched upright, pleased to see them despite the

grimace that overran his expression. Pippa thought he looked like he had been in a fight. He *had* been in a fight. Twice.

"Morning, Pippa, you look tired."

"It's afternoon now," she replied.

"Afternoon, Nelson. Your mum's been on the phone," he said, cheeking the last inch of Peperami and signalling his mobile. "You'd just left. She asked if I'd let you call her when we met up. Wondered if I knew anything about a man who's been helping you? Then she had a chat with my mum to thank her for letting you stay, or rather to make sure you actually had stayed."

"I've already spoken to her, thanks. She called Pippa, too, while we were walking."

"You can't blame her for being concerned," Pippa interjected.

"I know, I know. So…" Nelson turned to Roland, "what did you say about the man?"

"Turned out it was a terrible line. I didn't want to put my foot in it with both feet, me."

"Thanks."

"She's a clever clogs, your mum, though."

"How do you mean?"

"Remembering my number after just one telling at your house. Doesn't know her own, though?"

The cenotaph's greetings now played out, there followed an uncomfortable lull as each distractedly awaited the next move (*was that Gandhi near his left foot?*). Two minutes' silence and Roland was first to crumble.

"White rabbits!"

"Sorry?"

"First of November. I'm the winner."

"All Saints' Day," said Pippa.

"Is it?"

Quiet.

"Pippa knows everything," said Nelson, "I didn't want to lie to her. Again." And as he spoke, she teased back her hair and played with the lost earring his detour had recovered from The Gallery.

"Oh."

The heavy hush returned.

"Hey, what a day last night was!" *There seemed little point in pretence now.* And he fingered the tombstone scorch on his palm he had explained away as a dare to touch the DJ's lights.

"It was terrifying. I wasn't sure if it was the rain, or if I'd wet myself."

"Worse than that, me," Roland countered. "When he lifted me up by the head, I was definitely pushing cotton. Straight in the laundry basket with those beauties. And then that tongue thing got me around the neck…" And he slung an arm across his own throat.

"Listen," said Nelson, working again at the scrunch of jacket sleeves, "I haven't thanked you properly for not leaving me last night, and for letting me stay. You're a good friend."

"You'd have done the same. And the best bit is that we haven't told your mum a lie."

"Apart from the Halloween Disco part."

"Technically true, Pippa," Roland chuckled.

"And when you two have quite finished with the Butch and Sundance routine, we had a crash coming to your rescue."

"A crash!" Roland caught Nelson's face; it was not the

expression of someone hearing the news for the first time. "Are you all right?"

"The car's a disaster and Dad's got a terribly bruised ego. He's never been in trouble with the police in his life."

"The police?"

"Oh, yes. Breathalysed in the street like a common crook. He was under the limit, of course – that's own-brand sherry for you, Mum said – then towed away by some triple-time pick-up swindler. And *you* promised."

"True again," Roland conceded, now firm-faced. "But Nelson needed me and I couldn't leave him to ride the tiger alone…"

Pippa found Nelson's eye. "I'll explain later," he said.

"Yes, well… you were both lucky. For a second, I thought he was going to tell the officer everything, but he took the huff when the breathalyser appeared. It was name and rank only after that. *Foul* mood this morning. He's composing one of his specials to the chief constable as we speak."

"About being breathalysed?"

"That and other things. When I left, he was venting about the 'Keep focused on the road' sign flashing outside the fire station."

"I'm really sor—" Roland's mumbled stab at apology was dismissed mid-syllable.

"The only reason I am still talking to you both," Pippa continued, "is because I have something very, very important to discuss. But we can't do it here."

"We thought we might go to America," said Nelson. "Want to come?"

"How much have we got?"

"I've got a pound left that I didn't spend in the disco."

"I've got five," said Pippa.

"And with a crisp new twenty straight from my wages that should be more than enough."

*

"So, just to recap, guys. That's the two Amish burgers, both with relish, one Grand Canyon with extra fries and three *diet* sodas."

They nodded agreement.

"Any side orders?" The platinum blonde, clacking loud on her gum – as per the training – and swaying woozily despite the toe brake wedged firm to the ground, waited, pencil hovering.

Roland initially failed to realise that she was talking to him. "Oh, why not?" he beamed out from the Corvette. "Onion rings, please."

The scribble was made, and the notepad dropped into the red and white hooped pouch slung low around her waist. Hands emptied, she reached around her back to adjust its knot, thrusting proud the spangling stars, at nipple point, on her pullover.

"Take your coat, Sir?"

"T-thank you," Roland blushed.

"And you guys?"

"Thanks," said Pippa.

"I'll keep mine, thank you." Nelson, embarrassed, had abandoned at Roland's the remains of his pullover. He was about to set off for town wearing just his T-shirt when Mrs

Grange insisted he borrow a spare jacket. This garment was not his to lose.

"Okay, guys, thank you for your order. As I said, my name's Marilyn and I'll be happy to meet your requirements during your time with us." And she pushed away, freewheeling for the pass.

"Got a bit of lazy eye, hasn't she?" said Roland.

"Sure you were looking at her eyes?" Pippa was sliding the Laurel and Hardy cruet set and Statue of Liberty vinegar pot to the exposed brickwork. The flap of her soft leather briefcase was unclipped and the contents laid out.

She turned first to the journal and recounted in giddy breaths how Bastet had uncovered the hidden days. "*The brown colouration suggests a citrus ink. Invisible until reacting with heat or light.*"

The first of the new pages were shared. "What do you notice about the handwriting?"

"It's very neat," offered Roland.

"Precisely."

"But his arm," said Nelson. "How is he writing so neatly with his wrong arm?"

"It wasn't his wrong arm."

"How do you make that out?"

"The spidery scribble *was* his writing arm."

"So, he never lost an arm?"

"Oh, yes. The camera didn't lie. But that was later. Just before they murdered him."

*

The blue pleats of a skimpy skirt parked to the side of their car, and the order was deposited. Each booth was fitted with a gaudy plywood profile of a classic automobile – on arrival Roland had requested the Kennedy Continental, but staff had been mid-sponging some prankster's bolognaise from the upholstery.

Lounging opposite his friends with a bench to himself, Roland jabbed a napkin 'California – The Golden State!' into his collar, parted his cutlery and pulled the Grand Canyon towards him. He took a moment to admire lunch's steaming majesty: a yard-long baton roll stuffed its entire length with hot dogs and topped by a Colorado River of mustard.

"Will that be all?"

"Can I get some extra sauces, please?" asked Roland, a first crispy ring already necked.

A couple of slides later Marilyn was back with a bust of Abraham Lincoln, stovepipe sachet-stuffed.

"Enjoy, y'all!" And she was away again.

"You know, I'm not too sure roller-boots are the safest footwear while transporting hot food," said Pippa.

Unwaitressed, at last.

"Murdered him!" Nelson hissed through his first vegetable bite.

"I'll come to that. To begin at the beginning…"

*

Between knife-and-fork mouthfuls Pippa ran rapidly through the revelations of the previous evening: the serendipity of stumbling across the first secret entry, 4G's visit to Septimus the undertaker, the fight, the shattered arm, the braggadocio confession, The Orbis, the Critch alter-ego, the solubility of chloroform in whiskey, the Book of Shadows, the painting as host for transmutation, the photograph of Sheldan at the mayor's inauguration…

"There's two days' silence from the end of the visible diary until its invisible resumption, clearly accounted for by his recovery from the operation. The hiatus *before* the scribble page was merely the result of the journal being marooned in 4G's desk as he was escorted from the police station. It was out of his hands until Richards retrieved it on the day everything unravelled."

"Operation?" Roland belched.

"4G writes how he staggered home in agony, just about able to carry his overcoat and jacket, then staged a riotous fall. His cries for help roused the neighbours and he was discovered apparently dazed and terribly wounded at the foot of the stairs. There was no blood, and so no trail back to the undertaker's. A surgeon was summoned and the arm lopped within the hour. He would have been laid up for the next few days, drifting in and out of consciousness."

"Hey, 4G lost an arm and one hundred years later so did you, Nelson," said Roland.

"And that's not all that connects them."

"So, what was with the spidery stuff?" Nelson interjected.

"Neurasthenia."

"What?"

"While recuperating, 4G self-diagnoses Neurasthenia. Nervous breakdown, we would call it. I Googled it:

desperation, guilt, loneliness, exhaustion…" The diary was turned. "Just listen to this, 4th November…"

For months I endured torment beyond comprehension. Each waiting day, tumult and disorder gathered about me like a miasma. I could not sleep, eat, think, breathe...

"I think the prospect of confronting Critch, far from providing a sense of triumph, brought the crippling realisation that his journey of hope was finally over. He knew the day must end with the confirmation of his worst fear and his handwriting was that agony manifest.

"As for the secret diary, I'm not sure he ever planned it, rather events overtook him. Looking down from the window that night he saw the mayor and the chief inspector arrive to escort Critch to the train. And I'd be willing to bet the coroner was waiting on the platform. 4G had given them a vanishing of their own and it was simply a matter of time before The Orbis came for him. Trusting no one was his only option."

"So, why didn't they get rid of him straight away? I would have done, me."

"Ironically, his physical weakness now proved his greatest strength. People rallied round. He notes a constant stream of visitors on his return from the infirmary, neighbours sleeping downstairs should he cry out in the night, fresh fruit delivered daily. He knew The Orbis had to bide its time. And all the while he was calculating his next move… and composing the hidden pages.

"But news that the police planned to re-examine the

undertaker's cottage panicked him. Fearing the painting would be discovered, he crept from his sick bed after dark and attempted to raze the place with embers from his pipe. Miraculously, a passing officer was on hand to apprehend him in the act."

"*Very* convenient," said Roland.

"It was enough to discredit him. They made a show of commendation for the sake of appearances, hence the retirement portrait and certificate, but he was now isolated and watched from the sidelines. When they finally realised he was never going to lead them to their missing Critch, I think they decided to guarantee his silence. They conspired to quash any inquest and slipped free. And in the end, everyone's secrets went to the grave."

"What was he waiting for? Why didn't he just tell someone?"

"A glimpse from a window hardly constitutes proof. Until he had the means to square this particular circle, the hidden pages were his way of documenting the conspiracy. No matter what fate befell him, he hoped the disinfectant of sunlight would expose the guilty."

"And all these years the diary was in a cupboard, tied with a bow," said Nelson.

"An unopened gift," Pippa mouthed the last forkful of burger. "Do you know the irony of it all?" she added, wiping her mouth with the tip of 'Oregon – The Bear State!'. "He had already given us Critch's identity."

"How?"

"Remember 'If eaned wands talks the mall'... that final line?"

"Yes."

"We misread the handwriting. Not much of a crime considering its deterioration. What we thought were *ens* were actually *ars*." She scribbled it down.

"So… 'If eared wards talks the mall'," said Nelson.

"Septimus the undertaker, his surname was Edward."

Nelson nodded along, not sure why.

"Read it again. Slowly. 'I fear… Edward… stalks… them… all'."

"Oh my God."

"It gets better. Know of anyone else with the surname?"

There was a moment of mull.

"You're joking!"

"No. Plainly enough, given its graveyard location, The Cottage was once the undertaker's residence. Critch tells 4G he had already sold it to his 'idiot' cousin. Has to be: Septimus Edward, self-confessed killer and abductor for hire, is Norton's ancestor. Makes perfect sense given the bad blood running through that family."

"So, the painting has been hidden in Norton's house for a hundred years?" said Roland.

"And that's where you come into the picture, Nelson."

"How do you mean?"

"Without the Book of Shadows, I suppose we'll never know the exact mechanism for reversing the spell. However, many spiritualists at the time were intrigued by the concept of infinity. Using a willing scion – you, Nelson – to transport the picture to the exact spot portrayed within it would provide that sense of closing the loop.

"My guess is that Halloween, too, would have been

significant as it's traditionally the time when the barrier between the living and the dead is most porous. And I shouldn't be surprised if the centenary has more consequence than we comprehend."

"One hundred years later," puffed Roland. "It's always one hundred years later in these tales. Grim."

"But beyond all, Nelson, your blood is 4G's."

Roland noisily slurped the dregs from his Pepsi pot then tipped backwards to get at the ice. "Fresh fruit?"

Heads were shaken and stomachs patted. "No thanks, Roland, I'm stuffed."

"You did well, finishing that lot," said Pippa.

"No problemo," he said, gurgling again on his straw. "Good appetite, see. I've always been big, me. Even when I was little. Excuse me miss… er Marilyn…" he was now calling through a second mouthful of cold crunch, "can we have the bill, please?" A circling finger the universal gesture.

The waitress rolled up to deliver a slip-on-a-saucer and retrieve the crockery. "How was your meal?"

"Lovely, thank you."

"Peachy." She was *good* at this. "Be back in a moment."

Roland was first to the folded bill, flipping its upper half. "Eighteen pounds," he announced, reaching into his jeans pocket, "I'll get this."

Marilyn was back before counter-offers could be submitted. "This is for you," she said, proffering a glossy card. "We don't give out many."

"Really?" said Roland, taking it up and eyeing it proudly. "I've never won a certificate before." And he held it across his chest, mugshot-style, its cartoon rock formation declaring,

'I've gorged on the Grand Canyon!'

"May I take this?"

"Yes, thank you. Keep the change," he added.

"Why, thank *you*."

*

Pippa was elbow-deep in the briefcase again, pulling out blank playing cards. "I want to show you my final discovery. Now, this one gave me goosebumps."

She waited while Rita Hayworth rolled by, then popped the top from a felt-tipped pen and scribed individual letters on each of thirteen rectangles. A row was laid across the table: '*Sheldan Critch*'.

"Have you heard of transposition?"

They had not.

"This is how I like to do my anagrams." A shuffle of jump and leap and arch began. "I thought there was something not quite right about that name. Just *too* unusual."

Then chop and change stilled: the secret revealed. The boys' stares narrowed, pointed.

Sleight of hand? A trick?

"How about that for the final insult?" said Pippa, sitting back triumphantly.

Astonished, they said nothing. Instead, Roland swashed each card in turn away from his eyeline and against the wall. And still the letters read the same.

"It fits," she added, as if they didn't believe. "It really was a game to him, wasn't it?"

*

The heavy, palm-pressed glass of the diner door swung behind them and they were out once more onto the cobbles. They had departed America in a rush after Nelson had spied a top-hatted silhouette striding past the window. It was not *him*. Just Jack the Ripper, bag full of butcher's shop liver, making his way home after a Halloween stopover.

"I didn't know you were vegetarian," said Roland on the outside of the trio, hands stuffed into pockets and shoulders hunched (again!).

"I'm not, officially. I've been thinking about it—" Pippa replied.

"I think she liked me, that Marilyn."

"What makes you say that?"

"The way she said, 'Have a nice day,'" explained Roland, grinning.

"She meant all of us. In fact – in reality – she didn't mean any of us."

"But she was looking at me. Well, one of her eyes was."

All three laughed guiltily and Nelson almost claimed Pippa's hand as they brushed together to avoid a mobility trike.

"It's funny, isn't it?" said Pippa. "In the United States they say, 'Have a nice day.' In England we say, 'Thanks for waiting.' If we can be bothered."

The town centre crossroad was almost upon them and Nelson was anxious to confirm the direction of travel.

"So, are we decided?" he asked. "Cemetery or police station?"

They had tentatively discussed their destination while waiting for Nelson to re-roll, against the confines of the Corvette, the sleeves of his oversized loan. The vote had been split. *"It's all right for you! You weren't the one stealing from the mooseum!"*

"Have it your way, then. But we're straight to the police if there's nothing to be found," said Pippa.

"Deal."

Three abreast, they began to re-trace the earlier route. Up ahead, balloons bobbed overhead; the whine of accordion in crescendo.

"There's Podmore Street." Pippa pointed off to the left, where a terraced row hunkered. "The spiritualist meeting house was down there. 4G tried to disguise his visits as postscripts at the end of his diary entries, but anyone with slightest knowledge of the group's location would have easily tumbled his cipher. It was there he was given the Book of Shadows. And it was during one of their séances – the night after the infamous town hall meeting, Nelson – that the group is supposed to have made contact with some of the missing children, *'Where his oils become ground, the lost to be found...'*."

*

"Lima! Hey, Miss! Lima! Tell your big sister the answer's Lima!"

"Is he shouting to us?" asked Roland, nosing in the direction of the cocksure clipboard.

They were beyond the bike shop by the time the story had

been retold and polite chuckles were out of the way. Roland had played along (it was not *that* funny) but had otherwise been distracted by his friend: alone among the crowd.

"You okay, Nelson?" he asked.

"Wha? Oh, yeah, fine, thanks."

"Seemed miles away, that's all."

Nelson forced a semi-smile.

"I'm sorry about last night, your dad and everything," said Roland. "But don't give up. You'll see him again – wherever he is."

"Don't worry, Roland," Nelson replied. "I know exactly where he is."

*

Nelson slumped into the settee. Half-eaten toast abandoned, arms hard crossed, pinched eyes sheened.

"I hope you don't think I'm letting you stay over tonight. Not after this!" A folded dispatch (it resembled one of those comic-book giveaways – 'FREE INSIDE! Your Dennis the Menace Paper Banger!') was shaken at him. He had not been permitted to read the telltales within, but on the down stroke, when edges butterflied, the low-ink emerald mantling of St John's heraldry told him all he needed to know.

"Like to guess where I've been today?"

He did not like.

"I walked all the way to your Aunty Thom's – three miles! – to borrow £10 so I could call the school back. They'll be able to get in touch a damn sight quicker from now on. Happy?"

Happy he was not.

"Unauthorised absences! Playing truant! A *fight*!"

A shrug.

"Is that it? Nothing? Couldn't care less?"

The letter was flung at him in rising temper, though Mum's mood had been little short of apoplectic since the postman's plodding birdsong that lunchtime. Nelson lengthened the sheet and began to read.

Dear Mrs Hitchcock,

Having failed on several occasions to contact you by telephone, I write to regretfully inform you of some extremely serious iss—

That was as far as he reached before the words were wrenched back.

"So, would you like to explain yourself because the Nelson mentioned in that letter – this letter! – is not the Nelson I know."

Once more he said nothing, though this was not obduracy.

"I…"

"Go on!"

"It's…"

"I'm waiting!"

"At…"

"At? At what? At where?"

He watched the agitated blur of her foot. "You wouldn't understand."

"Well, why don't you try me?"

Nelson caught her glare before ducking behind the crook of his sleeve. He could see her still, clear as day. "And I hate these *bloody* jumpers! You're making me a laughing stock! No wonder…"

"No wonder what?"

"No wonder I've been having trouble at school."

"I can see that!"

"No, I mean someone's been picking on me. Hitting me and stuff. An *idiot*." He pointed to the proof of his shiner.

A pause.

"Why didn't you say something? Who is it?" The agitation in Harry's voice gave way to quiet disquiet.

"I needed…"

"Needed what? What? What was it, son?"

If she'd let him finish! "…I needed my dad."

"But *I* could have helped."

"Dad would have sorted it."

"*I* would have sorted it. You know that. I'm always here fo—"

"I wanted my dad!"

Harry stepped back: give them both space.

Time.

She spoke more calmly now. "I know I'm not your dad, son, but I would've wanted to help."

"Well, don't worry, someone's been helping me find him." Tears were glistening Nelson's features.

"Find him?"

"My dad! Someone's been helping me find my dad!"

"Really?" Now there was concern. "Who?"

"No one you know. But he's going to find him with me."

"He?"

"Yes, *he*."

"Who is it, Nelson?"

"A man."

"What man?" Thorns in her tone.

"A man I met."

"Met where?"

"Please! Just stop with all the questions!" Clear, wet snot had descended the length of his philtrum to breach his top lip, a slug-string bridging the parted mouth.

"Who is this man, Nelson?"

"Mum!" The filament snapped.

"Nelson!"

"Look, I'm missing my dad and you're not my dad, Mum!" The swipe of an upper arm gathered in the mucus.

"And you should be grateful for that!" Her voice was sturdy, but Harry was quaking. "I'm twice the man your father is."

"How can you say that when you knit all day, and he works for MI6?"

"MI6? He shared a ruddy desk in the tax office."

"That's what you think. He's an operative. He trusted me with his secret. We swore a pact."

"Well, that's strange because he'd spout that flannel to anyone who'd listen – all the better if they were wearing a skirt – and now it turns out he's been lying to his own son as well. The man's a bloody fantasist."

"He's been captured!"

"What?"

"He was on a mission, he told me. But he must have been captured, or lost, and the government came to search his things."

"When? The burglary?"

Nelson nodded.

"Did you ever stop to consider, then, why the government took the telly? Your savings tin? My jewellery?"

"That was part of the cover-up. They really came for his photos. They were looking for clues in them. People watching us in the background and stuff."

They both stared at each other, insides hammering.

"And that's why the police weren't interested when you called them. And that's why there wasn't a shit on the rug."

"What?" Harry, suddenly calmed, sat down heavy next to Nelson and rubbed a hand, comfort for both, around his knee. "The police took no action because they were told not to."

"See!"

"By me."

"What?"

"The reason the door wasn't smashed in was not because I mistakenly left it unlocked. He used his key. And even your father wouldn't resort to defecating on his own floor. It wasn't a burglar. It was your dad. Finishing what he'd started: I'd been taken a long time ago."

"So, *Dad* stole his own photos?" His voice steeped with scorn.

"Oh, come on. Use your head. I got rid of them. I couldn't stand the bloody sight of him."

She was never going to tell Nelson the burglar's identity, never define the charades played out. The *Bond* movie nights, beer garden afternoons, the interminable cars shows – always what *he* wanted. Never their choice. Always his. The Scoobys, the *Goldfinger* poster…

Keeping her truths from Nelson would let him make up his own mind when the time came. Make his own choices. That was only fair. Yet *fair* had brought them to this. "Your dad stole anything not tied down that day. And this was after he sold that watch he had always promised you. And do you want to know why?"

A tear bounced off the raging red of her face.

*

"I don't believe you!"

Nelson was up and through the door with Harry careening after him, bouncing from wall to staircase, a drone of clippety-claps. By the time she had made the airlock, he was beyond the squeal of the front gate.

"Nelson! Nelson!"

He was not listening. She was about to tell him the photos were boxed in the loft for when he was older, that she would get the ladder this minute and fetch them down. But he had leapt before the words came, and now he was not listening.

Why had she been so stupid?

Harry watched frozen, and burning, as his silhouette was smothered by the gloom. Stepping back, she closed the door behind her and brushed into fingertips the grief at her cheeks.

At her feet on the floor, a mesh of greens. She bent to retrieve it and as she plucked at its edge it lengthened slinky-like. A sleeve from his jumper. He must have wrenched it free in rage. She gathered together the wool and, eyes closed, held it redolently warm to her face.

Why have I been so stupid?

"…I'll stop knitting," she said to the corridor as the latch clicked home. "I'll stop the bloody knitting."

*

All three were now deep within the shanty town of the open-air market. "*You reckon Calvin Klein knows he's selling all these underpants?*"

"Do you believe her, your mum?"

Nelson had relayed mum's explanation: the money grab from the house, the note on the fireplace with its slurry of apology and justification, the airport assignation, the part-time barmaid (she worked on the buses during the day – "*That explains a lot*"), managing an English bar-cum-love nest in Magaluf, her unanswered letters pleading with him to at least contact Nelson, the unheeded birthday reminders and school reports. And secreting his photos because she could not bear to look at him for emptying all they had.

"He's probably still there," Harry had said, "if you want to see him."

"I don't believe you!" he yelled back from the door. "*Fucking hell*, Mum!"

*

"Dad used to always say that Mum knew nothing about his other work. And he told me once that if anything happened, they might come for his things."

"Well, Harry seems absolutely honest to me," said Pippa.

"I'm sure she thought she was doing what was best. Perhaps she hoped that if she avoided mentioning him, you wouldn't be reminded, wouldn't get upset."

"That worked, then." ("*Sarky!*" Mum would have said.)

"As a matter of interest, I'd just assumed it was Harriet."

"Ariadne."

"That's a beautiful name. *She* was a bit of a whizz, too, with the old thread." His hand was slyly squeezed. "She was trying her best, you know. She loves you."

"Iknowbut…"

"But?"

"But I deserve a dad."

"I wonder if he's changed addresses," said Pippa.

"I've not."

"Then, perhaps your dad doesn't deserve you."

*

They had paused at a stall pushing paintings, prints and garish, plastic-perimetered portraits: The King of Pop, David Sneddon, Daniel Bedingfield, Gareth Gates, and a dusty old Elton John. Each was hallmarked '*OFFICIAL*', the size of font in inverse proportion to the degree of endorsement.

"I've read of certain cultures that believe allowing someone to capture your likeness means your soul is surrendered," said Pippa. "But surely the opposite is the reality."

"I don't understand."

"Picture an image of a famished infant, or a moment of triumph, or a doe-eyed puppy. It is not the subject beguiled; it's us, the observer. We surrender *our* soul."

"So, the photograph controls us?"

"Or the painting does…"

*

In addition to pop culture, the stallholder, a young woman overrun by gingham and held together by several kilos of studs, sleepers and bars, had set aside a section of trestle for her own paintwork. To its front, she prostituted parochial landscapes – the only ones that ever sold in this lowbrow dump, this vulgarian hotspot – and, behind, shyly offered up the art that really touched her. Cat-bagged canals, emphysemic mills and other civic idylls, set incongruously before a mêlée of Surrealist impudence.

Nelson moved ahead to stare into her depictions of early-death locals going about their golden age (that stuff she was selling at the back was just *weird*). "Every time I look now, I can't help wondering," he said.

"Will any of us ever again trust that voice in our heads?" asked Pippa.

And, for that moment, all three stood and listened…

*

"Hey, did you hear about that old lady getting mugged this morning?"

Heads were shaken.

"Just up there," and Roland pointed to where they had been. "Bet it was him. Any money."

"What do you think he'll do next?" asked Nelson.

"I'm afraid the genie is out of the bottle," said Pippa. "I think he'll come for you."

"What?"

"He has no choice," she explained. "Nature abhors a vacuum. For him to be safe, he can't afford to leave you out of the picture. Literally. There'll be no happily ever after today."

Nelson was already scanning the Saturday crowd. "D'you know what? How about we skip the cemetery and go straight to the police?"

*

At the hem of a fabric stall, they found a zinc pole radiating blue arrows. An overnight crop had sprouted earlier in the year. It had been almost April, and planners had presumably run out of gutters and grids to re-brand as cycle paths (so *The Respecter* had speculated). They had just found the pointer marked 'Police Station 10 mins' – though only tourists would have required that information, and there were never any of those – when a grip reached out to Nelson and snapped tight. "I've been searching for you."

The hand released and all three spun.

Him.

*

"Have you seen Norton?"

And his eyes told them he knew all about it.

"No. S-sorry," Nelson stammered.

Each was handed a business card in turn. "If you do,

could you call any of these numbers? Please."

"Sure."

And, not glancing back, he shuffled off numb, though the painkillers were again ebbing. He slid his hand, hanging from a road-scuffed sleeve, into a pocket and kneaded the mobile phone he had recovered early that morning from the graveyard. Its call history logged his own number – 5.22pm, 31.10.03 – as the last contact. He had called him a tit.

Nelson looked down at the pristine white and red rectangle. *The Respecter* masthead across the top, and stacked towards its lower edge Office and Mobile. And there, sandwiched between, in golden Copperplate, 'Heath Edward, Editor'.

"What was all that about?" asked Roland.

"You know our crash?" whispered Pippa. "You're not going to believe this."

*

"Hey, did you bring the cards?"

"I thought you had them," said Roland.

"You were messing with them last."

"But they weren't mine."

"It's your fault for distracting me: '*Can I put my certificate in your briefcase?*'"

"That Jack the Ripper distracted *me*. We all jumped up."

*

At the other end of town, a waitress trundled nonchalantly to a halt, cloth palmed, anti-bacterial cocked. "Sheena," her gaze scanned for watchers in the diner, "come and have a look at this."

Rita the redhead rolled across. "What's the matter? Oh my God."

Was it an accusation? She had nothing to hide. Reaching down, and looking everywhere but the cards, Marilyn shuffled together the letters and stuffed them deep and untidy into the dark of her pouch. Why would anyone do that? What does it mean? Who were those three?

And why would anyone write…?

Epilogue

In the cemetery, away from the rubbers and roamers, a bench. And on that bench, a bush-bearded tramp, sprawled, slumped asleep (*or unconscious*); a nub on his head, an ooze of blood and missing his outermost layer. And under that bench, a top hat: a fine example, polished and trim and, bar the merest of grass stains, untouched by the century passed.

Nearby, a grave. And at the edge of that grave, pressed into a narrow channel newly excavated then sod-hidden, a dog-torn frockcoat wrapped around an ornate wooden frame, lighter now that the four golden ingots had been prised from the grooves in its back.

And held within that shrouded timber, a painting. A painting of the town cemetery in its Edwardian heyday: trim and spruce and soldier-straight.

And at the painting's centre, a figure.

Frozen. Stock still.

Trapped.

A figure with a sickle-shaped scar to scythe around its right eye.